Taskers End

Alan Reynolds

Fisher King Publishing

The distance between insanity and genius is measured only by success

The author is indebted to Deborah O'Byrne
BSc (Adult Nursing) RN for her assistance
with the specialist medical aspects of this book

Thanks also to Rick Armstrong for his
continued support, guidance and friendship
which has made the writing process so much
easier and to Sam and Rachel at Fisher King
Publishing.

To my friends and family for their
love and support.

Finally, to the many new friends and
supporters who have encouraged my writing, a
massive thank you.

Chapter One

Doctor Martin Young carried his tray with his empty plate, sandwich wrapper and bottle of mineral water to the trolley by the exit of the staff canteen and placed it with the rest of the neatly stacked trays. A heavy-set middle-aged woman, uniformed in an apron of a kitchen assistant, thanked him and started wheeling the trolley containing the remnants of people's lunches through the door marked 'Kitchen' for washing.

He turned to address his colleague. "I don't know how people can eat a three-course meal at lunch time; I'd be asleep by two-thirty."

His co-panellist, Doctor Jane Melrose, a fellow criminal psychiatrist who was holding the door open for him, smiled in acknowledgment. "What time are we reconvening?"

"Two o'clock, this afternoon's case is an interesting one and I want us to make a good start; we may not finish it today." He looked back towards the canteen. "Where's Peter?"

"Gone for some fresh air I think," replied Doctor Melrose.

"Can you chase him for me? I've just got to make a couple of calls... I'll meet you back at the room?"

Doctor Young punched a number into his phone and walked down the corridor with his mobile seemingly attached to his ear. Doctor Melrose headed in the opposite direction towards the hospital entrance.

Trenton Court is classed as a medium secure mental hospital, a refurbished facility dating back to the thirties; not as high a category as Broadmoor or Rampton but acts as an intermediate stage for those who have progressed to the rehabilitation phase of their treatment. It is nevertheless a secure unit.

The administration area is quite separate from the main hospital which is surrounded by a high fence, with its own supervised entrance. The modernisation of the accommodation block has been managed in a way that it now resembles less of the old-fashioned sanatorium it once was. It has excellent facilities including a library with internet access, spacious common room, canteen and a specialised medical unit. In keeping with the need to gradually integrate inmates back to society there are outdoor as well as indoor sports facilities available for the patients - they are not called prisoners, including a small 5-a-side soccer pitch and basketball court; interactive activities are encouraged. Visitors are generally allowed.

The whole complex is not visible to any casual passer-by; trees surround the facility and a long drive leads from the main road to the administration block where a large car park caters for staff and visitors. A shuttle bus visits at lunch time and at both ends of the day to ferry non-car users to and from the nearby town some three miles away. The grounds are well-kept and provide a welcome relief to the rather austere external visage. It was a bright late spring afternoon 2007 and the lawns looked immaculate.

Doctor Melrose spotted the other panellist Doctor Peter Campbell, a dapper, fifty-something academic with a flamboyant taste in clothes, who was finishing the final drag of his cigarette.

"Peter," she called, "Martin wants us back in five minutes."

"I'll be right with you," said Campbell, stubbing out his cigarette and dropping it into the receptacle to the right of the front door. Other admin staff were similarly engaged, eking out every last second of their lunch hour before reconvening their duties.

Back in the admin block, they made their way to the room where the Board was in session. Martin was at the table shifting files from his leather document bag; Peter ushered Jane through and shut the door behind them and took his seat. The room, not large but would comfortably sit ten people, was light and airy and Doctor Young had opened one of the windows which allowed a welcome draft of fresh air to filter through from the grounds. The smell of newly-cut grass was evident as was the distant sound of lawn mowing. Campbell took off his jacket to reveal a garish red and white striped shirt; he had dispensed with a tie.

"You look like a deck chair, Peter," teased Jane with a smile.

"Right, we best get cracking," said Martin, a tall man in his fifties with lean angular features who as senior psychiatrist was officially chairing the panel. He was acknowledged in his field as a leading expert on criminal behaviour, an authority which commanded respect. His research spanned over twenty years specialising in cases where insanity had been offered as a defence for perpetration and had chaired a number of similar panels in recent years.

The role of the tribunal was to examine case notes and medical evidence from a variety of sources, including witness statements if necessary, which would lead to a decision whether to release a patient back into the community or, for those who had committed serious crimes, referred back to the courts to continue their sentence in a normal prison.

They had three options: deferment, where the decision would be put on hold for a further period; decline where the evidence did not warrant release in the foreseeable future, that is, they still posed a potential threat to the public; or third, release.

The release option did have strings attached. With the Government keen to get 'care in the community' working, there was growing pressure to free as many patients as was possible. To help this happen, some form of supervision would in most cases be necessary. It was not a question of just unlocking the door and allowing the patient to get a taxi to the nearest station. Many in-mates had no homes or relatives and had become institutionalised. Many long-term patients also had no money. Half-way houses had been set up with the task of rehabilitating those released on parole and a social worker provided by the Local Authority would work with them to ensure their well-being and monitor their progress.

Doctor Young continued. "Our next patient is Gerald Perry, both of you know the case... We have a recommendation from the hospital board that he is now ready for release to the community. Who wants to go first?"

Jane Melrose was the youngest of the three panellists, an academic and in her mid-thirties, recently returned from maternity leave. This was her first tribunal but had many years' experience as a psychiatrist, again having worked with some extremely difficult and violent offenders. Martin Young had specifically asked for her for this particular case as she had some first-hand background knowledge of Perry.

"I'll kick off, Martin, if you like. As you know I worked with Perry two years ago and I can give you a good insight into his background and where I think we are."

"Thank you, Jane... please carry on," said Doctor Young and started taking notes on an A4 writing pad.

Jane started her briefing. "Perry was transferred to Trenton three years ago from a high secure unit following several assessments on his progress. He was no longer considered a high category risk. My role with him was participating in the talking-treatment programme that was recommended as part of his rehabilitation to run alongside the medicinal support which Peter will be able to outline. I had several sessions with him over an eight-month period and found him to be articulate, with an air of confidence... not cockiness exactly, but self-assured, certainly.

He's very intelligent; when I was interviewing him, he appeared to analyse every word I was saying. He was also what

I would call 'savvy'; he definitely knew what was going on around the hospital. He told me the nurses would regularly ask him for advice."

Martin looked up, raised his eyebrows then carried on writing.

Doctor Melrose continued. "He is, or was, an avid reader, always in the library, and was a keen observer of world events. This, of course, gave him a great deal of power around the hospital; I'm not sure whether that's still the case having not seen him for a while. I occasionally found him unsettling if I'm honest, he had a gaze that was not always comfortable. I'm sure he could be manipulative, but that's just an opinion, I have no factual evidence to back that up."

"Just for the record, can you give us some background into what caused him to be placed in Trenton?" asked Doctor Young, momentarily breaking Jane Melrose's recall.

"Of course," said Doctor Melrose quickly, and closed her folder, able to recite from memory. She looked at her fellow panellists in turn, maintaining eye contact which added an unintended dramatic effect to the proceedings.

"Gerald Perry's was an extremely sad case." She paused and poured herself a glass of water from the jug on the table and took a sip before continuing, partly to quench a dry mouth but also to galvanize herself for her recollections.

She continued. "You may remember the incident; it was widely reported in the press."

There were no looks of acknowledgement from her colleagues.

"He was just ten-years-old when his father shot Perry's mother, then blew his own head off with a twelve-bore shotgun." She took another sip. "I don't think you can imagine the scene the young boy would have witnessed when he returned from school that afternoon. He just let himself in and found the carnage in his parents' bedroom."

More water; Doctor Melrose looked down at her desk, relating the account as if telling a story. "There had been family problems, of course. At the inquest, some of Mrs Perry's friends said that Mr Perry senior was something of a control freak and routinely beat his wife and the boy. In the weeks leading up to the incident, she had confided in a close friend that she was having an affair with a work colleague. We will never know the true facts for certain, just hearsay."

She paused again, and then continued. "Gerald was very close to his mother... a bit of a 'mummy's boy' he was called, so as you can imagine the circumstances of her death had left him with severe trauma. Sadly, he blamed himself for his mother's murder, which, as you know, is not unusual with children."

Her two colleagues' attention was total.

"How long ago was that?" asked Doctor Young.

"That would be... 1985, the day before "Live Aid" – July 12th. I remember Perry telling me he was looking forward to seeing all the groups. He had taken up the piano, and music was his only hobby at the time."

Doctor Melrose looked up, her face reflecting the sadness having recalled the events and remembering her emotional interviews with Perry.

"What about his parents, what did they do for a living?" asked Doctor Young.

Doctor Melrose took another drink and continued; her voice now more composed and assertive.

"His father was a technician at the local Aerospace works, a responsible job by all accounts. His mother worked in a building society; it was the manager she was allegedly having the affair with. They seemed comfortable enough, nice house, nothing ostentatious, a three-bedroomed detached in a good neighbourhood; several witnesses said they were honest, hardworking, and outwardly stable, but, from what I gleaned in my interviews with Perry, not what I would call an affectionate family."

"What do you mean?" asked Doctor Young.

"Well, as I said, at the inquest Gerald's father was painted as a domineering bully but, interestingly, his work colleagues didn't see him that way at all. They said that no-one seemed to know him that well; he had no close friends and didn't mix with them socially. Not standoffish or anything, he was a good worker, just got on with his job and went home, you know, kept himself to himself." Doctor Young nodded.

Jane continued. "His work colleagues said the incident had come out of the blue, completely out of character. They were really shocked that he would do such a thing. According to his GP there was no history of depression or any mental illness in the family; no-one could have predicted the events, but this was clearly premeditated. Perry senior had written what amounted to a suicide note saying that he couldn't go on living a lie and if he couldn't have his wife, no-one else was going to; all very sad. He must have just sat there waiting for his wife to come home and then...." she let the words resonate around the room.

"This affection issue you mentioned," prompted Doctor Young. "Can you expand further; this could be important?"

Doctor Melrose replenished her glass from the jug of water and half-filled the other two glasses to the gratitude of her colleagues.

She continued. "At my meetings, Perry would never talk about his father, only his mother; and it was clear that she was the affectionate one of the family; as I said they were very close. It's possible there might have been some jealousy of the boy from the husband which could have contributed to the beatings but its pure speculation, we can't tell."

"What about his recovery from the shootings, how did he

cope with that?" asked Doctor Young.

"I looked up some old case notes from the time and it appears he was referred to a counsellor to get him through the tragedy but only attended a couple of sessions. Not much information to add. Luckily his grandparents on his mother's side were still alive and he went to live with them just outside Sheffield after the funeral and he made a gradual recovery."

The room was warm, despite the air from the open window, and her colleagues were now taking on water.

"Despite everything, he actually went on to do well in his exams; became a bit of a swot it seems. He didn't socialise much and there was a suggestion of bullying at school, according to his notes… no real friends until he got to University. He told me after the shooting he gave up his music and just concentrating on his studies."

"He went to university?" said Doctor Young, with a look of surprise. Campbell was also making notes and listening intently to Doctor Melrose's account.

"Yes, did well. Studied forensic science at Leeds and was training to be a doctor. Showed a talent for it, according to his tutor at his trial."

"Ah yes, the trial... as you've mentioned it, we better start looking at this in some detail, can you give us some background into the events that led to his arrest?" asked Doctor Young, who by now had made a couple of pages of notes.

"Of course," said Doctor Melrose, again without referring to her notes.

"June 2001, he was two years into his course at Leeds Medical School."

"So, he'd left the University and moved to the Medical School?" asked Doctor Young.

"That's right," replied Doctor Melrose. "He got a 2.1 BSc with Honours in forensic science and then continued his studies in Medicine."

Doctor Young looked up from his notes and looked at Peter Campbell, clearly impressed not just at the achievements of Gerald Perry but also Doctor Melrose's powers of recollection.

She continued. "While at Medical School he met a fellow student called Lindsey Jones and they started a physical relationship."

"Was this his first?" asked Doctor Young.

"It's difficult to say. Perry was extremely reticent to talk about his relationships even when I explained it was part of the procedure to try to get to the root of his illness. He would tend to just clam up when I broached the subject."

"Can we pick that up later, Jane, I want to concentrate on the trial for the moment?" said Doctor Young.

"Of course, where was I?" said Jane.

Doctor Young checked his notes. "You were saying about a relationship with this Lindsey... Jones girl."

"Ah yes," she recovered her thread. "As I said, when I tried to introduce the subject with him during counselling sessions it was very difficult for me to get anything from him; all the information I had, came from the trial transcripts. As you probably know Lindsey was chief witness for the prosecution and in her testimony, she said she'd become wary of Perry in the weeks leading up to the attack. His behaviour had changed."

"In what way?" asked Martin.

"Apparently, he was becoming more and more obsessive. They had been going out for about six months, but the relationship was starting to show signs of strain. He started drinking and became abusive. She had begun seeing another student who was also a friend of Perry's called Andrew Caldwell, known to everyone as 'Drew'. After a bitter row, Lindsey confessed she was seeing Caldwell and wanted to end their relationship. Perry went mad, literally. Something snapped, he tried to throttle her, and she lost consciousness. Luckily, he fell short of killing her and left her in her flat to go after Caldwell. Lindsey's flatmate found her lying on the sofa and called the ambulance and the paramedics saved her. Drew Caldwell was not so lucky. Perry went around to the house Caldwell shared with three other students just around the corner. It's not clear for certain what happened but, according to the police, he forced his way in when Caldwell opened the door and plunged a screw driver into his eye."

Young and Campbell looked at each other and Campbell made a wincing sound.

"He hit him with so much force it punctured his brain and he died almost instantly."

"What happened next?" asked Doctor Young.

"According to the police, Perry went back to his flat and ran a bath. As soon as Lindsey had regained consciousness she was able to tell the police what had happened, and they went around to Perry's place and found him in the bath singing loudly."

"What was he singing?" asked Doctor Young. "Do we know?"

"Afraid not; is that relevant, Martin?"

"Possibly not," he replied, "but there has been some research done in the States about the affect certain types of music, like thrash metal for instance, has on vulnerable minds, and some people claim to have heard voices in songs telling them to kill. That's all," said Doctor Young.

"There's nothing documented," said Jane.

"Going back to the trial, when did they decide to use the 'fitness to plead' defence?"

"Very early on in the trial. It became clear that Perry had or was having a complete breakdown. After Lindsey's testimony he began to mumble incoherently, and started reciting the Ying Tong Song," Young looked at Campbell.

"You know the one by the Goons," clarified Jane, noticing the glances.

"I know the song," replied Doctor Young.

"The more the trial went on, the worse Perry became, to the extent that the judge accepted that he was unfit to continue. There was overwhelming evidence that he had killed Drew Caldwell and tried to strangle Lindsey, the motive was jealousy according to the prosecution, but the court accepted a 'murder' charge was not appropriate and 'manslaughter on the grounds of diminished responsibility' was recorded. After extensive medical reports and tests, he was sent to a high secure unit for an indefinite term. That was in February 2002. He was transferred to Trenton in 2004."

"I see, so, he's been here for around three years… Where are we in terms of his medication, treatment and present prognosis by the medical team?" asked Doctor Young. "Peter this is your domain, I believe."

"Yes," said Doctor Campbell. "But before I continue can I suggest we take a break"

Doctor Young looked at his watch. "Good idea; its three fifteen. Reconvene in say fifteen minutes."

Doctor Young put down his pen and joined his two colleagues for the walk to the coffee machine.

"Just going outside," said Campbell waving a packet of cigarettes. Doctor Young was back on his mobile.

Fifteen minutes later and they were back in the room.

"Before we start," Doctor Young referred to his notes. "Jane, can I just go back to something that you said earlier about the trial. You mentioned that it was after Lindsey Jones' testimony that Perry started showing signs of distress. Is there anything that might suggest that this girl might still be in danger?"

"Nothing from my interviews and observations; although the last I heard she had married and moved away. She's a GP now somewhere so I don't think that will be an issue."

"Thanks, Jane... Peter?" and it was Doctor Campbell's turn to brief the panel.

"As Jane has said Perry was committed to a high security unit after his trial and he was examined by a number of practitioners both medical and psychiatric and was diagnosed with schizophrenia. All the symptoms and his family background fit this diagnosis. In one interview..." Campbell referred to his notes, "June 2002, he said at the time of the incident he felt an overwhelming compulsion to kill; his emotional detachment from the act was quite remarkable... just going home and running a bath. No sense of guilt or any differentiation between right and wrong... just this... need to kill, that's how he described it."

"Were these urges specific or general?" asked Doctor Young.

"How do you mean?" asked Campbell.

"Well was he compelled to kill indiscriminately or specifically?"

"Ah, I see what you mean. No, it was triggered by the girlfriend's infidelity, so it was quite specific. He felt he needed to seek retribution in some way. There was a striking similarity to his father's actions except Perry didn't try to take his own life as his father had done," said Campbell. Doctor Melrose listened intently, and she too took notes.

Doctor Young clarified. "So, just to confirm, his behaviour was prompted by a specific event, in this case his girlfriend's affair."

"Yes, that's right," Campbell confirmed.

"Well, there's no question he demonstrates the classic signs of schizophrenia. From what you say, he was quite clearly detached from reality."

Doctor Young paused and wrote something on his pad. "What about paranoia was there any sign or symptoms?"

"You mean thoughts of mind control or voices?" clarified Campbell. "No, as Jane has said, only this 'uncontrollable compulsion' was how he described it."

"Thank you," said Doctor Young and continued to write vigorously on his notepad. He finished and looked at Campbell.

"I have read the notes relating to his release from the high secure unit and transfer to Trenton. It appears he has made good progress in the time he has been here," said Doctor Young. "Can you give us a brief outline of the treatment?"

"You will have seen from the notes, when he first arrived at the previous facility after the trial, he was given neuroleptic drugs to control the 'positive' symptoms; but, as you know, they do have unpleasant side effects, particularly in high doses. Unfortunately, he suffered a great deal with shaking and muscle stiffness as well as blurred vision and rapid heartbeat. The muscle spasms were a real problem, and he came off those drugs after a few months. He had various other medicinal interventions but responded better to talking therapy and the drug programme was gradually withdrawn. After the success of the combined treatment he was eventually reassessed as a low category risk and transferred here."

Campbell referred again to his notes before continuing. "Since arriving at Trenton he has been on an extensive course of cognitive behaviour therapy. No continual requirement for drugs apart from the usual sexual depressants. He now enjoys human interaction; very different to his time at the secure unit and even before that to his college days. He was considered quite remote by his fellow students, although they did say he began to come out of his shell after he started his relationship with Lindsey Jones. It seems to have been a bit of a turning point for him."

He looked again at his notes. "His records do say he could be capricious at times and as a result was prescribed less invasive drugs, but his mood swings have gradually subsided."

Jane interjected. "Yes, I can confirm this. The sessions I had with him were always positive, apart from any mention of the relationship with Lindsey when he would just close up, but he was starting to show signs of recognising his problems. Before I left he was doing well with developing coping strategies; and learning how to prevent crisis situations from happening."

"Given the same circumstances what are the chances of him regressing and having the same reaction?" asked Doctor Young.

Doctor Melrose answered. "This is a difficult one to predict; the circumstances surrounding his breakdown could be classed as unique and extremely unlikely to recur."

"He could get rejected again," said Doctor Young.

"But it is almost impossible to measure the degree of risk that he would respond in the same way," said Doctor Melrose.

"But this is the crux of the decision, trying to establish the likelihood of him re-offending," said Doctor Young. "Can you throw any light on this Peter?"

"I agree with Jane. It would be impossible to say he would never react in the same way again, but he has responded well to the treatment," said Doctor Campbell. "I have seen him recently and I can see why the hospital board have recommended him for review. Talking to him you would have no idea that he was or had been schizophrenic."

"So, are we saying he is cured?" asked Doctor Young.

His two colleagues looked at each other and Doctor Melrose took over. "Cured is a difficult definition to apply. All we can do is to try to assess the degree of risk that the patient poses and in my professional opinion it is very small."

"I would concur with that," said Doctor Campbell.

"You talked about him enjoying social interaction earlier; what about visitors, since he arrived. Did he get any, you know, family, old friends?" asked Doctor Young.

"He has no family, he was an only child and the grandparents who brought him up are both dead, killed in a fire a couple of years ago," replied Doctor Melrose.

"How did he react to that?" asked Doctor Young.

"Well, he wasn't told the full circumstances for obvious reasons, but he seemed to just accept it. He had had no contact from them for three or four years, but his solicitor is a regular visitor, at least once a month since the accident. Gerald has inherited their house and rumour has it that he is quite wealthy now. How right that is I don't know, but the ward nurses seemed to think so."

"Hmm, that's interesting." The chairman made more notes. "As you've mentioned it, what about his relationship with the nurses and staff here, have we any information on that? How does he interact with them?" asked Doctor Young.

"Funny you should say that; I don't know whether you picked up on this Peter, but they seemed almost reverential when speaking about him. One called him the 'Guvnor'," said Doctor Melrose.

"I know what you mean," said Campbell. "He does have a certain aura about the place now you come to mention it."

"Thank you," said Doctor Young who was looking down continuing to make notes without eye-contact.

"One final point before we break. Jane, you mentioned that he would..." he checked his notes for the correct wording and looked at Doctor Melrose, "'close up' when you mentioned his relationship to Lindsey Jones. Is he still reticent? If he's still repressing these feelings it could still be a problem."

"Well, from the notes I've read, he does appear much more open in recent sessions. It could be he felt more comfortable discussing it with a male counsellor. Derek Filbert took over the case while I was on maternity. Or, of course, it could just be his treatment was working," replied Doctor Melrose.

"Thanks Jane, I'll give Derek a call to get his thoughts."

Doctor Young was starting to shuffle the papers in front of him into some sort of order.

"There was something else," said Doctor Melrose. "Something from the trial that has always interested me. In her testimony, Lindsey Jones said that the physical side of their relationship was 'primeval', which was a strange word to use. According to her account there was little sign of emotion or affection, just a functional, process. He could also be quite rough, not beating up or anything; just very... aggressive, I think she said. I recall this was one of the reasons for the break up. My guess is, he has difficulty in expressing emotion, particularly when it comes to physical relationships with women."

Doctor Young digested the information. "Yes, that would make sense and entirely consistent with his behaviour patterns."

He looked at his watch; it was five o'clock, and then to his colleagues.

"Thank you very much; we'll call it a day there. We've got a great deal of information to pore over."

He picked up his notes from the desk and started fiddling with his briefcase.

"We'll reconvene tomorrow, nine o'clock. Everybody happy with that?" There were nods of concurrence from his two colleagues.

The panel met again the following day to complete their deliberations and, over the next few weeks, Doctor Young compiled a detailed report of their findings.

In his summary, he wrote that in the panel's view Gerald Perry posed little threat to society and recommended him for release subject to him reporting to a social worker, who would continue to monitor his progress for twelve months, and regular sessions with a psychiatrist.

Given the criminal offence, the courts would also have to concur.

The report went around the various interested agencies before, eventually, a final decision was made to confirm Gerald Perry's release.

Chapter Two

Gerald Perry looked around his room. It was stark but functional; bland magnolia walls, a small window just above eye level from which, on tip-toe, he could see the grounds and the area where daily exercises would take place for those who were capable.

September 17, 2007, three years, two months, twenty-three days since he arrived at Trenton Court and, as usual at this time of day, post-lunch, he was lay on his bed staring at the ceiling. He could make patterns with the Artex texturing, shapes depicting animals and other things. There was one special one he liked to visit. If he screwed his eyes it resembled a human form, female, definitely; waist, breasts, buttocks, no question.

As a long-term patient, he had acquired some personal belongings, books mainly, and his small collection was stacked neatly on top of his desk in order of size from right to left. It was on here that he wrote his notes, details of his research from the library. His study was arbitrary and would be anything that took his fancy. He had an interest in a wide range of issues from fundamentalism to the Berlin Wall which had struck a particular chord bearing in mind his present situation. He felt he had plenty in common with those wishing to escape from an authoritarian regime. The notes were filed in alphabetical order in plastic sleeves that he managed to acquire from one of the nurses. The files were in the cupboard at the side of the desk in three file boxes labelled, 'Research A-J; K-R; S-Z'.

He was allowed supervised computer time including use of the internet which helped no end with his investigations, but he was not permitted any outside communication, email or social networking sites which were blocked. He had however managed to keep updated on research into his latest interest, Neuro-Linguistic Programming. He was fascinated by the idea of the power of the mind and how it could be used positively, or negatively.

In fact, he loved all science. Science represented order, facts, black and white, no grey, no room for ambiguity it either was or wasn't. Like his desk, everything had its place; it was just so.

He enjoyed a debate, but all of his fellow patients, and it had to be said, most of the nursing staff as well, were out of his league when it came to mental dexterity. Even the visiting pastor, Father Jacob, was no match for Gerald's intellect when it came to deliberating religion, or the mind control of the masses, as he preferred to call it; routinely quoting from John William Draper's book, '*History of the conflict between religion and science*', which he had read several times.

A ward nurse knocked on his room door. It was open; Gerald was annoyed at being interrupted from his ruminations.

"Sorry to disturb you, Gerald, the Director wants to see you; could be good news," said the nurse.

Gerald quickly shook off his irritation. "Thanks David, on my way. Can you tidy up in here while I'm gone?"

The nurse looked round the room bemused at the question. The room was tidy, meticulous even, as ever nothing out of place.

"Yeah, will do," said the nurse to humour him.

This could be the news Gerald had been waiting for.

Patients at Trenton were more or less free to come and go as they pleased; those who were considered to be no threat at least. There was a secure wing where more dangerous or less stable in-mates were housed. Gerald was considered a model patient and enjoyed a certain status. He was so well-read and had views on just about anything which meant he was always being consulted by fellow patients and even the nurses, eager for an 'expert' opinion.

He walked along the corridor from his room in the direction of the Director's office. Fellow patients were roaming about trying to overcome the sheer boredom of their enforced detention. Some were completely in another world, others wide-eyed and wary, some were inquisitive. "Hi Gerald, where are you going?" asked one in a child-like voice, as he passed by the open lounge. Gerald just smiled.

He reached the double security gates and spoke to the attendant. "The director wants to see me," he said with some authority.

"Hi Gerald... you know the way," replied the man, swiping a plastic card over a pad releasing the gates.

Down a corridor, following the signs which indicated 'Reception', he climbed the stairway to a large open area on the second floor. There were seats dotted around the outside of the room with small coffee tables where visitors would wait for their meets. A large picture window gave an extensive vista of the grounds. He made his way to the far end where a stern looking woman of indeterminate age was manning the main desk. This wing had been redeveloped four years ago, not long before Gerald arrived and the whole area was bathed in the afternoon sun. Gerald looked at the wide expanse, any moment, he thought he would be able to end the nightmare of the last five years and spread his wings like a bird and soar into open space. He never wanted to be confined again.

"The Director wants to see me, Edna," said Gerald to the matronly woman on the desk.

"Oh, hi Gerald, how are you today?" she said, flashing her eyes in a flirtatious manner; her V-neck top revealing more of her body than was really appropriate in such an environment.

"Fine thank you," replied Gerald.

She picked up the phone beside her, dialled two numbers and spoke. Gerald couldn't hear the conversation.

"The Director will be with you in a moment," she said and disappeared into her paper-work. She leaned forward revealing more of her chest to Gerald, knowing full-well the effect it would have.

What the regime did not know was that Gerald had never actually swallowed his prescribed medication to restrict his sexual desires. He knew exactly what they were and would either spit them out when no-one was looking or, if he was being closely supervised, regurgitate them later like a bulimic.

He had no desire to become a legalised eunuch.

"Gerald, how are you today? Come in," said a voice, which made Gerald jump; his mind was on other things.

He turned around to acknowledge the Director and followed him down a short corridor to the first office on the left which had a name plate with the words 'Dr Oscar Klein, PHD., FRCPsych,' appended.

The Director led the way and indicated with his hands for Gerald to sit on the sole chair in front of a large desk. Gerald had been in this room once before on his arrival, and it was just as he remembered it. The furniture was expensive looking, a large leather chair the other side of the desk, noticeably bigger than the one Gerald was sitting in; by the window a couple of armchairs flanking a coffee table and a 1970's throwback potted cheese-plant in the corner which was snaking its way up the wall like some enormous Triffid. The room had the same sweeping vista visible from the reception area Gerald had just left.

In front of him the Director had a folder which he proceeded to open, and he scanned the page of the first document as if reading it for the first time.

"Gerald, I have received the final report from your assessment and a letter today from the Justice Department confirming your release into Community Care."

Gerald tried hard to stymie a scream. "When?" asked Gerald, just about maintaining his composure.

"Well, we'll need to arrange a Social Worker to work alongside you and there'll be some administration to sort out, but I would say within the week," replied the Director. "You'll also need to spend some time with the resident care worker, take some trips into town and get familiar with being around crowds, shopping, that sort of thing."

He paused to look at the file and then locked eye contact again. "Is there anyone you want me to call?"

"Yes, can you call Arthur Cathcart of Cathcart Rivers; my solicitor in Sheffield, Edna has the number, and let him know? He'll need to make some arrangements for me," said Gerald.

"Yes of course, I'll arrange that for you. Anything else?" asked the Director.

"Not for now; when will the transition process start?" asked Gerald, aware of the appropriate jargon.

"Eh...?" the terminology surprised the Director and he peered at Gerald, his eyes squinting as if trying to weigh up the enquiry. "Tomorrow, Gerald, I'll get Daniel to take you into town for your first visit and he'll look after you. You can take the shuttle bus after it's dropped off the last morning shift."

"That's great... do I get some money to spend? Otherwise I can't see the point," said Gerald.

"Yes, there's a £50 allowance which I'll give to Daniel."

"Thank you, Dr Klein," said Gerald with feigned respect.

Gerald got up and was shown to the door by the director. "I'll contact Mr Cathcart for you in a few minutes," he said as Gerald walked past.

Back through reception, he made a point of waving to Edna on his way past. She responded with an exaggerated wave and equally dramatic smile.

"We all dance to a mysterious tune, intoned in the distance

by an invisible piper," He recited one of Einstein's famous quotations to himself which seemed to reflect the moment admirably. He was the invisible piper now, everyone playing to his tune and yet nobody realised.

Down the stairs he reached the security gates again. "Any news?" asked the attendant.

"Yes, all good," replied Gerald without elaboration and he waited for the swish of the opening of the first security gate and walked through. It closed behind him before the second opened allowing him back to his wing.

"Where have you been, Gerald?" came a voice from the lounge; the same obsequious patient who had made the earlier enquiry.

"See a man about a horse," said Gerald, his polite way of saying 'mind your own business'.

"Goodie, goodie gum drops, I like horses," said the inquisitor. Gerald smiled and walked on.

Back in his room he was returned to his bed and examination of the Artex ceiling and found his erotic shape. A familiar tune suddenly came to mind. "*Ying tong, ying tong, ying tong, ying tong, ying tong iddle I po*," he quietly chanted to himself.

The following day the shuttle bus was waiting at the entrance to the admin block as Gerald and Daniel made their way from the hospital wing. All security checks had been carried out and Gerald was taking his first journey in the outside world for over five years including the time he had spent while on remand. He smelt the clean air and then the diesel fumes as he approached the bus.

Daniel was a stocky lad, younger than Gerald with a close-cropped haircut and an earring in his left ear. He was wearing jeans and a badly creased denim jacket. Scruffy, thought Gerald, disapprovingly. Daniel was someone he had seen about the place but often wondered what his function was; most of the time he seemed to be just sitting around talking to staff or patients.

"The bus will take us to the interchange in town and we can have a look around the mall. Let me know if you feel any anxiety, anything at all," said Daniel, and they boarded the single decker.

Daniel spoke to the driver out of earshot as Gerald chose a window seat. It was completely empty having dropped off the previous passengers earlier. Daniel made his way down the bus and sat next to Gerald, row seven, lucky seven. It was no accident; it was exactly halfway down the fourteen rows of seats, on the left-hand side. It would be closer to the pavement, so Gerald would have a better view.

The bus pulled away and Gerald felt a degree of excitement as they made their way down the long drive and through the main entrance gates which had opened automatically for them. It was three miles to the City Centre and they made good time having missed the worst of the rush hour. Gerald soaked in the views, the trees still in full bloom, blue sky with wispy clouds, the houses neat and well maintained in the suburbs, but then unkempt and dowdy as they approached the environs of the city centre.

The bus eventually stopped at the transport interchange which was close to a recently completed indoor shopping mall. Gerald watched. He found the sight of people milling about fascinating. He would be storing them in his brain's database for later analysis.

"Meet you here at one o'clock," said Daniel to the driver and led Gerald towards the shops.

"I have the money with me so if there is anywhere in particular you want to visit let me know."

"A clothes shop would be good, I only have a limited

wardrobe," Gerald said, with deliberate understatement. His trainers, casual shirt and cords had been his staple apparel for almost three years.

Gerald noticed the shear pace of everything, rush, rush, rush; everyone seemed to have so little time. It was ten o'clock and it was mostly mothers with young children, or elderly people who had come into town to spend their pensions, but it was the same story. He looked at them with a degree of pity. What meaningless lives they led, no better than hamsters on a wheel. Gerald was thinking back trying to recall his last forays into a shopping mall, was it really this busy? He couldn't remember clearly. Having nothing but time on his hands for five years this would be a necessary adjustment. He noticed a group of giggly teenagers huddled outside a faux-Italian coffee shop; bunked off school no doubt. If only they knew what they were doing; no wonder the standard of education was falling. He never believed the statistics and the so-called improvements in "A" level results: it was just political rhetoric. He'd had this discussion many times with one of the nurses whose wife was a teacher.

There was one girl in the group who looked a bit older than the rest, taller, long legs, short skirt. Unnoticed, his gaze scanned her from top to bottom as if she were a bar code. He made a mental note; she could be his fantasy for later.

"What about this place?" said Daniel, as they came to a store that specialised in various casual attire for men.

"Yes, fine," said Gerald, and they went inside.

"What are you looking for?" asked Daniel.

"I don't know, but I thought a new pair of jeans and a top of some sort... something like that."

"You won't get much change for your fifty in here."

Gerald looked at the prices in the first rail of shirts. "Hmm, you could be right there."

There was, however, a sale on, and they spent half an hour going through the reduced-price stock looking for something suitable. Eventually, Gerald decided on a new pair of jeans and a sweatshirt similar to those worn by rugby players. He had noticed several young men wearing them and he didn't want to look out of place on his release. He had shopped wisely, the items coming to just under forty-five pounds, and he congratulated himself on his selection. Daniel gave Gerald the money which he took with the articles to the cash desk.

As he reached his turn in the queue to pay Gerald greeted the sales girl with a broad smile and fixed his eyes on hers. He noticed her badge which said 'Aisha'.

"How are you, Aisha?" he asked. "What a lovely name."

The girl smiled back. "Fine, thanks," she said warmly, but didn't acknowledge the compliment.

He watched the sales girl as she put the articles in a large carrier bag and took the money from him. Despite it being encased in the store's uniform; he could still make out the contours of her body under the less-than-flattering apron. He decided he liked Asian girls. She counted out his change in his hand and he fixed his eyes again.

"Thank you, Aisha," he said, and the girl smiled demurely and looked down from his stare.

"Have a nice day," she replied, and watched him leave the shop. He glanced back, catching her gaze and smiled.

The time went quickly and after sampling the wares of the coffee shop which had taken the rest of the money the pair headed back to catch the bus.

"What did you think?" asked Daniel.

"About what?" asked Gerald.

"The experience... how are you feeling? I mean, this is the first time you've been out for over five years."

"Fine," said Gerald, not really appreciating the relevance of the question.

It was a true statement; Gerald's social skills had developed considerably since moving to Trenton Court following his therapy. He had become more gregarious and confident, and it was his apparent determination in dealing with his 'problems' that had led to the recommendation for his release. Wandering around the shopping mall with a tame minder had provided no challenge at all; he was relishing the opportunity of being set free to roam as he wished. There would, however, be more challenging times ahead.

His casualness did not readily concern Daniel; no patients were the same, but Gerald had been different to most. He was unable to put his finger on it, but Gerald's degree of confidence, almost arrogance at times, was unnerving, given his period of detention. Daniel could understand why Gerald had been chosen as 'ready for release', but then again...

He put all thoughts of doubt firmly to the back of his mind. His report to the director on his return would be clean. No reason to rock the boat. Better minds than his had agreed Gerald Perry was ready.

Gerald, on the other hand, had not given it a moment's thought. He *was* ready, he was invincible.

The bus back to Trenton contained several administration staff who had travelled into town to do shopping on the first lunch hour. A second bus would be leaving in the opposite direction with the later shift. Row seven was empty and Gerald made his way to it and sat down with the carrier bag containing his purchases on his lap. Admin Edna was in row eight.

Gerald turned around and they exchanged greetings.

"How did it go today?" asked Edna warmly.

"Fine," said Gerald sharply and turned back to face the front. Why was everyone treating him like a five-year-old on his first day at school, he thought, misunderstanding a genuine enquiry.

The remainder of the journey was spent in silence and, back at Trenton, Daniel escorted Gerald through security and into the residential block, as the unit which housed the patients was euphemistically called. Edna followed a few paces behind, bemused at Gerald's apparent coldness.

As they walked past the open lounge a high-pitched voice called out, "have you been to see the horses, Gerald?"

Gerald walked on, not acknowledging the enquiry.

Daniel escorted Gerald to his room door. "Your social worker will be calling to meet you tomorrow and I can take you out again on Thursday... any questions?"

"No, it was fine today. I'll see you Thursday."

Daniel turned, annoyed at the lack of courtesy.

Gerald was oblivious to his rudeness and went into his room. He took out his new jeans and shirt from his carrier bag and folded them neatly before putting them into his small wardrobe, doubling his attire. He would remedy this as soon as he got out. Not long now, he thought.

He shut the door and lay on the bed staring at the ceiling recalling the sights and sounds of the morning. He thought of the long-legged sixth former and the Asian cashier; his mind wandered off into a different world of erotic possibilities. Not long now, not long now.

The following day he was called to the administration block to meet his social worker who had driven the forty miles from Sheffield. Reaching the reception area, he smiled genially at Edna who was behind the desk as usual. She responded but not as warmly as she had in the past still upset at the apparent snub the previous day. Gerald was unaware of the impact of his earlier behaviour.

"Dorinda is waiting for you over there," she said, pointing to a young woman of West Indian origin sat reading a nursing magazine in the corner of the reception area. Gerald walked towards her. She looked up at the approaching figure and stood up leaving her magazine on the coffee table next to the chair.

"You must be Gerald, I'm Dorinda Walcott, your Social Worker," she said in a soft voice with just a hint of a Yorkshire accent.

"Hello," said Gerald. "Pleased to meet you," and they shook hands. He was keen to make a good impression.

He looked at her quickly assimilating her appearance; in her thirties, about five-feet six, well built, gold band third finger left hand, married; two children he surmised.

"Shall we go through," she said and picked up a large holdall and her handbag. She led the way to one of the interview rooms down the corridor.

"Can I carry that for you?" asked Gerald, desperately trying to make a favourable impression.

"No, it's ok," said Dorinda. "Would you like a coffee?" she added, as they passed a vending machine.

"Yes please," said Gerald. He liked coffee, the caffeine was a stimulant and he enjoyed being stimulated; increase in brain activity, sharpens the mind.

The Social Worker took out a card from her handbag and placed it in the slot on the machine and keyed in a number.

"How do you like it?"

"White, no sugar please," replied Gerald without a moment's hesitation.

A cup dropped into the receptacle at the front of the machine and the machine began dispensing the drink. Gerald took his coffee and waited for the second cup to fill.

"I'll take these," he said. "You've got your hands full."

"Thank you," said Dorinda.

The interview room was small and a bit claustrophobic. There was a desk and two chairs, one either side. Gerald was not comfortable in enclosed spaces, a legacy of his incarceration, but he knew he would have to put up with it. Not long now, not long now, he thought, close enough to touch.

Dorinda took a laptop from her holdall and plugged it into a wall socket, the lead curling over the small desk which separated them. It sprang into life. Gerald took a sip of the coffee and watched her intently as the social worker keyed in her password.

"Won't be a moment," she said removing a pair of spectacles from her handbag and putting them on.

"I have plenty of time," he said jokingly. She looked up and smiled.

"What do you know about the transition process?" asked the social worker.

"Not much, just what the director told me."

This wasn't entirely true; he had studied the procedure intently over recent weeks in anticipation of his possible release.

"Well my role is to help you integrate into society and monitor your progress. I'll also need to update the authorities and advise them of any concerns I might have."

"Concerns?" interjected Gerald.

"Well, if you encounter any problems. Some patients find it difficult to get back into the swing of things after experiencing a period of..." She paused for an appropriate phrase, "exclusion."

'Exclusion!' what sort of euphemism is that? thought Gerald but kept his counsel.

"We'll have regular meetings, certainly in the first few months, then gradually these will be less frequent until they stop altogether."

"How long will that be?" asked Gerald.

"Depends, everyone is different; background, education, financial status, all play a part. The key is getting you back to full recovery. You may feel you are there already but the treatment you have had here is only part of it. As I said, after a time out of the system it takes a while to get used to things again. Managing a budget, getting a job, dealing with relationships, it all takes time. I'm here to help you through this."

"Oh, ok, yes, I see," said Gerald. "So, what happens when I leave here?"

"Well, I see from my notes that you want to return to Sheffield, which is why I'm involved; I look after the South Yorkshire area. We've got a couple of what we call 'halfway houses' in the city, sort of hostels where you can come and go as you please, somewhere to live until you find somewhere more permanent."

"But I have a house," said Gerald. "I've already given instructions to my solicitor to arrange for me to move back in... it's let at the moment," he added.

"I see," said Dorinda. She was writing on a notepad "Hmm, I'll have to make enquiries, but it *is* usual for new releasers to spend some time at the hostel until they are ready to move on. There'll be someone available for you on site should you need help; it will also give us the opportunity to assess your progress."

Gerald was trying to hide his disappointment; it was really just an extension of where he was now but without the gates. After five years being under scrutiny, he didn't want to spend any longer than necessary under so called 'supervision'.

"Whereabouts is the house?" she asked.

"Just outside Sheffield... Rivelin Valley."

"Hmm, nice area... Look, I can't promise anything, but I'll make enquiries for you."

Gerald could feel a sense of overwhelming depression sweeping over him after the earlier optimism, and meekly uttered, "Yeah, thanks."

Dorinda's fingers skated over her laptop keyboard and pecked at the letters. "Just making some notes."

Gerald looked at her screen-saver as she exited the 'notes' programme.

"Nice children," he said glancing at the picture of a family group which looked as though it had been taken on holiday.

"Thanks."

"What age are they?" he asked out of interest.

"Seven and five," she said without elaborating.

She folded the laptop down appearing uneasy at Gerald's interest.

"Any more questions?" she asked.

"Only the obvious one, when do I get to leave?"

"I don't know. The director will be in touch, but it shouldn't be long."

This did nothing to assuage his depression, but it would have to do for now.

Dorinda put her laptop into her hold all and got up from the chair.

"Once the date's been confirmed I'll be in touch about what happens next," she said and extended her hand.

"Thank you," said Gerald responding limply to the handshake and they left the room.

Dorinda hovered around the admin area to be signed out, Edna was busy, and Gerald made his way back to his room, his mind totally focussed on his pending release making mental notes of things to do. David, the duty nurse, stopped him in the corridor. "The Director was looking for you, he told me to tell you that your solicitor's visiting tomorrow at three o'clock."

"Thanks David," said Gerald

He snapped out of his melancholy; maybe things were moving along ok. He was looking forward to seeing his solicitor, he would discuss the situation with him; he could swing things.

That night Gerald lay in bed listening to the familiar shouts of other less fortunate inmates. The rants, the pleading, the confused, the crying; he felt no sympathy just an inward celebration that soon he would be away from all this. He shut it out once more and curled up in his own cocoon. The power of the mind; he imagined he was a chrysalis and soon he would burst open and take to the air like a butterfly.

The following day he had his second trip to town with Daniel and it went much the same as the first. Having blown the budget on the first trip there was little to do apart from wander around which Gerald found boring. On the way back on the bus, he kept staring out of the window and wishing he didn't have to return to his cell.

At three o'clock David knocked on Gerald's door.

"Visitor for you Gerald."

Gerald leapt off his bed and the nurse led the way to the reception area to meet Arthur Cathcart of Cathcart Rivers, solicitors and commissioners for oaths.

The solicitor was waiting in his dark grey suit, white shirt and black tie, looking more like a funeral director. He had a black briefcase and rolled up umbrella in his hands. He was a small man, about five-feet two, balding, and with an almost a circular face. He reminded Gerald of the Dickensian character, Mr Micawber, with his half-rimmed glasses which made him look a lot older than he probably was.

He greeted Gerald with a smile; at least that's how he interpreted it; it was difficult to tell, he only appeared to have one expression. The solicitor peered over his spectacles to look at Gerald. They shook hands and Cathcart led the way to one of the meeting rooms which had been made available to them. Gerald followed and noticed what looked like snow on Cathcart's shoulders. He should try a different shampoo he thought.

"Sit down Gerald, dear boy, we have a lot to discuss."

Gerald looked at him. Arthur Cathcart was the family retainer having represented Gerald's grandparents for many years.

Suddenly a recollection flashed through Gerald's mind. He vaguely remembered Cathcart visiting the house years ago to see his grandparents. He could picture him quite clearly, younger, of course, entering the house; it had been raining and his grandmother took his coat and umbrella in the hallway. He shuddered, then quickly discounted the memory. Dwelling on the past was uncomfortable; it was part of his coping strategy.

They made themselves comfortable and Cathcart opened his briefcase and took out two manila folders and a pile of papers. Gerald sat opposite as the solicitor scrutinised the first document.

"Good news, dear boy, you can leave tomorrow. I have the confirmation here," and he passed a piece of paper across to Gerald. He was speechless and for a moment just stared at the document.

"But that's fantastic," was all he could say.

"Yes, apparently they need the room so once the assessment had been concluded and they were happy with your rehabilitation programme there was no need for you to stay any longer. I've arranged for a car to pick you up at ten o'clock and take you to my office in Sheffield where we can sort out one or two legal requirements. We can also go over the conditions of your release and arrange a contact schedule with your social worker. Do you know her?"

"Yes, I met her yesterday. She said I would need to do that."

"Good, no doubt she will have explained everything," said the solicitor.

"Well, there were a couple of things she couldn't answer,

like when can I move back home."

"Well, according to my notes there's nothing stopping you once the social worker thinks you can manage on your own."

"I can, I can," said Gerald anxiously.

"That's not for you to decide," said the solicitor sharply. "As I said, I'll need to speak to the social worker. I'll phone her later and see what she says. I know there's a shortage of secure accommodation, so they may be willing to let you move back home straight away."

"What about the tenants?" asked Gerald.

"Moved out last weekend. Once I knew your release was imminent I gave notice immediately and, in accordance with your instructions, I've had decorators in there all week. They should be finished by tomorrow. I've had new curtains, carpets and a new kitchen installed; the other furnishings you asked for have also been delivered. All the old furniture has gone with the exception of the valuable items."

Cathcart looked up from his notes.

"I've not been today, but I called in yesterday and it was looking very good. I think you will be pleased. It's been quite an effort to arrange in the time but there is no shortage of willing workers in town. Oh, there's a new computer being installed today with an Internet connection and I am arranging a mobile phone which will be ready for you to pick up tomorrow."

"What about the other thing?" asked Gerald.

"Ah, yes, the change of name, well, all the paperwork's gone off. As we hold a Power of Attorney, everything's in the firm's name until you are ready to change it. The TV license, phone and internet contract, house deeds, council tax and utilities, driver's license will need changing. Once the new name has been confirmed, we can switch them over. You will of course need to advise the authorities."

Gerald nodded. "Ok...What about the finances?"

"They're in good order. You have a healthy portfolio of well-spread assets at present worth..." he looked at one of the sheets in front of him... "Just over one million six hundred thousand; there is also around sixty thousand pounds in a Client's deposit account in your name. The house deeds will eventually be transferred into your new name. Present market value would be two, maybe two and a half, million. Your grandparents have left you well-provided for."

Gerald reflected for a moment. Despite their wealth they were surrounded by tragedy and the phrase, 'money doesn't buy you happiness', was never more apt. But now he needed to look forward not back.

"Any other questions?" asked the solicitor. Gerald shook his head still trying to take it all in.

"In which case, I'll see you at the office tomorrow around eleven-thirty, and, in the meantime, I'll speak to the social worker and chase up any loose ends."

Cathcart stood up having completed his business and they shook hands. "Thank you for all your help," said Gerald.

Chapter Three

Gerald looked around his room for the last time. It was nine forty-five, Friday morning 21st September 2007. He had difficulty in keeping his emotions in check; excitement, some apprehension, which surprised him, but mostly the determination to make up for lost time. He held no resentment for those who had 'excluded' him, to use Dorinda's word, for the last five years. His earlier troubles were not of his making; he had been ill, that was the verdict of all his counsellors. Now he was better; time to get on with the rest of his life.

David, the duty ward nurse, came to meet him. "Have you got everything?"

Gerald looked down at his two carrier bags which contained his meagre wardrobe and research files and smiled, "I think so, but send on anything I might have left."

David closed the door behind them and locked it and led Gerald to the exit.

"Hi Gerald, are you going to see the horses?" said a voice from the lounge as he walked by. He made no acknowledgement; the sooner he got out of this place and away from the poor wretches it housed the better. He didn't belong here.

David took Gerald up to reception where the Director was waiting for him to say goodbye.

He approached Gerald and extended his hand. "Gerald, so glad you're leaving us. It sounds strange to say that, but you know what I mean. I wish you every success for the future and hope that you'll remember your time here at Trenton as a positive experience. I believe we have, in no small way, contributed to your recovery."

Gerald mulled over the last comment; he wouldn't have called it a positive experience but smiled politely.

"Thank you, Dr Klein, I'll always remember my time here."

He caught a glimpse of Edna behind her reception desk looking at him and smiled in her direction. She returned the smile and she appeared to mouth 'good luck'. Gerald waved in acknowledgement.

The car was waiting outside the main entrance and, after passing through security for the last time, Gerald had one final look at the building that had been home for the last three years. Never again, he vowed.

Gerald sat in the front with his two carrier bags on his lap, despite the offer to put them in the boot, and they headed off down the long drive. The trip up to Sheffield would take just over an hour. Traffic on the M1 was busy through the inevitable road works. He thought about the last time he was on a motorway. It must have been driving down from Leeds to see his grandparents; Lindsey was away that week-end, he remembered.

'Lindsey?!' He sat upright with a jolt. The driver looked across at him. "Are you ok, mate?" he enquired. Gerald nodded.

Where had that come from? Why had he thought of Lindsey, that wasn't allowed? He had erased all thoughts of her from his data banks; why had her name suddenly crept through his defences?

He shook his head as if trying to physically remove the intrusion from his brain. It must be the association with the journey. It came back again. Lindsey was definitely away that week-end, probably with HIM!!

Gerald curled up in a ball clutching his bags and shut his eyes. His coping strategies were already at breaking point.

The driver looked at him still concerned, but that was more to do with the pick-up point. Another nutter let loose into the community, he thought.

The rest of the journey was spent in silence with the occasional glances at Gerald from the driver. Gradually the feeling disappeared, and Gerald began to relax as they left the M1 and headed down the Parkway into the City Centre. Gerald looked at all the new developments, a business park, a hotel complex; it was not how he remembered it; a lot had changed in five years.

The taxi threaded its way through the traffic and ended up in the back streets behind the cathedral where all the professionals were based. Numerous solicitors, accountants, architects, barristers all had their offices there; it was like a club. The car pulled up outside the office of Cathcart Rivers, the brass name plate, worn from years of abrasive cleaning, proudly shining in the autumn sunshine.

The office was in a long row of terrace houses with early 1900's origins and had been tastefully converted. There was an Accountants next door separated by a covered alleyway and a Mortgage Consultants after that. It was just turned eleven and the area was a hive of activity. Barristers in their wigs heading to the law courts; clerks with briefcases crammed with important documents scurried here and there. After the solitude of Trenton this was very different.

Gerald thanked the driver and the taxi pulled away leaving him surveying the scene. Being a small practice with a selective clientele there was no visible means of entry, the door was locked, just a bell push which Gerald rang. After a few moments a very attractive young lady opened the door and greeted him.

"You must be Mr Perry," she said. "Mr Cathcart is expecting you."

Gerald stood there in his recently acquired outfit carrying all his present worldly possessions and smiled warmly.

"Yes," he said.

"Come through," said the girl and she led the way through a small vestibule, trailing an exquisite smell of perfume, into a larger room. Gerald surveyed his environment. There was a desk and small reception area with a couple of brown studded leather chairs and various financial magazines on a low walnut veneered coffee table.

Gerald was hypnotized as the receptionist made her way back towards her desk and watched as she took her position behind the reception desk. He banked the sight in his mind, skirt just above the knee, three-inch heels, long legs, slim. She dialled a number and a few moments later Arthur Cathcart appeared looking even more obsequious than ever.

He peered over his glasses.

"Come in Gerald, dear boy, would you like a coffee?"

"Yes please, white no sugar, if that's ok," he replied, politely.

He was for the moment in an alien environment and his self-confidence had taken a beating; this was unexpected.

"Maureen, could you get two coffees please and maybe some biscuits?"

The beauty from reception smiled at Gerald. "Yes, Mr Cathcart, I'll bring them through."

Gerald was intrigued by the formality; it was definitely a throwback to the sixties. He noticed with some surprise a computer with one of the new flat-screen monitors behind the reception desk where the lovely Maureen worked; incongruous, he thought. He followed Arthur down a narrow corridor to an office. The dandruff was no better he noted.

The office was as he could have imagined, a large desk with an in-tray and an out-tray and a leather 'executive' chair behind which matched those in reception. There was a smaller chair in front, just like the Director's office at Trenton. It was obviously an authority thing.

There were a couple of filing cabinets against the wall and a calendar with an anonymous seascape next to them. The windows were the old sash-type, but looked as though they had never been opened, certainly not in a long time. The cream coloured paint had been layered to a degree that the gaps in the frames were invisible. Still, keeps out the droughts, Gerald thought.

The view from the office was even less inspiring surveying the back yard of an adjoining property. There was probably an outside privy somewhere, he mused.

"Sit down, dear boy, sit down," said the solicitor pointing to the seat in front of the desk. "Let's get down to business."

He picked up a file from the in-tray which had the name 'Perry' written in felt tip pen on it. Gerald unconsciously started fiddling with the sleeve of his sweatshirt; he was inexplicably feeling some nerves.

As he had done at Trenton, Arthur scanned the first document. "I've had a letter from Mrs Walcott, your social worker. It seems she's happy for you to move back home. I spoke to her briefly yesterday after our chat and, as I thought, she was very amenable to the suggestion. I put it to her that the reports all show you were fit to manage on your own, but you *will* need to see her next week." He looked at the letter. "Wednesday is your first meeting. I cannot stress the importance of keeping these appointments. If you fail to attend without good reason you may end up back in Trenton Court or worse."

Gerald twitched. "Yes, I get that."

The solicitor continued. "Not heard anything yet from the change of name but it shouldn't be much longer, and we can get everything transferred to Greg Jensen..." he paused. "Out of curiosity what made you choose that name?"

"Jensen's my grandmother's maiden name. Her family were large land owners, way back. Her father diversified into engineering which is where their money came from. My grandfather was managing director of the family business. They sold out when he retired."

"Yes, the firm dealt with that transaction. Our association with your family goes back generations. Josiah Rivers was the original partner and I am sure he had connections."

There was a knock on the door and Maureen came in with a tray, two cups and saucers and a cafetière and milk. Gerald was grateful for the interruption; the family history lesson was not high on his agenda. It was also nice to admire the wonderful figure of the lovely Maureen once again. She caught his gaze and smiled at him as she put the tray on the table in front of the solicitor. Gerald was transfixed and had difficulty in averting his eyes. It was probably the same look that had disturbed Doctor Melrose.

"How long have you worked here, Maureen?" he asked, trying to engage with her.

"Three years," she replied, trying to return Gerald's eye contact whilst pouring the coffee.

"Damn," she said under her breath as she breached the lip of Cathcart's cup and it overflowed into the saucer.

Cathcart saw what had happened. "Don't worry, I'll see to it," he said, but with obvious disapproval.

Gerald was watching for signals, the odd glance, a touch of her hair or back of the neck, which were positive signs according to his research on male/female attraction.

Sure enough, as she poured Gerald's coffee, she caught his eyes before putting the cup in front of him and then immediately brushed her hair from her face. Gerald noticed it straightaway.

"Thanks," he said and once again fixed his gaze.

"My pleasure," she said and smiled.

Gerald picked up on the words and wondered if it was a deliberate innuendo. He continued watching her as she walked towards the door, then the subtle glance back over her shoulder before leaving the room. He smiled back.

The solicitor was totally absorbed in his files and oblivious to the subtle courting rituals that were being played out before him.

They both took a sip of the coffee. The solicitor continued, still half-reading the correspondence and not properly concentrating on what he was saying.

"So good news then, you don't have to go to any hostel and you're free to go back to the house." He looked up from the papers and glanced at Gerald. "But, I should mention, there's still a lot of work going on there and if I were you, I would find yourself a good hotel and base yourself there for a few days. Maureen can book one for you if you like."

Gerald was disappointed, he was desperate to get back to his former home.

"That's a shame, I was hoping to start arranging the house, but if you say so."

"Yes, sorry about that, but it will be better," said Cathcart. "It will give the workmen time to finish the job."

Gerald's concentration had wavered; his mind was still distracted by the lovely Maureen.

"Oh, that reminds me, I've got something for you," said Cathcart. He produced a box from one of the drawers and handed it to Gerald. His eyes lit up.

"A mobile phone," he said, looking at the picture of the latest must-have gadget on the front. "That's great, thanks."

While Gerald was drooling over his latest acquisition the solicitor made a call. "Maureen, can you make a reservation at the City Imperial for..." He put his hands over the receiver and looked at Gerald and mouthed, 'three?', Gerald nodded... "Three nights for Mr Perry. Get the best deal on a suite; there shouldn't be much call for one on a weekend. Book it in the practice name," and he replaced the receiver in its cradle.

"We've set up a contract for the phone for you in the firm's name, but we can transfer everything once the name change has been confirmed. I presume you will be needing a car?"

Gerald hadn't thought about that, he hadn't driven for over five years and had no idea what had happened to his old 'banger' that he regularly trudged up and down the M1 in while he was at University.

"I'll get something arranged next week. Audi do a nice range which I think would suit you, but you can let me know. We can purchase it in the firm's name until everything is in order. The Power of Attorney's still operative until you rescind it now you've got the 'all-clear', so to speak."

Gerald sat there feeling overwhelmed, but he would never admit it; he just wanted to leave and be on his own. Suddenly he had been transported into a different world. He had become conditioned to regimentation and conformity; everything provided for him. He was accustomed to his solitary world, alone with his thoughts and deliberations, and, in truth, he preferred it that way. There had been a lot to take in today and it had taken more than he had anticipated to cope.

It took another thirty-five minutes to conclude their business and it was almost lunch time. As he was about to leave there was a knock on the door and Maureen appeared.

"Would you like any sandwiches, Mr Cathcart, Mr Perry? I'm popping across to 'Wedges'."

Gerald looked confused.

"The sandwich shop in the precinct," she clarified, seeing Gerald's quizzical look.

"Nothing for me, thank you, and Mr Perry is just leaving," said the solicitor. "Can you show him out for me please?"

The solicitor stood up and shook Gerald's hand. "Call back on Monday at ten and we can finalise your return to 'Tasker's End. We may have had some news on your change of name as well."

The words 'Tasker's End,' the name of his grandparents' house, echoed in his head, his reactive brain triggered and stalled for a moment. Blood flowed from his face and he started to shake.

"Are you alright?" said Cathcart. "You've gone quite white."

"What, oh, oh... yes, sorry," said Gerald, quickly recovering as the rational side of his brain took control.

"Yes, yes, I will... and thank you... for all your help," said Gerald falteringly.

Gerald picked up his carrier bags, the mobile phone balancing precariously on top, and walked down the corridor. Maureen was already in the reception area and had not witnessed his momentary lapse.

She went to the desk and moved some papers and put them in a drawer, locked it and then switched the phone to 'answer machine'. Gerald just stood there just watching her go about her business.

"Hang on a sec, I'll just get my coat," said Maureen and she disappeared into a room behind the reception desk.

Gerald felt uneasy stood in the middle of the office. It was as if he were on a stage, highlighted in a spotlight. He moved to the corner next to the two chairs in the waiting area.

Just then Cathcart came out from his office.

"Ah, you're still here, dear boy. Thank goodness you haven't left yet. I nearly forgot, you'll need this," and the solicitor gave him an envelope. Gerald looked inside and could see a number of twenty-pound notes.

"You'll need some money to last you through until we can get your bank account finalised. It should be enough to see you over the weekend,"

"Thanks again, Mr Cathcart... for everything," said Gerald, a little annoyed at himself for not thinking about this himself.

He put the envelope in his jacket pocket and stood waiting, still feeling self-conscious.

A couple of minutes later Maureen re-appeared in a short leather jacket. She had also freshened up her make-up Gerald noticed.

She opened the front door and waited while Gerald passed. He caught the strong scent of her perfume. There was the merest of touches as he squeezed by her.

"Sorry," he said instinctively.

He walked down the two stone steps to the pavement and waited for Maureen to shut the door.

"Hey, I've got a better idea," she said as she joined Gerald. "Do you fancy a coffee and a bite to eat? There's a place around the corner that does great jacket potatoes."

"Yes... ok... that would be good," said Gerald, hardly able to take in the invitation.

"Great, this way," and Maureen strode off.

He walked beside her, down the street before turning right towards the main centre shopping area.

"Just here," she said, pointing to a shop with the sign 'Spudmania' above. The clue was probably in the title, he thought.

She led the way past people queuing for takeaways and into an area at the back which had been reserved for 'eat-ins'. It was very busy but one or two were beginning to prepare to leave to get back to their banks and offices which, in the main, serviced the shop.

"Can you find a seat and I'll get the food? What would you like?"

Gerald stared at the array of fare. If it could be fitted into a potato it seemed to be covered.

"Just cheese will be fine."

"Anything to drink?"

"Coffee... white, no sugar please," replied Gerald.

A couple got up from a table and Gerald made a move for the vacant seats. He put his carrier bags underneath the wooden table out of the way. His new mobile phone was visible on top of one of the bags and he pushed it out of site to deter any would-be thieves.

It was at least five minutes before Maureen returned with a tray containing their meal.

"The queues in here are hideous but the food's great," she said, as she put the tray on the table.

The perfume returned and attacked his senses even managing to overpower the smell of cooking. Gerald took in as much of the fragrance as he could. He had never smelled anything as good.

She took off her jacket and placed it neatly on an adjoining chair and placed her handbag on top. Gerald looked at her. Up close she was even more beautiful. Dark hair, green eyes, white complexion, his eyes strayed downwards then quickly moved back again. He logged the smart blouse with the three top buttons undone; the curve of her breasts putting a strain on the fourth. He almost gasped.

Trying to compose himself he made conversation.

"Thank you for this," he said, looking at the large steaming potato with a pile of cheese perched on top which reminded him of the Leaning Tower of Pisa; it seemed to be defying gravity. "How much do I owe you?"

"Nothing, it's fine, I'll claim it back as 'entertainment' on expenses later."

Gerald plunged his plastic fork into the pile of cheese.

"So, Mr Perry, what do you do? Mr Cathcart tells me you have been working away."

Gerald wasn't prepared for this; he naturally assumed, working in the office, she would know all about him.

"Please call me Greg," he managed to say but didn't know why. He hadn't thought about using his new name yet.

He wiped his mouth with a napkin giving him time to consider his response.

"Yes, over six years, returned this morning. Mr Cathcart's been looking after everything while I've been away."

"What do you do?" she asked, looking directly into his eyes again which he found unnerving.

"Forensic science," he replied without elaboration.

"Sounds interesting."

"Can be," he said; the conversation becoming a little awkward. He was finding it difficult in keeping his attention, distracted by her appearance. The fourth button was proving to be a magnet and he hoped she hadn't noticed.

He changed the subject.

"What do you do at the office?" he said, just as she leaned forward to put a fork full of potato into her mouth. She stifled a laugh.

"Sorry," she said as she cleared the offending morsel.

She leaned back and wiped her lips with a tissue.

"Anything, from making the tea, running errands, answering the phones and, occasionally, I get to go over the files with David."

Gerald looked quizzically.

"David Chapman... he's the other partner. I don't normally have much to do with Mr Cathcart; I'm just covering today. He's the senior partner and tends to look after the important clients."

That answered the earlier question; she obviously didn't know anything about him.

"I see," said Gerald, somewhat relieved.

"I used to work for another law firm as a legal secretary, but I met David at a law function."

Gerald noticed the informality, in complete contrast to Mr Cathcart.

"He asked if I would be interested in a PA role with more responsibility and quite a hike in salary. It was a no-brainer."

"No brainer," thought Gerald. That was a phrase he hadn't heard before; must be a new one on the office circuit; he would log it. He could listen to Maureen for hours; her voice was low and seductive, and he could watch her for even longer.

Maureen put her knife and fork down on her plate indicated she had finished although there was at least half her lunch remaining. Gerald had hardly touched his. He didn't feel hungry; his appetite having been overtaken by other thoughts.

"Excuse me for a moment, need to pop to the little girl's room; can you keep an eye on my things for me?" she said and smiled at Gerald.

"Of course."

She walked towards the sign that said 'Toilets', and Gerald followed her with his eyes all the way. He watched other people come and go and was drinking his coffee when Maureen returned. The perfume seemed to precede her.

"Your perfume is incredible," he said.

"Thank you," she said as she took her seat. "'Black Orchid,' not very common in the UK. I normally get it when I go on holiday, comes from Milan."

Gerald looked up and noticed something different. He nearly choked on a mouthful of coffee. The fourth button was undone, and the top of a black bra was visible. He tried not to look but too late, she had caught his gaze and she just smiled.

"It's warm in here," she said as if to emphasis the point.

Gerald was still sat with his jacket and sweatshirt on.

"Yes," he said.

"So, have you got a wife, partner or someone?" she asked; a question which came out of the blue.

"No, no-one," he said confidently. "What about you?"

"No, split up with my partner three years ago... Mr Cathcart mentioned this morning you live at Tasker's End," she said, quickly changing the subject.

"Not yet, but I will do, as soon as the renovations are finished; hopefully early next week."

"He says it's very nice."

"Yes, it's my home, I was brought up there. It belonged to my grandparents before they died."

The earlier awkwardness was slowly abating, and the conversation was starting to flow more easily.

Apart from his solicitor, his only social contact for over five years had been with medical staff, counsellors or fellow patients, many of whom had been incoherent. Her presence and attentiveness were giving him much needed confidence, but he had to be careful; he had plenty to hide. He had no intention of scaring her off. Now was not the right time to talk about his 'secret'.

She picked up her coffee and started to drink. Gerald's eyes went south again, and he was sure she leaned forward a fraction, but he could have imagined it. She finished her drink and a waitress came over and started to clear the plates.

"These finished with?" she asked, looking disparagingly at the virtually untouched meals.

"Yes," they answered together.

"Well, I suppose I'd better be getting back," she said, looking at her Gucci watch.

"Right, of course," said Gerald finishing the last of his drink and trying not to look too disappointed. "Oh, I forgot to ask, did you sort out the hotel for me?"

"Oh, yes, City Imperial Hotel, the Imperial suite, check-out Monday morning; it's one of the better ones, should be very comfortable."

"I'm sure it will be. Where is it? I don't think it was built when I was here last."

"Not far, five-minutes, just off West Street," and she gave Gerald some directions.

She stood up and took her jacket from the back of the chair. Gerald watched as she put it on, more glimpse of bra, and she smiled at the attention. She could almost feel his eyes watching her and she was more than happy to play along.

Outside the café, Maureen looked at Gerald. "See you soon," she said.

"I hope so… and thanks for lunch," replied Gerald.

She smiled again and headed back towards the office.

Gerald walked in the opposite direction carrying his bags. but turned around a couple of times to see if she was looking back but she had already turned the corner.

It was only a few minutes to the hotel as Maureen had said, and Gerald was impressed. It was a new building and was extremely well appointed, as an estate agent would say. The frontage was contemporary glass with the signage 'City Imperial Hotel' prominent across the entrance. The reception area was spacious and airy with large windows giving a wide view of the drop-off car-bay and street in the front of the hotel. There were easy chairs with other guests reading or slouched over a lap-top. Potted plants were dotted around to give a more relaxed feel. Gerald followed the signs to reception. A smart young man called Keith was manning the desk.

"You have a reservation in the name of Cathcart Rivers, my name's Perry," Gerald said in reply to the inquisitive look from the receptionist.

Keith scanned the list on the computer screen.

"Ah yes, the Imperial Suite, three nights," he said and rattled on his keyboard.

"Any luggage, Mr Perry?"

Gerald looked at his two carrier bags. "No," he answered.

"Wake-up call, newspapers?

"No wake-up call. Daily Telegraph, please."

Keith made a note and summarised. "Three nights in the Imperial Suite, account being settled by Cathcart Rivers, Daily Telegraph, correct?" checked Keith.

"That's right," said Gerald.

"Can I book you in for dinner this evening?" added the ever-attentive receptionist.

"I'll let you know," said Gerald. The thought of food was not in the forefront of his mind.

Keith directed Gerald with suitable hand signals.

"The lifts are down the corridor to the left, seventh floor, turn right out of the lift, Imperial Suite's in front of you. Would you like a hand with your bags?"

"I think I can manage," said Gerald without a hint of sarcasm and he made his way along the corridor as instructed to the lifts.

The suite was as grand as the name suggests and it didn't seem possible that only twenty-four hours earlier he was cooped up in a tiny room like a battery chicken.

The top floor gave him a panoramic view of the city. There was a large, state-of-the-art flat screen TV on the wall, two four-seater leather sofas, a dining table that would cater for six, a drinks cabinet, fully stocked and a complimentary bottle of red wine and two glasses on the writing desk. There was a separate bedroom with an enormous four poster bed and another TV on the wall. The bathroom had a sunken whirlpool bath and a walk-in shower; no bucket under the bed tonight, thought Gerald.

He opened the double wardrobe in the bedroom and deposited his two carrier bags, removed his jacket and hung it on a peg. He took out Cathcart's envelope from his inside pocket and checked the contents, four hundred pounds.

He found the kettle and cups in one of the drawers and made himself a cup of tea; much more refreshing this time of day.

As he sat on the sofa with his warm drink, his mind wondered back to Maureen; she had made quite an impact, and, if he were not mistaken, seemed genuinely interested.

He snapped out of his day-dream and considered what he needed to do. Priority was to set up his phone. He put down his mug on the coffee table and removed the box containing his new toy from the carrier bag. He loved gadgets and stared at the picture with a degree of excitement. It had been a long time since he had had access to a mobile phone and this one was far more complicated than his old Nokia; goodness knows what had happened to that.

He finished his tea and started to open the cardboard container like a kid on Christmas Day. He took the phone from the compartment in and looked at it. He was amazed at how small it was. He ignored the instructions and soon had the SIM card in place. He plugged the phone into the wall socket and watched as the indicator showed it was charging. A welcome text appeared from his mobile phone operator. Yes!!

He would leave the phone charging. He started to think about his next move.

He checked his watch, three-ten, plenty of time; his meagre wardrobe was in desperate need of attention. He looked out of the window and could see the shops and the myriad of people milling about. Apart from his brief trip out with his carer earlier in the week, shopping was another routine he had not done in a while and he suddenly felt anxious, but it had to be done.

He went back to the bedroom to retrieve his jacket, picked up his key-card and left the suite. He was still feeling apprehensive as he walked down the corridor to the lifts. He pressed the call button and waited for the elevator to arrive; then watched the floors change on the small adjacent indicator screen; 5… 6… 7. There was a ping and the doors opened. He walked inside and pressed the 'lobby' button and exhaled dramatically.

The reception area was quiet, he noticed, as he walked past the desk where Keith was stood waiting for the next client, looking bored. Gerald nodded as he made eye-contact, then walked out of the hotel and headed for the neighbouring precinct.

He was close to the place where he had enjoyed the lunch with Maureen and smiled as saw the sign. The area was all new to him and had no idea where he was going, but eventually he found a shop specialising in men's apparel.

It was an independent store called 'Jermaine's', not one of the ubiquitous chains, with a good range of clothes visible from the outside displays. Gerald walked in and the sole occupant approached him.

"How can I help you sir?" he said in a slightly camp voice.

"I need a complete makeover," Gerald replied.

"Of course, sir, it will be my pleasure," said the proprietor with flashing eyes and just a touch of blusher.

For the next hour Gerald, with Jermaine's undivided attention, managed the purchase of a new wardrobe.

Underwear and socks were a priority; he did not want to spend time washing the same pair over and over again as he had done at Trenton; he had better things to do with his time now. Five shirts, two pairs of slacks and a pair of jeans, a good pair of loafers and trainers and enough socks and boxer shorts to last him two weeks; that would do for now. Once everything was finalised he would be making further additions. He managed to do a good deal on the price and came away with fifty pounds which he felt would last the weekend until he could get more cash from the solicitor. He wasn't planning on spending anything else.

He left the shop with a feeling of elation. He felt invigorated, alive, his freedom had given him independence and he could sense a change… in everything. The earlier feelings of nervousness and anxiety had gone, replaced by the confident self of Trenton; it was as though his mind was gradually re-tuning, adjusting to the new conditions.

He retraced his steps back to the hotel; as he approached, the concierge opened the glass front door. Gerald noticed the lobby was much busier, and Keith had three people waiting.

He took the lift to the top floor, back to the suite. In his room he emptied the contents of his carrier bags on the bed. Each piece was folded neatly; he shook them out and put them on coat hangers in the wardrobe. Socks and boxers went into the drawer in the dressing table. He liked to put them in order of the colour spectrum, reds through to green.

He checked the time; five-twenty; a whirlpool bath, totally chill out, then some food.

Having mastered the settings and taps that controlled the bath he relaxed in the water, deep in contemplation. He was pleased with progress despite the 'Lindsay incident' in the taxi which he was convinced was a momentary lapse. He was sure he would be able to deal with it if it happened again.

The water was starting to get cold, and his fingers wrinkled by the time he got out. He dried off and went back to the lounge in the complimentary bathrobe, turned on the TV and started watching the news.

He was still recounting his day; the trip up the motorway, the meeting with the solicitor… and Maureen. He could still picture that fourth button in his mind and could only imagine the delights of what lay beneath. His pulse raced at the thought. Then he was asleep.

He was awakened by a noise; tap, tap, tap… and again tap… tap… tap… but couldn't immediately place where it was coming from. He was disorientated by his deep sleep. He tried to focus and checked the clock on the wall, just turned eight o'clock. Still not fully compus mentus, he sleepily got off the sofa, walked out of the lounge to the entrance hall. Without bothering to check through the spyhole, he half-opened the room door.

He stood there for a second in his bathrobe not able to speak.

"Maureen...! What are you doing here?" was all he could manage.

Chapter Four

"Hello Greg, I hope you don't mind me dropping by unannounced."

"No... No... Of course not," he stammered. He was now wide awake.

He stood there for a moment, like a rabbit in a headlight. He caught the perfume. He suddenly felt strange, his mouth turned powder dry and his stomach started to churn; butterflies... big time.

During his time at Trenton, particularly over recent months, he'd enjoyed a certain amount of status. He was considerably more intelligent than his fellow patients and was almost revered by them; they had viewed him as some sort of leader. He was not above abusing that power when he wanted something and could be extremely manipulative, although he would not view it as such; he just liked getting his own way. He had basked in this role as top dog; but suddenly this had been shattered into a thousand pieces. New game, new rules; this was the real world. The hunter had become the hunted momentarily. He had lost control and was desperately searching for his coping strategies, but this situation had not been foreseen or programmed.

It had been well over six years and a lot of therapy since he had been alone, properly alone, with a woman; panic was setting in. It was one thing watching and imagining, playing out his fantasies in his own protected world where there was no threat, no pressure, no rejection, no ritual courtship to be observed; but this...

"Come in... Come in."

He tried to compose himself.

"It's really good to see you," he managed to say, totally understating his real feelings.

He turned and led her into the room; he had difficulty in

looking at her but at least he seemed to be saying the right things. His mind was all over the place trying to compute, trying to find some point of reference. He could find none.

"You must excuse me, I've just had a bath and was chilling out," he said from somewhere.

"I hope I haven't disturbed you. It was a bit of an impulse thing," she said, "I can go if you like."

Impulse, he loved the idea, spur of the moment, recklessness, away from the norm; but it was outside his comprehension. His world was orderly, programmed, routine... predictable.

"No... No," he said quicker than he would have liked. "I'm really glad to see you it's just so... unexpected."

"Never do the expected," said Maureen. "Life is for living, I think, don't you?"

Gerald couldn't get out a reply.

She looked round the room. "Wow, this is great."

Gerald ushered her to the sofa. "Sit down; make yourself at home... I'll just go and change. There's a bottle of wine, you can open it if you like. It's on the desk, there, with the glasses."

The break would give him a chance to escape for a moment and regroup his thoughts. The nerves had made him speak quickly.

Gerald disappeared into the bedroom. He anxiously grabbed one of his new shirts from the rail in the wardrobe and put it round his shoulders; his arms flayed about trying to find the openings. He tried to fasten the buttons, but his hands were shaking and having difficulty in obeying the command from his brain. He slipped on a pair of slacks and wrestled with the buckle; he wouldn't bother with shoes and socks.

He stood up and instinctively looked at himself in the mirror but the reflective image hardly registered; he took a deep breath. The breathing exercises, he suddenly remembered calms nerves. One of his counsellors had prescribed it for overcoming anxiety. He took in another couple of deep breaths and exhaled slowly. Better...

He went back into the lounge and Maureen was sat on one of the sofas she had taken her jacket off and was sipping a glass of red wine; another full glass was on the coffee table next to the opened bottle.

"You're supposed to let it breathe," she said. "But I find it difficult to wait," she said, with an unintended double entendre.

Gerald picked up on it; he was speechless. He looked at her; she was dressed in a white top, low V-neck, gathered at the front, no fourth button this time, and the sides of her breasts visible in a patterned bra. He tried to take it all in; her dark hair and make-up perfect. The skinny jeans were tight, and she smiled as she took in his admiring glances. Her outfit was clearly having the desired effect.

A frisson overcame him; he started to shake again. Suddenly he was like a little boy lost. He took another breath. Maureen sensed his nervousness.

"Come and sit down... I like your shirt. Is it new?"

"Yes... I... I ... bought it this afternoon," he stammered.

"It suits you."

"Thanks," he managed to reply.

Gerald sat down next to her and took a sip from the other glass of red wine trying to hold his hands steady. He would need to be careful; alcohol was something else he hadn't had for over five years.

Maureen took another large sip of her drink. "Nice wine."

"Yes, with the hotel's compliments as well. I thought I was going to have to drink it on my own."

"You're pleased to see me then?"

"Yes, very much, I've been thinking about you this afternoon… I can't believe you're here," said Gerald.

"I've been thinking about you too, I couldn't concentrate

at work… so, as I wasn't doing anything tonight, I took a chance…" She took a sip of her wine. "I would've called, but I didn't have your phone number; so, I thought, what the hell. As I said, it was just on impulse."

Gerald had difficulty taking all this in. The behaviour pattern was not something with which he could identify.

"I knew which room you were in; there's only one Imperial Suite, so I didn't have to ask at reception, which might have been a problem…" She took another sip; the glass was nearly empty.

"I don't normally do this by the way."

Gerald didn't register the comment straightway; he was still taking in the sight, smell and sound of his visitor.

"No, no, it's fine… I'm really glad to see you," he managed to say.

There was a moment of awkward silence. He looked at her again. "You look wonderful."

"Thank you… you like to look, don't you?"

He was embarrassed; he had no desire to be considered a Peeping Tom. For the last six years or so that is all he could do; look and imagine, in his own safe, fantasy world.

In his private moments he had longed to touch; deep down he was a tactile person like his mother, but during his 'exclusion' he had detached himself from those thoughts. His treatment had revealed all kinds of taboos, things that were frowned upon in social interaction. That was part of his conditioning to integrate him back into society. The warmth of another human being had been out of his reach for a long time. It was something he would need to learn all over again.

"I like looking at you," he said, hoping his bold approach would alleviate any negativity in the connotation.

He was holding his wine glass, mainly because he didn't know what to do with his hands; he'd only taken a couple of sips.

She smiled and put her glass down on the table, then took his and placed it next to hers. She leant forward and kissed him. Gerald responded. It was natural; some things never leave you despite pills, potions and therapy.

She could sense his tenseness and anxiety; it was as though he was being kissed for the first time... awkward and unsure. Gradually though, she could feel him relax and the kiss became tender and sensual. She felt her own needs beginning to surface.

They paused for air and she picked up Gerald's glass and handed it to him. He took a drink and handed it back. She took a mouthful from the same glass and placed it back on the table and they resumed their kiss, this time with more urgency. Her right hand strayed to Gerald's thigh and he watched as she gently rubbed him through his Chinos. He could feel his cheeks flush and his manhood begin to stir.

She broke away and stood up. She looked directly into his eyes as she carefully and deliberately lifted her top over her head, her hair entangling in the fabric and dishevelling her immaculate styling; then she reached behind her back to unclip her bra. He watched open mouthed as her breasts spilled out; he gasped. She noticed and smiled.

She kicked off her shoes and reached for the zip that ran down the front of her jeans and pulled the fastener downwards slowly, taking her time. She eased them over her bottom, down her legs. She stepped out of them and stood there in just her panties. Gerald wished he was a camera. He could blink his eyes and the vision would be captured forever.

She walked to him and pulled his hand indicating for him to stand up. He obeyed the unspoken command. She wrapped his arms round his neck and engaged in another deep, passionate kiss. She was totally in control and knew it. She held his hand and drew it to her breasts and taking this as an invitation, slowly Gerald started to caress them. Instinctively he broke away from the kiss and moved down to suck her nipples and she arched her back in response. Her breathing was becoming more urgent.

She broke away for a moment and took his hand and led him towards the bedroom; the door was open and the fourposter was clearly visible from the lounge.

"We have plenty of time," she said, her face flushed; her lips full and inviting.

They reached the bed and she started to undo his shirt, then she unbuckled his belt and unzipped his trousers. Gerald was in danger of finishing before he had even started and somehow, she sensed this. She broke away and got on the bed.

"Come and lie down."

Gerald complied.

He was just laid there in his boxer shorts. She removed her panties and he feasted his eyes on the tuft of dark hair. Gerald wanted to touch her, but for the moment she wanted him just to watch. She continued her performance totally engrossed in her own world.

She could see he was aroused and leaned towards him and removed his shorts.

Gerald was searching in his mind; he had not been conditioned for any appropriate response he was freewheeling, completely overwhelmed by the occasion. Nature and instinct took over. She held his erection for a moment and then straddled him, slowly guiding him into her. Now she would be able to control the rhythm to her own needs.

He could hear her softly moaning; the noises gradually increasing; then she shouted …

"Yes, yes, fuck me Greg, make me cum."

He watched as she rode him, faster and faster, until he was unable to hold any longer and bucked as his orgasm shot into her. She gave a high-pitched scream and collapsed on top of him.

Gerald lay holding Maureen in his arms; he had so many questions... not just for her. He was unable to take in the latest turn of events. He wondered if this was some kind of reward for the last six years of exclusion from some higher force. Was this even real? Perhaps he was still asleep... but he could feel her and smell her perfume which intermingled with the musk of their lovemaking.

"Thank you," he said, with a total lack of adequacy.

"My pleasure," she said and smiled, her eyes locked on his. "I knew it would be good."

Gerald didn't know what to say, he was still grappling with what had happened.

"Where's the bathroom?"

"Just through there." He pointed to an adjoining door.

After a couple of minutes Maureen returned.

"Wow... now that's what I call a bathroom."

Gerald just stared. "You are so beautiful."

"Thank you... you're not so bad yourself," she replied as she approached the bed.

She lay down beside him, kissed him then broke away.

"Have you eaten yet?" she asked, changing intensity of the moment.

"No," he replied.

"Nor me... I'm starving. Can we get something to eat?"

"Of course, I can ring room service... we can eat in the room. How does that sound?"

"That would be great."

Gerald swung his legs round and sat on the side of the bed; he reached for the white-towelling bathrobe which was on the floor where he had left it earlier, and, rather self-consciously, put it on. He went into the lounge and returned with the room service menu and passed it to her. She sat up, still naked, and scanned the card.

"What do you fancy?" said Gerald.

"Pasta, definitely pasta... gives you energy."

"In that case I'll have the same."

"What about another bottle of wine, a nice Chablis, perhaps?"

"Ok, yeah, great," he said, bowing to her wider knowledge and he went back to the lounge and ordered the food.

He returned to the bedroom and Maureen was still lying on the bed. Gerald lay down beside her and wanted to say something but couldn't find the right words.

She propped her head up on one elbow.

"So, while you were away for six years did you have plenty of girls chasing you?".

Gerald didn't understand the reason for the question but answered truthfully.

"No, no-one."

She was intrigued. "Are you saying you haven't had a girlfriend for six years?"

"Yes... six years, three months, twenty-three days."

"That's very precise."

"Give or take," he quickly added, thinking it may seem a bit strange and smiled. She clearly thought he was joking and didn't press the subject.

"So where were you during your time away?"

Gerald wasn't ready for any third degree.

"Oh, various places," he replied, which he hoped would head off any further questions.

Saved by the bell or should that be 'bell-boy'; there was a knock on the door.

"Our dinner," he said, and got up from the bed and went to answer the door.

The meal was pushed in on a trolley. Two plates covered with metal trays, an ice bucket containing the wine and a single rose in a small vase. The waiter set the table.

"There're condiments underneath the trolley, salt pepper, three kinds of mustard. Just ring if you need anything, Mr Perry."

He hovered for a moment expecting a tip, but quickly realised one was not going to be forthcoming and he turned and left.

"Dinner's ready," shouted Gerald, and Maureen walked into the room, wearing the other bathrobe.

She walked over and kissed him passionately before sitting at the table. Gerald felt a stirring in his loins; the effect she was having on him was visible. As she sat down the robe gaped open and her breasts were clearly visible.

"Careful you don't spill anything hot down your front," said Gerald.

How was he supposed to eat with Maureen sat there virtually naked across the table wrestling with her tagliatelle and chicken? His appetite had disappeared, and he was struggling with his pasta.

Gerald left his unfinished red wine and took a sip of the Chablis; it was crisp and refreshing and went well with the pasta. He thought for a moment; he had never had the chance to study the social graces - food, wine and so on. He put that on his agenda, it had been an omission in his education. He looked across at Maureen who had clearly been hungry, her plate was almost empty. His feast was more ethereal as he continued to devour the beautiful Maureen with his eyes.

She finished her meal and looked at Gerald.

"What do you think of the wine?"

"Yes, good, very good."

With the red wine he'd drank earlier, he was starting to feel a bit light-headed. He eventually managed to eat most of his dinner and crossed his cutlery over the remnants of the pasta.

"Would you like a coffee? I can ring down for some or there's a tray in the cupboard."

"The tray would be fine."

Gerald got up slightly unsteadily and went to the cupboard with the kettle and various sachets of tea and coffee.

"Not a great selection I'm afraid... coffee, decaf or some teas."

"Coffee will be fine."

As the kettle boiled he could see his new mobile phone still plugged into the adjoining socket and noticed it had finished charging.

He watched her from across the room. She was sat at the table drinking her wine appearing totally in control of herself. He wondered how people developed that self-assurance, the confidence that together with her undoubted beauty made her a formidable force. Nature had certainly been kind to Maureen. He inexplicably thought of the poems of Homer and Helen of Troy, daughter of the gods, the face that launched a thousand ships. Somehow it made sense. Did she have such presence?

He took the two coffees to the table. Maureen had moved the plates to the catering trolley.

"So, what you do... forensic science, is it like that programme on the television, you know, what's it called...? 'Silent Witness'."

"I don't know, I haven't seen it," Gerald replied.

"Dissecting dead bodies, finding out how they died, that kind of thing," she clarified.

"Sort of."

"How did you get into it?"

"I studied it at University."

"Where was that?"

"Leeds."

He was not giving anything away and she sensed that and changed the subject. She took a sip of her coffee.

"So, why did you come back to Sheffield?"

"Well, my contract's finished, so I decided it was time to move back to the house."

He was still thinking on his feet.

"It was let while I was away, Mr Cathcart's been looking after things for me."

He realised he hadn't rehearsed any answers for such enquiries. He definitely needed to do more work to perfect his story.

The coffee was giving him the mental and physical stimulus he needed and his mind retuned to more basic desires. He watched her again and took in the curves and shape of her neck, the fold of the white towelling bathrobe which was still gaping forward revealing her breasts. He could see her nipples were erect. This time he took the initiative.

She put her glass of wine on the table, aware of the interest and slowly undid the tie to the bathrobe and let it fall behind her. This time Gerald was on her, pushing her down on the sofa. She responded immediately, and, in a moment, they were together. It was he who was now in control.

When it was finished he collapsed on her totally exhausted and they lay together for some time. She looked at him and started to rub his chest in an affectionate way.

"Would you like me to stay?"

Gerald was still in uncharted waters; it had been a long time since he had slept with a woman.

"Yes, if you like," he said, somewhat feebly. "I would like that, very much," he quickly corrected himself.

"Me too," she said.

Gerald slept the sleep of a baby, his head heavy from the alcohol, but dreams and flashbacks intervened at regular intervals. At one point he saw a big house and Maureen dressed in a white smock riding a horse, galloping across a field, but suddenly it wasn't Maureen; she had changed, it was someone else.

Maureen was aware that Gerald was stirring. "Fancy a coffee...? It's eight-thirty."

Gerald was gradually regaining his consciousness; the makings of a headache dulled his senses. Maureen was still here.

"Mmm, a cup of tea would be nice," he said, still in the throes of focussing his mind.

"Won't be a minute," she said, then got out of bed and wandered to the bathroom.

Gerald was now wide awake watching her naked body disappear into the adjoining room. A few minutes later Maureen appeared in her bathrobe with two mugs and a newspaper. Saturday morning was never this good.

Gerald sat up and took the drink. "Oh, that's just what I needed," he said after taking the first sip.

Maureen got into bed and her perfume hung in the air.

That wonderful smell again, she had freshened up.

She glanced at the headlines. "Anything interesting?"

"Don't think so," said Gerald.

"Did you sleep ok?"

"Like a baby."

"You seemed very restless; you were having some bad dreams I think..." She paused. "Who is Lindsey?"

The mention of the name shook him, and the tea slopped onto the bed sheet.

"Shit," he said, and reprimanded himself for the profanity.

"Sorry, only you shouted her name a couple of times, that's

all. It's ok, it's none of my business."

She picked up the newspaper again and was scanning the inside pages.

Gerald was momentarily stunned. That name, the apparition in the dream; it was Lindsey. She was not allowed into his mind, not allowed, not allowed. He was becoming agitated. Maureen put down the paper and looked at him.

"Are you alright, Greg?"

Greg who's Greg? His mind was in freefall; he felt like he was on a bungee-jump but then the elastic reached its limits and he started moving upwards again. He composed himself and took a deep breath and exhaled.

"Sorry, it was a long time ago."

"Your girlfriend?" she proffered.

"Yes... but we split up... before I went away."

His mind was beginning to re-file things in order.

"It was a long time ago," he repeated, and he sipped at the dregs of his tea and stared into the empty mug. "In the past."

It was Maureen's turn to be reflective and she was beginning to wonder if she had made a mistake in her impulsive dalliance.

"Look, it's been fun but perhaps we should leave it at that."

"No... no, please don't say that." The little boy had returned. "I want to see you again. I'm sorry, it's all been a bit..." He tailed off not really knowing what it had been like. Unexpected, exciting, yes, but the words were inadequate. In the last few hours he had begun to feel 'normal' again.

"Quick?" she said trying to finish his sentence.

It was beginning to sound like a post-mortem and he wanted to retrieve the situation.

"Look... I really want to see you again."

"I'm not Lindsey."

Surprisingly, this time, Gerald did not react to the mention of her name.

"I know, I know. I'm sorry, I'm sorry. It's just... you're the first girl I have been with for over six years. I'm not used..."

"I know," she said cutting him off, trying to relieve the pressure. "As I said it's none of my business."

She looked at the digital clock by the bed. "I really need to go; I've got things to do today."

"Of course," he said. "Will I see you again?"

"Give me your number. I'll phone you."

Gerald got out of bed and went to retrieve his new phone from the lounge. He had to access the 'settings' menu to extract the number. He returned to the bedroom and watched as Maureen dressed and flicked on the memory buttons in his mind; it was a vision he wanted to keep, forever. He wrote the number down on the hotel notepad by the bed and she popped it in her handbag and walked towards the lounge.

"You will phone?" it was almost a statement.

"Yes, I'll call you later. I need to get some housework done."

Housework...? It suddenly occurred to Gerald he knew nothing about Maureen, not even her second name.

She kissed him on the lips like a partner would do before setting off to work; comfortable and affectionate.

"I'll be in touch."

She picked up her jacket which was lying on the floor by one of the sofas and put it on. She opened the door and left without a backward glance leaving Gerald with a mountain of emotions.

The sudden emptiness was palpable. He walked into the bathroom and started running a bath. He poured in some foam from one of the complimentary containers and watched the water bubble; rising and popping, rising and popping.

There was an analogy there somewhere, he thought.

He pressed the whirlpool button and the maelstrom swirled round his body. He disappeared under the water until he couldn't hold his breath anymore and then started to sing to himself.

"*Ying tong, ying tong, ying tong, ying tong, ying tong iddle I po*".

The syllables of the words bounced around the walls of the bathroom the acoustics making them echo.

Louder and louder he sang and then stopped.

The water was cold before he got out and he looked at his hands which were like prunes and then his stomach made a growling noise which reminded that he had not had breakfast. He put a towel around himself and went into the lounge; he dialled room service. Cereals, fruit, a croissant and some coffee would be his breakfast.

The trolley arrived in about twenty minutes and in the interim he had shaved and dressed. His mind was still firmly fixed on last night and Maureen as he tucked into his muesli. Her perfume still hung in the air and he took in the heady aroma and connected the sensation with the passion that had taken place just a few short hours before. His repast seemed to stare back at him in mock defiance; his appetite had ebbed.

He hadn't thought about what he was going to do today. His idea yesterday was just to laze about and enjoy his freedom, maybe watch some sport. Maureen for some reason had changed everything; his whole value system had been shaken. He thought back to some of the therapy sessions and considered some of the mental exercises he had been given.

He knew he had got to get his head straight and congratulated himself on this self-diagnosis.

Another shopping trip perhaps, but with only fifty pounds it wouldn't last too long. He wanted to get one of the new MP3 players he'd read about; he would love to hear some different music, maybe get himself a keyboard and start playing again, but that would have to wait.

He could do with a suitcase now he had a wardrobe of sorts; he would have difficulty in carrying all his gear in the two carriers he had arrived with. He would have a walk around, he decided; he could do with some fresh air. He looked at the clock ten o'clock, the city would be full of shoppers, but no bad thing; he could always lose himself in a crowd.

He put on his jacket and headed down to reception. No keys to hand in; plastic cards were now the order of the day. That was a change from the last time he stayed in a hotel; a trip to Whitby he remembered... with Lindsey.

He couldn't believe her name had found its way in again. He swore to himself and quickened his pace and was soon outside the hotel mingling with shoppers.

Too many memories, too many memories; back in Trenton he had been sheltered from such things, but there was no hiding place in the real world and he would have to come to terms with it if he was going to survive. He would never go back to Trenton, he would kill himself first he vowed.

He checked his pocket; the envelope was there with the rest of his money, but it was the walk more than the shopping he needed. He thought about heading for the Peaks, Baslow was nice; his grandparents used to take him there when he was a little boy. He couldn't remember his parents taking him anywhere; another part of his past erased from his mind by his 'treatment'. But he would need a taxi to get there; he didn't fancy the bus, and it would cost more than he could afford at the moment. That was all about to change; maybe another day. Maybe he would take Maureen out there in his new car. He liked the sound of that.

He spotted a suitcase in a charity shop window and he went inside. It was packed with people sifting through second hand clothing, shoes, books, in fact an array of paraphernalia. He looked at the suitcase and it was good condition, certainly big enough to hold his now expanding collection of worldly goods and at five pounds it was not going to put too much strain on his resources. He took it to the counter where one of the volunteers was taking money, an elderly lady, grey/blue hair. Gerald admired what she was doing; the selfless dedication to others and he felt humbled having been mixed up in his own world for so long. His turn came, and he held the suitcase up for the lady to see. She spotted the label.

"Five pounds, love," she said.

Gerald produced a ten-pound note from his envelope.

"Keep the change," he said in an effort to assuage his guilt.

"Thank you, love, that's very generous of you," she said, and Gerald left the shop with his latest acquisition.

"Coffee time," he said to himself and found one of the new café-bars which were starting to spring up everywhere he noticed. He went in and found a seat placing his valise under the table. A couple of minutes later a waitress came over and took his order. He took his new phone out and started playing with the settings, experimenting. Ring tone, wallpaper, volume, he soon had it set to his preference. He just needed it to ring.

The waitress returned with the coffee and he sat there for half an hour just soaking up the atmosphere and fiddling with his new gadget. Rather than wander around, he decided to return to the hotel feeling a bit self-conscious with the suitcase; he had a picture in his mind of a black-market salesman from the old war-time films his mother used to watch. He suddenly had the urge to shout. "Stockings, cigarettes, perfume?"

It was another reference from his past that had scraped under the wire, but this time he didn't feel any threat. It also occurred to him that he hadn't eyed up the girl in the coffee shop; Maureen had fulfilled all his fantasies and there was no place for anyone else.

Back in his room he placed the case in the wardrobe beneath his hanging shirts and trousers and checked the time. He put on the TV to watch a football match; he enjoyed watching the odd game when he was allowed at Trenton. Usually it was just the big International matches; there was no Sky coverage, budgets and all that. He rang room service and ordered a sandwich and settled down for the afternoon. He wondered how Maureen was getting on with her housework.

Chapter Five

The afternoon went by and Gerald was beginning to get restless. The football scores were being announced on the TV, but he was not interested and began pacing the room. He went to the window and gazed down on the people scuttling around with their urgent stuff, into the shops, out of the shops, back and forth; there was no discernible pattern that would make the behaviour... orderly, give it shape it was just... random.

Gerald didn't do random; he liked things as they should be. He would love a giant remote control where he could put all the people in lines and move them from place to place like on a giant chess-board. That would be... cool, he thought.

"Cool?" now there's a new word, everyone was using it. Need to look cool, need to be cool, be accepted; Gerald needed to be cool.

As the minutes ticked by his depression increased and he was experiencing his own 'Black Dog', the same feeling, he speculated, that would inflict Winston Churchill from time to time, not that he could compare himself with the great man, just empathise. He made himself another cup of tea to give him a lift but after ten minutes the refreshing drink had failed to lift his spirits.

The evening came; he ordered a bar meal and a bottle of wine from room service but couldn't eat much, and the remainder of the club sandwich lay on the plate gradually curling in the heat of the room. The wine bottle remained unopened.

He went to the window again and looked out over the City, the lights shining, winking, blinking; traffic lights red, red-amber, green and back. Spots of rain streaked the window which seemed to match his mood. He tried to watch a hospital drama on the TV. He could test his memory of some of the procedures, but he found it difficult to concentrate. He opened the bottle of wine and drunk a glass, but that made him feel nauseous and he decided against another.

Then, twelve-minutes past ten he heard a noise which he didn't immediately recognise; a tinny rendition of some unrecognisable pre-programmed tune. His phone!!

"Where did I put it...? Where is it...? Wait, wait... don't ring off," he said out loud.

He followed the sound to his jacket and berated himself for not putting it somewhere more accessible. He extracted it from the depths of his pocket and hit the green button.

"Hello," he said.

"Hi, its Maureen," said the voice on the other end.

His mind raced, and his stomach churned again.

"I didn't think you were going to phone," he said, too subserviently he quickly recognised. Must be more confident, he told himself. Play it cool.

"I've been busy," she said. "You ok?"

"Yes, I am now," he said, still not following his own advice.

"I'm in town, I can come up... if you like," she said, and he sat on the sofa digesting the words for a split second. "Yes!!" he said silently to himself.

"Yes... yes, that would be great."

"About ten minutes. Need to find a place to park."

"Great, see you then..." and she rang off leaving Gerald with a feeling of elation and excitement; his depression had vanished in a flash.

"Shit!" he said, then remonstrated himself again for the expletive; profanities were the sign of a lazy mind he remembered. He looked at the state of the room. He couldn't believe he'd allowed it to become so untidy. He picked up the towelling bath robe from the floor and put it in the bedroom. He quickly buffed up the cushions and got them in their right place, at the same angle pointing towards the centre of the room.

He put the remnants of his meal on the tray and took it down the corridor away from his front door. He put the wine bottle and two glasses on the table. He took the cork out; he would let it... breathe; he smiled at Maureen's comments from last night.

"There!" he exclaimed, looking at the now orderly room.

Gerald went to the bathroom and jumped in the shower to freshen up and afterwards, as he dried himself off, he glanced in the mirror, this time paying more attention.

He had a good physique, lean and sculptured, quite muscular, the kind of shape that attracts women. At thirty-two he was probably the fittest he had ever been thanks to the gym work he was encouraged to put in at Trenton. "Gets the endorphins going," he was told.

He should have visited the leisure centre at the hotel earlier he thought, but of course he didn't have any kit. He put on another new shirt and slacks.

Gerald was suddenly overcome by insecurity again and started to feel nervous; self-doubt began to consume him.

He looked at his watch again, any minute now he thought. He wished he had some music, and then remembered. He flicked through the TV channels on the remote and found Radio 1; music he didn't recognise. Hip hop, hip hop. He flicked further, Radio 2, smooth jazz... that's better he thought, more in tune with the moment. He chuckled at the unintended pun. He adjusted the volume until it was ambient. There were speakers built in around the suite and even in the toilet, now that is luxury he thought.

Ten twenty-five and there was a tap, tap on the door. It made him jump; he took another deep breath and made his way to the door. He opened it and the perfume hit him.

He suddenly recounted one of Rome's finest romantic poets, Catullus. He enjoyed reading Roman and Greek literature. He was trying to recount the exact words which went along the lines of, '*so great was the power of her scent that he wished he could have been all nose.*' He could relate to that.

"Hi," he said, unable to think of anything else, and he followed her into the room taking in that incredible aroma.

"Hi Greg."

Gerald had to readjust; he was now Greg, the confident lover, cool and in control. He suddenly realised that this was the answer, the new coping mechanism; from now on he would be 'cool' Greg.

He looked at her; she was wearing the same jacket, a short denim skirt and an orange check shirt. The fourth button was undone, revealing a white, lacy bra.

She took off her jacket and gave it to 'Greg' and he put it in the wardrobe.

"You look stunning," he said and kissed her affectionately and led her to one of the sofas. "Would you like a glass of wine, Australian red, cabinet sauvignon... 2005 a good vintage, apparently?"

He repeated authoritatively the words of the wine waiter who had delivered the meal earlier.

"Yes great..." she said. "You look different."

"Probably the shirt."

"No... something else," but left it there.

Greg handed her the wine and clinked his glass. 'Cheers, they said together.

"What have you done today?" she asked, taking her first sip and they exchanged stories.

Gradually the mood became more relaxed. Cool Greg was now in charge; his former coping mechanisms had been replaced by a new, more confident, persona. The uncertainties of the previous day appeared to have gone.

They continued chatting and he discovered more about her; it was he who was asking the questions.

She told him she lived just outside the City boundaries in Derbyshire; it was a good deal cheaper, she said. She rented a two-bedroomed flat above a shop and drove a mini cooper. He was attentive, and, in conversation, she recognised his growing self-belief and that was the difference. He seemed to be more confident, something she found very attractive. She was used to being surrounded by strong personalities.

As they talked his attention was drawn once again to Maureen. Her blouse was straining at button five he noticed, and she caught his gaze. She looked at him and smiled.

The conversation stopped, she put her wine glass on the table and undid button five... and six. Gerald nearly fainted. She pushed the shirt back over her shoulders and it dropped on the sofa behind her.

"God you're beautiful," was all he could say, picturing her breasts encased in the diaphanous bra.

The music on the radio was playing quietly in the background and they sat there without talking for a while; words had become superfluous. She took another sip of her wine and then stood up and started swaying to the music. She watched him as she removed her bra and continued the tease until she was completely naked.

At her beckoning he stood up and she helped him remove his clothes and then once more she led him to the bedroom.

That night Gerald completed the mental transition; he was now Greg, cool, smooth and in control. He would banish Gerald forever and as he lay there holding Maureen, he realised how much his 'exclusion' had cost him.

He slept the carefree sleep of a child, as if his demons had been exorcised by some unseen priest.

Sunday morning and it was eight o'clock before he stirred, and Maureen was still asleep. He gently eased himself from the bed trying not to wake her and went into the lounge to make some tea. While the kettle was boiling he went to the entrance door and opened it; the complimentary newspaper was hanging on the door handle. He walked back in the bedroom in a bathrobe with the tray with two mugs of tea, the newspaper and the glass with the single rose.

"Madam, your tea is served," he said, doing his finest butler impression and she slowly opened her eyes and smiled.

"Mmm, what time is it?"

"Quarter to nine."

"It's early," she said sleepily and slowly raised herself from her pillow to take the tea from him.

'Greg' still couldn't get over the events of the last couple of days. Even in her waking she was beautiful. Her perfume still hung in the air and he watched her as she drank her tea, totally naked but completely at ease with herself.

"Have you got any plans today?" he asked.

"Nothing special," she said, still trying to acclimatise herself to the new day.

"I was thinking of going out to the Peaks, Baslow perhaps; it's been ages since I've been there. Would you like to come with me?"

She thought for a moment.

"Yeah, ok, why not... but I'll need to pop back home to change; I'm not geared up for any walking."

"Is it ok if we use your car...? I don't pick mine up till tomorrow... or we can go by bus, I don't mind.".

Maureen looked at him, "Yes, of course... no problem."

"That's great... would you like some breakfast? I'll ring down."

"Yeah, thanks, just some toast and tea please. While you do that I need a shower."

She got out of bed and disappeared into the bathroom.

After breakfast, Maureen was sat on the sofa in the lounge reading the paper in her outfit from the previous night. Greg was still heady from the recent experiences and tried not to stare at her; he thought she looked incredible. Her perfume, only a hint of make-up, her shirt, more demurely fastened, and denim skirt. He quickly came out of his trance and reminded himself he was now cool Greg.

He was scanning through the supplements when Maureen got up.

She looked at her watch. "I'd better get going… I'll pick you up outside about midday. Ok?"

"Yeah, ok, that's great," and he kissed her warmly.

She put her jacket on, put her bag over her shoulder and left.

Greg needed to regroup his emotions; he could feel Gerald trying to re-enter now that Maureen had left. Somehow, he was going to have to overcome this battle.

It was ten-thirty and he had an hour and a half to kill before her return; he decided to go for a walk to clear his head.

It was about twelve-fifteen when the brown and cream Mini-Cooper pulled up at the drop-off point in front of the hotel. Greg had been waiting for twenty-five minutes in case she was early.

She was dressed in jeans and a dark top with a yellow design in Chinese characters.

"Hi," said Greg and he got in. The weather was fine after last night's rain and the late summer sun played hide and seek among the clouds.

It took about half-an-hour to reach the small town which was packed with sight-seers and walkers. Maureen steered the mini into a public car park and fed the meter. Greg had no change; his remaining money was still in the envelope.

After a look around, they found a small cafe, and Greg bought lunch, two plates of sandwiches and two coffees.

Maureen wanted to know more about her enigmatic lover.

"So, what are you going to do now you're back?" she asked, in between bites of her tuna and mayo.

"Not sure, yet. I'll be spending some time at the house; there's a lot to do there, then I'll decide."

"Will you go back to forensic science?"

"Yes, possibly, if the right opportunity crops up."

"Where was your last job?"

She was moving into difficult territory for Greg, but he'd had time to concoct a believable story.

Although the transition between Gerald and Greg was still fragile, he could feel it strengthening all the time. The coping strategies seemed to be working and in 'cool' Greg he had found an alter-ego that he could manage and develop.

"New York," he said.

"Wow, you mean as in... 'CSI New York'?"

"What do you mean?" asked Greg.

"Crime Scene Investigation, New York... the TV series."

Greg looked blank.

"Hmm. You've been away *too* long, Greg Perry," she said with a smile.

Greg Perry…? Now he was confused. Then he remembered, she'd called him Mr Perry at the solicitors.

Now he was really in a quandary, cool Greg was 'Jensen', the same as the famous Interceptor car. He decided it best to leave it for now; he would explain things when the time was right.

He had no recollection of Baslow. He knew he had been there as a child, but none of the landmarks struck a chord; there was no familiarity; it was as though the memory had been wiped clean. The rest of the afternoon was spent wandering around the village and walking up into the hills.

Greg had a new tune in his mind and was singing it to himself. Lou Reed's 'Perfect Day'; it didn't get any better than this, he thought, as he walked hand in hand with Maureen, just like a real couple. He couldn't remember ever being this contented.

Lindsey's name did flash into his mind for a nano-second, but he was able to block it from his mind. In fact, he was beginning to feel more comfortable with the odd flash backs. He imagined a computer firewall. He would erect his own imaginary barrier to keep 'Gerald' at bay; he would be confined to history; dead and buried, out of his mind forever.

They got back to the hotel at around five o'clock and Maureen dropped him off outside the front entrance. He had of course asked her if she wanted to stay for a meal, but, with work in the morning, Greg would be on his own tonight. Somehow, it didn't feel so bad. She said she would see him again and was interested in the house. He would invite her over as soon as possible. Today had been his perfect day, and he was in positive mode; the possibilities seemed endless, he was 'cool' Greg and on fire.

Monday morning ten o'clock, and Greg was waiting outside the offices of Cathcart Rivers. He was carrying his suitcase containing most of his belongings, but he had a carrier bag with his toiletries and shoes. He did not want to run the risk of soiling his new clothes.

He rang the bell and waited in anticipation for Maureen to answer. He wondered what she would be wearing today. The security chain rattled, and the door opened.

"Hi..." said Greg but was stopped in his tracks. It wasn't Maureen but a more mature lady, probably in her late fifties, with hairs growing from moles on her chin. She was wearing a twin set and pearls, much more in keeping with the firm.

"Mr Jensen?" she enquired in a rather formal post-war BBC accent, "Mr Cathcart *is* expecting you".

"Thank you," he said, and followed her into the reception area, carrying his suitcase and carriers. He had been momentarily distracted, concerned with the whereabouts of Maureen.

Then he realised the woman had used his new name; it could be good news, he thought. The sooner Gerald Perry was buried the better; he could move on.

She went behind the desk and dialled a number and told Greg to take a seat. "Mr Cathcart will be with you in a moment. Do you want to leave your things with me? They will be quite safe."

"Yes, thank you," said Greg, and passed over his belongings."

He looked around the reception area; it was as quiet as a morgue, no phones, nothing, just the hum of the neon light fittings.

A few minutes later Arthur Cathcart and his dandruff greeted Greg.

"Come through, dear boy, come through," he said, and lead him down the corridor to his office.

"How are you today, Gerald…? Or should that be Greg?"

He indicated for him to sit down.

"What... you mean?"

"Yes, dear boy, all the paperwork came through this morning; you are now officially, Greg Jensen. Congratulations, we can now sort everything out."

"That's great," said Greg. The transition was now complete.

There was a knock on the door and the receptionist put her head around the door.

"Coffee, gentlemen?"

"Yes please, just milk for me," said Greg.

"Usual, Mr Cathcart?" she said to Cathcart. He grunted a response which she took as an affirmative and closed the door.

"Where's Maureen?" asked Greg.

"Dentists, she phoned in earlier. I'm expecting her back later this morning," replied Cathcart.

Greg exhaled; he had felt anxious for some reason.

"There's a lot to get through, but I'll explain everything as we go along, and if there's anything you don't understand you must tell me."

Greg nodded his mind still not totally focussed.

"I have all your bank details here; the account numbers are on this sheet. We've set up a current account and savings account where you can keep any surplus to get some interest; you can transfer in and out as you need. Clear?" Greg was trying to take in all the information and nodded again.

"The annuities which were set up on your inheritance are still in operation and presently returning about…" He checked his notes. "Just over two thousand pounds a month, so you'll have some income to help you run the house. If you stay there you're going to need it. It's very expensive to run."

"I do intend to stay," said Greg.

The solicitor looked up from his file. "That's your decision, but, as I say, it will be a costly business."

"I do intend to get a job," countered Greg.

Cathcart made a grunting noise in acknowledgment and went back to his file.

"This is your cheque book and this, your debit card, which you'll need to make purchases. Nobody uses cheques anymore."

Greg did remember debit cards. "Yes, I know how to use them."

The solicitor handed Greg more documents. "Here's your new passport and driver's licence. I've checked and it's still valid; you won't have to take your test again, but we'll need to sort out insurance before you can drive."

"That's a relief," said Greg. "I was hoping to get a hire-car today I can use until I get around to buying one. It's a bit of a trek to the house and I don't want to keep using taxis."

"I'll get Joan to ring Auto-hire, for you; we use them quite regularly. We can register one in the firm's name until we sort something out permanently."

Cathcart picked up the phone and gave Joan her instructions about the car-hire.

He continued. "Good that's done. Now the house... I've spoken to the architect and project manager; the work's virtually complete. There is still some scaffolding up, so you will need to be careful when moving about outside. There's some repair work which the builders have noticed which wasn't done properly after the fire."

"What fire?" asked Greg, only half listening, as he took his cup and saucer from the tray on the desk.

Cathcart looked at him in incredulity for a moment. "Of course, you don't know, do you?"

"Know what?" said Greg taking a sip of coffee still distracted with his refreshment.

"How your grandparents died... the circumstances," replied the solicitor, solemnly.

The words hit Greg with a jolt; he was suddenly very attentive.

"Only what they told me at Trenton. I didn't take it in much at the time; they just said there'd been an accident. I hadn't seen them for over three years; they never visited. I thought they'd abandoned me."

"Far from it, dear boy, far from it; in fact, they blamed themselves for your... illness. I had many conversations with them after... the incident," he euphemised. "They wanted to make sure you were looked after which is why they left you everything. They felt very guilty."

Greg tried to take this all in. He realised he had been

sheltered from the real world at Trenton; treated with kid-gloves and wrapped in cotton wool, so as not to disturb him into a regression. He wondered if, in reality, this had helped; it certainly hadn't prepared him for life outside.

Cathcart could see Greg was deep in thought but continued.

"I'm sorry, but I was told not to say anything about the fire. I was asked to keep our discussions upbeat and positive... which, of course, wasn't easy when dealing with your family estate."

This answered a lot of questions. Greg had found the solicitor somewhat weasel-like and didn't really warm to him, but he was beginning to change his opinion. Gerald often tried to manipulate him; it had become a game, but it was very obvious that Arthur Cathcart had done a great deal for him.

"So, what did happen?" asked Greg.

Cathcart took his time searching for the right words. He peered over the top of his spectacles, giving him a sinister appearance.

"It was over two years ago, July 2005... the 17th, if I remember correctly. Nobody knows for sure what happened, the fire brigade and forensic examinations were inconclusive. Some locals were even talking about spontaneous combustion, which was a bit fanciful. A woman was walking her dog through the woods at the back of the house and noticed smoke coming through the window on the third floor and she called the police and fire brigade. It was about nine o'clock in the evening. They managed to contain the fire, but the back bedroom was badly damaged. Your grandparents were found dead in bed. They had suffocated according to the coroner."

Greg looked quizzical trying to take it all in; his forensic mind suddenly sprang into action.

"How did the fire start, did they say?

"Too much damage, it was impossible to tell, but your grandfather smoked a pipe and it is thought he either fell asleep or had a heart attack and the embers caught fire to the bedclothes."

"But that can't be right... It would be almost impossible for tobacco ash to cause a flash fire, it would just smoulder."

Greg's earlier education was coming back to him.

"And what about my grandmother...? She would never let him smoke in the bedroom. In fact, the only time I saw him smoking a pipe was in the garden, and in the downstairs toilet. She hated the smell..." Greg paused for a moment. "And why didn't she wake up? In fact, why were they in bed at that time of night at all? They never used to go to bed until gone eleven after my grandfather retired."

"That's something we will never know, dear boy; the coroner's verdict was accidental death."

Greg was deep in thought... He sensed Gerald was trying hard to intervene, but Greg managed to stay in control.

"How long did they investigate?" he asked.

"Not too long. There was no evidence to suggest foul play. No motive. They were well liked. Everybody said so at the inquest."

"Inquest...!? When was this...? Why wasn't I consulted...? I could have told them a lot about their routines and stuff." Gerald was trying to resurface again.

"I think it was thought, how can I put it...? Inappropriate to call you as a witness... you understand." said Cathcart, sagely.

Greg nodded. "Yeah... I guess so."

Cathcart looked at Greg, sensing a level of distress.

"Are you alright...?" he enquired.

Greg took another drink of coffee digesting this recent information.

"Yeah, I'm ok."

The solicitor, seeing his client was calmer, continued.

"Let's move on..." said the solicitor. "We have a lot to

cover."

"Ok," replied Greg, but his mind was still on his grandparents" death.

"Wednesday... you're seeing your social worker, right?"

Greg shook himself out of his retrospection.

"Yes... yes, ten o'clock."

"Right, this is very important; under the Mental Health Act you have to undergo a period of supervision. This is fairly routine, but it's important for two reasons; to ensure you are integrating... settling in successfully..." he clarified. "And, to not put too fine a point on it, ensure you pose no threat to the public. It *is* a condition of your release."

Greg at first found this insulting but realised what the solicitor was saying.

"Yeah, I understand."

"As I said, you cannot miss these appointments, or you'll be recalled. Do you understand?"

Greg nodded.

"You'll also have to meet with your psychiatrist once a month. You know Doctor Melrose, don't you?"

"Yes, I remember her," He, or more correctly, Gerald, liked Doctor Melrose.

"For the time, being I've asked her to contact me to arrange the appointments. You can use a room here instead of the General for your meetings... more comfortable," he said, referring to the Northern General Hospital's mental health wing.

"One final thing ..." he paused again; this was a sensitive issue. "On no account are you to contact or try to contact ..." he referred to his notes, "Lindsey Jones."

Greg shuddered at the mention of her name but very quickly composed himself. There was no sign of Gerald; this was progress.

"Of course not; I have no interest in her."

"Good, we'll leave it there. I've informed your social worker where you're staying, and you must tell her, or me, if you decide to move. You'll also have to inform her of the change of name and she'll advise the Justice department, so everything's above board."

"Can you do that for me?" asked Greg.

"Yes, I'll send a letter today with a copy of the deed."

"When are you intending to move back to the house?" asked Cathcart.

"Today, I want to go there after I leave here. There'll be a lot to do."

"Right... one or two things. All the furnishings which we discussed are in, and your computer and Internet connection were installed over the weekend... I called and confirmed with the project manager earlier this morning. All your grandparent's belongings were auctioned. Some of the ornaments and paintings were quite valuable; the sale moneys were added to the estate. I have a note of them somewhere I can let you have. There is however a trunk of personal belongings and some bits and pieces in the scullery under the stairs... I had them put there after your grandparents died. They've not been touched; I have kept it locked and have the keys. The recent tenants didn't have access. I thought you could have a look through sometime. It's mostly old photos and letters. You can get rid of anything you don't want to keep..."

Cathcart was still holding a sheet of paper to make sure he hadn't missed anything.

"Oh yes, one final thing, I've managed to get you a housekeeper; you can't manage that place on your own. I've suggested she does three days a week, but you can of course change that if you wish. I've asked her to go in today to do some tidying up; builders do tend to make a lot of mess...

She'll stock up the fridge with some basics as well."

"Thank you... for everything," said Greg and Cathcart grimaced in way that could have been a smile.

"Good luck," he said. "Oh... nearly forgot, you will need these," and he passed Greg a ring with a number of keys attached to it. There was a plastic label with 'Taskers End' written on it in black ink.

Greg looked at them and then at the solicitor.

"Why is the house called 'Taskers End'...? Do you know...? I've often wondered; my grandparents never told me."

"Hmm, it's a long story but briefly, the building work for the house was started by your grandmother's great grandfather Cornelius Tasker in 1865, but he never finished it. According to legend, a stone from one of the turrets fell on him and crushed his skull."

"So much for health and safety," said Greg.

"Quite... as I understand it the house was named by his son Stanley, who finished it in 1867 but he too died shortly after from T.B... all very tragic. In fact, some say the house is cursed."

He looked at Greg over his half-rimmed spectacles in a way which Greg found a bit unsettling, chilling almost.

"I was very happy there," said Greg.

"Of course you were, dear boy, of course you were," said Cathcart, quickly back tracking.

"Well, if there's nothing else, I'll see if Joan has managed to fix you up with transport."

The solicitor got out of his chair and handed over the various papers to Greg.

Cathcart led the way down the corridor to reception and Joan was sat at the reception desk busy typing.

"Any news on the car-hire, Joan?" he said, disturbing her concentration.

"Yes," she said, without looking up. She finished what she was doing and made eye contact with Greg.

"They said they would try and get it here at around eleven-thirty... I managed to get you an Audi, Mr Jensen, hope that's alright… The firm's insurance brokers are going to issue a cover note and they're going to send it to your house"

"That's great, thank you very much."

Greg turned to his solicitor.

"And thank you, Mr Cathcart, I appreciate everything you've done for me. I don't know what I'd have done without you."

He extended his hand which Cathcart shook warmly.

"Let me know if you have any problems, dear boy... any problems at all."

Greg looked around; there was no sign of Maureen.

Joan appeared with Greg's suitcase and carriers and noticed his interest. "Not back yet, shouldn't be long, I wouldn't think," she said, and handed over his things.

Greg smiled and walked towards the front door with his suitcase and carrier. Joan got up from her desk and caught him up. She opened the door.

"Bye, Mr Jensen."

Greg walked down the three steps and stood on the pavement with his belongings. He checked his watch it was eleven twenty-four. There was a vacant parking bay immediately in front of him. He would wait.

A couple of minutes later, he noticed a silver 'five-series' BMW pull up on the other side of the road with two occupants. A middle-aged man was driving, and a younger woman was in the passenger seat. The sun was reflecting on the windscreen and he couldn't make it out clearly, but the woman leaned over and kissed the man before getting out.

The car pulled away and his heart went into his mouth.

It was Maureen.

Chapter Six

The alleyway between the solicitors and the accountants next door was used as access to the rear of the properties, mostly by bin-men to collect the rubbish from the offices every Friday. Greg quickly hid in there out of sight until he heard Maureen enter the building. The door closed, and he returned to his vantage point waiting for his car; his mind was in overdrive.

It didn't compute. He could feel Gerald trying to make an appearance. He fiddled with a button on his jacket, he had the urge to curl up, but social programming prevented that. He could not afford any lapses, not now.

He managed to bring back some composure; his firewall idea seemed to be working. He chastened himself; this was cool Greg now, Gerald must be banished, forever. He would have to think this through later. His meanderings were brought back to focus when a black Audi A3 pulled up in the parking bay in front of him. The driver turned off the engine and got out. He looked at Greg.

"Mr Jensen?" he enquired.

"Yes," said Greg.

"Scott Farmer, from Auto-hire."

They completed the paperwork on top of the car and he signed as Greg Jensen for the first time. He hadn't practiced a signature and only just stopped himself from signing 'Gerald Perry'.

The salesman explained the controls then opened the boot, so Greg could stow his luggage. He was given a receipt and then Scott walked off to get a taxi back to his office. He hadn't asked for a lift and it didn't occur to Greg to offer one.

A fine motor, he thought as he sat on the leatherette seat looking at the impressive array of dials in front of him. He checked the gear gate and practised, first, down to second, across the third, down to fourth and across to fifth. He reminded himself to remember the fifth gear; all his previous cars had four. He corrected the rear view and side mirrors and was ready. Seat position fine, he turned the ignition key and the car roared to life. He then thought about the route.

It had been a long time since he driven in town and there had been a huge change in the road system by the local council all designed to keep the traffic moving but serving only to confuse the unwary or unfamiliar motorist. He waited until the road was completely clear and then set off very carefully.

He could feel the pull; it was like trying to hold back a rampant stallion in sight of a mare. Gingerly he manoeuvred the car around the back streets until he came to the junction with the main A57 which would take him almost to the door. He indicated left and merged into the traffic flow, negotiated a couple of roundabouts. It was like he had never been away.

The road was clear as he left the city-centre behind him and he soon reached a familiar landmark, his old school. He shivered as he had another flash-back. Classmates... singing, "Gerry Perry's a fairy"; "Gerry Perry's a fairy". He remembered the humiliation of the ritual 'de-bagging'- having his trousers and pants forcibly removed and draped over the teacher's chair. Then there were the cruel jibes about his parents. The bullying greatly affected him at the time, but he told no-one, not even his grandparents. He had sought solace in his books.

He quickly dispatched his reminiscences and his firewall remained intact, shutting out any unwanted visit from his former self. He was cool Greg now, not Gerald.

It was a good six or seven miles out of town to Taskers End but the car was making light work of the journey and after about ten minutes or so he came round a bend to a familiar land mark. There was a turning to the right with a large house on the corner; his nearest neighbour, he recalled. He seemed to remember it being a B & B, a small hotel, but couldn't be certain. There was an impressive sign outside; 'The Pines, Residential Home for the Elderly', it said. Now *that* was new.

The care home was blessed with impressive gardens with sweeping green lawns and vibrant shrubbery. Large rhododendrons were in full bloom adding a colourful back-drop to the landscape. Luxuriant pine-trees added shape and height to the grounds. He moved slowly along the road curious to see what other changes had taken place in his neighbourhood.

As he passed the Pines' boundary fence, he came to a new development where the former wooded area had been cleared and two substantial houses had been built, set back among the trees. It had been completed fairly recently judging by the freshness of the tarmac in the drives and the light colour of the stonework, not yet weathered by the elements; new neighbours.

A short distance past the houses, the road narrowed, and the trees thickened into a copse. He suddenly caught a glance of the top of one of the turrets appearing above the hedging; it was like a siren beckoning a stricken sailor. He could almost hear it calling him; welcome home, welcome home. A chill ran down his spine; he checked the car's air conditioning; it was fine.

There were two stone gateposts with the words 'Taskers End' ornately chiselled on each of them, a credit to the stone mason's art. They were original and had suffered at the ravages of time with lichen and moss providing a green tinge. He slowly made the left turn through them and a thirty-metre gravel drive brought him in front of the house. He got out and stared up at the old building; he again felt a shiver run the length of his body, so many memories.

Surprisingly, there was no sign of Gerald. Greg seemed to have mastered the art of keeping him away; stay calm and confident... 'cool' Greg.

He parked the Audi in front of the large garage which was

set back from the main building and he walked round to the front door.

There was a skip full of the detritus of the building work in the corner of the parking area. There was also a pile of stone rocks, the same type as was used to build the house and a quantity of sand. He looked up at the two turrets on the roof looking like church steeples. He could recall climbing up inside them when he was younger; he flinched slightly at the memory. There was scaffolding still erected at the side which appeared to run around the back of the house; he would check later.

He opened the front door and was hit by the smell of paint and new carpets. He went through the small vestibule into the hallway which was entirely wood-panelled, just as he had remembered it. To the left was the old library which his grandfather used as a study/sitting room, next to that the large living room/lounge which overlooked the drive and, at the far end of the hall to the right, the kitchen. The wide stairway which spiralled up to the first floor was opposite the kitchen, past the lounge. Greg checked them in turn and as he stood looking around each of the rooms. Memories were being played out in his mind some happy, some not so.

He noticed all the old paintings had gone but he was not unhappy with that. Some used to frighten him when he was younger. There was a Victorian etching of a Punch and Judy show which would give him nightmares.

He was pleased with the building and decorating work; it appeared to have been carried out to the high standard that he had insisted. There were no scratches on the expensive panelling and no tell-tale specs of paint. All the rooms, except the kitchen, were carpeted, but they were quite stark in appearance; minimal clutter, just functional furnishings.

He instinctively took his shoes off before he went into the living room, something his grandmother had instilled in him;

the deep-seated conditioning of old habits dies hard.

There was a large leather sofa facing a new flat-screen TV on the wall; there was also a coffee table, bookcase and two arm chairs, which were new. Three central heating radiators would provide warmth and there was also a gas fire which must have been installed after he had left. There was originally a coal fire, he recalled. The new oat-meal colour carpet matched the room well; he was pleased with his choices. He walked back and into the study; the large bookshelves dominated the room. The books were intact as far as he could tell, as if they had never been touched.

The kitchen had been completely renovated and had the latest 'white goods' - dishwasher, large range, American style fridge, freezer and washing machine and tumble dryer in the utility-room which was in an adjoining area beyond the kitchen. There was also a TV on the wall which would enable him to watch while he was cooking or having breakfast. From the utility room a door opened out onto the back garden.

He came out of the kitchen and went up the stairs and looked in each of the four bedrooms on the first floor. On his instructions none had been furnished; he had decided to 'mothball' these rooms to save heat.

He went up a further flight of stairs to the top of the house. One of the old bedrooms on this floor which looked out over the front drive had been converted into an office/computer room. Next to his new office was a large bathroom with shower, tub complete with whirlpool bath and toilet. On the opposite side of the corridor was his bedroom which he realised was his grandparents' old room in which they had died two years earlier.

He opened the door and looked around. The bed was a large 'queen-size' with a bedside table either side; in front against the wall, a dressing table with mirror and there was a walk-in wardrobe which he hoped to fill over the coming weeks. In hindsight, he might have chosen a different room for himself had he known about the fire.

Surveying the room, he was filled with a great sadness and found himself playing the same question over and over again in his mind; how had they died?

The account from his solicitor this morning just didn't add up. He just wished he had been around at the time; he would have certainly been able to shed more light on the matter and perhaps a more detailed investigation would have been carried out. There would be no forensic evidence left now; none that could be relied on in court anyway.

He went to the window and peered out; it was quite a long way down, probably thirty-feet or more. He gazed across the large lawn to the woods at the bottom of the garden beyond the boundary fence, where the dog-walker would have been. He looked at the grass and grimaced; he was going to need a gardener. As he had thought, the scaffolding was still up on this side of the house which detracted from the view but that would be gone shortly. He was amazed at what had been achieved in such a short time; they must have worked twenty-four-hour shifts, he surmised.

He went back downstairs and into the kitchen. He looked in the fridge and it had been stocked up by the housekeeper, as the solicitor had said. Greg was keen to meet her and discuss cleaning arrangements which would be quite onerous with his exacting standards. She would be calling three mornings a week, Monday, Wednesday and Friday. With his appointment on Wednesday it would probably not be until the end of the week.

He took out some milk and made himself a coffee. As he opened the cupboard over the worktop he looked at the rows of jars and tinned produce, he would need to make some adjustments; it was not in order. He opened the cutlery drawer and made sure all the knives, forks and spoons were in the right compartment.

He sat on one of the kitchen stools at the breakfast bar topping up his caffeine and started thinking. Maureen, what was happening there? He wound back to the previous day and their trip to Baslow; it had been 'perfect', she couldn't have betrayed him surely. He managed to suppress any excursions from Gerald; Greg stayed firmly in charge. Don't jump to conclusions, he told himself; the firewall was still intact.

Early afternoon and, after a sandwich, he decided to have a look round the outside of the house; he was interested to see what work had been carried out. He checked that he had his phone in his pocket just in case he had a call. He went to the garage and on the ring of keys was a fob which worked the automatic door. He aimed it at the garage and pressed the button and slowly the wide garage door rolled upwards. Greg went inside.

The garage would comfortably accommodate two cars; it had been originally an outhouse of some sort, possibly a barn, made of the same stone as the main house and was also a solid construction. There was a long workbench down the right-hand side with various tools still hung on the wall on hooks; hammers, saws, socket sets and numerous screwdrivers of several different sizes in neat rows. Straight away Greg saw the inspection pit. He had forgotten that. His grandfather, as well as being an engineer, was a keen mechanic and did his own car servicing. Greg remembered him tinkering about underneath his cars for hours. His grandmother would be continually remonstrating with him not to get grease on the carpet. These memories were good memories and he smiled at the recall.

Where it stood now, however, the pit was a hazard and at almost five-feet deep, it would need to be filled in. He made a mental note. He got into the car and drove it into the garage with the pit underneath which would be a lot safer; he was not intending on driving again today. He left the garage and used the fob again to shut it.

He tracked around the outside of the house and from what he could see it looked in good condition. The downstairs rooms had been double glazed some time ago and the plastic frames were not warped or discoloured; the pointing was sound he noticed. Around the back a ladder was leant against the scaffolding that stretched to the top floor and instinctively he climbed up. He walked along the second-floor platform and it was fine, some remedial work had been carried out and was freshly painted. There was one area, however, in which he had a particular interest.

There was another shorter ladder from the second floor onto the third-floor platform and he climbed up and worked his way across to his bedroom window. It was a long way down and, without the benefit of safely rails, he moved slowly. He had earlier opened the bedroom window to help get rid of the paint smell and he carefully reached the sill and looked at it closely. He ran his hands down the frame. Sure enough he could feel that a piece of wood had been inserted down the side of the window where the opening latch was. A new latch had been screwed in; it was slightly different from the other window latches. He examined the bottom of the sill and again there was evidence of a repair. There was a longer piece of new wood which had been inserted where the casement stay that secured the window had been replaced. The two pieces had been painted over but the joins were quite clear to see. It would be difficult to tell how long ago the repairs had been made but it would be consistent with the window being forced open, presumably by the fire brigade on the night of the fire. They must have got a ladder up straight away, smashed the glass, pulled the frame to gain entry and extinguished the fire. Then they would have probably opened the front door from the inside to get the grandparents out. That would fit, he said to himself running through a possible sequence of events.

He didn't know the relevance of this information, just curiosity, a chance to test out his skills of reasoning and logic he had learned from his study of forensics. It was interesting.

Greg carefully went back down the ladder and went around the front of the house just as a van pulled up, "Air Satellite Systems," according to the logo. The driver got out; he was wearing a company overall with the same logo on the front.

"Mr Jensen?" asked the man.

"Yes," replied Greg.

"Satellite dish and box to install."

"Great," said Greg and he led the man into the lounge and showed him the TV.

"I'll leave you to it. Would you like a drink? I was just going to make some tea."

"Yeah, great ta, two sugars please," replied the satellite man.

Greg went to the kitchen and started to boil a kettle. While it was boiling he decided to answer the call of nature and went to the downstairs toilet next to the front door. As he was relieving himself he remembered his grandfather used to spend ages in there after breakfast with his pipe and newspaper and his grandmother would always go in and open the window. That was the only time he was ever allowed to smoke in the house, never in the bedroom.

Then something flashed into his mind. The window was of the old-style, lead-diamond construction and, after he had flushed the toilet, he opened the window and inspected the frame. Two new pieces of wood had been added, one along the side where the catch was and another, longer one, along the bottom; it was exactly the same repair as the one on his grandparent's bedroom window. The casement stay was much newer than the catch although it had been over-painted by heavy metallic paint. Someone had broken in, he was convinced.

He looked at the size of the window and it was certainly large enough for a man to get through, although it would be tight. Greg left the window open and went through the front door to look at it from the outside. It was probably four, maybe five feet from the ground but a step ladder would be all that was needed to reach it and possibly get in. His grandparents had a security system, but they would not have turned it on until they had gone to bed.

He went back inside as the satellite man was coming out.

"Just going to set up the dish," he said.

"I'll bring your tea out in a minute," said Greg, having completely forgotten his hospitality.

Greg was mulling everything over as he re-boiled the kettle and made the tea.

After half an hour the satellite dish was installed, and the van had left. Greg went back to the downstairs toilet window and made a further inspection. He took a screwdriver and poked at the paint which was beginning to flake. Underneath it was clearly a much more recent addition. The wood on the rest of the frame was dark and weather-beaten, probably original, he thought. He wished he had his equipment in the lab to examine it in more detail; although he wasn't really sure what it would tell him.

Greg shut the window and went into the lounge to test his new gadget and flicked through the now myriad of channels available for his viewing. He sat watching a programme on North American black bears which was visually stunning, but his interest quickly waned as thoughts returned to his grandparents' deaths.

He thought through his new 'evidence'. It could be nothing,

but it was quite possible that someone had broken in and perhaps started the fire; it would make more sense than what the inquest had concluded. He still couldn't understand why a more thorough investigation had not taken place.

After a few minutes, he was getting restless again and decided it was time to set up his computer, and he climbed the stairs to the third floor and his study. It was well set out with a large desk with a flexible lamp and a flat screen monitor on top. The computer was in a purpose-built slot under the desk next to the printer and modem. He spent the next couple of hours or so setting up his system.

His thoughts started turning to Maureen again and he wondered if she would ring. Maybe she had someone else, although she had said she hadn't in the cafe. He was in the kitchen making his dinner when the phone rang. It was in his pocket of his jeans so there was no danger in him missing any calls.

"Number withheld" it said on the screen.

"Hi Greg." It was Maureen.

Greg tried to play cool but couldn't hide his excitement.

"Hi Maureen, how are you? How are your teeth? Are you ok?"

He had probably overdone the concern, but it was sincere.

"Better now, thank goodness," she said. "I was up half the night with toothache. I had to get an emergency appointment this morning... I managed to get my Dad to take me, it was so bad. I didn't feel like driving."

The BMW, Greg thought with some relief.

"I was thinking about you. I thought about calling you at the office, but I didn't know what the situation was for private calls... I didn't want to get you into trouble or anything and I haven't got your mobile number."

"Yes, I realised that later... I wondered if you would call," she said.

"I wanted to," he said.

"You better have my number then," and she reeled off the numbers. Greg quickly wrote it down and would soon have it in his phone contact list along with his solicitor; friends were in short supply.

"How's the house?" she asked, and he explained his day but did not say anything about his investigation.

"Wow, it sounds fantastic. I can't wait to see it."

This was music to Greg's ears. He had no idea where he stood with Maureen despite the weekend, but there was obviously a connection there.

"If you don't feel up to it tonight, what about tomorrow? I can cook us a meal."

"That would be lovely. I need to get to get some sleep after last night... and the weekend," she added with a giggle.

"What time do you finish?" asked Greg.

"I'll start early tomorrow... I can be with you around five."

"That's great. Do you like Chinese Food?".

"Love it," she replied.

Greg gave her directions which she wrote down on a note pad.

"Just ring if you get lost," he said, and they carried on chatting about nothing in particular for twenty minutes before she eventually had to go.

Greg came away elated. There was no doubt that, although at a very early stage, his affection for Maureen was high, and without realising it, she had provided him with some emotional stability. Cool Greg can achieve anything he believed.

After watching a film on the movie channel, Greg decided to turn in. He went around the downstairs checking all the windows were shut before making his way to the third floor. The alarm system had been upgraded and he could now set the controls from his bedroom as well as from the panel by the front door. There were front and rear motion-sensitive lights as well which would give added security.

He got into bed and closed his eyes and could hear the familiar sound of the trees rustling and for a moment he was transported back to his childhood with his grandparents. He did not believe in ghosts, but he thought their spirits were still in the house. He wished it could speak; he wanted to know its dark secrets. How did his beloved guardians die?

He drifted off, but the nightmares returned; flames and suffocation seemed to dominate his dreams. At three o'clock he woke in a cold sweat, ligatures constricting his throat; he thought he was being strangled. His demons were mocking him; they had not left him, merely being contained.

Tuesday morning eight o'clock and Greg wandered downstairs still groggy from his fitful sleep. He turned on the TV on in the kitchen and was watching the news drinking a refreshing tea when there was the sound of a vehicle in the drive and Greg looked through the lounge window. A small lorry with the name 'Robinsons Scaffolders' was parked, and two men got out. Greg went to see what their business was.

The driver and a youth got out and were making their way around the back when Greg called out to them. The driver went back and spoke to Greg.

"Just come to take down the scaffolding, mate. Got another job in Barnsley later."

"Great, it'll be good to get the house back to normal. Would you like some tea?"

"Yeah, cheers mate, if it's no bother... white two sugars; same for the lad if that's ok."

"Ok, I'll bring them out," said Greg, who was not about to have muddy scaffolders' boots soiling his new carpets.

Ten minutes later Greg took two mugs of tea, as prescribed,

to the men. He had turned the corner at the back of the house when there was a piercing shriek.

"Look-out!!"

There was a loud crash as one of the extremely heavy metal scaffolding connectors landed on the ground not six inches away from him, cracking the paving slab at his feet. Greg jumped back dropping one mug and spilling most of the other.

The scaffolder came rushing down from the second-floor platform and looked at Greg.

"You ok, mate? You ok? It just slipped... I'm really sorry. Please don't tell my boss, he'll give me the push."

Greg stood there frozen for a moment, the blood rushing from his face. He looked at the paving slab, not only cracked, but with a large dent in the middle. The ugly metal connector had bounced on the hard surface and was lying on the grass. He couldn't imagine what would have happened had it hit him on the head,

"I'm ok," said Greg and gradually composed himself. He started picking up the bits of the broken mug from the path. The scaffolder helped, still protesting and pleading.

"T'were an accident, mate, honest; just an accident."

Greg's mind raced back to something his solicitor had said about Cornelius Tasker and the stone block from the turret. Another few inches and history would have been repeated. Was it some sort of sign? Greg dismissed the thought; he did not believe in ghosts.

He walked back to the kitchen with the attentive scaffolder and his buddy who continued their protestations of innocence.

"I don't know how it happened... it just fell off the end," said the lad, who was also clearly shaken.

"No harm done," said Greg composing himself. "Better get you another drink, eh?" and walked towards the front door.

The scaffolder and his mate looked at each other and

breathed a sigh of relief.

"We'll drink it here, if that's ok," shouted the scaffolder.

After taking the two men their tea, Greg left them to finish the removal. He had recovered from his near miss and went up to his office to get on the Internet. He wanted to do some more investigation, hoping to have a look at the Coroner's report on the fire at the house.

He searched and found some useful information on the website. He read the blurb. According to the narrative he would have to apply to the coroner to get permission for access, but, as a close relative, he 'should not normally encounter any difficulty in obtaining permission,' it said, unless there was an issue of national security which in this case was unlikely. He would have to travel to where it was filed to consult it, which, presumably, would be Sheffield so that wouldn't be a problem. He decided to make further enquiries and found the number of the local coroner's office and made a call.

He spoke to a very helpful lady who, after some delving, was able to confirm that the report was indeed filed there, but he would have to write to the coroner. Fortunately, they would accept an email request which would save time; Greg was on a roll and didn't want to lose momentum. She gave him the appropriate contact details and he sent off an email.

It was a couple of hours before he received a reply and the coroner had agreed to his request. He phoned back and made an appointment for the following day after his meeting with Dorinda, the social worker.

After lunch his thoughts turned to his dinner date and he was beginning to get excited at Maureen's prospective visit. He thought about the meal. He would need to do some shopping; his house-keeper hadn't catered for his more adventurous tastes. He was drawn back to his time whilst at university, he remembered he used to enjoy cooking and had regularly entertained his flat mates... and Lindsey. He thought about that for a moment and realised he was no longer shaking; cool Greg had definitely taken over.

He grabbed his jacket which was hung up on the row of pegs in the hall; it looked quite forlorn hanging there on its own, he noticed. He would remedy that in time.

As he walked to the garage, a thought occurred to him; he couldn't believe he hadn't thought about it before. Where was his stuff, his old clothes and things? He had no idea; he would ask the solicitor next time he saw him. He had a CD collection, lots of clothes, books, even his keyboard, loads of bits and pieces accumulated since his childhood. Some of it had been kept at his grandparents' house; there had not been much room in the flat in Leeds.

He opened the garage, reversed out the Audi and closed it again. Then he recalled Cathcart mentioning a trunk in the scullery. He hadn't been down there since he arrived. He would do that tomorrow but for now his attention would be firmly focused on his dinner guest.

Chapter Seven

There was a large retail park on the outskirts of the city about a ten-minute drive away which housed the usual stores found across the country. There was a 'mega', according to the sign, supermarket called 'Brandwood's' and Greg parked the Audi in the huge car park and went in search of their deli counter.

Greg was trying to remember what it was like seven years ago, the memory had faded, but he was pretty sure that the complex was not built when he was last here. He grabbed a basket and looked at the rows and rows of produce; there were twenty-seven check-outs according to the numbering! He couldn't recall going into anything as large as this store and it took him a while to acclimatise to the place.

He quickly overcame any initial apprehension; he was cool Greg after all, and eventually found what he was looking for among the aisles. He stocked up with the necessary ingredients for his stir fry.

On the way back, he took more notice of the 'Pines Residential Home for the Elderly'. It seemed busy again judging by the car park; there must have been twenty or thirty cars outside the frontage.

It had always been an impressive building, larger than Taskers End and he wondered if the original owners had been competing to see who could build the grandest house. It did happen; egos in Victorian time were no different from today. It wasn't called the 'Pines' when he lived at Taskers and he wracked his brain for the original name, but it wouldn't come to him.

The two new large properties were also interesting. He drove by slowly for a closer inspection. Judging by their position, they would have been built on some of the land between the Pines and Taskers End, but he had no idea who owned it; presumably the land belonged to the Pines. They too were fine buildings, six bedrooms, double garages, stone, in keeping with the area, but without the character of the Victorian structures they bisected.

The new builds were separated from Taskers End by a small wood which he now owned. He had not had chance to look around there yet. The distance from the nearest house to his gate posts would be at least two hundred yards he guessed.

He pulled into his drive and took out his produce. He had used his new debit card for the first time; it wouldn't be the last!

After garaging the car, he went to the kitchen and started to prepare for his guest. The cooking area was in the centre of the room where there was a large range with six gas rings of different intensity. Above it hung various cooking utensils. There were worktops around the outside with cupboards above and underneath which were used for storing food and cleaning materials. The sink and double drainer were below the window. Whilst washing up, there was a good view of the back garden and the trees at the bottom. In the corner of the kitchen there was a rustic looking dining table for breakfast and less formal meals with four matching chairs and a TV to keep the chef occupied while he cooked.

He set out all the ingredients on the central worktop and started preparing his dish, chopping onions, mushrooms and garlic and the various spices he would need. He diced two chicken breasts and put them in the fridge away from any predatory insects.

He checked his watch, four-thirty, and having completed the preparation, he went upstairs to shower and change. He put the radio on in the kitchen and lounge to give some background music. By five o'clock he was ready. He kept looking at his watch and realised he was getting anxious again and he tried to calm himself down with a few breathing exercises.

At twelve minutes past five he heard the crunching of gravel on the drive. He looked through the lounge window and could see Maureen's Mini Cooper.

He watched her get out and go to the boot of the car and retrieve a small valise and a carrier bag. He went to the front door and opened it just as she reached it.

"Wow, what a place," she said. "Sorry I'm a bit late the traffic was awful getting out of town."

She leant forward, and he kissed her.

"You look great," he said, admiring her smart two-piece suit which was in keeping with her work in the solicitor's office.

"Thank you," she said. "But I need to change and freshen up if that's ok."

"Of course," he said and led her up the stairs to the third-floor bathroom. She was enthralled by the house and kept saying, "wow" as they worked their way upwards. He showed her how to work the shower and gave her a clean pair of towels from the airing cupboard.

"I'll wait for you downstairs," he said.

After twenty minutes, Greg was reading the evening paper at the table when he heard her coming down the stairs; he left the kitchen to meet her. He looked at her; she was wearing a smart pair of jeans and a white tee shirt; the sight almost took his breath away. Her perfume once more permeated the air, even overcoming the smell of the new carpet, evoking memories of their weekend encounter. He ushered her into the lounge.

"This is amazing," she said, looking around the room. "I've put my stuff in the bedroom. Hope that's ok,"

For a second, Greg felt a shiver run down his spine. There had been no discussion about Maureen staying over, and he had not made this assumption; but he had hoped.

"Of course, would you like a drink?"

"Have you got any white wine?"

"Yes, I stocked up on some Chablis today; I got some red too, just in case. Won't be a minute."

He turned to leave the room. "Oh, I forgot to ask; how're your teeth?"

"Much better, fine now, thanks... Do you mind if I have a look around?"

"Of course, help yourself... I'll carry on with the dinner," and Greg went back to the kitchen to continue his cooking.

After about ten minutes, Maureen returned from her tour and walked into the kitchen. Greg was attending a wok.

"This is a fantastic place," she said struggling for superlatives.

What she had noticed, however, was the starkness of the interior; very minimal, with nothing out of place, functional rather than homely.

She walked up to him and put her arms around his waist, in an affectionate hug; Greg turned and kissed her. He continued stirring the meal.

"Hope you like it. Chicken in black bean sauce with stir fry vegetables. Be ready in five minutes."

"Smells great," she said and lent against the worktop watching him. "Do you know any of the history... of the house?"

He gave her a rundown of what he knew, and she was captivated by his description of events. He left out any stories of ghosts and curses.

Maureen felt at home sipping her Chablis and watching her new lover cooking for her.

Another few minutes, and Greg was ready.

"Do you want to sit down, and I'll serve up?"

He'd bought some spring rolls from the deli-counter as a starter and added some fresh lettuce and cucumber and carrot and a sweet chilli dip. Main course would be served with rice. Greg had even remembered the chop-sticks.

Maureen sat down and watched as Greg presented the starter and sat down opposite her.

"Hmm, these are nice," she said, after taking the first bite of the deli-fare.

"Ah, yes, those are not mine; Brandwood specials I'm afraid!"

"They taste good," said Maureen, and dipped the eaten end of the spring-roll into the chilli-dip with her fingers and took another bite. Greg couldn't help feasting his eyes on her.

They finished the starter and Greg cleared the plates and then served the main course. Maureen watched; she couldn't recall anyone cooking for her, apart from her mum.

"Hey, this looks great," said Maureen.

"I hope you like it," said Greg, firmly in control and confident.

She took a mouthful… "Mmm, delicious," she said and blew him a kiss.

"So, how long did you live in this house?"

"Moved here when I was ten... after my parents died," he replied.

"Oh sorry, I didn't mean to pry."

"No that's ok. It's no secret... my parents were killed in 1985. We were living in Preston at the time."

"What was it... a car accident?"

Greg was not sure he knew how to answer it. His mind was starting to trip back, and Gerald was showing an interest, but he held himself together.

"No... Nothing like that ..." There was a long pause.

"It's ok if you don't want to talk about it," said Maureen, seeing that Greg was struggling with the question.

"No... It's just..." he paused again. "It's something I haven't spoken about."

Greg was starting to show signs of anxiety. She noticed his hands were shaking.

"That's ok, I'm sorry; I didn't mean to upset you," she said.

He put his chop sticks down and started to speak.

"It was July 12th, 1985, the day before Live Aid... I was looking forward to seeing the bands, I remember."

A great deal of clarity entered Greg's mind, it was as though he had been transported back there. He was staring at his plate.

"I'd just started to play the piano, so I was well into my music and it was all everybody at school was talking about. I loved Queen, I thought they were great... I really wanted to see them."

He lifted his head and looked straight ahead, blankly, trance-like, as the vivid pictures came back to him. Maureen was beginning to worry.

"It was about half-past three, I'd got home after school... I'd got my own key and let myself in ..." He paused before carrying on.

"I remember going into the kitchen to get a drink. It was a warm day and I was hot from the walk home. I remember running the tap. Cold... lovely and cold, and I got a bottle of lemon juice from the larder, you know the stuff that you dilute with water... I got a glass from the cupboard..."

He made a motion with his hands as if he was re-enacting the physical opening of the cupboard.

"I put some of the lemonade in the bottom of the glass and filled it with water from the tap."

He continued his impromptu mime; Maureen watched transfixed.

"Are you ok? Please stop if it's too painful."

"No... no I want to tell you it's just..."

He snapped himself out of the trance and Greg was back in

control; he looked at Maureen and continued his account with more confidence.

"I... I went into the lounge to put the TV on before I did my homework and realised that no-one was around. Mum would normally be in on a Friday afternoon... she usually had a half day. She liked to get the washing out of the way so she would have the weekend to herself... She worked at the big building society in the precinct." He paused for a moment.

"I remember calling her... But there was no reply." He looked at Maureen who was engrossed by his account.

"I thought she'd probably gone shopping or had to work later. I remember putting my satchel down on the floor by the sofa."

He again acted out the process again.

"The TV was still on. I remember, and I went upstairs to get changed. That's when I saw them."

Greg closed his eyes; the pain was obvious and Maureen could sense the torment he was going through. She put her chopsticks down and went around the table and cuddled Greg's head into her stomach; rubbing her hands through his hair as cradling a baby who had woken from a nightmare.

"Shhh, it's ok," she said.

"No... I need to finish, then you'll understand... Their bedroom door was open, and Mum was sort of sprawled on the bed and my Dad was on the floor. There was a shotgun beside him and blood everywhere. It was if someone had sprayed red paint all over the walls, the bed, the floor, everywhere."

Greg was trying to hold it together and Maureen was doing her best to comfort him. But this was not Gerald this was 'cool' Greg coming to terms with the past which was something that, until now, only therapy and drugs had enabled him to do. His coping mechanisms were working and despite the emotional turmoil, he was completely in control.

"I'm so sorry," she said. "I'm so sorry."

Greg moved his head away and wiped his face.

"No, no, it's ok. It is about time I trusted someone. I've never told anyone before. It's right that I should tell you."

He composed himself and then continued.

"I ran downstairs and called the ambulance and then ran next door; the lady there was my Mum's friend and she came around and looked after me until the ambulance came… and that was that. They said that Dad had shot Mum and then himself. I knew things weren't very good; they were always rowing, but I never for one-minute thought that Dad would ever do something like that. My grandparents brought me here and I've never been back to Preston to this day."

"I don't know what to say," said Maureen, and seeing Greg was now more composed, she returned to her seat.

"There's nothing to say… but thank you for listening; I've always found it difficult to talk about it. I was offered counselling at the time, but after a couple of sessions I thought it was a waste of time, so I didn't go any more. Perhaps I should have continued, instead of me bottling it up."

He changed the subject. "Hope I haven't put you off your meal," he said, "I've got a cheesecake in the fridge, if you'd like."

"Yes please," she said, still concerned at Greg. "That was great. Where did you learn to cook Chinese?" she asked, keeping away from the earlier conversation.

"I did quite a bit of cooking when I was at Uni; none of my flat mates could cook but I quite enjoyed it. So, I did the cooking and the others did the washing up or keeping the place clean… division of labour. It worked well."

Greg went to the fridge and brought out a cheesecake which he cut into four slices.

"Help yourself, there's some cream as well if you like."

"No this is fine," she said and helped herself to a portion. Greg did the same.

"What about you, did you go to University?"

"Economics at Sheffield," she said, and she gave Greg a synopsis of her time at university.

After they'd finished, Maureen started clearing the dishes away. "Come on I'll help you clear up."

"You don't have to. I've got a housekeeper coming tomorrow. I'll need to make sure she's got something to do."

"Now that *is* impressive," she said with a smile, and they put all the dishes into the dishwasher.

"Mr Cathcart arranged it; he said I would need some help in looking after the place... Would you like a coffee?"

"Yes please," said Maureen and Greg went to the cupboard and took out a cafetière.

Whilst the coffee was percolating, Maureen talked more about her background. Her parents had split up when she was fourteen and her mother moved to Scotland. She had very little contact with her, just the odd Christmas and birthday card which Greg found rather sad. She was however close to her father who was a partner with a large firm of accountants in the city. He had remarried and lived in the up-market suburb of Dore. Her step mother was only three years older than Maureen, but she got on well with her. The subject of former relationships was not raised.

Maureen watched as Greg put the used mugs in the dishwasher and rinsed the cafetière under the tap. The earlier revelations were still in her mind, but, if anything, they had drawn her closer to him. There was something about Greg that she found attractive, not just his physical appearance but his vulnerability; different from the usual macho-men who would try to seduce her. She could sense that Greg had not been used to talking about his earlier life and she felt a sense of responsibility which had developed the growing bond between them.

Greg poured out the rest of the wine and led Maureen by the hand back to the lounge and they continued swapping stories. For Greg, the earlier revelations had been a cathartic experience and he felt almost liberated. He managed to deflect explorations into his more recent past despite Maureen's natural inquisitiveness. "New York... not very exciting, lab-work mostly," seemed to satisfy her curiosity. Now was not the time for any further disclosures. There had been enough emotions for one night and Greg had no intention of scaring Maureen away. The truth of the last six years would remain locked away in the recesses of his mind.

Being able to share his background with someone who was not trying to judge or assess him had been better than any cognitive therapy sessions, but, unwittingly, the proxy counselling had also served to cement his growing dependency on Maureen for his mental stability.

Maureen did stay over that night and for both of them it was a warm and fulfilling experience. The lovemaking was tender and sensual, different from the more lustful exploits of the weekend. As they lay together before giving way to sleep Maureen could hear the noises of the house; the surrounding trees creating an eeriness which she found frightening, but in Greg's arms she felt safe. She wasn't sure whether she would want to stay at the house on her own.

Wednesday was going to be busy. Greg had his first official meeting with his Social Worker, Dorinda Walcott, and then his appointment at the Coroner's Office; but first he would meet his new housekeeper.

Maureen left around eight o'clock to face the rush hour

traffic into town. Greg felt quite empty as he watched the Mini pull out of the drive, but he soon shook himself out of any depressive thoughts.

Ten minutes later there was another sound of crunching gravel and an old Peugeot parked in front of the garage and a middle-aged lady got out. Greg watched her from the lounge window. He heard the front door open, then remembered she had a set of keys from the solicitors. He walked into the hall to greet her and the lady nearly collapsed with fright when she saw him.

"Good grief, you frightened the life out of me...You must be Mr Jensen. I'm Mrs Asquith. People call me Queenie."

Greg walked towards her and held out his hand in greeting.

"Yes, Greg Jensen. Pleased to meet you... Queenie."

She had two large bags of shopping and her apron. She took off her coat and hung it in the entrance hall and gave the shopping bags to Greg.

"Mr Cathcart suggested I do some more stocking up. I've bought a load of cleaning stuff, and there's some toilet rolls, kitchen towels and other bits and pieces to keep you going."

"That's very good of you... Queenie. How much do I owe you?"

"Nothing, Mr Cathcart settles the bill. The firm's got an account at the wholesalers, so if you need anything extra anytime, you let me know and I'll call in and get it. It's not far from where I live so it's easy enough."

Greg immediately liked Queenie, she was, he tried to think of the right word... wholesome. Yes, wholesome would be close. There was a familiarity about her which he couldn't place; she reminded him of his mother. She had a kind face and looked as though she had raised a number of children... four guessed Greg which was later confirmed. Greg didn't know where his insight into people came from.

Greg went through the house with Queenie and explained his cleaning requirements with which she seemed quite happy.

"You should hear what some of them want," she said and laughed.

"The kitchen will need a bit of attention, I had a guest staying last night," he said, which intrigued her.

"A lady friend?" she speculated, but Greg would not elaborate.

"And the bed linen will need changing and washing," he added, which made her even more curious.

"I'll be going out shortly and won't be back till later this afternoon, so you'll probably have finished before I get back but if there is anything you need, let me know. This is my number," and Greg gave her his mobile details.

Greg was away by nine-fifteen; Queenie had to move her car, so he could get the Audi from the garage.

The drive into town was busy with the remnants of the rush-hour traffic, but he was back at Cathcart Rivers by quarter-to-ten, in good time to see Dorinda.

Seeing his social worker at the solicitors had caused a problem. He couldn't tell Maureen the truth; it would have opened up a can of worms, so he'd told her he was meeting someone to discuss investments; a bit weak but the best he could come up with at the time.

Outside the office, Greg rang the doorbell and it was Maureen who opened the door; her perfume seemed to hang in the air. He wanted to kiss her but thought it would be unprofessional. What a difference since his last visit on Friday. His whole world had changed in just a few days.

Maureen led the way to a small conference room which had been made available for the meeting; a large flask of coffee and two cups, a bowl of sugar and a covered milk-jug were on the table. Greg thanked her. "Shall I see you later?" he whispered, as she was about to leave the room.

"I'll call and let you know. I may have one or two things I need to catch up on," she replied.

"Ok," he said trying not to let his disappointment show.

He poured himself a coffee and sat down. His mind started drifting but was jolted back as the door opened and Dorinda was ushered in by Maureen. He got up and they shook hands and the social worker took out her laptop from her bag and plugged it into the socket as she had done at Trenton. He poured her a coffee while she set up.

"So, Gerald," she looked up at him for a second from her screen and then back to her laptop as she searched for the appropriate file. "How are you?"

"Fine... but it's Greg now. I thought Mr Cathcart had told you."

"Yes of course... I'm sorry... ah... here we are," she said, clearly engrossed in the computer and not really listening to what he was saying. Greg was annoyed at her rudeness but didn't let it show.

"Right... now, where were we?" she said, seemingly satisfied with her laptop's configuration.

"You asked how I was," said Greg displaying a little irritation.

"So, how are you settling in?"

"Fine, like I said."

"Any problems?"

"No."

The conversation was going nowhere, and Dorinda tried to open up the discussion.

"What about the basics, shopping, getting around, that sort of thing?"

"Fine, I have a car," he said without a hint of smugness.

"And things at the house, you are coping there?"

"Yes, fine, I've got a housekeeper. She's looking after the house."

Greg was getting tired of this cat and mouse game and didn't know why he needed to be here; he thought Dorinda probably felt the same. She sensed his frustration.

"I'm sorry if these questions seem a bit ..." she thought for the right word. "Rudimentary... but I *am* required by law to ensure your wellbeing as far as I can. So, I have to ask these questions and report any problems. Do I make myself clear?"

Greg thought that her response was a little aggressive but then reasoned she was only doing her job and he had no intention of rocking the boat. He was not going back to Trenton under any circumstances.

"Yes, sorry, I understand but, as I said, things couldn't be better. I'm being well looked-after and feel really positive about the future for the first time."

Dorinda liked that answer and she relaxed. She explained the practicalities of her role and outlined the calling programme.

"We'll meet again next week and then two weeks after that, then one month and then every month for a year... This can be extended if I think you are having problems."

Greg appreciated that Dorinda was not someone he would want to cross and decided he would play the game as he had at Trenton. It did after all get results.

She gave him the dates of future appointments on an official appointment card.

"You must let me know straight away if you can't make any of these arrangements. Do you have a contact telephone number... just in case I need to contact you, change dates, things like that?"

He gave the social worker his new mobile-phone number and for the first time she smiled.

"You seem to be making very good progress... Greg," she

made a point of emphasising his name. "Not all my clients have your resources and they struggle in the outside world after being away for a long time, but you appear to be fairly resilient."

Greg picked up on her turn of phrase... 'resilient' that was a good word... he liked that.

"I think so, it's been a difficult time but all that's behind me now," he said playing the game. He was telling her what she wanted to hear.

"Well, I think we can leave it there," she said and started typing a few notes on her laptop, then closed it down. "We'll meet again same time next week," she said, authoritatively.

"Fine... but can we make it somewhere else... if that's ok," he added.

"Have you anywhere in mind?"

"Well, I have an idea, why don't you come up to the house? You'll be able to see how I'm managing at first hand."

"Yes... ok, good idea," and Greg gave her directions.

"You can't miss it."

The meeting concluded, and they shook hands.

"Oh, I nearly forgot, I've arranged for you to meet your psychiatrist, Doctor Melrose, next Monday at two o'clock. She'll be in touch to make arrangements, but it will probably be at the hospital unless you hear otherwise. I'll pass on your phone number. I'm seeing her later this week."

"Mr Cathcart said I could use a room here if I wanted," said Greg, then suddenly thought about Maureen.

"I'll leave it with you to sort out with Jane."

Greg made a mental note; he would need to write it on his calendar when he got home. He would consider the implications regarding Maureen; he could always use the same excuse.

"See you next week," she said, and opened the door and left.

Greg sat for a moment contemplating the discussions and was reasonably satisfied with how it went. He helped himself to another coffee before eventually making his way back to reception hoping to see Maureen, but Joan was behind the desk typing. He asked her where the toilets were; he needed to make himself comfortable before heading onto his next appointment at the Coroner's Office.

"Just down the corridor and up the stairs on the left," she said indicating the opposite end of the building from the conference room. It would be on the same side as Cathcart's office but on the first floor. He'd not ventured upstairs before and the narrow wooden boards on the spiral staircase creaked, a sign of their age, as he made his way to the facilities.

He completed his ablutions and as he came out he noticed a door on the opposite side of the first-floor passage.

It had the name D.G. Chapman MA. LLB (Honours) on a small silver nameplate on the door. It was slightly ajar, and he could hear raised voices, one of which was Maureen's. He couldn't make out the dialogue.

Greg's immediate response was to go in and protect her, but something held him back. He waited there for a few minutes until the voices had lowered and then Maureen came out, seemingly in tears. Instead of going to her and offering comfort which was his immediate reaction he dodged back into the toilet and Maureen went back downstairs, not seeing him, and went into another room.

Greg took the opportunity of heading back downstairs to reception and Joan escorted him to the front door.

What was all that about, he wondered, as he walked to the Coroner's Office only a few minutes away. He was processing the information as he covered the journey with all kinds of permutations going through his mind.

He reached his destination and followed the signs for

'enquiries'; for the moment his attention was on his immediate goal; the report into the death of his grandparents.

Chapter Eight

Greg went to reception.

"Can I help you?" asked the lady at the desk.

Greg explained his requirements and produced the email confirmation he had received earlier.

"Won't be a moment," she said, and disappeared into a back office.

A few minutes later she returned with a file with the name 'Sinclair' on it.

"There's a viewing room you can use; or we can supply copies of the files if you'd prefer," said the receptionist. "We can post them to you."

"Can I have some time now and you send me the copies?" asked Greg.

"Yes, we can do that," and she led him to a small private room across the room from the reception desk.

There was just a table and a single chair and Greg sat down and made himself comfortable. He had a small notepad and pen in his jacket pocket and he took a moment to look at the document file which was secured by a pink ribbon. Greg untied the fastening and took out the contents. The report itself looked only to be a few pages long and he began to wonder if there was going to be any meaningful information.

He looked at the first page headed Coroner's Report. There was a royal seal and various admin boxes that had been ticked or crossed then in bold type; *In the matter of James and Martha Sinclair deceased July 17th, 2005.*

Before reading it in detail, Greg looked at the other documents in the file. There was a copy of the Post Mortem signed by a Dr Schuman, an 'Interim Certificate of Fact of Death', which is what the Coroner would have issued prior to the inquest thus enabling the funeral to take place. There were also several 'Notes of Evidence', effectively witness statements from those on the scene or other parties having a bearing on the outcome of the hearing. There was one from the Chief Fire Officer which gave details of the fire and conclusions on how it started plus a summary of the police investigation, such as it was.

Greg became fascinated by all the information and with his forensic background he was able to make sense of even the most complex of statements. It took him two hours to go through all the documents and had made copious notes, but at one o'clock he decided to call it a day and get some lunch.

He took the file back to reception and paid the copy fee.

"The documents should be with you within forty-eight hours," said the receptionist.

Greg thanked her for the information and her help and set off for some food. His mind returned to Maureen and her apparent distress earlier and he keyed her number into his mobile; it was answered on the third ring.

"Hi Greg," it was good to hear her voice.

"I'm still in town, wondered if you fancied a bite to eat. I was just going for a sandwich."

"Yeah, that's great... I could do with a break."

"Spudmania...? I can be there in two minutes."

"Yeah ok, get a seat I'll be with you in a few minutes," and she rang off.

Greg made his way to the cafe and managed to find a seat. It was not as busy as last Friday but it was still doing a good trade. He joined the queue and while he waited he noticed the blackboard behind the counter and was amazed at the range of the menu that had been lovingly painted on it for all to see. His turn came, and he ordered a coffee before finding a seat in the corner. He was still reflecting the visit to the coroner's office, but his main concern was centred on Maureen and he wondered at the cause of her upset.

It was another ten minutes before Maureen arrived and she looked back to normal. She had obviously repaired her makeup and, judging by the fact that her perfume had managed to overpower the smell of cooking, she had freshened that as well. Greg leaned over and kissed her as any couple would, with fondness and affection. Greg had finished his coffee.

"What would you like?" he said.

"Cheese and chives fill, please, and a coffee", and she took off her jacket and put it on the back of a chair.

Greg went to the counter to order then returned to the table. "You look great."

"Thank you. How did your meeting go?"

He had to think for a minute he had been so engrossed at the Coroner's Office he had almost forgotten.

"Oh, yes, fine... fine," he said. "Didn't last long I was out by quarter to eleven."

"What about you, how was your morning?" he asked, waiting to see if she was going to say anything.

"Oh... you know..." and her voice tailed off as if not wanting to say anymore.

Greg needed to confront this properly which is something Gerald would never have done. He searched for the right words.

"Look... I know this is none of my business, but I was outside the upstairs rooms earlier... I went to use the loo after my meeting and I saw you come out of one of the offices. I was about to call you, but you seemed upset. I didn't know what to do, so I went back into the toilet. I didn't want to embarrass you or anything."

Maureen looked down on the table and fiddled with her cutlery. Just then the waitress came over with their food and disturbed the moment.

"I can't talk here; can I call round later? I'll explain

everything… There's something I need to talk to you about."

"Of course, I just needed to know you were ok. I was concerned that's all," said Greg.

This was great progress for Greg in his recuperation. Gerald would have flipped by now but not Greg, not cool Greg.

"I'll make you some dinner, if you like, something quick," and Maureen smiled at him in a way that said more than words could ever do. Their eyes locked. Was this really the look of love? Greg had no benchmark, he was in uncharted waters, but it felt good.

"Yes, that would be great," she said.

They ate their food in relative silence; Greg was deep in thought on two accounts, of course concerned by what it was that Maureen had to say, but also engrossed in his findings from the Coroner's Office, chewing over the facts like a dog with a bone. Maureen was also contemplating but was not disclosing anything at this time.

By two o'clock the pair walked back towards the office, Greg had parked his car in the multi-story close by and as they reached the door of Cathcart and Rivers Greg leaned across to Maureen and kissed her. She responded warmly, and Greg felt a twinge of excitement as though he had touched a live wire.

"See you about five," she said, and rang the doorbell. She didn't have a key Greg noticed.

He waited for her to go inside and went to find his car in the car park, on the sixth floor, he thought; he was trying to remember.

On the way back to the house he called into the mega Supermarket again and bought some more food. He wanted something quick; he sensed there would be more talking than eating tonight. He bought some pasta sauces he would do a chicken dish in the oven. It could be cooking while he continued his research.

He got back to Taskers End around three and noticed the place was spotless, Queenie had weaved her magic. He would have to thank his solicitor for his selection; he had chosen well.

After a quick change he went into the kitchen and prepared his chicken dish. He sliced two chicken breasts, chopped an onion, couple of garlic cloves and added some mushrooms and cooked the ingredients in white wine for a few minutes with some oregano then poured the sauce over the top. He put it in the oven and set the timer for four-thirty when it would be simmering on a low heat.

He sat at the table and started looking through the notes he'd made from the Coroner's Report. In some ways he was disappointed as it didn't say much more than what the solicitor had told him but there was a lot more detail he would have to sift through before he could draw any conclusions. The summary he noted had deduced that the cause of death for both of his grandparents was asphyxiation due to smoke inhalation. He started making visual summaries like flow charts so he could make sense of it all. He put question marks where there was still investigation to be done.

The cause of the fire was inconclusive according to the fire-officer's witness statement, but it was consistent with being started by a cigarette or in this case, most probably his grandfather's pipe. Greg discounted this straight away; as he had deduced earlier, smouldering tobacco ash was unlikely to cause this sort of fire unless it had come into contact with some particularly flammable material; there was no mention of that in the report. So, whilst it was just about feasible, it was not probable. It also did not fit in with their routine and his grandmother's moratorium on his grandfather's pipe smoking. He would never be allowed to smoke in the bedroom.

The report confirmed that firefighters had, as Greg had worked out, broken in through the bedroom window from a long ladder and eventually opened the front door from the inside. They must have got one of the fire appliances around the back of the house. There was no mention of any forced entry from the front which did nothing to explain the repairs to the downstairs toilet window.

The police witness statement was just as inconclusive and if anything, Greg thought, evasive. They had relied solely on the Fire Officer's report and had not looked for any signs of a break in. Greg was beset with anger, at himself mainly. If he had not been in 'hospital' he could have explained the inconsistencies with his grandparents' behaviour patterns and the smoking ban.

Then there was the time of death, nine-ten; what on earth were they doing in bed at that time? He made a note on his pad with a question mark. Perhaps one of them was ill; it was a possibility, but that still didn't account for the broken window frame in the downstairs toilet.

It could of course have been a coincidence but why would anyone break in, particularly in what would have been broad daylight; they could have just rang the doorbell and overpowered them when they answered. It didn't add up.

There was something else he needed to look at, the local press coverage. It would have been a high-profile event, he thought; there were not many double death stories; probably made the front page. He made a note to research this later.

It was all going around in his head when he noticed the time. It was four-fifty and he needed to check the dinner. He went to the kitchen and gave the chicken and sauce a stir. He would do the pasta later. Then suddenly he remembered the appointment with Doctor Melrose on Monday and wrote her name on the calendar. He'd almost forgotten with everything else going on, and that would have meant real trouble.

Just turned five and the familiar sound of crunching gravel announced Maureen's arrival.

He went to the front door and let her in. She was carrying her business handbag and a carrier bag. He took her jacket and they walked through to the lounge. She was in her business attire and Greg filled his lungs with her perfume as they walked through the hall, he could never get enough.

"Can I get you anything?" he asked. "Glass of wine, coffee perhaps?"

"Coffee will be great, thanks," she said, and Greg went to the kitchen.

"I'll just go and change if that's ok," she said.

"Of course, help yourself."

Maureen took her things and went upstairs.

Greg gave the dinner another stir while the coffee percolated before returning to the lounge with two mugs. He had decided to join her; he was anxious to hear what she had to say.

After a few minutes she came down the stairs in her jeans and tee shirt that she had worn the previous night. She hadn't had chance to go home, Greg realised.

"So, not a good day then?" he asked as she sat down in an attempt to lighten the atmosphere.

"You could say that," she said and smiled but in an ironic way.

She took her first sip of coffee. "Mmm, that's good," she said.

"So, do you want to talk about it?"

"Later, I just need to relax for a while... something smells good," she said, changing the subject.

"Chicken again I'm afraid; I wanted to do something quick."

"No, that's great," she said and continued drinking her coffee.

The silence wasn't awkward exactly, but it was clear she was preoccupied with her thoughts. Greg realised that the lounge was not the best place for an intimate conversation

"Come on, let's go through to the kitchen, I need to put the pasta on. Don't want the dinner to overcook."

She followed Greg into the kitchen and sat at the table Greg went to the radio and put on some music.

"Still haven't got any CD's yet," he said, and started to measure out some Fettuccine into a saucepan.

"What are you doing with that?" she asked pointing to a bottle of olive oil.

"Just a little trick I learned. If you add a drop of oil to the pasta it stops it sticking."

"I must try it sometime," she said.

The pasta was cooking as Greg stirred the chicken.

"Five minutes," he said. "Would you like a glass of wine with your meal?"

"Yes please... but only a small one; I'll need to drive later."

A tinge of disappointment ran through him momentarily, but he had not expected her to stay; he knew she would need to go home tonight.

Greg dished up the pasta a few minutes later.

"I'm afraid I cheated with the sauce, it's from the supermarket, but I've added my magic touch," he said with a smile.

She returned the smile and started to eat.

"Mmm, this is wonderful, you certainly have got a magic touch," she said after a couple of mouthfuls.

They ate in relative silence only broken by the radio and the occasional traffic reports.

"Busy on the roads tonight," Greg proffered, trying to make conversation.

They finished their meal.

"There's some cheesecake from last night to finish off if you'd like?"

"No thanks, that's just enough," she said and she took a

deep breath.

"Right, here goes," she said, sensing the time was right for her exposé.

Greg was sitting opposite her with his empty plate in front of him.

"I told you I started with Cathcart Rivers three years ago," Greg nodded, not knowing what to expect.

"Well, as I told you, I met David... Chapman at a Law Society do just over three years ago. What I didn't tell you was he started flirting with me, and one thing led to another and we started an affair. I knew he was married but I thought what the heck, I was single, and he did have a certain charisma." She took a sip of her wine. "I wasn't particularly looking for a long-term relationship, it was meant to be just a bit of fun. Later he offered me a job, 'keep me on tap', he said." She made a grimace at the expression. "It was more money and he promised to involve me with client cases and so on. Seemed ideal and in a way, it was."

Greg took a sip of wine and topped up his glass. He was not finding this easy and he felt Gerald stirring trying to get over his firewall, but he fought back.

She continued. "I soon discovered he was a control freak. A few times I wanted to end the relationship, I would meet someone I thought I might want to go out with but each time he would threaten me – how would I manage the mortgage without a job, that sort of thing. Not physical violence, although he had hinted that he had 'friends' who could make life difficult for me. So, I stayed but last week was when things changed. As soon as I saw you I knew you were... different."

Greg had to stop himself from reacting at the word, recognising an alternative context.

"And after the week-end and yesterday, I knew I had to break away for good."

The emotion starting to get the better of her.

She recovered her composure and continued. "So, this morning I told him that it was over, and I was seeing someone else."

"What did he say," asked Greg.

"At first, he went mad, shouting and threatening again but he knew this time I meant it and he started pleading; said he would leave his wife and we could buy a place together but I told him it was too late. I'd made up my mind and there was no going back, and I said that if he would not leave me alone I would tell his wife everything."

"What did he say then?" asked Greg.

"He just ranted again and that's when I left his office. I was upset, but I was not going to let him control me ever again."

Greg was in turmoil listening to her story but something strange happened. His normal instincts would have been to lash out in some way; he could feel Gerald trying to escape again and do just that, but cool Greg was still in charge and instead of his usual self-centred defence mechanism, he went around the other side of the table and took Maureen in his arms as if to protect her. She was starting to cry but quickly recovered; she was a strong character and did not want to succumb to this emotion, not as a result of what David Chapman had done.

She got up and sat on his lap and he held her tight.

"It's ok, it's ok," he said trying to give her some reassurance. "I'll help you, I'll protect you. I won't let anyone ever hurt you."

She looked up at him and they kissed. "I love you Greg, I've never felt this way about anyone else before."

"I love you too," he said.

They stayed together in silence for a few minutes with Maureen still sat on his lap on the kitchen chair; her finished meal in front of her.

"So, what are you going to do about work. You can't continue to stay there, surely?"

"For the moment I've swopped roles with Joan, she'll look after David and I'll look after Mr Cathcart. As it happens David is on holiday now for ten days. He flies off to Dubai tomorrow, but I've had to switch my mobile off, I've had three missed calls from him already."

There was a long pause and she picked up her wine glass and took another sip.

"There's another thing", she paused again as if unsure she should continue, "I'm not convinced that all his dealings have been above board. There were times when he would be very secretive; you know... shut the door and ask not to be disturbed, that kind of thing; and there were some clients that I was not allowed access to. He has some secret files which he always keeps locked away."

"Does Cathcart know about this?"

"I honestly don't know... They do have totally different clients; it's like two separate practices sharing the same office. How much they talk about each other's clients, I don't know, but I've never seen them. They certainly don't socialise."

"What about the change of roles, won't that seem a bit odd?" asked Greg.

"Mr Cathcart never said anything when I suggested it and Joan was happy enough. She thought the change would do her good; doesn't really get on with him. He doesn't do relationships, only interested in getting the work done."

That certainly fitted in with Greg's assessment.

"Well we need a plan," said Greg. "Have you any idea what he will do?"

"Not really, I think he could be capable of anything, I've seen him operate. He can be nasty when he wants to be."

"Do you think you might be in any danger?"

"I don't think so. I could probably do as much damage to him."

"That's my point, if he thinks you're a threat, might he not take some sort of preventative action?"

"I hadn't thought so, but he was certainly angry this morning. He doesn't like losing, anything. He even cheats when he plays his kids at Scrabble. He told me that. I thought he was joking."

"How many children does he have?"

"Three, the eldest is thirteen, the youngest six."

Greg sat for a moment, thinking. Maureen was still holding onto him.

"Does he know where you live?" he asked, which was probably a silly question, but he wanted to make sure.

"Well, he'll know my address, but he hasn't been there; I only moved in a couple of months ago."

"Why don't you move in here, at least for the time being? You'd be quite safe and, as you see, I have enough room."

She smiled and thought for a moment.

"I'm not sure, things have moved so quickly for me."

"Me too," said Greg. "But in the short term, we need to make sure you're safe, at least until things cool down. You could stay for a couple of weeks and see how it goes. At least you won't be looking over your shoulder wondering."

She could see the logic in Greg's argument and frankly she didn't want to be on her own.

"When?" she asked.

"Now," said Greg. "I can take you back to your place and help you pack a few things. We can collect the rest at the weekend."

She looked at him and kissed him again.

"Yes, you're right. Let's do it," and she got up off Greg's lap.

"Oo that's better," he said jokingly, and she gave him a

playful smack before kissing him again.

They grabbed their jackets and left the house; Greg locked up and opened the garage. "We'll take my car, we can get more stuff in."

He reversed out and headed for Maureen's flat.

Maureen provided directions and it took about half an hour to reach the row of shops. Greg parked in the lay-by outside a hairdresser's. The parade looked a bit run down and there was litter scattered around the pavement and graffiti adorned the walls. There were four other shops including an off-license which was still open and a mini supermarket. They got out and walked towards a door with flaking green paint between the salon and a baker's.

"This is it," said Maureen and she opened the door and led the way up the stairs. Although it was still light outside, the stairway was dark.

"Careful, the bulb's broken," she said before opening the door at the top.

They went inside. It was a small flat and Greg straightaway noticed it was neat and tidy which appealed to his sense of order. They were going to get along just fine, he thought.

"I won't be long, have a seat," she said.

It took almost half an hour but gradually she had collected all the things she would need for the rest of the week plus a few personal things, a teddy bear and some pictures of her family.

"I take these everywhere."

Greg started taking the things down to the car and put them in the boot. There was a smart dress and some trousers which he folded neatly and placed on the back seat.

He went back up the stairs.

"That's everything I need for now," she said, bringing in a couple of boxes and carrier bags from what appeared to be a spare bedroom.

Greg carried the two boxes stacked on top of one another and slowly made his way downstairs.

"You ok, Greg?" Maureen asked as he struggled down the stairs.

"So far," he said after a few steps. "I'll let you know when I get to the bottom," and she laughed.

They put the rest of the things in the car which was now looking extremely loaded up. They got in and Greg was about to pull away when he noticed a car pulling up on the other side of the road opposite the flat. The light was fading, and it was difficult to make out his features, but the driver seemed to be taking a particular interest in what was going on.

"Do you know anyone with a silver Mercedes?"

"David's got a silver Mercedes," she said.

"Is that him over there?" Greg asked, indicating to his left with his head. His view of the man was obscured by his passenger. She looked across the road and recognised the car.

"Oh my God, yes, it is. I don't want to speak to him," she said.

"He's getting out. What do you want to do?" asked Greg.

"Just drive, I don't want anything more to do with him."

Greg waited until the figure was well away from the Mercedes and had started to cross the road towards them and then hit the accelerator. The Audi roared out of the parking spot with gravel flying up from the tyres and headed out into the country. He made a left turn and after a few hundred yards another left which brought him onto one of the main roads back into the city. There was no sign of the Mercedes.

Once in town, they headed through the city centre and back out onto the road to Taskers End.

Returning to the house, Greg helped Maureen get her belongings in and upstairs to the bedroom. He opened the walk-in wardrobe which contained his meagre selection of clothes;

trousers, followed by shirts, followed by his two jackets, all in order.

"You can have this side if you like, I won't be needing it for some time."

"You know, you're really tidy, for a man," she said, looking at the neat row of clothes.

"I like order; it helps the mind process information. I think I read that somewhere."

"I thought it had been excluded from a man's DNA," she said with a smile.

It took over an hour to sort everything out and they went back to the kitchen to clear the dishes.

"I'll put them in the dishwasher," said Greg. "What about some cheesecake?"

"I'd prefer a glass of red."

Greg produced a bottle of Cabinet Sauvignon from the wine rack and two glasses and put them on the table.

As he poured the drink, Maureen looked at him.

"Thank you… for everything."

"That's ok, I just want you safe," he said, as he poured the drinks. He led her into the lounge.

"I need to tell my Dad."

"What are you going to say?"

"I'll just tell him I'm staying with a friend for a while. He'll be fine."

Maureen made the call.

It was starting to get quite dark and Greg went around the ground floor closing the curtains.

Once settled, they stayed in the lounge chatting for ages before going to bed; the bond between them growing stronger all the time. Greg felt completely at home with the situation. He never wanted it to end; he had never felt this good.

Thursday morning and Maureen left for work at eight o'clock as she'd done the previous day. Greg suggested she stayed at home and call in sick, but she was adamant she needed to go in.

"Keep an eye out for any strange cars or anyone following you, and if you get any problems, or notice anything strange, ring me straight away." He was really concerned for her safety.

As he ate his breakfast, he suddenly had had a thought; the trunk in the scullery; there might be some answers there.

He finished his toast and took the large key which he'd hung on a hook in the kitchen. It was old and showing signs of rust, probably original he thought, and went to the door under the stairs.

Chapter Nine

Greg turned the sturdy iron key. It was an old-fashioned mortise lock, quite stiff and he had to use pressure to make the turn; it had clearly not been used for some time. The door made a creaking sound as it slowly opened; the wood had warped into the frame. He looked down the dark staircase.

A large spider's web clung to his face as he took his first step into the darkness. He flicked on the light switch. Click, click, nothing; the bulb had long since expired. He went back to the kitchen, wiping the sticky thread from his face, to get a torch. As he made his way down the twelve concrete stairs, eerie shadows danced on the wall from the flash light.

He reached the bottom and scanned the scullery. It felt dank and clammy; there was a musty smell. It was not a large area, maybe twenty-feet long by sixteen and, like the rest of the building, had stone walls but they had not been plastered and were just bare. There was a small fanlight right at the top of the wall on the opposite side of the room which let in a small shaft of light but not enough to obviate the need of a torch. More spiders' webs festooned the room as he walked across floor. He couldn't believe what he was seeing.

At the back against the wall there was a clothes rail with men's apparel hanging, several cardboard boxes and a keyboard which he recognised straight away was his old Yamaha DX7. It had cost his grandparents a fortune in 1984, he remembered. It was his pride and joy at the time, but his parents had baulked at the cost. He went over to it and wiped some of the dust away. Holding the torch in his left, he made chord structures with his right hand and imagined the sound which used to emanate from it. Despite being a relative novice could almost make it sing.

He went to the clothes rail and examined them in more detail. They were his most recent, the ones from his flat in

Leeds; someone must have collected them. He opened one of the boxes and found his lost CD collection. He flicked through, mostly 80's electronic, the Smiths, then Nirvana, Oasis, Blur; his teen years encapsulated in music. He would get a new hi-fi system as soon as he could and give them an airing. He realised how much he had missed music; it had been his refuge when the bullying and abuse was at its worst.

He shook himself out of his retrospection; he had other, more important matters to attend to. He swept around with the torch, the beam of light making a circle on the wall then distorted as it came to a corner.

Then he saw it, almost concealed by a blanket which had been draped over the top, a large metal trunk. He went across to it, more spiders' webs stuck to his face. He shone his torch over the chest. On the side were the initials 'J.S.' stencilled in gold lettering. James Sinclair, his grandfather. As he looked at it he felt a sudden chill and shivered, it was a good ten degrees cooler in the scullery.

Greg tried opening it but it was locked. He decided that he would need to get it upstairs; he could not go through it in the basement, but a problem immediately arose. He tried lifting it, but it wouldn't budge. He looked at it in consternation; how was he going to get it up to the sitting room?

On each side there was a metal handle and he grabbed the nearest one and started to pull. After at least two years' incarceration in this dungeon it had embedded itself into the ground and there was some initial resistance to his efforts to move it. But once unsettled, it started to slide across the floor bit by bit making a hideous grating noise which set Greg's teeth on edge, leaving scrape marks on the tiling of the scullery floor.

Gradually using all his strength, he was able to manoeuvre the trunk to the bottom of the stairs. He looked up and could see the light of the hallway at the top. Twelve steep stone steps separated him. He went upstairs and adjusted his eyes to the light. He put down the torch, wiped away the arachnid residue and went into the kitchen. Think, think, he said to himself. He went through the kitchen cupboards for inspiration, nothing; and then the drawers, most of which were empty but in one of them he found a plastic washing line; that would be strong enough.

He went back down the stairs to the chest. He doubled the line and threaded it through one of the handles. He was able to lift up one side of the chest onto the bottom step, so it was at a forty-five-degree angle and he walked up three steps and took the strain. Sure enough, the box started to slide upwards and with only the edges of the stairs offering any resistance it was easier than he had expected and, after five minutes of effort, the trunk was safely at the top of the staircase.

He found an old blanket to put underneath it which would make it easier to move and would also stop it scratching the floor or damaging the carpet.

He slowly negotiated the chest into the sitting room. He'd had hardly used this room since he had been back. As well as the family library it had been his grandfather's study; there was a large book shelf to the right which contained hundreds of books. The previous tenants had obviously not taken much interest in them as none appeared to have been removed from their confines. They were all in alphabetical order by authors; Granddad Sinclair was almost as fastidious as his grandson.

Memories kept coming back; he could see his grandparents playing Bridge and Gin Rummy on many a Saturday night on the old card table in the corner. Occasionally he would join them he remembered. He particularly enjoyed Canasta which they had to play with a dummy hand as there was never a fourth to make up the right numbers. He smiled at the thought. The reminiscences were warm and fond, and he realised that, despite the emotional references, once again Gerald had stayed away; this was significant progress.

The study would now be his centre of operations, he decided. He put the trunk by the window, then went to the kitchen and returned with a bunch of keys and a duster. He cleared off the two years' debris of dead insects and grime and revealed a shiny black container.

There was no more lettering apart from the initials and Greg rummaged through the keys to see if he could find the right one. Fortunately, they were nearly all labelled so he was able to discount most of them but there was one on its own and Greg tried it in the lock. "Voila," he said to himself as the key turned and the lid of the trunk lifted; freed from the pressure of its contents.

He opened the box and it was filled with books, papers, old ledgers, photographs and greeting cards, remarkable dry considering the climate they had been stored in for all this time. Greg was anxious to dive in but decided to think first and went to the kitchen to make a coffee.

He called Maureen to see how she was. In all the excitement of the discovery of the trunk, he still hadn't forgotten her situation. She was pleased to hear from him and everything seemed to be fine. There were no strange men hanging around; "no stranger than usual," she joked, which was a good sign. After a brief catch up, Maureen confirmed she would be 'home'- her words, by five. Greg would have a meal ready; he hadn't worked out what yet.

Back to the trunk, and he decided to take out the contents and put them on the table, so he could see more clearly what was there. He made a pile of letters, one of books and one of photographs.

He had a quick look through some of the photos and although most were black and white there were some in colour typical of the rather intense hues caused by the developer fluid that was used in mass film processing in the 70's. Many had lost their colour for the same reason. Some had been bound by elastic bands which had become perished and hard and disintegrated to the touch.

He glanced through them and recognised scenes of past visits to Taskers End when he was a child. There were some from his parent's wedding, Greg tried to recall the date – 1970 sometime.

Going through these old photos brought back many memories of his childhood and seeing his parents again caused him great sadness, but he was dealing with it in a different way, a normal way; he had no feeling of anger at the world or himself. He felt no inclination to hit out. Gerald was nowhere to be found.

He put the photos to one side; they were not what he was after. The letters were more likely to reveal something.

There were three piles of correspondence of various description; invoices for building work, letters from the bank, private letters, and so on. He sorted out the letters and organised them into categories as far as he could, which would make it easier to extract information. The private letters he put in date order; he decided to examine these first.

He picked up one which had a Preston post mark, in what looked like his mother's handwriting; there were several from 1985, including one dated two days before the 'incident'. He read it and sure enough it was from his mother; it was addressed to Martha Sinclair, Taskers End.

Dear Mum

I hope you are well. Thank you for your lovely letter. I know it's easier to phone but there's always something special in getting a letter and I look forward to yours so much. I do have some news though which I did not want to speak about over the phone.

I don't think I can go on much longer. John's becoming more and more aggressive. I have never said anything before, but he's always been free with his fists. I guess most of the time I've deserved the beatings, but I never mean to make him angry. He just gets worried about things. But no more; I have to put a stop to it. John doesn't know but I have been seeing someone else. He works at the building society where I work. It only started a couple of months ago, but I love him and he loves me. I'm going to tell John that I am going to leave him. I would have gone before but I have to protect Gerald, but the rows are getting worse now and I have to do something.

I will call you as soon as I have more news.

All my love

Denise

Greg read it again and felt a huge weight on his shoulders. He had no idea how bad things were between his father and mother and having not been at the inquest knew nothing of the course of events that had preceded the shooting. He knew they had been rowing but tended to shut himself away when the voices were raised. His memory returned to him sitting on the bed with his hands over his ears as his parents shouted abuse at each other. He remembered it had got worse before the incident but at ten years of age could not account for it. He thought of his mother's courage and her need to shelter him from the realities of the marital relationship.

Greg decided that reading more of his mother's letters would be too upsetting for him and so he sifted out the more recent correspondence addressed to his grandparents. There could be something that might help him with his investigation into their deaths.

His grandmother was also meticulous in her organisation and had kept the letters in date order. He wanted to see if there was anything in the run up to the fire. He went back to May 2005 and found one letter, locally postmarked, with the name 'Dacombe Properties' as part of the franking.

He opened it and it was headed 'Taskers End'. It went as follows:

Dacombe Properties Ltd
The Pines,
High Peak Lane
Rivelin
Sheffield
Dear Mr & Mrs Sinclair,

I am writing following our conversation today regarding the possible sale of Taskers End. I am sorry that we were not able to reach an amicable conclusion but feel that a figure of £750,000 is a fair and reasonable price in today's market. We hope that after careful consideration you will have a more positive viewpoint on this generous offer.

I look forward to meeting you again in the future,
Yours sincerely
Peter Dacombe,
Managing director, Dacombe Properties Ltd.

Greg read the letter in disbelief. He knew that his grandparents would never sell Taskers End; they always said it should stay in the family and they had told him many times that he was the sole beneficiary in their will for this reason. What had triggered this, he wondered.

He looked at the address again, 'The Pines'. Of course, the large house on the corner. He then thought about the two new houses. Taskers End was next door and planning consent for rebuilding or conversion into flats would almost certainly be a formality with them being close by, irrespective of the strict planning regulations in this area of the Peak District.

He did some calculations. If Taskers End was demolished you could get three or, if you were to clear the woods, possibly four similar properties on the site. They would be worth at least a million each, given the area. Greg had discovered a possible motive.

But why kill his grandparents? It didn't make sense; perhaps they hoped that whoever inherited the property would be more inclined to sell; now that was a possibility.

Then he had another thought, Cathcart Rivers had a Power of Attorney, so, after his grandparents had died, they could have sold the property without his consent. Perhaps Cathcart wouldn't sell; so many questions.

He sat at the table with his head in his hands trying to make sense of it all. He read the letter again and noticed something that sent a shiver down his spine. At the foot of the paper there were the usual company details, VAT number, registered office and so on.

The list of directors read, P.K. Dacombe, J.S. Dacombe, D.G. Chapman MA. LLB (Honours), Company Secretary. The registered office was Cathcart Rivers' address.

Chapman! What on earth was he up to? Greg could feel Gerald stirring, but quickly calmed down. Maybe Maureen might know, but this did throw another pebble into the pond and ripples were heading out in all directions.

Greg was trying to remember his own legal training from his University days. He was certain there would have been a conflict of interest with Chapman being a partner in Cathcart Rivers; although that would not necessarily have been a deterrent if he was as ruthless as Maureen had said.

He picked up another letter with the same red franking.

This one was dated 22nd May 2005, two weeks after the earlier one. The text went as follows:

Dear Mr & Mrs Sinclair,

Following my visit today I have to say I am very surprised at your intransigence. From what you say your grandson is working away and has no interest in Taskers End and unlikely to want to live there.

As I explained we are prepared to increase our already generous offer to £800,000 which would be more than enough for you to buy a new property that would be more manageable for you as you get older and leave you a nice sum to provide you with an income.

I urge you to consider your options very carefully.

Yours sincerely ...

What does that mean 'consider your options'? Sounds like a threat, or it could be just clever wording, but there is an implication there, surely.

Greg mulled over this letter but then his attention was drawn to the pile of books. Most of them were old and quite historical company records from the family business but also among them he could see his grandmother's diaries.

Greg remembered his grandmother being very disciplined and before going to bed would always write a few lines. Some would be more interesting than others; 'had cheese on toast at lunch', or 'went into town with James', were not the most interesting of topics, but they reflected the pattern of their lives, mostly humdrum but occasionally there were special moments.

Greg found 2005, which of course finished on July 16th. The diary would normally have been in her bedside cabinet, but it obviously had survived the fire; so, where was it on that night? Greg examined it more closely, no signs of scorching, nothing to suggest it had been in a heated environment. She must have left it downstairs, in the library most probably. He remembered she did sometime make entries the following day if they had been late to bed but he was certain she would have taken it upstairs if they were going to turn in for the night.

Why was it not by the bedside, he pondered?

He wondered who would have collected all the belongings together and put them in the trunk after the fire. It could only be his solicitor, but why? Why would he go to all that trouble?

Greg remembered that it was Cathcart who had told him about the trunk; if he hadn't he might never have gone into the scullery. Perhaps he wanted him to discover something; he would be aware of Greg's keen analytical mind. It was difficult to make sense of it.

Greg went and made another coffee and took the diary into the kitchen with him. He flicked through the pages until he got to May and sure enough there was an entry on the day of the visit described in the first letter.

We had a visit today from one of our neighbours, Mr Dacombe from The Pines. Didn't much care for him. Told us he wanted to buy Taskers End. Offered seven hundred and fifty thousand pounds. James gave him short shrift and told him it was not for sale at any price. He seemed right put out I must say. Said we were being foolish. He said he would put the offer in writing and we should consider it carefully. James told him to leave and not come back.

Greg skipped some pages which weren't of interest until he got to the entry on 22nd May.

That nasty man Dacombe called again today, the cheek of the man. He didn't get further than the door. Said he would increase the price to £800,000 which was his final offer. He tried to be nice, but James told him to go to hell. I have never known James get so angry or use such language before. He said we hasn't heard the last of it.

There were a couple more letters in June, the last one increasing the 'final offer' to £900,000. Dacombe appeared to be getting desperate and the letters more threatening, but subtly, nothing that would stand up in court. It was the diary entries that made the most interesting reading.

June 4th – someone emptied a lorry load of sand across the driveway and left.

June 7th – I am sure someone was outside the kitchen window when I drew the curtains tonight

June 10th – more deliveries – 6.30am a pile of bricks dumped right outside the front door. James saw the lorry as it left but there was no name on it and he couldn't see the number.

June 15th – someone is watching the house from the woods with binoculars. James spotted him when he was looking at a Tawny Owl with his telescope. I am beginning to worry.

June 22nd – someone tried to break in through the little toilet window. When James went in there for his morning smoke it was open and had been forced. We had to call a builder to fix it. I have told James we must call the police, but he said they couldn't do anything we have no proof it's Dacombe.

Greg stopped at this entry. So, someone did try to break in, or was it just a warning to scare his grandparents? But he had been right; unfortunately, it appeared to have nothing to do with the fire.

July 3rd – we have started to get strange phone calls. It rings and there is no-one there. James has called the telephone company and they are going to monitor all calls which is a relief. I wish Gerald was here he would know what to do.

Greg was quite emotional on reading this passage he realised what they must have been going through and he was not there to help them, after everything they had done for him.

He decided on another break to calm down and have a sandwich for lunch; he would also ring Maureen again to make sure she was ok.

"Hi Greg," she said when he called. "You ok?"

"Yeah, I'm fine, how're things?"

"Everything's fine here" she said.

"Have you heard anything from Chapman?"

"Nothing, I don't think he's called. He's not contacted the office either as far as I know."

"That's good, see you later and *be* careful," he said.

After lunch it was back to the trunk.

He continued the diary which had given him a good insight into what was happening to them around the time they died. What he couldn't understand is, why the police didn't check through the papers.

July 7th – a very unpleasant man called said he was selling insurance although he didn't look like an insurance man, very scruffy individual. James told him quite forcibly to leave.

July 10th – another letter from Dacombe, increasing the offer to one million. I told James perhaps we should think about it. Gerald would have the money and could buy a house somewhere else. He might not want to live at Taskers in any case. I do think of him all the time cooped up in that hospital. Heaven knows what they are doing to him. You read in the papers about experimenting with electric shocks all kinds of things. It is so worrying; I do hope he is alright.

If Greg had any doubts about his grandmother's love for him, they were dispelled at that moment. He had to stop to prevent him from becoming emotional. It was so upsetting he wasn't sure if he wanted to continue but there were only a few more entries left. This was not Gerald trying to intervene, this was cool Greg responding as anyone would have done in the same circumstance.

The next three were fairly mundane shopping trips but there was one on 14th July which was disturbing.

Went shopping this morning and James thought we were being followed. When we came out of the supermarket the tyres of the car had been slashed. We had to call the AA. I told James we must contact the police, but he refused. Said if we ignore them they will soon get fed up and leave us alone. I hope he is right.

July 15th – Someone drove onto the drive tonight playing really loud music and drove away again. I was in the kitchen making our Horlicks when I heard it. James went to the front door, but it was too late. Just kids he said. Still won't call the police. I said to him I want to sell but he would have none of it. Over my dead body he said, it's a matter of principle now.

I hope it doesn't come to that. I am so scared.

Greg read the final entry July 16th, 2005.

I wish Gerald was here. I am sure there was someone in the woods again. James thought he heard someone creeping around the back of the house. I have told him we must get some security lights and an alarm. He says I am being hysterical, but we must do something.

It was getting all too much for Greg and decided to take a break.

So many questions.

He gradually composed himself. He could feel Gerald knocking on the door of the firewall again, but he had a mission and he would not be distracted. He decided he would make a list of questions and try to work out the answers by deduction, possibilities or known facts. That would help take away the emotion.

What does Cathcart know?

Where does Chapman fit into all this?

The owner of the Pines, Dacombe, seems to have had the motive to kill his grandparents, but how was Greg going to prove he had?

He decided he would go and see the solicitor to try to find more information about events around the time of the fire. He would also ask Maureen about Chapman to see if she can throw any light on what happened. It might mean giving her a great deal of information, but it was not the right time to tell her about his 'illness', not yet anyway. He had no idea about how to tackle the third question but believed it would become clearer if he could get answers to the other two.

He looked at his watch; it was almost four o'clock. He decided he would take Maureen out for dinner it would save time and be a change.

The Mini pulled into the drive just before five and Greg went to the front door to let her in.

"I'll get you a key tomorrow," he said, and leaned over and kissed her.

"Thank you," she said and responded warmly; then took off her jacket and hung it on a peg in the hall.

"I thought we could go out for tea, how do you fancy a curry?" asked Greg attentively. "I'll drive."

Maureen thought for a second. "Yeah, great."

It was said without a great deal of enthusiasm Greg could tell, so he added. "I can rustle up something here if you prefer," he said.

"If you don't mind, I just need to chill out, if that's ok," she said, following Greg to the kitchen.

"Of course. You go and change; I'll see what I can find," and Greg went and opened the fridge to check the provisions as Maureen went upstairs to change.

Greg studied the contents; having not stocked up he would be reliant on what Queenie had left for him earlier in the week. There was a quiche which was still within its sell-by date and some salad and he could put some potatoes in the microwave. Menu settled.

Maureen came into the kitchen looking more refreshed.

Greg thought she looked beautiful, but she would disagree.

"Tea, coffee or a glass of wine?" he asked.

"A glass of red wine would be great," and Maureen started to tell Greg about her day.

"Nothing from Chapman then?"

"No. Which is a bit disturbing in itself. I didn't think he would give up this easily."

They continued talking as Greg finished preparing the meal and as they sat down to eat, he asked his first question.

"Have you heard of a company called Dacombe Properties?"

Chapter Ten

Maureen thought for a moment; then the recollection. "'Dacombe Properties', yes of course, it's one of David's special clients; you know, the ones I wasn't allowed to look at. Why do you ask?"

"I need to explain a lot of things and it will become clear."

Greg started to give Maureen the background into the 'accident' that killed his grandparents and his suspicions.

"I'm so sorry," she said when he described the fire.

"It just doesn't add up, and everyone just accepted the cause of the fire without any real investigation. I know it couldn't have started the way that they said. I've studied these things... Anyway, I've been doing some delving. I went to the Coroner's Office and seen a copy of the Coroner's Report. Today I've been going through some of my grandparents' old papers. I'll show you later."

Maureen listened closely. "So, what does all this mean?"

"I don't think my grandparents died by accident; I'm certain of it, and it is possible that this Peter Dacombe, he's the chap who owns the Pines... the care-home on the corner, was involved in some way. My grandmother says in her diary that he was putting pressure on them to sell Taskers End, so there's your motive. Then there's Chapman, he's Company Secretary of Dacombe Properties, so there's a link there; although it proves nothing, and I've got no idea whether he is involved or not."

"Why don't you go to the police?"

"Because there's no evidence, plus I'm not convinced they did a thorough enough job the first-time around. They're unlikely to admit that they cocked-up," he replied. "I need to get more evidence."

They finished their meal and Greg cleared the plates.

"Cheesecake?" he asked, with a smile. "It needs to be eaten today," and Greg went to the fridge.

After dinner, Greg took Maureen into the sitting room to show her all the papers and letters. He also showed her some of the photographs.

"You look lovely in short trousers," she teased.

Maureen read the diary entries and the letters that Greg had pored over earlier and agreed with him that something was not right.

"You should take these to the police; surely it would be enough."

"They are incriminating but not evidence," said Greg, "I need a lot more before there's a case."

"What are you going to do?" asked Maureen.

"Well, I need to speak to Cathcart; I am sure he can throw some light on things. Then I need to find out more about Dacombe." He looked at Maureen. "Which you may be able to help with. Can you get access to any papers in Chapman's office?"

Maureen folded her arms, defensively.

"I don't think so. The Dacombe files will be one of those under lock and key and I don't have one."

"What about Joan, does she have a key?"

"I wouldn't think so but..." Maureen was thinking. "There may be a way... The office duplicates are kept at the Bank for safe keeping. I might be able to get access. I have done before. David used to send me around with an authorisation slip when we needed to change the safe combination. I would bring the keys back and then return them when he had finished with them."

"What about Chapman's signature, won't you need that?"

"Yes, but I think I can find the authorisation slip I used last time. It will be filed somewhere. I can check."

"Can you do that? That would be brilliant. I just feel so frustrated; I had no idea what they were going through."

"Well, it's no use beating yourself up over it. You can't turn back the clock."

There was definitely a pragmatic side to Maureen which Greg liked.

"I know but..." his voice tailed off as he looked at a photograph of him and his mother.

"Is that your Mum?" asked Maureen.

"Yes, I would be about six, there."

"She's pretty."

She sensed Greg was starting to become distressed and changed the subject.

"Is it ok if I have a bath, I could do with washing my hair? You can scrub my back if you like."

Greg snapped out of his introspection straight away.

Friday morning, a week since Greg had left Trenton Court and he couldn't in his wildest dreams have foreseen the events that had unfolded in such a short time.

He believed he had finally overcome the mental scars which had still been lurking just under the surface when he left the hospital. Going through the old papers, confronting the past, had been therapeutic and Gerald Perry had now been consigned to history along with the name; cool Greg was now in complete control. Gerald would never have coped with the emotion of the letters in the trunk or the discovery of his grandparent's demise; he would have literally freaked out.

Maureen was just leaving as Queenie arrived for her house managing duties and Greg made the introductions. There was a nice banter between them before Maureen left for the office; something about keeping Greg tidy, which was ironic given his obsession with order.

With Chapman away, Maureen had offered to see if she could find anything which might throw some light into the fire tragedy. She wasn't sure about the duplicate key situation, she would check the lie of the land; she didn't want to jeopardise her job and Friday was normally pretty busy.

Greg went back to the trunk after breakfast and continued to go down to the scullery to retrieve his bits and pieces. He changed the light bulb which made life a lot easier and he found other things he thought had been lost forever. There were some of his old school books and stuff from his University days. He rummaged through looking for nothing in particular and found his old text books on forensic science. He picked up 'Forensic Science Laboratory Manual and Workbook' by Thomas Kubic and Nicholas Petraco. He remembered studying these books religiously, intrigued by the art of logic and the investigative process.

As he flicked through the academic tome a letter dropped out; he must have been using it as a book mark. He recognised the handwriting straight away; it was from Lindsey.

There was a momentary feeling of panic as if Gerald was starting to wake from his slumbers, but Greg took a deep breath and opened it. It was early on in their relationship judging by the date of the post mark; addressed to him at the University and posted in Devon. Greg recalled Lindsey going on holiday for a week over Easter while he stayed and did some revising. He remembered teasing her about it. He read the contents and it was not so much a love letter just a 'having a good time, hope you are well; look forward to seeing you when I get back,' kind of letter, nothing gushing or indicative of the trouble that lay ahead. It was signed, 'Love Lindsey'.

Greg reminisced for a while when a call disturbed him from the top of the stairs which made him jump.

"I'm just making a drink Mr Jensen, would you like a

coffee?"

It was Queenie.

"Yes please, I'll be up in a minute," and suddenly the spell was broken. Gerald was back in his box and Greg realised that whatever hold Lindsey had had on him was gone, forever.

He put the letter back in the book and picked up the box of CDs and carried it upstairs.

Queenie was there waiting for him with a mug of coffee.

"What have you got there?" she asked.

"My old CD collection I have been storing them there while I was away."

She handed him the coffee. "Any Frankie Sinatra?" she asked, "I like him."

"Afraid not," he said, and she looked disparagingly at the titles.

"Never heard of 'em," she said and went back to the kitchen.

Greg decided he would go into town later and acquire a hifi system. He wanted to give them an airing.

He finished his coffee and called Maureen to see how she was getting on. She was fine, very busy and hasn't had any chance to do any investigating but would do so in her lunch hour.

"While you're on, can you check if Mr Cathcart is available on Monday please, I need to speak to him?"

Maureen checked the diary. "He's free around eleven o'clock."

"Great, can you book me in?"

They concluded the conversation.

As soon as he had finished the call his phone went again. It was Doctor Melrose.

"Is that Gerald?" she asked.

"It's Greg now," he replied.

"This is Jane Melrose calling to confirm the appointment for Monday."

"Of course," said Greg. "Is it possible we can meet at my solicitor's office at say ten o'clock? Dorinda said you were fairly flexible."

The doctor was amazed at his confidence compared with the last time they had met.

"Yes, I think so, can you give me details," and Greg gave her the directions and where to park. She rang off and Greg went back to his CD's.

A few minutes later the crunching of gravel heralded the arrival of the postman and the doorbell rang.

"Package for Mr Jensen, can you sign please?" asked the postman.

Formalities completed Greg went inside with the package; it was from the Coroner's Office according to the franking.

Back at the solicitors Maureen was covering on reception as she had the previous week; it was Joan's day off. At lunch time Arthur Cathcart left the office to meet clients according to the diary, and she would have the place to herself. She switched the phones to answer machine and nervously went upstairs to Chapman's office. Although it was locked she was able to gain access; the key was on a small hook in the reception desk drawer in case of emergencies. She unlocked the door and entered the room anxiously looking around half-expecting someone to be lurking inside.

The office overlooked the street, not as big as Cathcart's and with a low ceiling, but still had the smart leather chair and large desk which dominated the room; there were two smaller chairs for clients' use. In the corner was another small table with two chairs that Chapman would use for his laptop and write his private letters.

Maureen looked at the two metal cabinets in the corner

which contained his private files. Then had a thought; had he taken his PC home?

She knew where he usually kept it, top drawer at the side of the desk. There were two other keys on the ring for Chapman's office and she knew which one opened it; she'd locked it for him many times. She felt really nervous now; her hands fumbling as she worked the key. The drawer opened and on the top was a basket with various papers. She lifted it out and sure enough underneath was his laptop.

"Yes," she said to herself.

She put it on the desk and opened it. Anxiety was really beginning to take over; she couldn't risk discovery; the consequences would be unthinkable. It was not just her job on the line she knew; her former lover was not a man to cross. Her hands were having difficulty co-ordinating. She pressed the 'on' button and the Windows logo appeared followed by a password request box. She knew his password and hoped that he hadn't changed it; her guess was he would have been too preoccupied to think about it. She entered the name of his eldest daughter and the year of her birth. 'Password accepted', and the desktop came into view.

The screensaver was a photograph of the Chapman family on a holiday taken three or four years earlier. Maureen remembered that she had challenged him about it; she thought it was degrading for her given their relationship, but he had insisted he needed to do that to allay any suspicions.

Maureen entered 'Dacombe' in the search box on the start menu and several files came up. She quickly went back down the stairs to reception and retrieved her phone from her handbag to call Greg. She was just about to return upstairs when she heard keys in the lock of the front door.

"Oh no!" she gasped.

Arthur Cathcart walked in and went through to his office

hardly giving her a glance.

"A coffee Miss Brown, when you have a minute," he said as he walked past.

"Yes, Mr Cathcart," said Maureen.

Checking Cathcart was still in his room she hurried back upstairs. The laptop was still on the desk but had 'timed-out'. "Shit, shit, shit," she said to herself. She re-entered the password and phoned Greg. "Come on, come on, come on," as she waited for him to answer.

"Greg, it's me. I've got into David's laptop and there are some files here that look interesting, what's your email address?" She was whispering despite the distance to Cathcart's office.

Greg gave her the information which she wrote on a doodle pad on the desk and hung up.

The laptop had automatically connected to the office's WIFI network. She opened Outlook and started a new mail message and attached the folders entitled 'Peter Dacombe' and 'Dacombe Properties'. She entered Greg's email address and hit send.

"Come on, come on, hurry, hurry," she said to herself as the mail slowly left the outbox. The seconds seemed to stretch into minutes. It's incredible how long thirty seconds can seem when you are in a hurry.

Zap! Gone.

She needed to cover her tracks and deleted the 'sent item', then cleared the 'deleted item' and logged off, closed the lid and put the laptop back in the drawer with the basket back on top. She locked it and started to head for the door. She had a quick look round to make sure nothing was out of place when she noticed the note pad. "Shit," she said to herself and rushed back to the desk and ripped off the top page with Greg's email address written on it; that would certainly have set the cat amongst the pigeons. She put it in her pocket, then left the room. She walked down the corridor and breathed a huge sigh of relief; then for good measure she went into the ladies' toilet and flushed it.

She made the coffee and took a cup on a tray to Cathcart.

Her legs still felt wobbly.

"Sorry for the delay Mr Cathcart, I had to visit the ladies' room."

Cathcart made what seemed to be a grunting noise as an acknowledgement.

"Thank you, Miss Brown; that will be all," and he went back to his papers.

As she returned to her desk she started to relax having completed her mission and hoped it had proved a worthwhile exercise. She couldn't help thinking about how easy it had been to access her former boss's laptop; there was a certain arrogance about him that said, "I am untouchable". She was beginning to despise him and berated herself for becoming so involved.

Back at Taskers End, Greg was upstairs in his own office waiting anxiously for the email to appear. After twenty minutes a blue box opened on the right-hand bottom corner of the screen *dchapman@...* and the familiar ping. "I have mail," he said in a whisper.

He saved the folders to his documents; they were in various file types including a couple of spread sheets.

He opened one folder and checked the dates; he was looking particularly for 2005. As it happened the earliest letter in the folder was dated 7th June 2005, so previous correspondence must be in paper format somewhere he reasoned.

He opened the letter; it was on Cathcart Rivers headed notepaper. It went:

Dear Peter,

I am writing following our conversation this morning. As you say it is disappointing that the Sinclairs are being so intransigent, but I am willing to increase my stake in the venture by £100,000 if this will give you additional leverage in your negotiations.

Let me know when you have a positive outcome and I will arrange the usual Bank transfer.

Yours etc...

"So, you were involved, you bastard," he said to himself. He went through the rest of the letters for 2005. There was one dated just after the fire on 21st July which was also of interest.

Dear Peter

The recent events at Taskers End have cast doubts on the viability of this project. Cathcart informs me that the whole estate passes to the Sinclair's grandson who is on indefinite detention in Trenton Court Mental Hospital with no indication of release. The firm holds a Power of Attorney and could sell but Cathcart won't have any of it, he is adamant that he will not agree to any sale while the grandson is still locked up and is intending to rent it out until he is released.

I suggest we leave things for now and maybe it is something we can revisit as and when Sinclair junior is freed and hope that house prices increase in the meantime.

Yours etc

Another bombshell and Cathcart's involvement was becoming clearer; he was on their side. He read the letter again; 'as and when... is freed'. What did that mean? Will they try again? He realised he could not show Maureen this letter with the mention of Trenton Court; it was not the right time for him to explain everything.

These were the only letters with any direct reference to Taskers End but there were many more details of property deals.

Out of curiosity he opened up one of the spreadsheets and it was a Funds-flow summary with moneys moving in and out of various accounts, presumably of Cathcart & Rivers. Greg studied the information; his accounting knowledge was fairly basic, but it was clear that a great deal of money was moving from the solicitors to Dacombe Properties and then back again, sometimes several months later. There was a 'surplus' box which Greg deduced was profit on the deal. He would check with Maureen, but it looked like Chapman was borrowing money from Clients' accounts and moving this into property dealings with Dacombe and then pocketing his share of the 'profit' when the transaction was completed. He looked at the running total; the latest figure, August 2007 in the 'surplus' column, £1,276,374.

"Wow" said Greg to himself. "Now that is serious money."

Greg was aware from his legal studies that solicitors using Clients' money for their personal gain was against The Law Society's principles and would get Chapman struck off at least, if not imprisoned. "Now there's a thought." He couldn't wait to tell Maureen.

There was a call about two-thirty from the Audi garage to say that his new car would be ready to pick up tomorrow. Greg had completely forgotten about it in the mayhem, Arthur Cathcart had obviously put in the order they had discussed. He would be around at ten o'clock, he told them. Greg decided to leave his investigation for a while and pop to the Retail Park and supermarket. He wanted to treat himself and there was something he needed to do for Maureen.

Back in the solicitor's office, by four-thirty Maureen was starting to tidy up ready to go home. The afternoon had been slow, and time had dragged, she was looking forward to seeing what was in the folders she had sent to Greg. She hoped they had been of use.

Cathcart walked through the reception area from his office, he was wearing his long raincoat and carrying his briefcase. "Goodnight Miss Brown, see you on Monday. Have a nice weekend," he said routinely with no real warmth in the wishes.

"Goodnight Mr Cathcart, you too," she said to his back as he headed for the front door.

She didn't need a key to get out; it was a Yale lock and would shut behind her when she left. There was an alarm system, but this would be set by the cleaners who would be arriving at six o'clock.

She quickly finished tidying up, locked the desk on reception and collected her jacket and handbag; she couldn't wait to get out. There had been enough excitement for one day.

She got outside the office and slammed the door behind her. It was four thirty-five and the rush hour traffic would be building. Behind the row of offices there was a large cobbled square with allocated parking spaces servicing the entire block; a narrow feeder road led to the street which ran past the front of the building. Cathcart Rivers had four reserved spaces and Maureen was the proud occupant of one of them. It was a luxury to have parking so close to the office paid for by your employers.

As she approached her car she became aware of someone watching her. A white van was parked on the pavement, nothing strange about that; workmen came and went all the time, but this was different. As she looked across the driver appeared to dodge down as if not wanting to be seen.

She thought quickly and walked straight past her car and up the hill towards the shops and once out of sight got on the phone. Greg was back at the house having completed his brief shopping excursion.

"Greg, it's me. I think I'm being watched."

"Where are you?"

"Just by the car park in Jesmond Street, outside the cafe."

"I know where you mean. Stay there, I'll be with you as soon as I can. Keep your phone on and ring me every five minutes, ok?"

"Ok".

Greg grabbed his jacket and car keys and headed into town.

Initially the Audi made good progress but, although going against the traffic flow, it still took half an hour to reach Maureen. She had called in every five minutes as Greg had asked and she was able to keep watch on the white van from a discreet vantage point. She had decided to wait in the small cafe and was able to see the vehicle quite clearly without being seen herself.

Greg parked on the pavement outside the cafe and went inside. Maureen got up and hugged Greg when he came in.

He sat opposite her and started to formulate a plan. He noticed that the van had parked on the pavement, as tradesmen tended to do, with its rear very close to a wall so there was no chance of it reversing.

"Here's what we do, I'm going to drive around the car park and block his exit. You go to your car and when I've boxed him in, drive away and get home. I'll meet you there.

"Ok?"

"Yes, ok, got it".

Maureen and Greg left the cafe. Greg got back in the Audi and drove into the square, initially not making any move towards the van. He approached it slowly from behind and timed his run so that Maureen was safely in her car. She started the engine and, just as she was about to drive off, Greg pulled in front of the white van and got out.

The driver went mad. Greg nonchalantly walked up to the driver's window and knocked on it. The driver was screaming at him to move. The window came down and expletives were vented.

"Sorry, no need for that language I'm just looking for Divers and Divers solicitors they're around here some place. I've got the address, but I can't seem to find it; the streets look all the same to me."

"Get out of the fucking way!" the driver screamed.

"Sorry, no need to be rude, I was only asking," and knowing that Maureen would have been safely away, Greg calmly walked back to the Audi and pulled away slowly as if looking at the buildings. The van pulled behind Greg and started flashing his lights, but Greg drove at walking pace until he joined the queue to the main road. It being Friday night, Greg had no difficulty in waiting for several cars to pass before pulling into the traffic irritating the white van man even more.

Greg drove round the block one more time to ensure he wasn't being followed before joining the main road out towards the Peaks and home. There was no sign of the van.

He pulled into the drive of Taskers End and Maureen was sat in her car in front of the house waiting for him. Greg opened the garage door and suggested she put the mini in the garage for tonight just in case.

"There's plenty of room but be careful of the inspection pit, it's very dangerous," he warned.

Maureen came out and Greg parked the Audi over the pit next to the Mini.

Once inside, Maureen hugged Greg again. "Thank you, thank you," she said, and he explained his diversionary tactics.

"Very clever," she said and kissed him warmly.

She left him to get changed and after a few minutes came down with some washing.

"You should have said. Queenie would have done that for you."

"It's ok, just a few bits," she said.

Greg joined Maureen in the kitchen, her washing now tumbling around in the machine.

"I've got something for you," he said. "Close your eyes," and Maureen complied.

"Hold out your hand." Maureen held out her hand, and Greg placed a set of house keys in her open hand.

"Thank you," she said and kissed him again.

"I went into town this afternoon and got them done. Oh, I also treated myself at the same time. What do you think?" and in the corner was his new favourite toy; a top-of-the-range sound system with digital radio.

"What do you think?"

"It's a CD player."

"Philistine," he said. "It's the new state-of-the-art CD and MP3 audio sensation, with digital radio I should add."

He was giving it a much bigger build up than it really deserved.

"Have a listen to this," and he pointed a remote control at the machine, coloured lights appeared closely followed by the haunting sounds of Pink Floyd's *'Wish you were here'*.

"Sounds good," said Maureen with no more than a passing interest as David Gilmour's haunting riff reverberated round the kitchen.

"It's brilliant," he said. "Here, sit down I've got so much to tell you."

He went to the wine rack.

"Red or white?" he asked.

"Red I think," she said, and he poured two glasses.

"I hope you don't mind, I've ordered a takeaway; it'll be here around seven if that's ok. Thought it would save time; I didn't get in till four o'clock."

"No, that's fine."

"I wasn't sure what you like so I have ordered a bit of a mixture."

"No, that's ok, I'm fairly easy," she said.

Maureen sipped her drink, clearly with her mind elsewhere.

"Who do you think they were?"

Greg was distracted with his gadget for a moment but refocused.

"I don't know, but I'm going to find out… and I don't want you worrying, we'll be fine, we'll get through this," he said with some assertiveness, and his reassurance seemed to placate Maureen as she gradually relaxed.

A few minutes later there was the sound of crunching gravel and a red van pulled into the drive with the words "Taj Mahal Restaurant," on the side.

"Dinner is served, m'lady," said Greg in his butler voice again, as he carried the plastic containers into the kitchen in the branded carrier bag.

"Smells delicious," she said as he dished out the meal.

She looked at him across the table as they started their dinner.

"Come on then tell me all the news. Was the stuff I sent through any use?" she asked.

Chapter Eleven

As they ate their dinner, Greg told Maureen about the Dacombe letter relating to the offer of money from Chapman, clearly implicating him with the deal to try to purchase the house.

"There's no evidence to suggest he was involved with any of the heavy stuff but, from what I've found out, it's certainly possible and in one of the letters after the fire he suggests, and I quote, 'revisiting it at a later date'."

"Are you saying they may try to buy the house again?" asked Maureen, as she tucked into her Chicken Tikka Masala.

"Sounds like it, but they'll have me to contend with now, not some elderly couple and I'll be waiting."

"This is delicious, where did you find the restaurant?" she asked as she took another mouthful.

"In the phone book... hope you like my choice."

"Yeah, it's great, really great."

"There's another thing which may be more relevant in handling Chapman... It seems you were right about his dodgy dealings, I am pretty sure he has been using clients' money to finance property purchases".

"But that's illegal," said Maureen.

"Well, it will certainly get him struck off, so we do have some leverage. The problem is I don't know how we can use it yet. I am not sure how hacking into someone's laptop and stealing files will go down in a court of law."

"Hmmm, I see what you mean."

"I might raise it with Cathcart. As senior partner he'll be obliged to report suspicions and get them investigated."

"But then he'll know we've accessed David's files, or at least someone's divulged confidential information... I'm not sure how that will go down."

"That's the problem and I don't want you to get into any

trouble. Is there any other way we can get some evidence on him that won't incriminate us…? Anything that he might have said or done that might not have seemed suspicious at the time but now we know what's been happening may seem not quite right?"

"Not off the top of my head, but I'll think about it."

"What about the client accounts, do you know if anyone audits them…? I had a thought, if we could get a look at the bank accounts there will have to be transfers to Dacombe somewhere down the line to cover the payments."

"I'm not sure but I'll check. We used to have an office manager who did all the banking transactions, but he left about six months ago. Joan does it now."

She paused for a moment. "It was very strange that, now you come to mention it. He'd been with the firm for a long time, over ten years, then one morning he turned up collected his things and left. No-one's seen him since. I asked David about it and he just said there'd been a difference of opinion, and that was that."

"Do you know his name?"

"Yes, Sam Davenport."

"Do you know where he lives? I'd like to pay him a visit."

"Fullwood, I think. I'll ask Joan, she'll know."

They continued their deliberations long after they finished their meal and after clearing up they retired to the lounge.

There was a burning question that Maureen wanted to ask.

"What are we going to do about the stalker? He's bound to try again. David's not going to give up that easy."

"I know, I've been thinking about that and I think it's time we went on the offensive," and he outlined his plan.

"Monday, I'll sort it."

Maureen felt a little more assured but was still uneasy.

Saturday morning and Greg was up early ready to collect his new car. Maureen said she wanted to go back to her flat after she had washed her hair and pick up some more things. Greg wanted to take her with him to the showroom to pick up his new car, but she passed on the opportunity. "It's a boy's thing," she said.

Greg was not at all happy leaving her on her own, but she was insistent and after promises of regular contact, Greg finally relented.

Over breakfast he'd been thinking about how he was going to tackle the stalker and as he was reversing the rented Audi out of the garage, he had an idea.

He went back inside and had a look around the work bench. In the corner he spotted his grandfather's old wooden box of nails and screws. It had been painstakingly hand-made with mini drawers each containing a different type and size. Greg rummaged through each in turn and chose a couple of roofing-felt tacks which he thought may come in useful and he put them in his pocket ready for Monday's proposed confrontation with the van-man.

He looked at the magnificent display of screwdrivers which his grandfather had kept pinned on the long wall. There were at least fifty different types for every eventuality; Phillips, Flat Heads, Cabinet, Robertson, Star, Hex, Clutch Heads and Nut Drivers all in order of length and purpose. Greg suddenly felt a shiver and Gerald was beginning to stir but didn't know why. He took one from the rack and put it in his pocket, just in case; of what, he wasn't sure.

Greg was firmly in control; Gerald had gone back to sleep.

He set off into town and made a stop at the supermarket to use a cash machine; his pocket float was almost exhausted, he drew out £300 which he thought would keep him going for a few days.

He arrived at the garage just before the allotted time and an ingratiating salesman gave him the usual spiel about what a fine choice he had made and so on. Greg was anxious to conclude the transaction and the salesman was surprised at Greg's blasé approach to the purchase. He had chosen the sportier TT and the new vehicle gleamed in the autumn sunshine. He'd arranged to leave the A3 with the dealer who would get it back to the car rental company. They spent some time talking about the controls and the assistant helped Greg 'pair' his phone with the car system which meant he would be able to use the hands-free phone kit.

It had taken over an hour to complete all the paperwork and induction but eventually Greg was able to ease his shiny TT slowly out of the forecourt. As he was heading back to the house a call came through on his mobile. Greg was still trying to work out the controls and found the button on the steering column. By the miracles of modern technology, the signal reached his phone in his jacket pocket and routed it to the car.

He pressed answer.

"Greg, it's me. The van... it's parked outside the flat." Maureen's voice echoed around the inside of the car.

"Where are you?" asked Greg.

"Just around the corner from the shops. I don't think he saw me."

"Ok, time to bring the plan forward I think... Stay where you are; I'll be with you as soon as I can. If he spots you or approaches the car, drive off as fast as you can then phone me."

"Will do," she said.

Greg did a left turn through a housing estate which would be a short cut. Speed bumps in the road slowed him down and did nothing to maintain the pristine condition of his new car but needs must.

It was twenty minutes before the row of shops came into

view. He could see Maureen's car parked in the road adjacent to the parade and the white van was still stationary in the layby where they had collected Maureen's stuff a few days earlier.

Greg turned left and pulled in behind Maureen's car. He got out of the Audi and opened the passenger door of the Mini and got in.

"Oh, am I pleased to see you," she said. "What are you going to do?"

"A little bit of negotiation. Wait here till I get back," and Greg got out and walked around the corner towards the white van.

The vehicle was pointing away from him which meant he could approach it without being seen if he kept out of the sight of the rear-view mirrors. He got up behind the van and then, stooping below the wing mirror line of sight, slowly made his way alongside the van until he was at the passenger door. He rummaged around in his pocket.

He bent down and wedged one of the roofing-felt tacks immediately in front of the rear wheel at a forty-five-degree angle with the sharp point sticking into the tyre, just as a precaution.

He took a deep breath and slid the door open and got in.

"What the fu... You!!" said the driver, spilling a flask of coffee down his trousers.

"Shut up," said Greg. He had clearly caught him off guard.

"How much is Chapman paying you?"

"What the fuck are you on about? Get out of my van before I do you an injury."

Greg was calm, assured and in charge.

"You're not going to do anything to me because you will want to know what I want."

"I'm warning you," said the low life.

"As I said, shut up and listen. I know what you're doing

and I'm willing to make you an offer that you shouldn't refuse. Chapman is a pussy-cat compared with what I can do."

This was not Gerald re-emerging; he would never have been able to maintain composure. This was cool Greg and definitely in control.

The man's nostrils were flaring like a wild stallion.

"Now calm down and listen to what I have to say. I repeat, how much is Chapman paying you?"

"And as I said, I don't know what the fuck you are talking about."

Greg could feel the screw driver in his hand and was ready to pounce if necessary.

"I see, well, let me see if I can enlighten you. Chapman is a solicitor in town and has hired you to keep watch on the lady who lives here. Now, I don't know whether you mean to do her harm or not, but I'm willing to double anything he is paying you and take over your employment... Consider it a career change."

The man was confused but was beginning to listen.

"Two hundred pounds," he said.

"Ok, what's your name?" asked Greg.

"Terry, Terry Baker," the man was becoming less aggressive and more compliant as Greg continued to work his pitch.

"Right Terry, so this is what we'll do. I'll pay you five-hundred pounds for two weeks' work; that's two hundred and fifty now, in your hand and the same again in two weeks' time. I may have some other work for you which you will find equally as rewarding. If there are any problems or if the girl is hurt in any way, the deal is off, and you'd better be very careful because I *will* find you."

Greg was full of menace and in full flow. This was all about protecting Maureen and he was prepared to go to any lengths to ensure her safety. It was reactive behaviour. He was not playacting; he could feel genuine anger, but this was Greg, cool Greg; not the weak and feeble Gerald. His many experiences at the hands of psychiatrists and his study in mind control were beginning to pay dividends.

"I'm listening," said the man.

"Now I don't know what Chapman told you, but he's a conniving bastard; he'll probably have you shot after he's done with you and you won't get your money."

"Don't worry, I know all about Chapman; why should I trust you?" asked Terry.

"Because at this moment you don't have an option," said Greg. "What did he tell you to do?"

"He just said to put the frighteners on the girl," said Terry... no hard stuff unless I got into trouble."

"Ok, ok... we can use that. When's he due to call you?"

"Tonight, he said he would call around nine," replied Terry. Greg digested this information.

"Ok, just tell him that the girl's been at the flat all day and that she's had no visitors. Oh, you can mention a silver BMW, that's her father's car. He would have expected him to meet her at some time over the week-end. I need him thinking that everything's normal and boring. Convince him you're waiting for the right moment and you'll sort her out, that kind of thing. Clear?"

"Yeah... ok. So, when do I get my money then?"

"Now," Greg counted out the money he'd drawn from the cash machine.

"Think of it this way, you'll get paid by him as well as me and you get to do nothing; seems a good deal... but do not cross me; I promise, you'll regret it."

"Yeah, ok, no drama."

Terry was looking directly ahead out of the van window, making no eye-contact; he seemed to be weighing up the situation. Greg watched him like a hawk; he trusted the low-life about as far as he could throw him; his hand was still fiddling with the screwdriver in his pocket.

Terry seemed to relax and turned to Greg.

"Right, you better have my phone number. Have you got some paper?" said Greg.

"Here, you can use this," and Terry passed Greg a cigarette packet from the top of the dashboard.

"A pen?"

Terry handed Greg a well-used ballpoint from his top pocket; Greg wrote down his number on the back of the pack and handed it back to Terry.

"You better let me have yours in case I need to contact you… Don't forget, if you get any problems, call me."

Terry gave Greg his number and he loaded it into the contacts on his phone.

"Right this meeting is concluded, and you might as well take the rest of the day off."

Greg offered his hand which Terry shook.

"Nice doing business with you Mr...?"

"Just call me Greg," he said, and got out of the van.

He decided to leave the nail where it was for the inconvenience.

He walked back to the car where Maureen was anxiously waiting; the white van pulled away.

Maureen got out and went to Greg. "Are you ok?" she asked and hugged him.

"Fine, I don't think he'll be causing you any problems."

"Really…? What did you do?"

"Just made him an offer he couldn't refuse," he said in his best mafia accent.

"Thank you… I don't know how I'd have managed without you."

"Do you need a hand with anything? Might as well make use of me while I'm here."

"Wouldn't mind," she replied.

So, for the next hour Greg helped Maureen sort through more of her gear and load it into the two cars before they left for the journey back.

They had only gone about five minutes when Greg turned a corner to find Terry's van parked-up while the hapless driver stood kicking a flat tyre. Greg smiled as he passed the stricken vehicle unnoticed.

Back at Taskers End, Greg helped Maureen get her clothes and belongings out of the cars and up to the bedroom. As Greg locked the Audi, Maureen made a passing comment about the new car. "That looks nice," she said, although Greg had not really had a chance to appreciate it. It was certainly a lot better than the old bangers he used to drive as a student in Leeds.

For the remainder of the day the two wallowed in blissful domesticity and both were feeling very comfortable in each other's company. After lunch Greg took a couple of chairs into the back garden to make the most of the warm autumn sunshine. He looked at the magnificent house and the way the sunlight caught the windows it was as though Taskers End was smiling on them.

Sunday was a similar day and for the time being they put their troubles and investigations to one side and just enjoyed life. Greg decided to take the new Audi out for a drive and took Maureen to Bakewell where they spent time walking along the river path while swopping stories. There was a funfair and Greg took Maureen on the waltzers and the dodgems. Greg tried his hand at the rifle shoot and came away with a coconut which he decided he was going to split in half and hang it in the garden for the birds; it was another perfect day.

As they were walking back to the car Greg reflected briefly on his time at Trenton Court and realised this was how he imagined life should be; he had never been happier and just wanted the moment to last forever.

Monday morning and it was back to work for Maureen and for her, too, the weekend had been special. She was starting to feel more comfortable with Greg, but it was too early to start thinking of Taskers End as home yet. It was like she was on holiday. She felt more relaxed now Greg had sorted out the stalker threat and she'd really enjoyed the trip to Bakewell. The love-making had been passionate and almost risqué at times as she recalled the frolic on the back lawn on Saturday afternoon. It was just as well they weren't overlooked! She smiled at the memory as she made her way through the rush hour traffic.

Today would be different.

Greg was deciding what to wear for his meeting with the consultant psychologist and checked his growing wardrobe. With the items rescued from the scullery, he now had a more varied collection but realised that some of the clothes looked dated and he would take them to the charity shop. He decided against wearing his only suit that he had last worn for his university interview; he probably wouldn't get into it in any case and the musty smell hadn't entirely disappeared.

So, it was one of his new shirts, smart pair of slacks and the jacket he had worn on Saturday morning. He put his hands in the pocket and felt the screwdriver and remaining nail. He took them out and put them on the kitchen table. He would return them to the garage later on his way out.

Queenie had arrived for her cleaning shift and they had a coffee together before Greg left for his first appointment at the solicitors. He had a lot of questions for him.

Greg parked up in the multi-story which was almost full,

and he found himself on the ninth floor. The lift down smelt of urine and disinfectant and it was difficult to know which was winning the struggle.

He arrived at the office just before ten and was greeted by Maureen; the fragrance of her perfume making up for the obnoxiousness of the lift.

"Hi," she said, her face giving away her pleasure at seeing Greg. "Mr Cathcart will be with you in a couple of minutes," she added, trying to be professional; her smile revealed otherwise. "Have a seat. Can I get you a coffee?"

"Yes please, white no sugar," replied Greg and winked.

Just then Cathcart came down the corridor and greeted Greg.

"Gerald dear boy... sorry, I should say Greg, shouldn't I? Still trying to get used to it. Come through, come through," and he led the way back down the corridor to his office. Luckily Maureen was making the coffee and hadn't heard the greeting. That might have been a problem.

"Have a seat dear boy, have a seat," and Cathcart sat behind his desk and looked at Greg like an approving school master with a favourite pupil.

"So, how are you settling in, dear boy, everything going well? The house in good order?" he quickly added, before allowing Greg to answer the first question.

"Yes, fine everything is fine."

"You have your new car, I understand, a good choice if I might say so. A bit sporty for me I'm afraid... definitely a young man's car."

Greg knew that Cathcart would have authorised the payment from the estate's account; Greg's own personal float would not have covered the purchase.

"Yes," it's very nice thank you."

Just then Maureen arrived with two bone china cups and a tray with a cafetière of hot coffee and a jug of milk.

"Thank you, Miss Brown. That will be all."

It felt strange to Greg hearing her being called 'Miss Brown'. Maureen smiled at him as she left the room. Cathcart was too busy pouring the coffee to notice.

Cathcart handed Greg a cup and looked at him with a grave expression.

"But you haven't come to discuss how you are settling in have you?"

"No," said Greg.

"You've been to the scullery and opened the trunk?"

"Yes," said Greg.

"Hmm, I thought so; I wondered how soon you'd be in touch, I *was* expecting this visit. What do you want to know?"

Greg picked up his cup and started drinking to give himself some thinking time.

"I have so many questions; about how my grandparents died and why the cause of their deaths was covered up. You know they were murdered, don't you?"

"Murdered...? That's a bit dramatic; let's just say I didn't think everything was fully explained," he said rather cryptically. "Like you, I did not have access to your grandparents' effects until well after the inquest by which time the verdict had already been reached."

"Why didn't you challenge it at the time?" asked Greg.

"As I said, it was too late. There was no evidence and no motive. I knew your grandparents and it just didn't seem right that they died in that way, that's all."

"Did you clear the house up and put the stuff in the trunk?" asked Greg.

"Yes, myself and Mr Davenport, he was the office manager here."

"Did you read any of the letters?"

"No, there were so many, there just wasn't time, but I did

wonder if there might be some information there."

"There was," replied Greg. "Why didn't the police check?"

"I have no idea, as far as they were concerned they just went with the fire officer's report. Probable cause of fire - lighted tobacco, from your grandfather's pipe. I did have some doubts; I knew that your grandmother didn't allow smoking in the house."

"Why didn't you say something?" asked Greg.

"It wouldn't have made any difference; they had it all tied up. Saved a great deal of money... a murder investigation would have cost a fortune... and as I said they were convinced it was an accident."

"I've read the Coroner's report and the fire officer's account and more questions should have been asked. Why was the fire contained in their bedroom, for instance? An old house like that should have burned to the ground."

"I can answer that. It was a piece of luck, that's all. The fire brigade was there very quickly. It was only by chance that an appliance was returning from a call out and was close by, otherwise, as you say, it would have been much worse. They broke in through the bedroom window where the fire was. They saw your grandparents on the bed and made the rescue but, I'm afraid, too late to save them… and there was a lot of damage; I had to deal with the repairs," said Cathcart gravely. "It was the smoke that killed them; they didn't burn or anything," he said, trying to ease any pain.

Greg put his hands in his head.

"If only I'd have been here… I would have made them listen."

"Dear boy, this is not your fault, you mustn't blame yourself. It was a difficult time for everyone, but nothing was going to bring them back... I just hoped that you would recover sufficiently to be released and pick up your rightful inheritance".

Greg thought about the next question.

"If you had suspected that foul play was a possibility, did you ever consider what the motive might be?" Greg had phrased the question carefully in a way that might open up the involvement of Chapman.

"That's the thing, dear boy, it didn't make any sense. They were such lovely people. I can't think of any reason why anyone would want to hurt them," replied the solicitor.

"I think it was about money" said Greg, and he described the letters and diary entries.

"Are you saying they were being pressured into selling Taskers End?"

"Yes, it seems so... There are letters that suggest that..." He paused for a moment and took another drink of coffee which was starting to go cold. "Does the name Dacombe Properties mean anything to you?"

"Dacombe, yes it's one of David Chapman's clients. He keeps his cards close to his chest with that one. Never discusses it."

"Did you know that Chapman's a director of Dacombe Properties?" Cathcart looked at Greg with an expression of surprise.

"Really? No, I didn't."

"It's on their letter heading," said Greg.

"I wouldn't know... but he should have declared that in a Partner's Meeting," said Cathcart.

"And did he?" countered Greg.

"I can't recall; I would need to check the minutes."

Greg wasn't sure whether Cathcart was being evasive or was genuinely ignorant; or perhaps he was just naive. Maybe he was under Chapman's control. All these thoughts were going around in his head. Greg felt short-changed; the meeting hadn't been as fruitful as he had hoped. He wasn't sure how much more information he could get from the solicitor. He decided not to mention the Clients' moneys at this stage; he wanted more proof.

"Ok, this is how I see it," said Greg, trying to summarise. "According to my grandmother's diary, my grandparents were being harassed by Peter Dacombe, he's the owner of Dacombe Properties, into selling Taskers End. He wanted to buy the property and build houses on the land. I have letters confirming that offers were made which were very persuasive... but not sufficient on their own to be considered as a threat or evidence of any wrong doing. However, the finger's definitely pointing at Dacombe. I don't know what, if any, involvement your partner has had in the matter."

He deliberately had not revealed the information he had gleaned from Maureen's laptop hacking enterprise. He paused.

"Just a thought, did Chapman ever ask you about selling Taskers End under the Power of Attorney after my grandparents were killed?"

This was a trick question, Greg already knew the answer.

Cathcart seemed uneasy, his body language was tense and on the defensive.

"I can't recall, but he might have done. It was a long time ago; but I would never have agreed to it. I knew what your grandparents had wanted and having visited you in hospital I thought you would be released sooner rather than later. You had made such good progress." He paused again. "Your grandparents were very proud of you, you know."

He looked down at his desk again. "My sole aim was to look after your interests as best as I could."

"Yes, and I must thank you for that. You *have* been very helpful. I couldn't have managed without you."

Greg paused again and finished his coffee.

"Just one thing, out of interest, how did my stuff get back from Leeds?"

"Your grandfather went up there one afternoon and collected your things. They were stored in the University somewhere. I met him at the house and helped him carry them down into the scullery."

Greg checked the time; he was due to meet Jane Melrose in a few minutes. Cathcart looked at Greg. "So dear boy, what are you going to do?"

"I don't know, but I do intend to find out what happened, whatever it takes. Someone killed my grandparents and I need justice, for them."

Greg went to stand up and Cathcart walked around his desk and shook his hand warmly. "So glad you are well, dear boy, and if there is any way I can help, any way, you must let me know."

"I will," replied Greg. "And thank you, thank you, for everything."

As they walked to his office door Cathcart asked, "How did it go with your Social Worker last week, she never said anything to me?"

"Fine, I think; she seemed happy enough. I've got to see her again on Wednesday."

"Good, very good, and you're seeing the psychiatrist this morning, am I right?"

"Yes, at eleven o'clock."

"Well I hope everything goes well. You deserve some happiness after all you have been through," said the solicitor.

Greg looked at Cathcart; he seemed to look older somehow; his hair, what was left of it, was so fine and white; he reminded him of a corpse.

Greg walked down the corridor and Maureen was waiting.

"Doctor Melrose is waiting for you in the conference room," she said in a voice which hinted at intrigue. "She's pretty," she added with a grin.

"Too old," said Greg. "Thanks, I'll catch up later. Do you want to do lunch?"

"Definitely, I want to know what went on with Cathcart, and who the mysterious woman is," she whispered, still smiling.

Greg would need to finalise his excuse. He had just told Maureen that he had arranged to meet someone after his chat with Cathcart but hadn't elaborated. He did have a more difficult problem, however. With Maureen working for Cathcart, she would have access to his files and Greg wondered how long he could keep his secret from her. He decided he would cross that bridge if it became necessary.

He walked into the conference room and the familiar face of Jane Melrose greeted him.

"Hello, Greg, how are you? Please have a seat."

Chapter Twelve

Greg, rather nervously, shook hands. He looked at Doctor Melrose, she was an attractive woman and recent motherhood hadn't diminished her presence. She was dressed in a dark two-piece suit, skirt, a fashionable length above the knee, and looked very smart, hair and make-up, just so. Gerald would have been devouring her with his eyes like some old letch, but Greg was much more professional, and the psychiatrist picked up on this straight away.

"You look... *well*," she said, emphasising the word to depersonalise the comment.

"Thank you," said Greg, "I feel well... Mr Cathcart tells me you've had a baby."

"Yes, a little girl."

"Congratulations," said Greg.

Greg sat opposite her at the small table; her laptop was already fired up and ready to go. Before they could get going there was a knock on the door and Maureen put her head around.

"Would you two like a coffee?"

"Not for me, thanks," said Greg.

"I'm fine," said Doctor Melrose and Maureen closed the door.

The psychiatrist started by outlining her role in the transition process.

"The purpose of these meetings is just to check on your progress and to help you work through any issues. I see it very much as part of a support mechanism."

She was keeping the discussion deliberately formal; this was no time for any familiarity.

"I will see you once a month to start with, or sooner if you feel you need it, and I'll keep a record of our discussions to track your progress. Is that all clear?"

She sounded officious.

"Yes, quite clear," said Greg.

Doctor Melrose quickly made an assessment based on her initial impression and noticed his confident demeanour. His body language was positive, and he talked with some assurance. She also noticed that his penetrating stare had gone; she'd always felt as though he was mentally undressing her but this time she felt more at ease in his presence. She was not however dropping her guard.

She took an A4 note pad from her briefcase.

"So, it's Greg now isn't it…? What made you change your name?"

The opening salvo; her pen poised for the answer. Greg was ready for this one.

"I felt I needed to move on and put Gerald behind me. That was a challenging time in my life, but I'm past that now. Changing my name was just part of that process."

The psychiatrist started writing furiously.

"And what has been the result... personally, I mean?"

"I'm not sure what you mean."

"Well has it helped you in making the adjustment to the outside world or have you started putting thoughts into compartments, some for Gerald, some for Greg?"

Greg knew where she was going with this; he had studied multi-personality and dissociative disorders whilst at Trenton. It was so good to talk to someone who was an intellectual equal.

"No, not at all," which was not completely true. "I just wanted to make a fresh start and changing my identity seemed the right thing to do. I discussed it with my solicitor and he thought it would be a good idea. There might be some people who would want revenge for what I did,"

This was his first real acknowledgement for his earlier

crime.

"And how do you feel about that?" she asked, not letting him off easily.

"I will deal with it, if necessary. I feel so much stronger in myself."

Doctor Melrose continued her note taking.

"How about socialising, shopping, the normal day to day things; how has that gone?"

"As I was telling Dorinda, it's been fine, no problems at all. I am a regular at the supermarket now," he joked.

The psychiatrist sort of smiled in acknowledgement; she was not about to engage in any flippancy.

"What about managing your house? You've moved back to..." she paused to look up the name, "Taskers End, I understand."

"Yes, it's not a problem at all. I have a housekeeper and my girlfriend's moved in; I couldn't be happier."

Greg had unwittingly opened floodgates.

"Girlfriend...? Girlfriend, you say. I didn't know you were in a relationship."

"Yes," said Greg, realising his error too late.

"So, how long have you been going out with her? Did you meet her while you were in Trenton?"

The questions were coming quickly.

Greg thought she might be thinking he had accessed some Internet Dating site while in hospital.

"No, I met her the first day I came home."

"And she's moved in already?" she said, in some disbelief.

"Yes," he said, without adding to the comment.

Greg could see the doctor writing feverously and there was a pause.

"Have you told her about your... history?"

"No... Not yet, but I will... when the time's right, we're still getting to know each other."

"How old is she?" asked Doctor Melrose.

Greg thought for a moment; he was concerned in case she thought he had groomed some adolescent for his carnal desires. Greg decided attack was the best form of defence.

"She's the same age as me. In fact, you've already met her."

"I have? who?

"Maureen."

"What... the receptionist?" she said in astonishment.

"Yes,"

More writing.

"I don't know what to say."

"You seem disapproving," said Greg.

"No.., No... Not at all." She quickly backtracked. "It's just a bit sudden, that's all."

"These things happen," said Greg.

"Yes... I suppose they do."

There was a pause while the doctor tried to evaluate this piece of information.

Greg sensed the time was right. He had a question.

"Can I ask you a question?"

She looked up from her notepad.

"Yes, of course."

"I assume these discussions are confidential?"

"Of course," she repeated.

Greg fired his own round. "What do you know about my grandparents' death?"

The doctor was a bit taken aback by this unexpected question.

"What do you mean?"

"Well you were around at Trenton when they told me about their deaths. You offered me counselling I remember. Why wasn't I told the truth?"

"What do you mean?"

"Well at the time I was told that they died in an accident, but nobody would tell me exactly what happened."

Doctor Melrose shuffled in her seat.

"We thought it best; you were still quite... fragile," she said, and outlined the rationale in more technical terms.

Greg felt frustrated at the lack of concern from the psychiatrist and fired back.

"Well I've been doing some investigation and I'm pretty sure they were murdered."

"Murdered?" said the psychiatrist, clearly shocked by the word.

Greg proceeded to outline his theory based on his investigations so far and the evidence he had discovered.

"What do the police say?"

"I can't tell them yet. I need more evidence. What I have wouldn't stand up in court, but I am determined to get justice for them."

Greg was quite forceful in his words which concerned the doctor and she was now well down her second page of notes.

"Well you must keep me updated with your investigations when we meet next time."

She checked her watch.

"Well I think that will do for today... unless you have anything else you want to share."

"No, thank you for listening; I'll let you know how I get on. It's good to be able to talk about it with someone who understands," replied Greg, which sounded more sycophantic than he had intended. Nor was it quite true; he had found the meeting quite frustrating, she obviously didn't believe the story and may even have been humouring him, which he found insulting.

They made their farewells with Doctor Melrose maintaining

her aloofness. Greg left the room and went to seek out Maureen.

The psychiatrist started writing her report.

Greg had a problem. Jane Melrose was a respected psychiatrist with many years' experience dealing with disturbed people which meant that every nuance, every word would be dissected for hidden or alternative meanings. This led to the most innocent of comments being construed so closely that interpretations far removed from intentions could be deduced. This was such a case.

Date: *1ˢᵗ October 2007*

Patient: *Gerald Perry aka Greg Jensen*

Purpose of report: *First post-release interview*

Conducted by: *Dr Jane Melrose MD, FRCPsych*

Interviewed at the offices of Messrs Cathcart Rivers, Solicitors. I found Greg Jensen, as he now prefers to be known, to be in good physical health. He showed a degree of confidence not present in earlier interviews and he articulated effectively. His body language was assured and there was a forcefulness which I have not noticed before. He has changed his name, he says to move on, but there are signs of dissociate behaviour. His coping strategy is to compartmentalise his 'old self' to history and he may well have difficulty in coming to terms with his past; he mentioned concern at possible retribution for his earlier deeds as a reason for changing his identity.

He presently seems preoccupied by investigating his grandparents' death to a degree that there is a suggestion of delusional behaviour bordering on paranoia possibly triggered by a guilt complex. He cannot come to terms with the fact that their demise was an accident, believing strongly that they were murdered. By his own admission, there is no corroborative evidence to support these suppositions. He has based his conspiracy theory on old papers found at his grandparents' house where he now lives. He expressed his determination to continue this fruitless investigation, to what end I am not sure.

More concerning is the news that he has not only started a relationship but that she has moved into his house with him. I know this man from previous meetings to be extremely manipulative and it could well be that this girl has been coerced into this relationship and could well be in danger.

I am flagging up an 'amber' alert on this patient and will see him again in a month's time to assess possible changes in his behavioural pattern. Meanwhile I will be discussing my concerns with his case worker.

Signed, Dr J D Melrose MD, FRCPsych.

Cc Dorinda Walcott, South Yorks Social Services

Greg would never see this report or learn the potential implications for him of its content.

While the doctor was writing up her report, Greg met Maureen in reception and took her to their usual haunt for lunch. She was keen to learn details of the two meetings.

Greg collected their baked potatoes and coffees; Maureen found a seat.

"Come on then, what did Cathcart say?" she asked excitedly, as Greg sat down with their meals.

"Frankly not as much as I'd hoped. He says he had suspicions about the cause of the fire at the time; he knew about my grandmother's rules about smoking in the house, but says the police ignored him. I think they just didn't want the expense of a murder investigation and took the easy option," he said.

"Did you tell him about the letters?"

"Yes, but he says he didn't read them at the time. He and Sam Davenport tidied the house and put all the correspondence in the trunk. That was about it."

"What about David, did he say anything about him?" she asked.

"No, not really, he was not evasive exactly, but not as forthcoming as I was expecting. He said that he didn't know that Chapman was a director of Dacombe Properties but knew that they were clients of his. I didn't say anything about the Client account money. I need to get more information. I don't think Cathcart is involved, but there could be implications for the practice. As senior partner he would have been expected to have had some control over the administration; and the partnership, I'm sure, would have some liability, not just Chapman, but I would have to check. I think the main priority now is trying to find Sam Davenport; he could hold the key."

"Oh, I nearly forgot," Maureen went to her handbag and pulled out a piece of paper. "His address, I was right, it is Fullwood."

Greg took the piece of paper and opened it. "That's great, I'll pay him a visit on the way back."

"And what about the lovely Doctor Melrose," she teased.

"Oh that, she's a forensic pathologist and I contacted her to see if there was any freelance work going. I need to get some work to pay the bills; can't stay at home all the time," he said, laughing nervously. He hoped his expression would not give away his untruth; he hated having to lie to her.

"And?" she said.

"And what?" he replied.

"Well, was there any work?"

"Oh, no... no, unfortunately, but she said she'd be in touch if anything comes up."

Greg was anxious to change the subject.

"So how has your morning been?".

"Apart from having to make coffees for visitors, you mean?" she said with a smile.

The persiflage between them was easy and relaxed as with two people who knew each other intimately.

There was a pause as she finished her jacket potato and tuna melt.

"Do you want me to do any more private investigation work? Only Joan's about and it won't be so easy. She can be very nosy."

"Let me see how I get on with Sam Davenport. I may have to follow things up depending on what he says, if I can find him that is."

"Well, Joan said that the address was the only one we have on file, so if he's not there we'll be stuck."

Greg loved the way she used the term 'we'; it seemed she was as committed as he was in finding out the truth.

"Have you had any more messages from Chapman?"

"No, nothing, I'm glad to say. I need him out of my life forever. I'm dreading his return next week."

Greg had finished his lunch and looked at her.

"Well, if the worst comes to the worst, you'll have to give your notice. I can look after you until you find somewhere else."

"But why should I? I've put in a lot of hours for that firm and I do enjoy the work."

"I know, but there's a bigger problem. He'll have expected the van man to have caused you grief in some way and if it hasn't succeeded he could try something else and that is a worry."

Maureen looked down at the remnants of her jacket potato and moved around the plate with her fork.

"What are we going to do, Greg? I can't let him rule my life anymore."

"He won't, I promise you. He won't," said Greg.

The mood had grown sombre and Greg wanted to change the subject.

"What do you fancy for dinner? I'll cook something nice for you," he asked.

"I don't mind," she said, showing an uncharacteristic lack of interest.

"It'll be a surprise then, but not chicken, eh?" and she smiled at him and leant over and kissed him.

"Thank you, I'm sure it will be wonderful."

She looked at her watch.

"I better get going, I don't want to be late. Cathcart's got back-to-back meetings this afternoon."

The couple got up and headed out the door. Greg walked Maureen back to the office and they kissed before going their separate ways.

Greg made his way to the multi-story car park and found his car. He checked the piece of paper. "Time to check the Sat-Nav works," he said to himself.

He got in and switched on the car's ignition and punched in the postcode from the address. 13 Ramscroft Road, Fullwood, showed on the screen. Greg pressed enter. "Proceed to the highlighted route," said a computer-generated voice; Greg complied.

Greg followed the Sat-Nav's instructions and eventually he was instructed to turn into a large estate of private houses. Neatly-cut lawns, perfect topiary, immaculate trees greeted him, nothing appeared out of place; a community that cared, it said.

The roads were a maze but the Sat Nav's authoritative commentator was not to be beaten and after several turns the Audi entered Ramscroft Road. "Your destination is straight ahead," said the automated voice.

The street had the same ambience as the rest of the estate, but the houses were all bungalows. There were a couple of elderly people tending to their gardens, otherwise it was as quiet as the grave. Greg remembered that the schools were still in session which could account for the apparent absence of life although it was difficult to imagine a less child-friendly environment. This was a street where people moved to... to die.

Greg got out of the car and looked at the three-bedroomed detached bungalow. The lawn had recently been cut, possibly with a pair of scissors he mused, and the paintwork gleamed in the early afternoon sunshine. A trellis of rambling roses traced their way up both sides of the front door. He rang the doorbell.

He could hear the distant sound of a radio from within, not loud enough of course to disturb the solemnity. He heard a security chain being affixed and the door opened the three inches allowed by the chain. A woman's quarter face appeared, squashed against the door frame to view the visitor.

"Can I help you?" she asked. "You're not selling anything are you?"

"No, nothing like that, I'm looking for Sam Davenport. I think he may be able to help me."

"I don't think so," she said.

"But it's very important, I'm trying to find some information about my grandparents, they lived at Taskers End."

There was a long pause and then the door closed before reopening minus the chain.

"You'd better come in," she said.

There was a hallway which stretched the length of the building and Greg could see the garden through the door at the end. It was slightly open. Greg followed the woman through a door to the right. Obviously, the living room, there was a sofa and two armchairs facing an old-style TV. On the right was a large bookcase with various nick-knacks and ornaments, family photos from different eras, black and white to colour; a large vase of artificial flowers stood next to the fireplace. A gas simulated coal fire and surround completed the scene.

"Have a seat Mr...?"

"Jensen, Greg Jensen, you must be Mrs Davenport."

"Dora, you can call me Dora," she said. "How can I help you?"

He looked at the woman, smartly dressed as if going shopping, grey hair, her face giving away her age. Her voice was typically middle England, not a trace of a local dialect.

"I've just returned to Sheffield and moved back to Taskers End and I was hoping Mr Davenport could help me tie-up some loose ends regarding the death of my grandparents."

"I didn't know the Sinclairs had a second grandson. Sam only talked about, now what was his name...? It'll come back to me."

"Gerald?" offered Greg.

"Yes, that's right Gerald, he murdered someone apparently; got sent to the loony bin, very sad. They never got over it you know, so Sam said. Blamed themselves, but I said to him, you can't hold yourself responsible for other people's actions."

She spoke very quickly as if she needed to talk to someone; the words falling out like parachutists from a plane. She was clearly a lonely woman and obviously valued the company; a welcome interruption to a drab life.

"That was me," said Greg, looking down at his feet and the light brown carpet.

It seemed to stop her in mid flow and there was an embarrassing silence as she took in this information before Greg spoke again; he could see concern appearing on her face.

"It's ok. I'm better now. It was a long time ago," he said, trying to allay any fears.

"Would you like a cup of tea, Mr Jensen?" she asked.

"Greg, please call me Greg," he said. "Yes please, that would be very kind."

The woman got up from her chair and disappeared into

another room. Greg looked around at the bookshelf and the pictures; so many memories. A few minutes later Dora returned with a tray, teapot, two cups and saucers, milk, sugar and a plate of biscuits. She put the tray down on a small coffee table in front of the sofa.

"Do you take sugar, Greg?"

"Just milk please," and she poured the tea and handed him a cup.

"Thank you, and I'm sorry to just turn up out of the blue like this, but I had no telephone number."

Greg could see that the woman was still anxious, so he knew he had to win her trust.

"As you rightly said, I've had many difficulties to overcome, but I am glad to say those are all behind me and I am trying to make a new start. Let me give you a bit of background and maybe you'll get a clearer idea of why I am here."

He realised there had been no mention yet of Mr Davenport, but it was clear that Dora had some familiarity with the situation; it was obvious as a couple they shared things.

"I moved back to Taskers End over a week ago and I've been going through some old letters and diaries that I think cast some doubt on how my grandparents died."

Dora was sitting upright listening intently to his recount.

"I understand your husband helped Mr Cathcart tidy up my grandparents' affairs following their deaths."

"Yes, he did. Sam often talked about it. I don't think Mr Cathcart was convinced the fire was started the way they said either, but no-one seemed to take him seriously and Sam wouldn't say anything, especially after Chapman threatened him."

"What do you mean 'threatened', what happened?" asked Greg, intrigued by this last comment.

"Sam told me that Mr Cathcart had told the police that he

had doubts about the cause of the fire, but they hadn't taken much notice of him. Sam didn't say why, but Chapman warned my husband not to get involved, if he knew what was good for him."

"Did he make any specific threats?" asked Greg.

"No, but Sam knew his reputation and he was in no doubt about the message. Chapman is a dangerous and very clever man. I can never forgive him for what he has done to this family."

"What do you mean?" asked Greg.

"You want to see my husband? Come with me". Dora got up and beckoned Greg to follow her out of the room through the kitchen and into the back garden. There was a small patio and a large lawn, so flat and well maintained a green-keeper would have been proud. Flower beds surrounded the grass. At the bottom of the garden there was a shed and next to that, in the corner, a small gazebo with a seat and Greg could see the figure of a man, bent at the waist with his head slumped onto his chest. A walking stick was resting against the side of the seat.

Greg followed Dora across the lawn and reached the man who appeared to be asleep or dead, it was difficult to tell. There was saliva dribbling from the corner of his mouth which was wetting his shirt.

"Sam always likes a nap in the afternoons. When it's sunny he likes to sit in the garden."

"Sam... Sam, wake up there's somebody here to see you," and the head slowly looked up, the eyes opened and started to focus.

"He's never been the same since the strokes," she said, as the man tried to regain consciousness.

"He'd only left Cathcart Rivers a couple of weeks when he had his first; crippled him down the left side. These last few months have been hell," she said, with venom in her voice.

"I'm so sorry," said Greg, looking at the pathetic figure.

"It's all Chapman's fault. He forced him out of his job and threatened to stop his pension if he said anything about what was going on... but Sam told me. There's plenty I could tell you about that man."

"I hope you will," said Greg, "I hope you will."

Dora looked at her husband who was now almost back from his slumbers.

"Sam, dear, this is the Sinclairs' grandson, you remember... Taskers End?"

The man tuned his eyes and stared at Greg, a ghostly stare, a manikin's stare, as if there was no life behind the gaze. He tried to speak but the sound was incoherent. Then the chilling words, "Taskers End," he said, very slowly and deliberately in a guttural voice as if chewing each vowel.

"Fire... fire... dead... they're all dead," he said, and appeared to shut down again. His head slumped down to his chest and he seemed to go back to sleep.

"He used to be full of life you know," she said, looking with pitiful eyes at the shell of a man who used to be her husband. "Hard to believe that now and it's all Chapman's fault. He took my Sam away from me."

There was a pause.

"I'll leave him for now, he'll be alright. He usually sleeps till four. He likes his routine; it upsets him when it's disturbed. Let's go back into the house. I may have something that will interest you."

Back in the living room, Dora went to one of the drawers in the bottom of the bookcase and took out what looked like two old cashbooks. She handed them to Greg.

"What do you know about my husband's work?" she asked.

"Only that Sam was the office administrator."

"Hmm, he was a lot more than that; he was the practice bookkeeper. He would also..." She paused searching for the right word. "Facilitate things."

"What do you mean 'facilitate'?" asked Greg.

"Well, he was a problem solver, he was good at making things disappear, difficulties, you know."

"Such as?" asked Greg.

"Well, Sam found out that Chapman was using Clients' money for property deals?"

Greg decided not to reveal what he knew preferring to hear what she had to say.

"Go on," he said.

She opened one of the books and it showed itemised entries of transactions in and out of the practice account.

"The accounts had been computerised for some time, but Sam was a belt and braces man and kept clerical records, in case the computer broke down he used to say... never trusted them, you know."

"So, these are duplicate copies of all the transactions that went through Cathcart Rivers' books?" observed Greg, flicking through one of the registers.

"Since January 2000, that's when they were fully computerised, until he left," she replied. "Before that, the records will be in the office vaults somewhere."

Greg thought about this; he could imagine an old firm being slow to make use of computer technology.

"You will see that there are many entries which he has indicated are for Chapman's personal use."

Greg quickly scanned through and chose a page at random and could see some large transactions red circled.

"You mean these with the red rings round them?" he asked.

"Yes," she replied.

"Why didn't he go to the police or just tell Cathcart?"

Dora looked down at the floor.

"He did a silly thing. Very early on when the first payment went through, Chapman told Sam that it was a special payment and when it was repaid Sam would get a bonus for all his hard work and for his discretion. He was paid a thousand pounds. The boys had just started University and money was tight and so he took it, then each time there was a 'special' transaction, he would get a bonus, mostly the same amount, but there was one for three thousand when Chapman made a real killing... I didn't know what he was doing until one day it all came out. I'd noticed he wasn't eating or sleeping so I asked him what was wrong. He told me everything, eventually. He was so worried about what was going on; he thought he would go to prison. I told him he must tell Chapman he wasn't going to cover up his payments any longer and he told Chapman the next day. They had a row and Chapman told him to leave. He agreed to a pension only if Sam kept his mouth shut, and that's what he did. Of course, when he had the stroke that put an end to any threat. He would never have been fit enough to give any evidence."

Greg tried to take it all in.

"Can I borrow these; I need to look at them in more detail, if that's ok?"

"If it will help get justice against that man, of course."

"You don't know anything about a company called Dacombe Properties, do you?" he asked, still flicking through the cashbooks.

She thought for a moment. "I'm sure it's mentioned in there somewhere... I'm sure Chapman was involved."

"Chapman's a director, and from what I can gather, he and Dacombe have been financing property deals together. I think it was Peter Dacombe, he's the owner, that had some involvement in my grandparents' death, but I can't prove it."

"Why don't you go to the police?" asked Dora.

"I haven't got enough evidence, it's all circumstantial," replied Greg. "But I'm determined to get justice for my grandparents."

"Well, if there's anything we can do you just have to say," replied Dora.

"Thank you so much; it means a lot. I can't imagine what you must've been going through… Look, this is my number. Phone me if you think of anything else that might help."

With that, he stood up and went to the front door. Dora held his hand when Greg offered it to say goodbye.

"Now you be careful, young Greg. That Chapman's a dangerous man and he has some nasty friends, that's what Sam always said."

"I will, and I will let you know how I get on," he replied.

"You must call again," said Dora as she opened the door.

"I will, and thank you for these," he said nodding to the ledgers he was holding. She gave him a warm smile.

She stayed at the front door and Greg waved as he got into the Audi.

He started the engine and headed out of the estate. He looked at the two cashbooks on the passenger seat; he had a lot of work ahead.

Chapter Thirteen

Greg called in at the supermarket; it was just turned three-thirty and was full of mothers with children recently released from school. He bought his ingredients he would need for tonight's meal, some steak, fresh cream, mushrooms and onions and some peppercorns. He would do peppered steak with French fries, he decided. Maureen needed a lift.

On his way back to the house, he was pondering his next move. He would need to go through the cash books and see if they gave him any more clues. He considered progress. At the moment, he probably had enough on Chapman to prove his use of Clients' money which would end his career as a solicitor, but it was not enough to link him with his grandparents' death. That was down to Dacombe, and his investigations would need to move in that direction.

When he got back to Taskers End he made a call.

"Terry? Greg here,"

"Ok, and you? What's the news? I see... and he bought that...? Good. Ok, thanks for that... I'll ring you later in the week; I may have some more work you can help me with. Yeah... and ring me if he contacts you again."

Greg rang off and considered the conversation. According to Terry he told Chapman that he had been following Maureen in a way that she was aware she was being watched and it was definitely unsettling her. This psychological approach seemed to appeal to Chapman and he appeared happy with that. Terry wasn't expecting another call from him in the short term.

Just after five and the sound of Maureen's Mini entering the drive had Greg with the meal cooking in the oven and a bottle of red wine waiting. He had put an Alison Moyet CD on the hi-fi; he knew Maureen was fond of her voice. He felt excited as he heard the key turn in the lock it was so good that she felt at home now. She appeared in the hallway with a bag of shopping and Greg went to greet her.

"Hi, how did you get on this afternoon?" she asked as she took her jacket off and hung it in the hallway.

"Very interesting, I've got loads to tell you."

As they walked from the hallway she handed him a carrier bag.

"I've bought some fruit; I thought we could do with some vitamin C."

He took the bag and went into the kitchen. Maureen followed and joined him at the table.

"Wow, something smells good... Do you know, no-one's cooked for me since my mother; it's quite a luxury."

"My pleasure, I enjoy looking after you," he said, handing her a glass of red.

Maureen took a sip of her wine before going upstairs to change leaving Greg to finish cooking the fries and mushrooms. By the time she returned the meal was ready to dish up.

In an atmosphere of complete domesticity, Greg related his meeting with the Davenports and she was shocked when Greg described Sam's condition.

"I can't believe he'll survive much longer and his poor wife having to look after him; it puts everything into perspective."

"Hmm, that's so sad... He was such an important part of the office; we were all shocked when he left. I wish I'd known the truth."

"I'll show you the cashbooks after dinner; I need to go through them in detail to see if there's anything else of interest."

"I can help you with that, if you like. I may be able to give you more information from working there."

After dinner Greg went into the study to have a closer look at the cashbooks, he also wanted to have another look at the Fire Officer's report; something was nagging at him.

Maureen decided to leave him to it and went into the lounge to watch TV.

Greg spent an hour going through the cashbooks before turning his attention to the Fire Officer's Report. It was a relatively brief document, describing the scene as presented to the first arrival, the decision to break in and eventual extinguishing of the fire, time taken, and number of appliances.

The investigation was not conclusive, using the word 'probable' when referring to the cause of the fire. There was no evidence of any accelerants that one might have expected in fires started deliberately. Cause of fire was typical of that caused by localised source such as a cigarette, or in this case, supposedly, grandfather's pipe.

But that was the problem, where was the pipe? Most pipes are briars, extremely hard-wood, or meerschaum, a clay material, both of which would have survived the fire. He was sure his grandfather used to use a briar, but there was no mention of it in the report.

Later, Maureen came to join him to see how he was getting on and Greg shared his thoughts with her. He went through the information in the ledgers. Greg had managed to tie up entries from Sam's records to those kept by Chapman on his laptop which corroborated everything that they had found.

"We can use this to get Cathcart to open up an internal investigation at the very least. There's enough information here to get Chapman struck off, but I don't want to show our hand yet. I'm sure there's more to unravel."

Maureen flicked through the pages.

Greg looked up at her, "I don't know how much further I can go with this now. Everything hinges on Dacombe, but I've had an idea… I'm going to arrange to see him."

He outlined his plan.

"What will you do then?" she asked.

"I don't know yet, I just want to meet him and see where it goes."

The following day Greg was up early. After Maureen had left for work he was on his computer and opened his internet browser. In the search line he added Dacombe Properties. The search engine took him to the main website and Greg read with interest.

Apart from 'The Pines', which had its own website – there was a link from the Dacombe Properties page, there were details of the various enterprises. It was clear that the company owned a number of properties; some that had been refurbished and subsequently let; others were being modernised for on-sale. The company was not directly involved with the building or construction work; there was another company called SYR Construction and again a link went to a separate website where there were details of ongoing developments. Overall it was a substantial enterprise.

On 'The Pines' website there were pictures of the house and the accommodation for the residents. The rooms appeared to be of a standard afforded to a luxury hotel with en-suite facilities, all geared up to cater for the elderly with a lot of money. There was a very pleasant-looking resident's lounge with French windows which opened up to a patio overlooking several substantial pine trees. There was even a picture of a grey squirrel which also appeared on the web page, obviously a logo. A doctor was on twenty-four-hour call and there was a resident nurse as well as catering staff and carers. There were no details of prices. Greg found the telephone number under the 'Contact us' page. He made the call.

A very pleasant lady answered the phone and was keen to respond to his request.

"Let me check his diary," said the receptionist. "Yes, Mr

Jensen, Mr Dacombe will be free this afternoon, shall we say three o'clock if that's convenient...? Good, see you then." Greg rang off and smiled to himself; it's starting.

Before then, he had a task which would mean another phone call; the City Library.

He explained he wanted to book a microfiche viewer to research a back issue of the Sheffield Evening News. The librarian was extremely helpful and efficient; one could be made available for him at eleven o'clock. He would need to go to the Local Studies Library section, upstairs in the main library building. Greg made a note.

By ten twenty-five Greg was heading into town and parked on a meter not far from the library; he had an hour which he thought would be sufficient. He took his notebook with him and after a short walk went inside.

It was very busy for a mid-morning and the coffee bar and Internet cafe were doing a steady trade. He made his way upstairs as he had been instructed and waited at the enquiries desk. An assistant, a woman probably in her late-twenties but looking much older, took his details and then escorted him to the microfiche machine. As he followed the assistant he looked at her with her long shapeless skirt, spectacles and sensible jumper and wondered if librarians were cloned somewhere.

"How far back would you like to go? We have records on the Rotherham Independent going back to 1819 and the Sheffield papers to 1855," said the woman.

This was really impressive, and she seemed a little disappointed when Greg explained he only needed to go back just over two years.

"The more recent editions will be on-line quite soon," she said, as she gave Greg a container labelled, 'Sheffield Evening News 2005, July – December'.

Greg thanked her and loaded the viewer. It was an old machine and judging by its condition, frequently in use. He flicked through until he came to the edition dated 18th July and, as he expected, there was a large banner headline that read *'Couple found dead in Rivelin Valley blaze'*.

He read the short leading article underneath a picture of the house.

'Two fire appliances last night attended a house fire at Taskers End, Rivelin Valley. An elderly couple were found dead at the scene. Police spokesman DS James Gilbraith told our reporter that the fire appears to have been contained to the bedroom area and that two bodies were recovered. DS Gilbraith said it was too early to confirm the cause of the fire but at this stage there was no evidence to suggest it was foul play, but investigations were continuing. Full story page 6.'

Greg turned to page six and there was a longer piece describing the house and the owners Mr and Mrs Sinclair. There was some background on Mr Sinclair's business interests – *former Managing Director of Sinclair Precision Tooling Ltd*, some comments from friends who Greg had never heard of, and then something that made Greg's blood run cold... *'Peter Dacombe owner of the nearby Pines Residential Home, said they were lovely people and would be sadly missed'.*

Greg could feel the swell of emotion, he wanted to lash out; Gerald had suddenly appeared from nowhere, but Greg fought to retain control from the burning rage he felt inside and after a few breathing exercises Gerald went back over the wall to his slumbers. It was only momentary, but for a second Greg felt he had a sudden urge to pick up the microfiche viewer and throw it over the balcony without regard for anyone walking beneath. The fury was like a tornado that springs to life and dies down again in the blink of an eye.

Greg was sweating. He had not realised how quickly he

had become affected by this man who he was due to meet this afternoon. He had to get his act together or it would put his plan in jeopardy.

"Are you alright?" came a voice from behind him.

It was the librarian who had noticed Greg's agitated state from the admin desk.

"Yes, I'm fine, thank you," said Greg, having quickly composed himself.

He flicked forward a couple of days and there was another lengthy piece profiling his grandparents; 'pillars of society, lovely people, and a report saying that police were satisfied that following an investigation the fire had not been started deliberately and appeared to be a tragic accident. There was one other piece that he was keen to view, and he flicked through the records until he reached Tuesday September 20th, the day after the inquest.

Again, there was a lengthy article more or less covering the coroner's report which Greg of course already had read. It talked about the possible cause, again quoting the fire officer who put forward the theory of it being 'most likely' his grandfather's smoking.

There was nothing new, but the feeling of frustration was still strong, and he texted Maureen to see if she could join him for lunch; he needed her company.

Maureen was pleased to get the text; she wasn't expecting it and quickly agreed to meet up at the usual cafe. Over the now familiar baked potatoes, Greg told her of his morning at the Library and article with the words from Dacombe.

"How dare he!" he said, raising his voice and causing other diners to look round.

He quickly calmed, but Maureen could fully understand his annoyance and she shared his frustration.

"Did you manage to get an appointment with him today?"

"Yes… three o'clock."

"How do you feel about the meeting?" she asked, seeing his agitation.

"Good question; I'm not sure if I'm honest and I probably won't know until I meet him."

"Well, if you want some advice, you must try to stay calm despite how you feel. Remember there's no rush."

Greg accepted Maureen's council and gradually calmed down.

"Yes, you're right, it's just so... difficult... you know, not knowing what really happened, and the thought that Dacombe could well be responsible. I hate the man for causing my grandparents so much pain and I haven't even met him."

She offered the voice of reason once more. There is no doubt they made a great team.

They finished their meal and they walked back to Maureen's office in relative silence, Greg clearly still troubled by his impending meeting. As they said their goodbyes, she looked at him and could see the concern in his eyes.

"I know, why don't I cook tonight?" Maureen said, trying to lighten his mood. "I'll pick up some provisions on the way home… I'll make it special," she added with a wink.

He was immediately shaken from his thoughts. "Mmm… yeah, that sounds great… Look forward to it, and I'll give you a full report on my meeting with Dacombe."

"Good luck," she said as they said their farewells and he headed off to the multi-story to pick up his car; he'd had to move it from the meter having exhausted his hour.

Greg went back to the house to prepare for his meeting and finalise his story.

At ten-to-three he got into the Audi and headed up the road and within a couple of minutes he was pulling into the drive of The Pines Residential Home for the Elderly. He could have walked of course but he had no intention of giving away any indication of his real identity; it was too early.

He looked up at the impressive building. Like Taskers End it was on three floors but it was much larger, stretching back probably double the size. Greg felt a touch nervous as he opened the door.

The entrance hall was clean and welcoming and there was a reception desk immediately to the left. It looked like a small hotel, like the ones prevalent in the Lake District he thought, but as he had only been there once as a boy, his memory may have been exaggerating. There was no-one on duty and he complied with the instruction that said, 'ring the bell for attention'. He dropped his palm on the old-fashioned brass bell on the desk and a loud 'clang' echoed round the room. Loud enough to wake the dead, he thought. Greg winced at the noise.

Curiosity had clearly got the better of an elderly woman who came out of the room immediately in front of him to have look; then went back inside, duly satisfied; she would pass the news around to her fellow residents.

A smart looking woman appeared from what looked like an office behind the desk. "Can I help you please?"

"Yes, my name's Jensen, Greg Jensen, I rang this morning... to see Mr Dacombe."

"Of course, take a seat; I'll let him know you're here."

There were two wooden chairs that appeared to have come from a dining room placed against the left-hand wall just after the reception desk; there was a small coffee table in front with some travel magazines advertising the Peak District on it.

Greg looked around. Across the entrance area in front of him were two rooms, to the right the door was labelled 'Manager', the other said 'Private', but judging by the sounds coming from within, probably the admin area. A corridor disappeared to the left. The decor was neutral, mostly magnolia but clean and recently refurbished according to Greg's keen eye for detail. There were slight traces of paint on the windows that had not been properly masked or cleaned. Botched job, thought Greg.

He thought about opening one of the magazines, when the manager's door opened, and he came face to face with his nemesis for the first time.

Greg was not sure what to expect, something like an arch-typical East End enforcer had come to mind... but evil doesn't do clichés. The man walking towards him was probably in his fifties, hair fashionably short and well-groomed, grey but in a distinguished way. His teeth were white and gleamed almost as if starbursts were emanating from them. Greg had to control a nervous fit of the giggles at the thought. He was wearing a smart, expensive two-piece suit with a blue striped shirt and a pink tie with matching pocket handkerchief. He resembled an American game show host, the smarmy sort!

"Mr Jensen," he gushed. "How lovely to meet you," his arm extended almost at ninety degrees in greeting. Greg inwardly gritted his teeth and shook the offered hand.

"Come in, come in; make yourself comfortable. Can I get you a drink, tea, coffee, something stronger?" he said, as he walked purposefully back to the manager's room.

"Coffee would be fine, thank you," Greg replied.

"Melissa, can you get two coffees please?" he said to the receptionist.

They entered his office and the air was one of opulence. The large walnut desk, mahogany veneer around the walls, leather chairs two in front and the obligatory slightly larger one behind. There was a seventeenth century, John Speede map of South Yorkshire on the wall immediately behind him in what looked like an original frame. A large window overlooked the manicured lawns.

"Take a seat, Mr Jensen, take a seat," and Greg complied.

Dacombe went around the other side of the table and took command.

"So, I understand you're looking to place a family member with us, is that right?"

"Yes, my grandmother. She lives on her own and she's finding it difficult to manage since my grandfather died. The house is far too big for her."

"Sorry to hear that," he said, without much conviction. "A large house, you say… local?"

"Yes, Loxley" replied Greg. "Eight bedrooms would you believe? I said they should have downsized years ago, but you know how stubborn these old people can be," he said, letting the words hang for a moment.

"Yes, indeed, yes indeed, very common," said smarmy. "So how can we help?"

"Well, I'm looking for a reputable nursing home, somewhere where she can see out the rest of her days in comfort," said Greg. "I've been telling her for ages, and... well, she's not keen on moving, but she knows she can't stay there forever. I keep telling her it will be a weight off her mind, but she keeps digging her heels in… You know what they're like… I thought if I could show her some pictures of how nice nursing homes are these days it will help her change her mind. I mean the cost of upkeep of the place is enormous. I told her she should sell it and have some capital to enjoy herself while she still can." Greg spoke quickly, partly from nerves, but it had the right impact.

"I see, I see," said Dacombe, becoming quite animated at the possibilities; the prospect of potential business was like a drug.

There was a knock on the door and Melissa brought in the coffees on a tray and left them on the table.

"Milk? Sugar?" asked Dacombe.

"Just milk," said Greg, and Dacombe poured milk into one of the cups and took a container of sweeteners from the desk drawer and dropped two into the other cup before topping it up with milk.

"How much is the house worth...? Just out of interest," Dacombe asked.

Greg accepted the drink from him and took a sip, deliberately slowing down the conversation.

"Hmm, I can't be precise, but I've spoken to a couple of estate agents recently, just to get an idea, like, and if we were to put it on the market today, probably one-point-three, may be even one-point-four, something like that."

The deliberate phraseology was like a magnet as Greg talked in terms of millions; it had certainly got his attention.

"It sounds like an excellent house," said Dacombe.

"It is... and there's a lot of land which would be worth a fair bit with planning permission," he said. Dacombe was practically drooling.

"Still, that's further down the line; I need to sort out my grandmother first."

"Of course, of course," said Dacombe. "Well, I can tell you a bit about The Pines and then I'll give you a guided tour and you can ask me any questions you like. I would want your grandmother to be very happy here."

"Thank you," replied Greg and as they drank their coffee, Dacombe gave him a brief history. The property was a similar age as Taskers End and, as Greg had concluded, there had been some local rivalry at the time. Dacombe had bought the property about ten years ago. It had been a hotel in the eighties and he had it converted to a nursing home. He believed there was more money in care homes and with the inevitability of death, a reasonable turnover of clients, as he preferred to call the residents. Greg smiled at the turn of phrase.

"We are actually full at the moment and, with a reputation like ours, we have quite a long waiting list but there could be ways of expediting things if necessary," he said, with what appeared to be a wink.

"That's very helpful," said Greg.

They had finished their drinks and Dacombe got up and led Greg back into the reception area towards the corridor. He pointed to the door next to his office.

"This is the admin office. I have three staff in there looking after the accounts, personnel, sales and marketing and procurement; quite a busy place."

The first room on the left, as they entered the corridor was the residents lounge. It was from where the elderly lady had appeared earlier. Dacombe opened the door and there were ten or twelve residents in various pursuits. A couple were playing cards, a woman knitting, several were reading. It was light and airy with a large window which appeared to open up to a patio.

The next room was the TV and dining room and there were half a dozen residents watching a gameshow.

"This tends to be the most popular room," said Dacombe. "Although there are TVs in all the bedrooms, they like the company, which of course we encourage. We have classes as well – the morning keep fit sessions are particularly well attended."

Opposite the community rooms were three private bedrooms; reserved for those who have difficulty with stairs, Dacombe explained.

They walked past the kitchen which they did not enter and came to a large staircase with an expensive looking stair-lift running its length and climbed to the next floor. Dacombe showed Greg the upstairs accommodation. All the rooms were self-contained and comfortable, and the decor was of a high standard. Whatever his faults, on the face of it he certainly ran a good business.

"Very impressive," said Greg as they moved from bedroom to bedroom. Some rooms were locked. "Some residents like an afternoon nap," he said. "We won't disturb them."

There were ten rooms on the second floor and the same again on the third.

Dacombe led Greg back to his office on the ground floor and returned to their seats.

"So, you don't live here," said Greg, more an observation than a question.

"No, we have a place in Ridge Lane... by the golf course."

Greg knew exactly where that would be; one of the most sought-after areas in the district; you would get little change from three million for any of the properties along that road.

"Do you play?" asked Dacombe.

"Sorry?" said Greg, still mulling over the last statement.

"Golf, do you play golf?" Dacombe repeated.

"No, sorry," replied Greg.

"A pity, I could have swung a membership, if you excuse the pun," he laughed. "We have a five-year waiting list, but I will be president next year, so I am not without influence... and there are always ways and means if you know what I mean," he said, tapping his finger against his nose in a 'nudge, nudge; wink, wink' kind of way.

"What about riding?" he asked. "You can always have the use of our paddock. We have four thoroughbreds which we're hoping to breed this year. You can't beat the thrill of riding a thoroughbred."

"Sorry, no," said Greg.

Dacombe spoke about his wealth in a 'matter of fact' way, not boastful exactly, but clearly wanted Greg to know he was dealing with a successful man.

"I've just had a thought..." he paused. "I'm having a drinks party at the house this Saturday, why don't you join us? You would be very welcome. Bring a friend if you like. Are you married, Greg? It's alright to call you Greg?"

"Of course, and no I'm not married," replied Greg, hardly believing his luck. He paused as if considering the invitation. "Well, if it's ok, that would be great. I haven't had chance to do much socialising since I came back to Sheffield."

Dacombe looked at Greg as though wanting more information.

"I've been working in the States," he said, answering the unasked question.

"And what do you do?" asked Dacombe.

"Research," said Greg without elaborating.

"What about fees?" asked Greg, quickly changing the subject?

"Sorry?" asked Dacombe, not following the direction of the conversation.

"How much do you charge, for the rooms?"

"Ah... yes... the important part. Well, full residency, and that includes private medical care and meals, laundry and so on, start from two-thousand, two-hundred pounds a month. Fees are reviewed annually with a minimum twelve-month contract."

"What if someone dies after the first two months?" said Greg out of interest.

"There's a two-month termination fee in the event of the contract not being fulfilled for any reason."

"Including death?" queried Greg.

"Including death," replied Dacombe. "It covers the cost of refurbishing the room and so on ready for the next client."

"Thank you," said Greg. "You mentioned a waiting list."

"Ah yes, there are twelve presently ahead of your grandmother."

"And your 'turnover' is what?" asked Greg.

Dacombe could see where this was heading.

"Well as I said, there are ways of, how shall I put it... moving up the list," replied Dacombe.

"Go on," said Greg.

"Well, it is a bit delicate and I wouldn't want this to be broadcast around," said Dacombe, looking around the room as if seeking an eavesdropper. "Shall we say... a sort of sliding scale?"

"What do you mean?" asked Greg, not letting him off the hook.

"A payment representing a place in the queue," he said, trying to look suitably embarrassed.

"How much?" asked Greg.

"Well, say a couple of grand a place, it's the going rate for a place of this quality," he quickly added.

No wonder he had a string of thoroughbreds, thought Greg.

"So, to get my grandmother to the top of the list will cost me twenty-four thousand pounds," said Greg, summarising.

"At the moment, yes, obviously the price comes down if the list gets smaller, but there's no sign of that; we're getting enquiries every day and then of course the list grows. It's a simple question of supply and demand."

"Yes, I can see that," said Greg.

"Well, I'll have to talk to my grandmother, the money won't be an issue. She's got investments which she can realise if necessary. Have you got a brochure I can let her have a look at?"

"Of course," and Dacombe opened the drawer in the desk and took out a glossy brochure which looked more like a fashion magazine. Greg scanned through the pages.

"Have you any more questions, Greg?" asked Dacombe half standing, clearly concluding the interview.

Greg stood up. "No... No," you have been very helpful, and I have to say the place is very impressive," he said with conviction; it was.

"And you *will* join us on Saturday? It will give you a chance to meet Barbara and the rest of the family. There'll be about ten of us, just a nice number," said Dacombe.

"Yes, if that's ok. Thank you. What time?"

"Seven-thirty for eight, if that suits. The Fairways, Ridge Lane, you can't miss it. Here's my number if things change," and Dacombe handed Greg a business card.

Greg made his farewells and Dacombe led him to the front porch of the building. It had started to spit with rain.

Dacombe looked up at the greying sky.

"Hope this doesn't come to anything, I was hoping for four holes this evening before it gets too dark."

Greg left him at the entrance and walked towards his car.

"Well, that went well," he thought.

Chapter Fourteen

It took Greg just the couple of minutes to get back to Taskers End and his mind was racing; the invite to the Dacombe house on Saturday was certainly a bonus and in keeping with the man's arrogance. He was clearly trying to impress a potential investor. Greg couldn't wait to tell Maureen.

It was just gone five when Maureen's mini pulled into the drive.

Maureen swept into the hall with two plastic Brandwood's supermarket carrier bags in one hand and two more what looked like boutique bags in the other.

"Hi," she said, sounding upbeat as if a weight had been lifted from her.

Greg went and greeted her with a warm hug and kiss.

"You sound cheerful," he said.

"Yes," she said, "I am."

"Any particular reason?" asked Greg as he took the shopping bags from her.

She removed her jacket and hung it on the nearest coat peg in the hall.

"No... No particular reason and that's what makes it so nice," said Maureen rather cryptically.

"I don't understand," said Greg.

"As I was driving up here, I just felt so happy, looking forward to seeing you, doing the cooking. I've never felt like this before, happy for no apparent reason."

Greg went to her and kissed her passionately. "I know what you mean."

"I want to give you a treat," she said and went to the kitchen and took the contents of her supermarket bags onto the work surface. "How do you fancy pan fried red snapper with spicy salad and sweet and sour dressing? Very healthy."

"Sounds brilliant," said Greg who was anxious to tell Maureen about his meeting with Dacombe but didn't want to spoil her excitement.

"How did you get on with Dacombe?" asked Maureen, as she began to relieve the shopping bags of their contents.

Despite his anxiety to relive his meeting he realised there was no rush.

"Very interesting, I'll tell you over dinner."

He went to the fridge and took a bottle of Chablis suitably chilled.

"Would you like a drink?" he asked and started to pour two glasses of wine before she had chance to answer.

"That would be great," she said, removing the fish from its packaging.

"Won't take long. I'll finish off then go and change."

Maureen explained the dish to Greg as she gathered all the ingredients and set them all out on the work top.

"There, that's all done, won't take long to cook," she said after about ten minutes and she disappeared upstairs with the two boutique bags.

Greg put the news on the TV in the kitchen and waited for her to return. There was a piece on the news about Care Home regulations which took his interest and he didn't immediately notice Maureen enter the room. The tee shirt and jeans quickly had his attention and Greg turned off the TV with the remote.

"Wow, you look incredible. Is that new?"

"Yes, bought it this afternoon. Do you like it?" she asked, modelling her outfit for him. "I'll need an apron, don't want to splash anything down me," she said, and Greg went to one of the kitchen cupboards and handed one to her.

Maureen wrapped it around her and for twenty minutes while she cooked, Greg described his meeting with Dacombe, the opulence of the Care Home and his offer of the drinks party on Saturday. She listened with interest.

"I said I would go; you don't mind, do you?" he said apologetically.

"No, of course not."

"He did say I could bring someone, but it did occur to me it's possible that Chapman might be there if he's returned from his holiday... and that would really put the cat among the pigeons," Greg continued.

"No, no, I'll be fine... You never know it could give you more evidence, and at least you'll have a better idea about what you're up against.".

Greg was grateful to Maureen for her common sense and practicality; it was such an important foil for his occasional impetuosity.

After the meal, they washed up together and continued to discuss the investigation; Greg outlined his next step.

"I still don't know how much involvement Chapman has had; the only thing we know for sure is that he has been using Clients' moneys illegally. I think I'll speak to Cathcart again." He was now using the 'we' word.

"I'm not looking forward to him coming back next week. It is going to be very difficult."

"I have an idea which may keep him under control," said Greg, and he outlined another potential plan which only marginally served to allay Maureen's fears.

The next morning Queenie arrived for her cleaning duties and Greg prepared for his second meeting with Dorinda, the social worker. He decided to use the study for the interview and was fairly relaxed about it; the last meeting seemed to go well. He had briefed the cleaner that he was expecting a visitor.

At just after ten o'clock, Greg heard the familiar crunching of gravel and he went to the window to see Dorinda getting out of a fairly ancient Citroen. He got to the door before she had chance to ring and showed her into the hall.

"Great place you have here, Greg."

She paused before using his name to show she had remembered his preferred address.

"Yes, thank you. Would you like a drink, tea, coffee, soft drink?"

"Coffee will be fine," she said as she took off her jacket; Greg hung it on a vacant peg.

Queenie appeared to see what was happening.

"Ah, Queenie, this is Dorinda; Dorinda this is Queenie... my life-saver," he said, trying to keep the mood light. "Queenie looks after me... Can we have two coffees, please?"

"Hello," said Queenie. "I'll bring your drinks through."

Greg led Dorinda into the study.

Dorinda was carrying her large bag containing her laptop and paraphernalia.

"Can I plug this in somewhere," she asked, waving the lead to her computer and Greg trailed the connection to a socket near the window. Greg had cleared the table and had put a chair either side which he thought would serve as a suitable interview space. Greg waited whilst Dorinda set up her stuff.

"Lovely room," she said, looking around.

"Thank you, this used to be the library. The bookshelves are original and so are some of the books."

Queenie came in with a tray with the two coffees and some biscuits and placed it on the table.

"Let me know if you need anything else," she said before leaving the room and closing the door.

"So how has it been?" asked Dorinda as she started up her laptop.

"Fine," said Greg, which seemed to be his stock answer.

"Any problems?" asked Dorinda trying to widen the

question.

"No, none at all; I was telling Doctor Melrose, I don't think I have ever been happier."

"Why do you think that is?" she asked.

"Well, obviously getting out of Trenton was a start but meeting my girlfriend has made a big difference," he expanded.

"Ah yes, Doctor Melrose mentioned you're in a relationship, all very quick," she said, but not in a judgemental way.

Greg thought about questioning the confidentiality, but then realised he was being naive; of course, Doctor Melrose would have told Dorinda everything.

"Yes, it happens…" he said. "I suppose she also told you about my suspicions concerning my grandparents' deaths."

"Yes, I do have a note of that," said Dorinda.

Greg continued, "Well, as I told her, I'm positive that my grandparents were murdered, and I think I'm close to finding out who was responsible."

"Why do you think someone killed them?"

"Because the fire didn't start the way they said it did… and I've discovered a motive."

"Do you feel a sense of guilt for their deaths?" she asked.

Greg hadn't really thought of it as guilt, but he had expressed his regrets on several occasions particularly to Arthur Cathcart, so it was a reasonable definition.

"No, not guilt exactly, but I certainly regret not being around when they needed me," he replied. He hoped he had headed off any negative implications.

Dorinda made some notes but didn't pursue the question further and this was the difference between Doctor Melrose and Dorinda. The psychiatrist was specifically looking for the slightest aberrant, Dorinda had responsibility for Greg's overall wellbeing and would view his behaviour much more objectively.

"I understand your girlfriend's moved in," said the social worker, changing the subject. "How is it working? Any problems?"

"No, it's fine; it's the best thing that's ever happened to me."

There was a pause while Dorinda made a note on her laptop.

"Would you like to have a look round the house?" Greg asked.

There was a motive in his question. He was desperate to reassure the 'authorities' that had the power over his life, personified by the social worker, that he was not only coping, but thriving, in the community.

"Yes, thank you, that would be great," she said, and Greg spent the next twenty minutes giving Dorinda a guided tour.

"Well, you certainly have a magnificent house," she said as they came back down the stairs after the look-round.

"Thank you," he said, and they went back to the study.

"Is it alright if I finish off my admin here before I go onto my next appointment?"

"Of course, I'll be next door in the lounge; just give me a shout when you are ready."

Dorinda Walcott's report was not exactly at odds with Doctor Melrose, but she did give a different perspective. Her report was as follows:

'Interviewed patient at his house today. As in previous meetings he was bright, confident and in good health. He is extremely well catered for with a substantial house and income. He has a housekeeper who visits three days a week and a girlfriend who has moved in. He seems extremely fond of her and I do not consider her in any kind of danger. His interest in his grandparents' deaths is understandable and probably stems from his guilt at not being around at the time. In my interview I did not find this obsessive or anything of concern.

Dorinda Walcott, Senior Social Worker, South Yorks Social

Services.

Cc Jane Melrose, Mental Health Division, South Yorks NHS Trust

Dorinda saved the document on her laptop and would send it later.

Greg showed Dorinda out and made arrangements for her to call in two weeks' time.

"At the house again, if you like," he said. She happily agreed.

After she had gone Greg made a phone call.

"Terry, it's Greg."

He was keen to hear if he had heard anything more from Chapman.

"Nah... it's all gone quiet, mate. Don't think I'll be hearing any more till I collect me money."

"Did he say when he was coming back?"

"Friday night, I think. He's flying into Manchester. I'm supposed to see him on Saturday afternoon to get further instructions."

Greg was anxious about the 'further instructions' bit. He thought quickly.

"Look, why don't we meet up on Saturday morning outside the shops where we met last time. I'll bring you the rest of your money and we can have a chat?"

Terry was happy with that, especially with the promise of his money, and they agreed on a time. Greg rang off and went to the kitchen where Queenie was just finishing the washing.

"How's that nice young lady of yours, Mr Jensen?"

Maureen had left for the office by the time Queenie arrived at the house earlier.

"She's well thank you," he said with a smile. "I'll tell her you were asking after her."

He loved the sound of the terminology 'nice young lady

of yours'; the thought of he and Maureen being considered a couple gave him a warm glow.

Greg went upstairs and took Sam's two cash registers with him. He had a boring but necessary job to do and for the next couple of hours or so, he laboriously copied pages of the books. Not all, just a chosen selection which would highlight Chapman's misdemeanours admirably. He also scanned the pages into his computer and copied them onto a memory stick. He was leaving nothing to chance. If Chapman was as ruthless as it had been suggested, these pages would be worth a great deal to him; certainly, his profession and possibly his liberty.

Queenie called him around one o'clock; she had made him a sandwich and coffee and the pair chatted in the kitchen while he ate his lunch. It was during this conversation that Queenie dropped another bombshell which would have repercussions.

"I do love this house you know", she said. "It brings back so many memories. It's so nice to be back, I can't tell you."

She stared blankly in a reminiscent sort of way; a faraway, day-dreamy sort of way.

Greg stopped his sandwich eating in mid-flow.

"Sorry," he spluttered. "What do you mean memories?"

"I used to come here with my mother, years ago... before I got married."

"I didn't know that."

"Well, why would you?"

"I thought I might remember her."

She was looking confused. Then Greg suddenly realised.

"You don't know who I am, do you?"

There was a pause. "I'm Gerald... Gerald Perry... the Sinclairs were my grandparents."

Queenie looked at him closely. "But I thought your name was Jensen."

"It is... now, but it used to be Perry. I changed it when I returned to Sheffield," he said without expanding further.

Queenie appeared to be in shock. "But weren't you..." she was looking for the right words. "Sent away?"

"Yes," said Greg. "But I'm fine now. That's all behind me, which is one of the reasons I changed my name."

"I can understand that," she said.

"So, when did you visit here then?"

"Oh, it would be a long time ago, I was a teenager." She was still staring at him. "You would only be about nine or ten. It was just after your Mum and Dad died."

She paused and apologised, "Sorry didn't mean to..."

"It's alright," said Greg.

"My Mum used to work for the Sinclairs, your grandparents. I used to help her sometimes. You would be at school, I suppose. I don't think we ever met, but Mum often talked about you... said what a nice, well-mannered boy you were."

She paused again still trying to take in Greg's revelation and looked at him inquisitively. Greg was speechless.

"You remember Alice, Alice Howley?" she asked, almost as a statement.

"Mrs Howley, of course, she used to clean for us. I remember her very well. Lovely lady, she used to bring me sweets and things. My grandparents didn't approve of treats." He paused for a moment to tune his mind. "And she was your mother?"

"Yes, that's how I got the job. Mr Cathcart looked after her, after the fire."

"What do you mean, 'looked after'?"

"Well he paid her for six months afterwards, I know that. She was so grateful. They even left her some money in their will, the Sinclairs; ten thousand pounds it was. Mum didn't have to work again."

Queenie paused and took a drink of tea before continuing.

"When Mr Cathcart knew you were moving in he rang me and asked if I'd be interested in taking over the cleaning and I said yes straight away. He didn't tell me you were Gerald... just said it was a new tenant. I used to clean for Mr Cathcart's niece over in Baslow, but this is far more convenient, pays more too."

Greg was trying to take this all in.

"So, your Mum is Alice Howley, who used to clean the house for my grandparents?"

"Over twenty years it was," she replied.

"Was she working at the time of the fire?".

"Of course, she worked every day, loved it she did, hardly took any holidays."

"Did she say anything about the fire?" asked Greg.

"No..." she paused, "That was the strangest thing. We all put it down to the shock. She would never speak about it."

"Where is she now?" asked Greg.

"Lives on the Isle of Wight. Moved there when she got the money from the will, sold her house in Dronfield and bought a bungalow in Seaview, overlooking the sea. Loves it there, says it was the best move she ever made, been there almost two years; got loads of friends."

"What about your father?" asked Greg.

"Oh, he died in 2003, got cancer from working with asbestos. Mum got compensation though, which is how she bought the house in Dronfield."

Greg continued to get their life history and he couldn't help thinking that Alice may be able to throw some light onto the tragedy.

"Does your mother come back at all?"

"Occasionally, but not for some time, she's got a man friend you know. I've not met him, but she does seem quite keen on him."

The words poured out as Queenie related story after story.

"I'll tell her we've had a chat. I told her I was working here; she couldn't believe it. Wanted to know what you'd done to the place. She used to say she knew every nook and cranny."

"Well she would be very welcome to come and have a look round when she next visits. It would be lovely to meet her again."

"I'll tell her that, and that you're back here, and you were asking after her, she'll be chuffed to death."

Greg left Queenie to finish off and wandered into the study. He wanted to talk to Alice. If necessary, he would go and visit her. He didn't want to speak over the phone, particularly if she was anxious about it in any way.

Greg made another decision; he phoned Maureen and managed to get an appointment with Cathcart for Friday morning.

That evening Greg told Maureen about his conversation with Terry, the low-life, and Queenie's revelations.

"I had no idea her mother was Mrs Howley who used to work here," he said. "She was working the day of the fire, according to Queenie; so, it's possible she may know something."

He also told her of his plan for Friday and his meeting with Cathcart.

Friday morning ten o'clock. and Greg was at the front door of Cathcart Rivers with a carrier bag. He rang the doorbell and he was sure he could smell Maureen's perfume before she opened the door. It reminded him of the first time he had called, two weeks ago, what a difference his life was now.

She smiled warmly and led him into the reception area.

"He won't be a minute, would you like a coffee?" she said, very professionally. Greg wanted to kiss her, but they had agreed to play it cool in the office.

A few minutes later Greg heard the door along the corridor

open and Cathcart walked into reception.

"Greg, my dear boy, lovely to see you again; come on through; would you like a drink?"

"Maureen's looking after me, thank you," said Greg, and he followed Cathcart to his office. Greg noticed several white hairs had mixed with the solicitor's dandruff on his shoulders and wondered if this was a sign he was under pressure.

He sat down with his carrier bag on his lap and Cathcart made small talk, such as it was.

"How are you getting on? Have you kept up with your appointments? Are you ok for money?" that kind of thing.

Maureen brought in the coffee and left them to their business.

"So, Greg, I'm still trying to get used to the name," Cathcart said. "What can I do for you?"

"Well, it's more what I can do for you."

Cathcart looked intrigued.

"Well, after our last meeting I've been looking into the activities of your partner David Chapman."

"Why would you want to do that, dear boy?" he said, looking quite uncomfortable.

"Well, as I told you last time, I know he has some involvement somewhere... so, I went to see Sam Davenport."

"Well you won't get much from him; he's a basket case."

This was a strange and uncharacteristic comment for Cathcart to make. He was always articulate and measured in his discussions with Greg. Perhaps he *was* feeling the strain.

"Actually, I didn't; as you say he is in a bad way, but his wife gave me these;" and Greg pulled out the two cash registers and handed them to him.

"What are these?" asked Cathcart, as he scanned quickly through the pages.

"Mrs Davenport told me that Sam didn't trust computers and was always concerned that they might break down, so he kept his own cash books. I think if you compare them with the practice computer version you should find they match; according to his wife anyway. Sam, it appears, was a perfectionist."

"He certainly was," commented Cathcart, still viewing the pages. "I don't see how this helps with your investigation."

"Maybe it does; maybe it doesn't, it's just something I've stumbled across. If you look carefully you will see that Chapman's been using Clients' money to finance deals, property I think, given his involvement with Dacombe. There are many entries going back several years, certainly before the fire. I did a quick calculation and I reckon he's pocketed over a million pounds."

Cathcart looked gravely at the files and was rubbing his palm and fingers across his face deep in thought. A look of anxiety swept over him and he began twitching nervously.

"This doesn't prove anything, dear boy," he said, which surprised Greg.

"Not about the fire perhaps, but they certainly show that Chapman has been illegally using clients" money and possibly embezzling practice funds. There's enough there to get him struck off and maybe even sent down."

Cathcart's demeanour was becoming even graver if that was possible.

"Have you showed these to anybody?"

"No," said Greg, deliberately not mentioning Maureen's involvement.

"Good, you have done the right thing bringing these to me."

"What are you going to do?" asked Greg.

"Give this a lot of thought," he replied, which did not satisfy Greg.

"But you are going to confront him with this, surely?" asked Greg somewhat exasperated.

"All in good time, dear boy, all in good time. There's a lot to consider," replied Cathcart. "I need to think about the clients and the possible bad press. As you have gathered we only have selected clients who appreciate discretion and we can't possibly be involved in any scandal."

"But it's too late for that now. Chapman has already seen to that."

"There are ways and means, dear boy; ways and means."

Cathcart opened one of the drawers on his desk and put the two registers in and locked it. I will look after these, they are practice property and we won't be taking any action against Mr Davenport over this you have my assurance."

"What do you mean action? Against Sam?"

"What I said, there won't be any. Sam has stolen practice property and, if he were not so unwell, I would have to consider legal proceedings very carefully."

"I can't believe I am hearing this," said Greg, getting quite animated. "It's Chapman who is the villain here not poor old Sam."

"Quite," said Cathcart. "And as I said, ways and means. Leave them with me, I will see that the appropriate action is taken."

Greg was crestfallen. He was sure Cathcart's reaction would have been different.

"I thought you were on my side."

"I am, dear boy, I am; but this does have much wider implications than you can imagine, and I need to cover everything before I take any precipitous action. Please trust me on this, now was there anything else?"

Greg was dumbfounded. "No, no that was all."

"Then leave it with me, I will see to everything," and he got up to escort Greg out.

Greg met Maureen in reception and she could see by his

demeanour that something was wrong and after Cathcart had said his farewells, she confronted him.

"What's the matter Greg, are you ok?"

"Can't talk here" he spoke quietly. "Can we talk at lunch time?"

"Of course, I'll meet you at one at the cafe."

"Ok, great, see you then. I'm off to do some shopping," and he rubbed her arm in an affectionate way. He wanted to hug her.

It was gone eleven, and while he waited for his rendezvous with Maureen he decided to buy some more clothes for his party on Saturday night. He thought it would be important to create an impression of wealth and that would need to be reflected in his appearance; the right clothes would to do that. He found a men's boutique that specialised in 'designer' labels and bought a new jacket, pair of slacks and shirt, all with the right logos to impress the nouveau-riche. It was not cheap, but he felt it would be an investment and he argued he would get good use out of them.

At one o'clock, he was sat at a table in the cafe waiting for Maureen laden with his purchases. It was very busy, normal for Friday lunchtime. He saw her coming through the door and still had that excited feeling as she walked towards him. They kissed, and Greg went to get the food whilst Maureen looked after the table and bags.

"You've been busy," she said. "Let's see what you've bought,"

Greg showed her the contents of the bags. "Very smart," she said.

After a brief catch-up Greg explained his disappointment at the meeting with Cathcart."

"I thought he would be more, I don't know, concerned. It was though I had presented him with an unwanted problem rather than exposing possible corruption in his office."

"That's probably it… 'his office'," Maureen made the emphasis. "He is extremely protective of the business. He has some very influential and high-profile clients including celebrities. Any hint of scandal or embarrassment would cause him a lot of worry and telling him that his partner has been cooking the books is not going to be welcome news. I've known Mr Cathcart for some time and I would say that, for all his gruffness, he is a man of integrity and if he says he will take action I'm sure he will, but he'll do it in a way that won't hurt the business and, he won't be rushed."

Extremely wise words again from Maureen, which went some way to placate Greg, but his underlying frustration in not being able to get to the bottom of his grandparents demise was palpable; it was becoming an obsession.

That evening it was again the main topic of conversation and Maureen was a willing listener and tried to offer the voice of reason.

Saturday morning and it was time for Greg to meet 'lowlife' Terry. The white van was waiting in the parking bay outside the shops by Maureen's flat when Greg arrived as arranged. There was a large pub adjacent to the parade and Greg tapped on the driver's window causing Terry to jump and indicated they decamp there for a drink.

The two of them walked towards the 'Dog and Duck' without speaking. Inside, it was virtually empty with just a couple of punters sat on high bar stools staring into the bottom of their pints. The floor was bare wood and their footsteps echoed around the soul-less room as they walked towards the bar. There was a nauseating smell of stale alcohol. Greg ordered an orange juice and a pint for Terry who started the conversation by bemoaning the recent smoking ban which he said was killing the pub trade.

Greg didn't comment.

"Have you heard any more from Chapman?" said Greg, not wishing to spend any longer in the man's company than was necessary.

"He phoned just before you turned up, he wants a meet this afternoon, two o'clock. Said he's got further instructions."

"Any indication what they might be?" asked Greg, clearly concerned.

"Nah, just said further instructions," replied Terry.

"Ok, this is what I want you to do," said Greg reaching for his wallet. "This is the remainder of the money I promised, a week early and I am prepared to pay you a hundred pounds a week to be at my disposal."

"What do you mean, disposal?"

"I may have a few jobs for you to do but mainly I need you to tell me what Chapman is doing, I need to keep one step ahead of him."

"Yeah ok, I can do that," said Terry

"But you mustn't underestimate him, he's no fool. You will have to be careful."

"I told you before, I know all about David Chapman; I can soon sort him out," said Terry. "I tell you what, for fifty-grand I can make sure he would never be a problem, ever."

That was an attractive proposition and Greg momentarily considered that option. It certainly would tie up that end quite nicely and avoid any worries for Maureen, once and for all.

"I'll think about that, it's a tempting offer, but I need to do more research first and find out what's going on," said Greg. "Two o'clock you're meeting him, right?"

"Yeah"

"Ok, I'll expect a call after your meeting and let me know what he wants you to do, we can take it from there."

Greg downed the last of his orange juice and almost gagged as the sugary liquid passed through his mouth and into his throat.

"Urgh," he said unintentionally. "Right I must get going, I'll hear from you later, ok?" and he put his drink down on the sticky surface of the bar and left. Terry ordered another pint.

Greg got into the Audi and headed back to the house to consider his next move.

Chapter Fifteen

Maureen was waiting for him back at the house.

"How did it go?" she asked as soon as he came through the door, clearly anxious.

Greg outlined what went on at the meeting and what was going to happen next in an effort to reassure her.

"Don't worry about Chapman, I've got everything under control," he said.

Later that afternoon Greg got a call.

"It's Terry," said the voice in the strong local accent.

"What's happening?" said Greg.

"Not a lot. I told him that I'd been following her like I said, and he just said that he would think about what to do next and would let me know."

"Thanks for that. Can you let me know as soon as he makes contact again?" Terry agreed.

"Cheers," said Greg emulating Terry and rang off.

This gave Greg a bit of breathing space and it didn't look as though Maureen was in any immediate danger, much to his relief. He still wasn't too keen on leaving her alone in the house though. He walked back to the kitchen where she was making a coffee.

"Are you sure you are ok about tonight?" he asked.

"Of course," she said, "I'll be fine. I'm going to have a long bath and watch some TV."

"There's some white wine in the fridge or some red in the rack if you feel like a drink."

"Thanks, and stop worrying, I'll be fine," and she walked over and kissed him.

Greg was ready in his new gear by seven-fifteen. He went into the lounge where Maureen was curled up on the sofa watching TV.

"You look nice," she said as he walked in the room.

"Thanks… I'm off now. Don't know what time I'll be back but it shouldn't be late. I'll call you from the car when I'm leaving."

"That's ok, I'll wait up," she replied, and got up to see him out.

"I've got my keys," he said, holding them up so she could see, and he kissed her then left the house. He heard her lock the door behind him.

Greg looked up at the sky; there was a distinct chill in the early October air and he could see the clouds scurrying across the sliver of an old moon. As he made his way to the car, the drive was bathed in the reassuring luminescence of the security lights.

It took about twenty minutes to get to Dacombe's substantial property. As he had said, you couldn't miss it. The name 'Fairways' was hanging from a post at the entrance off Ridge Lane indicating the long tarmac and pebble drive to the house in the distance. It was bathed in arc lights giving it an almost 'Oscar night' feel and was clearly visible from the road. It was completely open with no trees or plants bordering the track and electric lanterns lit the way to the frontage over a hundred yards from the main road. There was little natural light left but his headlights picked out the fields on both sides which he could see were used for grazing and riding horses. From what he could see it was a quite substantial dormer bungalow probably about twenty-years-old and reminded Greg of the Ewing ranch, 'Southfork' from the TV series 'Dallas' which he used to watch with his mother as a child.

He parked the Audi next to a Porsche 911 with the number plate 'IC 11'. There were four other cars on the drive including a top of the range Mercedes SLK convertible and Range Rover with plates 'BD 58' and 'PD 47'.

"His and hers, how sweet," thought Greg.

The trappings of wealth were everywhere. To the left of the main house there were other outbuildings and he could hear agitated horses calling, disturbed by his arrival. He could see expensive mini-tractors parked by the stables together with two horse boxes. He went up to the front door which was set back into an alcove. To the side there was a brass bell attached to a spring with a chain hanging down. He worked out the mechanism for a moment before pulling the chord; the bell echoed around the porch.

The door was opened by Peter Dacombe himself. What no butler, thought Greg!

"Greg, do come in, so pleased you could make it," he fawned. Dacombe was dressed casually as though he had just come off the golf-course. Light beige trousers with a garish diamond pattern, pink shirt and lime green jumper, white loafers. Greg bit his lip as he thought of a blancmange.

Greg followed Dacombe into the large reception where there were four other people talking with the familiarity of friendship. Trays of drinks were strategically placed on tables around the room. The decor was modern with what looked like original artwork on the walls. The red-patterned carpet was a high quality, probably Wilton, thought Greg, remembering his grandmother's taste for fine floor-covering.

"Go on through and I'll make some introductions," he said.

"What can I get you to drink?"

"Just an orange juice," said Greg. Dacombe looked a little disappointed.

"Can't tempt you with a cocktail or a beer perhaps? You're welcome to stay if you're worried about driving or we can always order you a taxi and you can pick up the car tomorrow.

We like our guests to relax and let their hair down."

"Maybe later," said Greg, wanting to maintain his sharpness; he wasn't here, for pleasure.

A glamorous looking woman about the same age as Dacombe joined them.

"Barbara darling, let me introduce you to Greg... the young man I was telling you about. You remember... wants to book a place at the Pines for his grandmother."

"Of course, darling," she said and leaned forward to offer her cheek for Greg to kiss. Not sure of the social etiquette, he went with his instincts and kissed one cheek and then the other. He didn't know whether a third was required but he thought that was French. The woman seemed satisfied with the greeting and looked at Greg.

"So, you're Greg, Peter told me about you. You live with your grandmother in, where was it? Loxley, that right? I'm Barbara by the way, but you can call me Babs, everybody does."

Greg looked at the present Mrs Dacombe, too much make up, and dressed in a low-cut top with a chiffon scarf wrapped around her shoulders, for decoration, not to protect her modesty. The skirt was probably three inches shorter than someone of her age would normally wear but she had good legs and poise, possibly a dancer in her earlier years, thought Greg. There had clearly been some enhancement cosmetically, judging by the way her breasts appeared to defy gravity and the taught skin under her chin.

"Nice place, you have here," said Greg making conversation.

"Thank you, yes, we're very happy here."

"I'll just get the drinks, darling," said Dacombe who left them to carry on their small talk.

"How long have you lived here?" asked Greg.

"Fourteen years," she said.

Greg noticed a photograph on an occasional table in the corner of room. It was of a family group in swimming gear on a boat somewhere.

"Is this the family?" asked Greg, pointing to the picture.

"Yes, that was taken on our yacht last year at Juan Les Pains. We have a small villa at Cavalier-sur-Mer".

Greg wasn't familiar with the resort.

"Near St Tropez," she clarified.

"That's Emma, she's at sixth form and that's Jessica, she's at Bath, doing law. Emma's on a stopover tonight at one of her friends in Dore. Not keen on parents' parties," she said and smiled.

Her husband returned with a long tumbler of orange juice, heavy with ice and what looked like a gin and tonic. He handed the gin to his wife.

"Thank you darling," she said.

There was something about their interaction that said something was not quite right. Their body language incompatible with that of a devoted couple, performed for the benefit of their guests, and Greg wondered what their relationship was really like. He also noticed that he called her 'Barbara' but she was 'Babs' to her friends; a lack of closeness he sensed.

Dacombe gave him the juice and said, "Come with me there's someone I want you to meet."

He walked across the room to another group who were chatting.

"Excuse me interrupting, but can I introduce you to Greg… Greg this is Nancy Hogarth and her partner Dawn." Greg shook hands.

"Nice to meet you," he said.

"And this is my business partner, David Chapman, and his wife Isabel, we call her Izzy."

Greg for a fraction of a second was paralysed. He had not

had a clear view of Chapman when he had tried to confront them outside Maureen's flat the previous week, he was concentrating on the road; Greg just hoped that Chapman had not recognised him, or it would all be over.

"Hello Greg," said Chapman, and Greg just managed to hold it together; he was hoping his anxiety wouldn't show.

"Hello," he said.

"Peter tells me you're into research," said Chapman, in a very amiable way, no sign of any cognisance.

Greg just stared for a second; the unexpected introduction had caught him off guard.

"Y... yes, that's right," he managed to stammer.

His wife took over the interrogation. "Where was this?"

"In the States," said Greg, recovering quickly and using his cover story.

He tried not to stare at Chapman, but his curiosity was getting the better of him. Although he knew it was a possibility, Greg had not thought about how he might react if he should finally meet Chapman face to face. He felt Gerald starting to stir.

Chapman was smartly dressed, as you would expect at a drinks party, not as tall as Dacombe, short stylish fair hair starting to thin into a widows peak, mid-forties probably, judging by the bulging waste line and lines on his face, slightly rugged and swarthier than his business partner; he looked like he may have played rugby by the slightly crooked nose. There was a definite 'no messing' air about him.

His wife was about the same age as her husband, dark hair, also with too much makeup and an expensive looking but rather unflatteringly tight pair of trousers. "Yes, your bum really does look big in that," Greg thought and had to stop himself from laughing. There seemed to be some friendly rivalry between the host's wife and Izzy Chapman in the glamour stakes.

"I'm very sorry, can you excuse me a moment." Greg quickly made an excuse to visit the men's room and was given directions by his host. The other guests did not appear to notice anything amiss and kept on chatting.

Greg went into one of the two 'downstairs' facilities and looked at himself in the mirror. He was shaking; his face pallid and his heart racing. Beads of sweat began to appear on his forehead. He wanted to be sick but instead he went into his breathing exercises and his pulse rate gradually reduced. After a few moments the colour returned to his face. He knew he was going to have to overcome this if he was going to get any further with his investigations tonight. He splashed water over his face and wiped himself dry before returning to the gathering. Gerald finally went back to sleep.

"Would you like that beer now?" asked Dacombe as Greg walked back to the reception.

"Yes, thank you," said Greg.

The groups had split up and there was a lot of activity coming from one room which Greg realised later was the kitchen. Dacombe returned with a bottle of lager.

"We'll be having some food in a moment. Why don't you make yourself comfortable in the dining room?"

Dacombe took Greg into an adjoining room which was blessed with a huge picture window overlooking the fields. The brightness from the arc lights cast eerie shadows which gently faded across grounds into the distance. There was a large dining table which had been set out for ten. The two women he had met earlier were in deep conversation and he sat next to Nancy who acknowledged his presence. Chapman and his wife came in and sat opposite him followed by Dacombe who sat next to her. There was a spare seat at the top of the table nearest the door which presumably would be taken by Barbara, another couple that Greg had not yet met, and then a young woman probably a couple of years younger than Greg came in. She was slim with long flowing fair hair wearing a pair of 'spray on' jeans and a low-cut top from which her breasts appeared to be making an escape.

"Ah Pippa, there you are. Why don't you sit next to Greg?" said Dacombe, and she made her way round the table and sat down. Gerald would have been in his element, but cool Greg was still in charge. She introduced herself.

"Hi, I'm Pippa," she said.

"Greg," he replied.

"I look after the horses here, do you ride at all?" she asked, looking directly into his eyes.

"No, never had the chance."

"Oh, you should, I love it, can't get enough," she said, licking her lips in a seductive way which unnerved Greg momentarily.

Barbara, and what looked to be a hired help, brought in the food.

"Nothing special just a few bits," she said, as the smoked salmon and foie-gras with various types of bread, quiche, taramasalata, cheeses, olives and an array of salad and dips, were ferried in from the kitchen.

"Thank you, Franciscka," said Barbara, and the Polish au pair went back to whatever duties had been allocated for her.

"Help yourself everyone," and plates were passed round for guests to serve themselves.

Greg didn't feel at all hungry but took a selection to be polite. As he helped himself to a portion of salmon and spooned some salad he tried not to stare at the man opposite but found it difficult. He started to picture his hands all over Maureen. Gerald was beginning to stir again.

He was shaken from his imaginings by a voice. "So, what do you do... work-wise I mean?"

It was Pippa with the big eyes and voluptuous body; she

seemed to flutter her eye lids as she spoke.

"Research," replied Greg for the umpteenth time to the same question. Nobody had bothered to pursue it further, preferring to talk about themselves.

"And what do you research?" she asked.

"All kinds of things," said Greg and the room at his end of the table had gone quiet seemingly intrigued by the possibilities.

"Forensic science is my speciality," he said, hoping that it would satisfy the inquisitor.

Chapman must have been eavesdropping and butted in.

"That sounds interesting, where did you do your research?"

"The States," replied Greg, hoping that would kill it.

"Whereabouts?" asked Chapman whose wife had also taken an interest.

"New York," said Greg.

"Really, that's interesting", said Izzy. "Were you attached to the police department? I love that CSI programme, have you seen it?"

"No, I was on attachment to Pace University."

Greg was struggling but remembered a student from Pace being attached to his department at Leeds. His memory from that era was now practically intact despite all the medical interventions and counselling of the last six years.

Everyone seemed satisfied and Chapman changed the story. "So, Peter tells me that you want to place your grandmother in the Pines.

"Yes, if I can, he's told me about the waiting list."

"Oh, I'm sure we can accommodate her," he said. "I understand she has a sizeable property."

"Yes," said Greg.

"Do you know what she intends to do with it?" asked Chapman.

This was more like it and Greg was now on familiar ground.

"Well, it will need to be sold. It's much too large for me and I want to buy my own place."

"And some land as well, Peter tells me," said Chapman as a statement.

"Yes, about ten acres I think."

"And this is in, Loxley?" asked Chapman.

"Yes," said Greg.

"I was trying to place it, we used to live not far away in Oughtibridge. I was a member at Glenborough Golf Club which backs onto the common."

"It's on the other side not far from the dams," he said, hoping to head off a potential disaster. He couldn't afford to be caught in a lie.

Izzy came to the rescue.

"And is there a lady on the scene?" she asked.

"I haven't had a lot of time for socialising since I got back," he said, dodging the question, hoping that it would close off that line of enquiry.

Chapman was keen to get back to business.

"When were you thinking of moving things forward?"

"Well as I said to Peter, I'm trying to persuade my grandmother she should move, but it's not easy, she's lived there most of her life and is very reluctant to leave but she seemed to like the brochure. What I was thinking was, if someone would let me know when there's a vacancy I would arrange for her to have a look around."

Greg realised too late that this might have been a step too far.

"Why don't you bring her over next week, I'm sure Peter would be delighted to show her around?" Chapman said as quick as a flash.

"Yes, I'll ask her," said Greg.

Chapman called out to Peter who was in conversation with

another guest at the other end of the table.

"Peter, I suggested Greg brings his grandmother over next week, have look at the Pines. What do you think?"

Dacombe looked up and across at Greg. "Of course, anytime, just give me a ring."

"So, what do you do?" Greg asked Chapman.

"I'm a solicitor… in town," Chapman replied.

Greg hadn't made himself clear.

"No, I'm sorry, I mean with the properties. How does it work?"

"Well, we have a number of options. Where possible we buy the property, convert it or renovate depending on planning and potential market and then sell it on."

"Seems to pay well," said Greg and smiled for the first time. He realised he might be coming across too defensive and he would get nowhere if he didn't build up some rapport, however distasteful he found it.

"Yes," said Chapman. "It does."

"What about the banking crisis. Isn't that going to affect property prices?" asked Greg, trying to imply some knowledge of the present economic situation.

"Possibly, in the short term, and it may have a bearing on funding if the banks start pulling back on property lending."

"So, you may be open to an investor?" asked Greg.

Chapman leant forward; he was listening intently, as if a beam of light had struck an antenna.

"Quite possibly, we have a couple of projects under consideration at the moment. Look, I suggest when we've finished eating we can chat to Peter, somewhere more private."

"Great," said Greg and helped himself to a bowl of fruit salad which the fresh-faced Franciscka had brought in.

Just then he felt a hand on his inner thigh, which understandably made him jump. He looked around and Pippa was looking at him in what could be described as a wanton way. Greg nearly swallowed a grape that he had just spooned into his mouth and wasn't sure how to handle this. The hand moved ever upwards and rested on his crotch. She smiled at him as her fingers rubbed his trousers and was starting to have an obvious effect.

The dilemma facing Greg was that he had no intention of pursuing her advances but at the same time didn't want to cause any possible scene by rejecting his new admirer – a woman scorned and all that. He took a risk and leaned over to her, but before he could speak she took the initiative.

"We could go upstairs," she whispered. "Nobody would mind."

"I'm gay," he said, "sorry."

This statement had a dramatic effect. Pippa swiftly removed her hand and stormed out of the room with a face like thunder, the chair tipping backwards onto the floor.

"What's wrong with Pippa?" asked Izzy.

"I think something disagreed with her," said Greg.

"I'll go and see if she's alright," said Izzy.

"I'm sure she'll be fine in a moment," said Greg and Izzy stayed put, not wishing to miss any of the gossip.

The chat continued for a while and then coffee and brandies were served.

"I'll join you in a moment, just going outside for a smoke," said Dacombe, as the guests started to vacate the dining room and disperse elsewhere. Chapman suggested that he and Greg adjourn to the study; Peter's 'den', he called it.

"Be back in a couple of minutes," said Dacombe and left the room.

Greg passed on the brandies. "Driving later," he explained.

It was clear that both Chapman and Dacombe had consumed liberally and were showing early signs of inebriation.

Loud music sounded from another room towards the back of the house. There was no sign of the ever-ready Pippa.

"There'll be some dancing later," said Chapman, as he took his brandy and led Greg into an adjoining room.

There were two substantial workstations with computers, printers, a fax machine, telephones and several filing cabinets, a large TV monitor and, by the window, an 'executive' table with two chairs. There was a settee in the middle of the room facing the TV with a small coffee-table in front. Greg and Chapman sat on the settee with Greg trying to be as far away from him as possible but within suitable hearing range.

Greg took a sip of his coffee before getting up from the settee; he found it difficult to keep still.

"Just popping to the men's room," he said.

As he was walking back from the toilet, Barbara was coming out of the kitchen and nearly collided with him. She grabbed his arm to stop herself falling over.

"Oh, you're a strong boy," she said, as he steadied her. The alcohol had certainly been flowing in her direction.

Just then Dacombe appeared through the front door and saw Greg with his wife who was holding onto him for balance.

"Never know when to stop, do you darling?" he said, with an edge to his voice.

Greg quickly went to her defence. "No... it was an accident, I bumped into her."

"Wish somebody would," he said, under his breath but loud enough for Greg to hear.

Another piece of research which would be stored.

"Anyway, Pippa's gone home," he said to his wife. "Says she's got a head-ache."

"That's a pity we thought Greg might enjoy her company," said Barbara, looking at Greg in a knowing sort of way.

Greg thought about that comment for a moment. Was he

being set up; a honey trap, perhaps? Still, he was not unhappy with the outcome; he would let it go for now.

Dacombe followed Greg into the study. Greg sat back down on the settee, again on the opposite end to Chapman. Dacombe opened the drawer to his desk on his workstation and dropped in a packet of King Edward cigars.

"Those will be the death of you, you know," said Chapman, and Dacombe deliberately ignored the comment.

"Do you play any sport at all, Greg?" asked Chapman, as Dacombe pulled up a chair opposite them. He put a glass of brandy down on the coffee table.

"I used to play squash at college but haven't played for a while."

"Really, we must have a game sometime; I'm a member at Abbey Fields."

Greg knew the club; it was quite expensive and used to have a reputation for being very selective in its membership.

"I play Monday's; Wednesday's and most weekends... maybe we can arrange a friendly sometime. I can get you a membership if you'd like."

"Thanks," said Greg. "That would be great."

Chapman spoke to Dacombe. "Greg was telling me he may have some capital to invest."

"Is that right?" asked Dacombe.

"For the right project," said Greg. "The return from equities isn't what it was. I've already taken a hit on Northern Rock and moved my assets out of financials. So yes, I do have some money on fixed term at the moment which I would consider putting up for an appropriate reward."

Greg had studied the financial press avidly since his return to the house; he did, after all, have some substantial assets being managed by Cathcart and was well aware of the present vagaries of the Stock Market.

Greg had established that Chapman was the brains of the organisation. Dacombe was very much a junior partner but obviously had the connections in construction and the property market. A good business combination.

Chapman looked at Dacombe and Chapman went first.

"Well, as I said earlier, we do have a couple of projects on the go. The first is over in Eccleshall, a large house which we are converting into flats but that one is nearing completion."

"Should realise half-a-million profit when it's finished, said Dacombe without a hint of boasting, just matter-of-fact. Greg looked impressed, which frankly, he was.

"The other one is more interesting; a bit of a story to it," said Chapman, pouring another glass from a bottle of Remy Martin. They were both singing like larks, thought Greg.

Dacombe intervened. "Yes, there's a big house near the Pines which we have been trying to get our hands on for some time, called Taskers End."

Greg was drinking mineral water and nearly spurted a mouthful on the floor. He quickly regained his composure.

"Go on," said Greg.

Dacombe looked at Chapman possibly for re-assurance. Chapman took over.

"We had a go about two or three years ago, an elderly couple owned it, lived in it just by themselves. Peter went around to see them and offered them a small fortune, but they wouldn't budge, despite a lot of encouragement."

Chapman cast a glance at Dacombe who appeared to, not smile exactly, more a smirk. "Said they were keeping it in the family."

"What happened?" asked Greg.

"There was a fire and they both died," said Dacombe.

Greg watched closely to see if there was any give away signs and he thought he noticed a look between them but if there was, it was very brief; he could have been mistaken.

"So, we thought, great we can buy it, but it turns out that the property was willed to a relative, a grandson, who just happened to be locked away in some loony-bin somewhere."

"What did you do?" asked Greg, trying desperately not to display outwardly the emotion he was feeling.

"We tried to buy it, as I said, made a good offer but in the end the solicitor who holds the Power of Attorney refused to sell, said he wanted to wait until the proper owner was fit enough to make the decision."

"What happened?" asked Greg.

"The property's been let, but a couple of weeks' ago we heard that the tenants had left and someone else has moved in. We haven't been able to find out who it is yet, but we have someone working on that."

"In fact, he's working on it tonight," said Dacombe, who flashed a knowing look at Chapman who grinned.

This had Greg extremely worried.

"What do you mean?" said Greg, anxiously. He could feel Gerald becoming interested.

Dacombe and Chapman just looked at each other.

"Well, we've got someone who works for us that sort of fixes things, and I've asked him if he can find out who's living there, that's all, just a recce around."

Against all his instincts Greg needed to find out more, but he was desperate to get home to Maureen.

"How likely is this deal...? Only, I wouldn't want to miss out."

"Well, that depends. First, we need to find out who's living there and, who knows? If it's the nutter returned, he might be willing to sell; we'll just have to see," said Chapman.

"How much are we talking about?" asked Dacombe. "Do you have to invest," he clarified.

"Well, I've got two-hundred-and-fifty k on overnight deposit on the money market, so I could definitely use that, but I could probably get another hundred k reasonable quickly, the remainder is in long term bonds and the penalties would not make withdrawal worthwhile."

"Remainder?" said Chapman. "You never know it could be very worthwhile..." and he looked at Dacombe and smiled.

Just then Greg's mobile rang. It was just turned eleven.

"Excuse me, sorry, I need to take this," he said, and walked out of the room for more privacy.

It was Maureen in a very distressed state.

"Greg, please get back here there's someone outside trying to get in. I'm so scared," then the phone went dead.

Greg was in panic mode. He went back into the study and addressed the business partners.

"Look, I am so sorry, but I have to get back; that was my grandmother, she's had a fall and can't get up. I hope you'll excuse me."

"Of course," said Dacombe standing up albeit rather unsteadily. "I've got your number and I'll call you as soon as we have more information."

Chapman also got to his feet rather gingerly.

"Nice to have met you Greg. I hope to have some information for you very soon."

"Thanks," said Greg and headed for the front door.

Barbara came out from the kitchen with Izzy who had been helping to tidy up while the men talked business.

"Going so soon Greg? We hoped you'd stay a bit longer we have all sorts of entertainment," she said with a strange look.

"Thank you, you have been very hospitable," said Greg, "but my grandmother's had a fall and I need to get back."

"Oh dear, I hope she's alright," said Izzy, seemingly sincere.

"Thank you," he said, shaking hands with everyone and left.

He got to the Audi and floored it; the roaring engine causing more agitation to the horses.

He rang Maureen from the car, but the call went direct to answer phone. Greg was really worried now.

Chapter Sixteen

Earlier at Taskers End, the evening had started very much as Maureen had planned.

She'd had a light dinner and then luxuriated in a long bath. She loved the bathroom it was probably her favourite room in the house and the whirlpool bath was something she could only have imagined owning. She had tried one once before on holiday some years ago and she was hooked; the height of pampering.

As she lay there relaxing in the soothing bubbles she took stock of where she was in terms of her relationship with Greg. She thought of previous lovers, not that there had been that many, and then her relationship with Chapman. How she regretted that now; the very thought made her skin crawl. She was not sure how she would be on Monday; she was already feeling anxious, but she tried to put it to one side. She trusted Greg implicitly and he said it would be alright.

In Greg, she was beginning to think that she had really found 'the one'. From the moment he walked into the office that Friday, looking a little lost, she wanted to get to know him. Then the jacket potato lunch at Spudmania; she couldn't help flirting with him. She had no idea what made her call at the hotel that evening. She winced at the thought; it had been the most outrageous thing she'd ever done in her life, and the most exciting.

No-one had ever made her feel the way he had, and she couldn't believe her luck, particularly as he seemed so unattached. There was always baggage, emotional baggage, from some failed marriage or past broken heart, but Greg seemed totally free of all that. When she admitted her affair with Chapman, some men would have been wracked by jealousy, but Greg seemed to just, deal with it. She loved his pragmatism. He was sensitive and a great lover with a streak of vulnerability which made her want to protect him. But he could be strong too; she felt safe with him.

It had happened so quickly, but the signs were good. She was a little concerned over his driving obsession to get justice for his grandparents. There had been times when it seemed all consuming and she had felt pushed aside. On the other hand it was understandable that he would want some remedy for his grandparents' deaths, anyone would.

As she lay there she felt warm and content it was as though the house had welcomed her into the fold and was looking after her till Greg got home. She did not feel in the slightest bit nervous... alone in such a big and secluded house.

After her bath she wrapped a bathrobe round her and went to the bedroom. There was another surprise coming Greg's way later. It was in the other shopping bag that she had bought back the previous day. She opened up the carrier and took out the most exquisite and delicate lingerie. She modelled it in the mirror and knew Greg would love it. She couldn't wait.

She put her bathrobe over the underwear and headed down the stairs. She'd left the TV on in the lounge and went to the kitchen and poured herself a glass of red wine. She looked out of the window. It was gone eight o'clock and quite dark; thick clouds had now obscured the waning moon. She could see the outline of the trees against the red-glow reflection of the distant city lights; a strong breeze had got up and they were swaying vigorously, creating a vision like rolling waves.

She returned to the lounge, closed the curtains and made herself comfortable. She flicked through the channels to find a film; she fancied a real girly one, maybe one that would make her cry, she didn't mind, Greg would make it better when he came back and then she would make him feel better! She smiled at the thought; it was making her tingle inside.

The film failed to keep her attention and in no time at all she had begun to doze. It was about ten-thirty when something woke her. It was only fleeting, but she thought she had caught a glimpse of the security light, a brief flash; more of an awareness really. No concern, it had happened before, foxes or even deer made excursions through the grounds of Taskers End. She was only half awake and could have imagined it but suddenly her impulses were on high alert.

She got up from the sofa, went to the window and opened the curtains to look out. It was very dark, nothing. The TV theme to Match of The Day echoed around the room and she went and switched channels having recovered from her momentary alarm.

She found the remote control on the settee and scrolled through the menu to another channel and then suddenly…

click.

She nearly jumped out of her skin; she'd been suddenly pitched into another world; a scary world. The darkness was total, as if she had been rendered blind. The lights had gone out… the TV was off… the power completely gone. Things we take for granted; they should always be there.

"That's all I need," she thought, and sat on the sofa waiting for the electricity to be restored. It won't be long, she told herself.

But it was long; it seemed so. The house had come alive; creaking, swirling noises; the tap, tap, tap of branches on roof tiles, a groan from the lone beech in the corner of the drive as it took the strain of the weight of its remaining leaves. Pit, pat, pit pat, the slow relentless sound of the start of a rain shower and then building faster and faster until it merged into one long crescendo. In the dark, black room it seemed like the roar of an express train. Another noise made Maureen jump but it was only a dustbin lid, lifted from its rightful place and now careering helplessly round the drive.

She sat there in the dark, the house had suddenly become a frightening place as if it had somehow decided she was some sort of threat, an interloper, she didn't belong. She told herself not to be silly... it's just a power cut... they happen, don't they? She wasn't going to just sit there and succumb to the fear.

Then she remembered... there was a torch, of course, there's a torch; Greg had used it to go down to the scullery.

She got up from the sofa and very slowly edged her way from the lounge, her eyes now more accustomed to the gloom and into the kitchen. She moved to each kitchen cupboard in turn, squinting to try to improve her vision. Unable to make out anything at the back of the cupboard, she put her hands deep inside and felt around searching for the plastic shape of what would be her light source.

Tins of food were knocked over; she banged her head backing out of the second cupboard causing a sharp pain. "Shit," she shouted. Then she reached the kitchen sink. It was slightly brighter on this side of the room; the ambient light from the garden had moved the luminosity up a couple of notches. She opened the cupboard underneath and felt around inside. She touched something plastic, the right shape; it was right in front of her. She took it out and switched it on and exhaled as the welcoming beam of light danced around the room.

She was about to close the cupboard door when she noticed something else right at the back behind the sink's drain pipe which she thought may come in handy. She reached in and pulled out a packet of candles; the short, stubby kind, not the long white ones you get in churches. She looked at the container which was covered in a cellophane wrapper. A box of six, the covering had been split in one corner, one had been used. She sniffed the box, a strong hint of vanilla. Must have been left by the previous tenants, she couldn't imagine Greg using scented candles, she smiled at the thought.

She read the label. "Relaxing, soothing, aids sleep; best before Jan 06". She put them back where she had found them for now, the torch would do. She knew where they were.

She was drawn through the utility room to the back door, illogically to see if there was any indication of the cause of the lack of power and moved towards it... and then... froze... she gasped for air; then uttered a shriek, one of fright. A face appeared at the window... looking in. The beam of the torch hit the apparition at an angle and gave it a long ghostly look like Munch's iconic picture, 'The Scream'.

The normal reaction to a sense of danger is fight or flight where the body's survival mechanism cuts in, but there is another, more extreme phenomenon called 'freeze' where the brain effectively shuts down. It can have fatal consequences as evidenced by road-kill; the rabbit in the headlights syndrome. Maureen was there.

Fortunately, the paralysis was temporary; Maureen dropped the torch and it hit the ground with a crash, extinguishing the light. Darkness resumed.

The face quickly vanished. Maureen knelt down and fumbled around on the floor feeling with her trembling hands looking for the light-source. She found bits of broken glass and the large PP9 battery, then the outer casing. She stood up shaking and slowly made her way out of the kitchen and back into the lounge. She banged her leg on the side of the coffee table and cursed again.

"Phone, must find my phone."

She had put it by her, so she could answer it when Greg called; must be on the sofa somewhere. She felt around in the black, her eyes still not attuned to the dimness. She swept her hand right the way across the seat... nothing. She slid her hand down between the seats and the back still nothing. She stopped for a second... a noise... then quiet. Her heart was almost bursting, and she was beginning to panic. Further random sweeps of the sofa failed to reveal her phone.

She stood up and turned around and knocked into the coffee table again, this time she heard the sound of breaking glass as her wineglass hit the floor. "Shit," she said again and got down on her hands and knees to pick up the broken pieces. For all that she could see she might as well have her eyes closed.

There was a damp patch on the carpet which warranted another expletive and then suddenly the familiar oblong shape... her phone. It was wet from the wine; she picked it up and instinctively blew on it then wiped it down her bathrobe. She pressed the on button and the screen illuminated, she breathed a sigh of relief.

She tried to visualise the configuration of the numbers and moved her index finger across the key pad as if she were reading Braille. The bottom row of three, the middle... press. A zero appeared on the display; then the next row up; left ... press. A seven appeared. She could feel liquid dropping down her hand. She completed the eleven numbers... call. She heard the comforting outgoing ringtone and then Greg's voice. She shouted into the phone

"Greg, please get back here there's someone trying to get in. I'm so scared." She was still speaking when she realised Greg wasn't replying; the screen was dead. She switched off the phone and switched it back on again... nothing... dead as the grave; an unfortunate figure of speech.

"Had he heard it? Had he heard the message?" was all Maureen could think. She got on the settee and curled up into a ball. "Go away... go away," she said.

The only noises were the rustling of the trees and the dustbin lid which continued to roll unfettered around the drive.

She stayed like that for what seemed a lifetime and then

suddenly the room was bathed in a powerful light.

Maureen looked up. "Greg," she shouted.

She slowly made her way out of the lounge, her eyes once more adjusted to the dark and edged her way to the front door. She waited until she heard the key in the lock and then slowly turn. The door opened.

"Greg... Greg," she shouted and flung her arms around him and held on.

"It's ok, it's ok... I'm here now... everything's going to be fine."

"There was someone at the window... There was someone at the window," she sobbed.

"It's ok," he said again, "I'll sort it," and she gradually let go. Greg shut the front door.

"I'll get the torch,"

"It's broken," she said, "I dropped it."

"Ok, ok, don't worry. I think there're some matches in the drawer in the kitchen. Wait here."

He spoke with authority and calmness. He was much more familiar with the house than Maureen and moved easily to the kitchen and the drawer containing the matches.

He came out of the kitchen and next to the door to the scullery there was another small door under the stairs which Greg opened. Maureen had managed to join him; she didn't want to leave his side.

"The circuit board and fuses are in here."

He lit a match and checked the board.

"There's the problem... ouch," he said, as the flame reached his fingers. He dropped the dead match.

"Here, can you light another one for me," he said, and passed the box of matches to her. Her trembling hands made heavy weather of opening the box and extracting a match. She managed to strike another, her hands still shaking uncontrollably. Greg looked across the row of switches. All except one was facing downwards.

"That's the one," and he switched the erring connector down and immediately the house came back to life.

The TV droned from the lounge.

"Oh Greg, I've been so scared... the face at the window... it was awful. It looked like a ghost."

"It's ok now; it's ok... What's this on your bathrobe?"

"Red wine," she said.

"Thank goodness, for a minute I thought it was blood."

"I think I might have made a mess on the carpet," and they headed back to the lounge and started clearing the broken wineglass and sponging the spilt red wine with some stain remover.

"I'm going to check round outside. I won't be a minute," he said.

Maureen looked up at him. "Be careful."

Greg got outside; it had stopped raining. He noticed the dustbin lid which had come to rest against the wall of the garage. He picked it up and put it back on top of the dustbin. He went to the pile of large stones in the corner of the drive, chose one and rested it on top of the dustbin.

He looked around trying to work out how they managed to cut the electricity; must have shorted it somewhere, he thought, but he would have to investigate further in daylight when he could see properly.

He went right around the house, which of course was now bathed in brightness from the security lights. He soon discovered footsteps in the mud all around the outside which would probably belong to the unwanted visitor who had frightened Maureen.

"If I find out who it was, I'll kill him," he said to himself, and he could feel the strength of his anger swelling inside.

Gerald had woken up. Aware of the feelings, Greg refocused and managed to return his adversary over the firewall.

Back indoors, the cleaning activity had helped Maureen and she was much calmer. Greg gave her that feeling of security you get in a close relationship.

Greg went to the kitchen where Maureen was clearing up the broken torch.

"Don't worry, I'll get a new one tomorrow," he said, and told her of the footprints.

He went to the wine rack and took another bottle of red wine.

"Come on," he said, "I feel like getting smashed," an inappropriate syntax, and he picked up two wine glasses from the kitchen cabinet and led Maureen back into the lounge.

"I think I'll join you," she said, and she snuggled up to him on the settee with a late film on TV.

Over two more glasses of wine Greg told Maureen all about his evening, except the incident with the eager Pippa.

Maureen was intrigued.

"And I reckon it was their man you saw at the window. Dacombe said someone was doing a recce tonight. They want to know who's moved in, so they can try to buy the house again.".

The wine and closeness were beginning to have the right effect and Maureen looked at Greg and, sensing the time was right, made an announcement. "I bought you a present."

"Great," he said. "What is it?"

"She dropped the bathrobe off her shoulders and stood up.

"This," she said, and Greg's eyes feasted on her amazing body encased in the diaphanous lingerie.

"Wow... you look amazing," was all he could say.

After the exploits of the previous night, they slept in till almost ten o'clock before Greg got up and made Maureen breakfast, a traditional English which he took up to her on a tray. The Sunday paper had been delivered and they spent the next half an hour reading the news and gossip.

About eleven-thirty, Greg was dressed and reading the colour supplement in the lounge when his phone rang.

"Greg...? Peter Dacombe."

Greg felt his stomach churn.

"Hope you enjoyed yourself last night. It was a shame you had to leave so early there was some interesting entertainment afterwards which we know you would have enjoyed."

He didn't embellish. "How's your grandmother by the way," he added as an afterthought.

"Eh? Oh... She's ok, thank you..." said Greg quickly adjusting to the situation. "And thanks again for the hospitality last night."

"That's fine, you must come again," he said. "I thought I would give you a quick call about the project we discussed."

"Go on," said Greg.

"Well, one of my lads had a look around the house last night, like I said, and someone's definitely moved in. There's certainly a woman there but we don't have any details yet; as soon as we know more I'll be in touch. If we can get the owner onside, then we could be looking at mega bucks."

"Thanks for letting me know," said Greg and rang off.

"'Owner onside'...? What sort of language is that?" he thought.

Greg went to find Maureen who was in the shower and he told her of the conversation.

"So, it was one of Dacombe's heavies that frightened you last night. Just having a look around."

This did little to reassure her.

After her shower, Maureen joined Greg in the lounge.

"I don't know whether you can do anything about this," she said, as she handed him her dead phone.

"Let me have a look," and he took it from her and slid off the back casing.

"It looks like the wine's got inside through the keys. We could try drying it out but it's not like water, it'll be sticky, so it still might not work."

He got up and went to the kitchen, Maureen followed him, and Greg was rummaging in his special drawer with his bits and pieces to see if he could find anything that might revive the ailing mobile.

"I need to go around to my Dad's this morning. Just to check if he's ok. I shouldn't be long."

"That's fine... I'll pop to the Phone Shop in the precinct to see if I can get yours fixed... I also want to have a closer look around the house; see if I can find how they cut the power."

He looked at her. "I'm going to have to upgrade the security system as well... I'll get some CCTV cameras fitted. I'll do some ringing around tomorrow.".

After Maureen had left, Greg went outside to have a more thorough look around, but there was nothing obvious he could see, and he was at a loss to understand how they had tripped the power. Then he noticed the box on the wall that contained the gas and electricity meters. There would be a special key to open it which the utility companies used. He looked closely at the hole where the key would go and noticed a recent scratch as if someone was trying to get into it in a hurry and missed with the first attempt. Greg smiled at his powers of logic; his forensic mind had not deserted him.

It still didn't answer the question of how they had cut the power or why; but then it occurred to him that they would need to shut off the security lights to avoid detection. As for the how, he didn't know exactly. He knew that there was a way of tampering with junction boxes that would enable someone to access other people's electricity. Maybe they had a gadget that was able to short circuit from the mains. He would never know, and it would remain a mystery.

Greg realised there was nothing more he could do to further secure the house for the moment, so decided to pop to the retail park to try to salvage Maureen's phone. He entered the Phone Shop and went to the sales counter and was immediately confronted by a spotty youth called 'Jamie', according to his name badge. Greg watched as the geeky assistant took the back off stared inside before declaring it was not worth the cost of repair and that various packages were available, including today's limited offer, etc., etc." Greg was not interested and decided to buy Maureen a new handset. He would swap the SIM card and, hey presto, she would be incommunicado no longer.

Meanwhile Maureen had arrived at her father's house in Dore, a large detached modern property set back from the road in keeping with this salubrious suburb. The gates of the short drive were open, and she parked outside the front door. Her father's BMW and stepmother's Golf were in front of the double garage and, judging by the soapy residue on the drive around them, both had recently been cleaned.

Her father opened the door before she had chance to ring the bell alerted by the sound of the Mini pulling up.

They embraced warmly.

"Come in... come in," said Mr Brown.

He was dressed in his Sunday best, a sloppy rugby shirt and jeans, a long way from his normal business attire. Her stepmother joined him, and they exchanged greetings.

"Would you like a coffee?" asked Katie, similarly dressed in jeans and casual top.

As her stepmother went to the kitchen Maureen followed

her father into the living room and made herself comfortable. It was a lovely house, but not one she could call home; she had never lived there. Her father had sold the original family home in Totley when he married Katie.

Maureen could sense the contentment and was pleased for them; she would never begrudge her father his happiness. He had selflessly looked after her following her mother's desertion. They had been difficult times coming right in the middle of her teenage years and all the angst that went along with them, but he had always treated her in an adult way and guided her through her years at sixth form and financed her University education. She owed him a great deal.

As for Katie, she saw her more of a sister than a stepmother. They regularly discussed fashion and had a similar interest in music; they had even talked about going to some concerts together.

Her father sat down in his armchair and wanted an update on her new man. Maureen had told him of her relationship with Greg in one of her regular phone calls; but not that she had moved in. She was concerned that he would think it a bit soon.

"You must bring him around for Sunday lunch next week, I would like to meet him," said her father.

Maureen agreed, "I'll ask him and ring you."

Katie brought in the coffees and sat and on the second armchair and the three engaged in conversation for the next hour.

It was nearly two o'clock before Maureen eventually left, having accepted the offer of a sandwich. Still anxious from last night's scare, as she pulled out of the drive and into the tree lined avenue, she checked to see if any cars were parked nearby. Coast clear, she eased along the street and out towards her flat, she wanted to pick up some more bits and pieces and the rest of her clothes. She had made another decision; having seen the closeness of her father and stepmother, she wanted to make the domestic arrangements with Greg permanent; if he would have her; she had no doubts in that direction.

It was only a brief diversion to her flat and she was no more than fifteen minutes collecting the stuff she wanted. After loading up her gear, she got in the Mini and pulled away from the parking bay in front of the parade of shops. Out of the thirty-mile-an-hour zone, she eased the car up the gears; forty, forty-five. After half a mile, the "T" junction loomed ahead, and Maureen instinctively applied the brake... her foot went straight to the floor, she tried again ...nothing and the car was going too fast. Hand brake... nothing. Quick thinking, she crashed the gears into third and then second but still too fast. The 'STOP' line was approaching... too quickly, too quickly; more frantic pedal pushing, still to no effect. Nothing she could do now and at twenty-five miles an hour she jumped the junction.

She held her breath; but fortune was with her and the road was clear. The hedge and sign-post on the other side of the road however were directly ahead of her and approaching very fast. She swung the steering wheel hard left instinctively to avoid them. Luckily the manoeuvre was not enough to roll the car, and it had slowed down, but she was now on the wrong side of the road facing the oncoming traffic and this time another car was coming... heading straight for her. Headlights flashed. She turned the steering wheel to the right missing the oncoming vehicle by a fraction. The Mini bounced onto the grass verge, and the upward slope mercifully did the rest and it came to a stop.

She opened the car door shaking like a leaf, her legs barely able to hold her weight. The opposing car had stopped a little further down the road and the driver got out to remonstrate with her.

"What the hell do you think you were doing?" the irate driver said, as he approached her; at which point Maureen who was steadying herself against the car, burst into tears.

"My brakes... my brakes," she sobbed.

The driver quickly calmed down seeing Maureen in obvious distress.

"Are you ok?"

"Yes... j... just a bit... sh... shaken."

"Do you want me to call someone for you?" he said chivalrously.

"Yes... yes p... please," she sobbed.

The driver took out his mobile and Maureen gave him Greg's number.

Greg was in the kitchen making a drink when the call came through. The driver had passed the phone to her.

"Greg... the car... my brakes..."

"Whatever's the matter?" asked Greg and Maureen managed to describe what had happened.

"Where are you?" She told him.

"Wait there." Which was a bit of an unnecessary statement given the circumstances, "I'll be there as soon as I can."

Maureen had given Greg directions and he raced out of the drive throwing up a spray of gravel which rattled against the wall of the house.

He arrived at the scene in about twenty minutes and the white knight had stayed with Maureen who was now much calmer.

Greg parked just in front of the Mini with his hazard lights flashing to warn other approaching vehicles. He thanked the man who had helped, and he gave Greg a business card. "In case you need a witness," he said, and he drove away.

Greg had a look under the car. Given it was low on the ground; it was difficult to tell what was wrong. He took the jack from the boot of the Audi and raised the car sufficiently to get his head underneath and have a look round.

Then his worst fears were realised.

"It looks like your brake lines have been cut."

He got from under the car.

"If I find out who did this... I'll fucking kill them," he exclaimed.

The vehemence in his voice shook Maureen. It was her first view of Gerald.

Greg quickly regained control. "We will need to get this into a garage," and he rang the breakdown company that was advertised on the reverse of Maureen's tax disc.

Maureen sat with Greg in the Audi and there was a silence for a while as she took in what had happened. She was in shock. Greg tried to calm her and gradually she recovered.

"How did they manage to do it?" she asked. "I wasn't very long."

Greg had had the same thought. "They must have been waiting. It wouldn't have taken long if they knew what they were doing... probably used a trolley jack. But in broad daylight... they've certainly got some nerve. Chapman must be paying them well."

It took an hour for the breakdown truck to arrive and winch the Mini onto the back. They had taken out the clothes and stuff and transferred it to the Audi. The truck would take the car to a local Mini garage, not far from the retail park and Maureen would phone Monday to find out the extent of the damage.

It was nearly five o'clock by the time they pulled into the drive at Taskers End in Greg's Audi and they went into the house. A few minutes later, Maureen reappeared with Greg to help her carry the rest of the stuff from the back seat.

They wouldn't see the zoom lens or hear the distant click, click, click of a camera motor-drive firing at seven frames a second; the neighbouring trees still sufficiently luxuriant to offer some cover despite last night's strong winds.

Back in the house, Greg made them both a coffee while Maureen described her time with her father and gave more detail of her ordeal. Greg was still wild with anger, but it was under control... it wouldn't take much however to have Gerald back over the wall.

Greg battled to retain his own composure. He was convinced it was Chapman, or one of his people and Maureen was also coming round to that way of thinking. "It wouldn't be Baker..." said Greg, "Chapman must have got someone else to do his dirty work. Whoever it was must have been staking out the flat again."

Greg had some serious thinking to do.

Later, when emotions had eased, Greg presented her with her new phone which he had charged up and took great delight in showing her the various features. She would soon get used to them, he had said.

An unheard phone call went from the woods; there was just enough signal.

"It's Les... I've got the pictures... yeah; I'll send them through to you in the morning. Yeah... will do."

Chapter Seventeen

Monday 8th October, and a day that would have significant consequences for everyone connected with Taskers End.

With the Mini being repaired in the garage, Greg offered to take Maureen to the office and they left the house just as Queenie was arriving to start work. The previous evening Maureen had told Greg of her intention to make the domestic arrangements permanent and he was thrilled.

"I'll speak to the Estate Agents later and give in my notice," she said. That call would never be made.

As they crawled through the rush hour traffic, Greg phoned the garage from the car to check the Mini's status and how long it would take to fix it. He was told that the car was on the ramp and they were in luck, they could replace the brake lines and the car would be ready by late afternoon. They confirmed the pipes had been severed deliberately and suggested that Greg called the police.

He looked at Maureen who shook her head. Greg passed on the message and asked if they could drop the car back to the Cathcart Rivers office... he would make it worth their while, and they agreed.

"As long as we don't hit any snags," was the usual proviso.

In the office, Cathcart had been in since seven, in fact he had spent most of the weekend there going through the accounts for the last four years; something that he had relied on others to do. He had Sam's two registers and as Greg had suggested they were an accurate reflection of the computer records, an exact copy in fact.

Cathcart Rivers was a small but very profitable practice. Arthur Cathcart specialised in contract law had acquired a number of high visibility clients, with the occasional family law remits; sorting out expensive divorce settlements to some of the rich and famous had been particularly lucrative. He would also take on the occasional criminal law case if one of his clients had got into trouble for instance. He had managed to get more than one of his 'celebrities' off a drink-drive charge on a technicality. His fees were substantial, and for that the client got peace of mind. It was this that was driving Cathcart in the direction he was about to go.

His partner specialised in property law which is where his connection with Dacombe had come about. He would negotiate and arrange deals but was not involved with the laborious paper chase that this line of work entailed; all conveyance work was outsourced to a specialist company. Again, Chapman had a number of well-established clients including many corporate customers where the serious money was earned.

Maureen arrived at her desk just before nine and made Cathcart a coffee; she assumed she would be continuing her new role as his assistant.

"Ah, Miss Brown, thank you," he said, interrupting himself as she handed him his coffee. "I want you to do something for me, in complete confidence you understand."

"Of course," she said.

"I want you to switch all incoming calls on Mr Chapman's phone to this one," he said pointing to the one on his desk. "And can you cancel all his appointments. He and I will be in conference for most of the day."

Maureen was intrigued; something was definitely happening. She couldn't wait to ring Greg.

"Anything else?" she said.

"Again, in confidence, there are going to be a few changes around here and, as the senior assistant, I will be relying on you a great deal. I have asked Joan not to come in today. I don't want anyone covering anything up."

"I'm not sure what you mean," said Maureen.

Cathcart did not expand. He continued, "I want you to look after any calls and enquiries today. If anyone wants to speak to Mr Chapman tell them he has taken another day's leave... is that clear?"

"Yes of course, anything I can do, you just have to say."

"I know that, which is why you are still here," said Cathcart abstrusely.

Maureen was on reception and on high alert dreading Chapman's return. A few minutes later sure enough the front door opened, and he walked in. She immediately ducked down and dashed into the back-office to avoid him. She listened anxiously as he ambled down the corridor and up the creaking wooden staircase and unlocked his office door. She returned to the reception desk and took a call.

Moments later Cathcart strode purposefully past her without making any eye contact and up the stairs towards Chapman's office carrying the two registers. His footsteps were heavy on the floorboards and echoed across the downstairs reception.

Maureen took her new phone from her bag and speed-dialled Greg. He had showed her how to use the facility the previous day. He thought that would be useful, particularly in emergencies.

"Hi... it's me... something's definitely happening. Cathcart's cancelled all David's appointments and phone calls... no I have no idea... I'll ring you later," she quickly put her phone back into her bag feeling like a naughty schoolgirl.

What Maureen could not hear was Cathcart's conversation with Chapman which would have considerable repercussions.

Before Chapman had a chance to take off his coat Cathcart had opened the door and walked in.

"Arthur?" Chapman said in surprise. "To what do I owe this pleasure?" he said, which sounded sarcastic.

Chapman took off his jacket and put it over one of the chairs and went to his desk and started unlocking the drawers.

"Hope this won't take long. I'll have a mountain of emails to clear this morning," he said, dismissively. He continued to rummage around his drawers retrieving files and putting his laptop on his desk as though his visitor wasn't there.

"I intend to relieve you of that chore," he said.

Chapman looked up at him "What do you mean?"

Cathcart put the two registers on the desk and sat down opposite his partner.

"Do you know what these are?"

"I have no idea," he said.

"No, you wouldn't have, would you…? They belong to Sam Davenport, or I should say they belong to me now."

Chapman looked at Cathcart in bemusement.

"Let me explain. Sam as you know was a meticulous and thorough man, but he didn't trust computers..." Cathcart let the words resonate. "So, he kept his own records of entries passing through the office accounts... including Clients' transactions."

Chapman was starting to turn pale; he had an idea where this was going.

"I was provided with these on Friday and over the weekend I have been comparing them with the accounts and they are an exact copy. As you know, I have never got involved with the book-keeping side; unwisely I had left that to Sam and lately to Mrs Unsworth." Chapman was looking anxious.

"There are certain transactions here, which I have been following through..."

Chapman cut in, "I can explain."

"Don't interrupt," admonished Cathcart. "There is no doubt in my mind that you have been using clients' money to gamble on property deals."

"It wasn't a gamble, I only borrowed the money," said Chapman. "No-one has lost out."

"If they had, you would have been in police custody by now. But that's not the point, it's about trust and integrity and I will not have Cathcart Rivers' name besmirched in this way."

Chapman was now ashen.

"I have been giving this a lot of careful consideration and I am taking appropriate action. I am going to outline what will happen. These are not proposals... You will sever all connections with this company forthwith. You can take your clients with you; I don't want anything to do with them. I suggest you start up on your own somewhere."

He paused to let his words sink in.

"In return you will forfeit any money on your partner's account which will revert to the practice and help finance another partner."

"But that's..."

"Yes, I know, over a million pounds, but look at it this way you're still practising and there is no alternative. I will report you to the Law Society if you breech any of these conditions. Do I make myself clear?" Chapman didn't respond. "As I said, you can take your grubby clients with you, so there should be plenty of work there to enable you to start again and, if my calculations are right, you've netted over a million pounds in profits from your shady deals in any case. You can put that towards your set up costs."

A mixture of shock and anger engulfed Chapman. He didn't know what to say.

"Do you understand what I am saying?"

"Yes," said Chapman.

"You may think you've got off lightly, and, in a way, you have, but I intend to protect the integrity of Cathcart Rivers at all costs, and I cannot afford to have the scandal of a practice partner involved in any underhand dealings... I have drawn up an agreement which you will sign. I have asked Glen Darby from Havers Dennison to call in at eleven o'clock to witness it."

Cathcart was grave and assertive in his delivery, leaving Chapman in no doubt about his earnestness.

Chapman looked a beaten man, not the suave and confident solicitor who enjoyed a high profile on the local business scene.

"As I said, you can have the rest of the day to get your accounts in order. Any moneys due and not paid up to the close of business will of course come to the practice, and then you can do what you like. You can leave your laptop as well. I have asked a computer engineer to call tomorrow to wipe it clean so if you have any files to transfer I suggest you get on with it."

Chapman was trying to come to terms with what was happening.

"I need to go outside for some fresh air," he said.

"That's alright but I will take your keys. Miss Brown will let you in."

Maureen's name hit him hard. "She's behind this, I'll bet, the bitch," he said under his breath.

He walked along the corridor and past reception, too quickly for Maureen to take evasive action. He looked at her with hate in his eyes. She looked down avoiding eye contact.

"Would you come in, Miss Brown," said Cathcart who had followed Chapman.

She walked along the corridor into his office.

"Sit down, Miss Brown..." Maureen complied. "I will tell you in confidence that Mr Chapman is leaving the practice today and will not be returning. Any calls after today should be either directed to me or the caller told that he is no longer a partner here and you have no forwarding details. Is that clear?"

"Perfectly," said Maureen.

"It's going to be a difficult few weeks until I decide what we will do next. It's possible I will appoint a new partner, but I will let you know. Can you get me another coffee please?"

Cathcart had shown a great deal of leadership in a difficult situation and he had definitely gone up in Maureen's estimation.

"Of course," said Maureen.

Outside the office Chapman made a call.

"Peter? It's David... Things have gone pear-shaped this end. Cathcart's found out about the property deals... No, he just told me to leave... No, I thought he would have gone to the police as well. Something to do with protecting the integrity of the practice... I'm not sure, probably set up on my own, I think. He's said I can take my clients with me, which I have to say is more than I could have expected under the circumstances..."

Dacombe cut him off and unloaded another bombshell.

There was a pause as Chapman digested the information.

"You what!? Greg... what from Saturday...? At Taskers End?"

Dacombe outlined the turn of events, then a further revelation.

"What do you mean there's something else?" He listened while Dacombe explained the photographs that had been taken and the investigations he had been doing that morning as a result.

Dacombe knew Maureen well; he regularly spoke to her in the office when he was visiting Chapman. In fact, he'd tried to chat her up on more than one occasion, unaware of her relationship with her boss.

Chapman summarised. "So, let me get this straight, you think that Maureen is living at Taskers End with Greg Jensen, who's really Gerald Perry. How on earth did you find that out? Connections, I see. Yes, I know all about Gerald Perry, he's the Sinclair's grandson, you remember Cathcart refused to sign the house over under the Power of Attorney... been stuck in Trenton Court for years, a right nutter, tried to throttle his girlfriend and killed one of his mates... No... I didn't know he was out."

There was another pause. "But what I don't understand is what are they up to and why did he lie about his grandmother? Wait a minute, you don't think they were behind... yeah... it would make sense... I agree... I think I will pay him a little visit later. We need to have a chat and I may need the disposal services later."

SYR Construction had a record of being able to hide the occasional embarrassment or obstruction in the foundations of its developments. Chapman smiled for the first time today.

"No thank you, that's very helpful... yeah... be in touch."

Chapman went back to his office and started sorting out his files on his laptop; Maureen was with Cathcart. He looked at his emails; the Inbox indicated seventy-six unread messages.

He started to go down, deleting those he considered irrelevant. He stopped at one from Graham Bedser, one of his important clients. He read it with interest and then went to make a coffee. He had no intention of confronting Maureen, yet.

Back at his desk, he opened up 'Outlook' and decided to write back to Bedser. He knew the email address and instead of just replying to the earlier note he opened a new mail message box. He entered the letter 'g' and a list of past recipients beginning with the letter 'g' was listed, a feature used by the programme to speed up the process. He entered the letter 'r' and the list narrowed to two – 'Graham Bedser' and 'greg.jensen@email. com'. He stared at the address. Although Maureen had deleted her email to Greg with the various files, she had forgotten about deleting the history which is why the email address was still visible, a potentially fatal error.

"How on earth?" he said under his breath. He sat there just gazing at the recipient options trying to work out how Greg's email address had got onto his computer. Maureen, the only conclusion; she must have accessed his laptop while he was away but why and what had she sent? There was no way he could tell that; it would have to be the subject of a discussion.

Chapman knew he had to confront her, but it would be difficult in the office. He would bide his time, no rush.

At eleven o'clock, Cathcart came into Chapman's office; he didn't knock, with Glen Darby from Havers Dennison, a neighbouring firm of solicitors who had close links with Cathcart Rivers.

Chapman knew him, so introductions were superfluous.

"Right, let's get down to business, shall we?" said Cathcart and produced a contract detailing the arrangement for dissolving the partnership between him and Chapman. It was a long document and, as expected, extremely thorough. Darby asked Chapman if he fully understood the document and its implications. Chapman said he did, and the signing took place.

"I will register this with the Law Society and all the other interested parties. I'm meeting with the Bank Manager this afternoon and changing all present signing instructions," said Cathcart very officiously. He had no liking for his former partner; the feeling of betrayal was raw.

Maureen had kept Greg updated with developments and he was naturally delighted with events. He was sorry he had doubted Cathcart's resolve.

"Just Dacombe to sort out," he said, satisfied that Chapman's ignominy would be a just punishment for his involvement with his grandparents" deaths. Dacombe was the real villain here, he had had no doubts.

At three o'clock, Cathcart left the office for his appointment with the Bank Manager, leaving Maureen on her own in the office with Chapman. This had made Maureen nervous, the earlier look had indicated some definite antipathy.

Sure enough, a matter of minutes after Cathcart had left Chapman came storming out of his office and into reception.

"You have a lot of explaining to do," he said wildly.

"I have nothing to explain to you," she said, more assertively than she was feeling inside.

"So why have you shacked up with a nutter, then... I thought you had more class," he said, trying to wound her with words; this was not the time for any physical stuff he had realised.

"I don't know what you are talking about."

"No, you wouldn't, he didn't tell you, did he?"

"Who didn't tell me what?" she replied.

"Oh, I'm going to love this," he said, mockingly. "Your new boyfriend, the head-case."

He was beginning to turn the metaphorical knife.

"I don't know what you're talking about." She looked at him as if he was talking in tongues.

"Greg, your new shag," Chapman was getting his money's worth. "Or should I say, Gerald?"

"Gerald, Gerald I don't know anybody called Gerald," she said.

"Ah but you do, only he doesn't call himself Gerald anymore. Calls himself Greg, manlier I suppose, than Gerald. Yes, Greg Jensen, formerly known as Gerald Perry."

This was beginning to strike a chord with Maureen, but she was now totally confused; Cathcart had introduced him as Mr Perry.

"So?" said Maureen.

"You really don't know do you? Well let me enlighten you. Gerald Perry, aka Greg Jensen, was sent to Rampton in 2001 for trying to throttle his girlfriend and killing one of his friends. He apparently found out she was having an affair with him. Stabbed him with a screwdriver in a fit of rage."

Maureen was beginning to worry. "You're making this up, because I dumped you," she said, defensively.

"You think? Check it out on the internet. It's all there, the trial, or lack of one; unfit to plead. Got an indefinite sentence, released a couple of weeks ago from Trenton Court. It's what they call a medium secure detention facility."

He was right in her face, she could smell his stale breath; she turned away.

"Yeah you might look away, but you have to ask yourself a couple of questions. What am I doing with this nutcase and will I be next?"

He laughed a sardonic laugh, more a guffaw. He was enjoying his revenge and could see she was hurting.

"Have a nice life, Maureen," he said, as he walked back down the corridor and started to sing, "*Always look on the bright side of life, tee dum, tee dum... tee dum, tee dum, tee dum*".

Maureen rushed into the back office visibly shaking and trying to make sense of it all. Some of it fitted. Greg had been away; he said so, in the States. His name was Perry but not Gerald. It was always Greg. She went back to her desk and to her computer screen. She accessed the internet browser and typed in 'Gerald Perry' in the search engine.

There were numerous hits; a painter and decorator in Darlington, a surfing instructor in Santa Rosa, California. Then she held her breath, BBC South Yorkshire News, 2001, '*Gerald Perry, local medical student, sentenced to indefinite detention at Rampton Secure Mental Hospital for the vicious killing of his girlfriend's lover.*' She didn't want to read anymore.

She felt sick and empty. The duplicity, how could he?

The office doorbell rang which distracted her from her thoughts momentarily.

She went to answer it and it was the garage returning her car. It had been given a clean bill of health and the bill had been settled over the phone with a debit card.

She took the keys in a daze and thanked the mechanic. She

would have to move the car to the parking area round the back but as Cathcart had the keys she would have to wait for his return.

It was a pointless exercise trying to concentrate on any work. Her mind just raced. She just couldn't believe it. How could she have trusted someone so totally?

She was convinced Greg was 'the one', had moved in with him. Apart from the temper he had shown yesterday with the brake incident, which was understandable, he had shown no indication for violence whatsoever. He was gentle, kind, considerate; a bit obsessive but nothing like the pictures painted about him. There was no way he was a killer, he couldn't be.

Cathcart came back around four o'clock and Maureen was able to move her car from the meter just before it was due to expire. She wanted to get back to the house, she was desperately anxious to speak to Greg; he would put things right, she just knew.

How slowly the clock moved; she could hear the tick of every minute. She had made Cathcart a drink and he had briefly passed the time of day with her but was not forthcoming about his immediate plans for the practice. After today Chapman was no longer a partner and she was not unhappy with that.

Around four-thirty, Chapman made his way to the front door loaded up with files and his briefcase. He glowered at Maureen as he walked past her desk. She ignored him.

Not soon enough, five o'clock arrived and Maureen made her way back to Taskers End. She had no idea what she was going to say to Greg. Should she just hint and see if he would come clean or should she just confront him and get his version of events? She found it difficult to gauge her feelings towards him. Just a few hours ago, he was her life and was going to be forever if she had anything to do with it, but now?

She pondered all the way back to the house but was still no

further forward.

As she pulled into the drive Greg was rinsing off the Audi with a hose. He was stood there in his old sweatshirt and jeans, and a pair of grey wellingtons looking very much the man of the house. She felt momentarily pleased to see him and wanted to sweep everything under the carpet. Just ignore it, it will go away. Let's get back to normal. But she couldn't.

He turned off the tap on the wall and walked purposefully to the Mini as she got out.

"How are the brakes?" he asked. "Everything ok?"

"They're fine," she said brusquely. Greg walked up to her and went to kiss her but for some reason she turned her head away.

Greg was confused. "What's the matter, you ok?" he asked.

"Not here, inside, we need to talk."

Greg was worried. He had not seen Maureen like this.

They got inside. "Whatever's wrong?"

"In the kitchen," she said. "I could do with a drink."

Greg still couldn't work out the apparent coldness. He poured her a glass of red wine and sat down.

"You must tell me, whatever's the matter? It's not Chapman is it? He hasn't threatened you or anything?"

She took a large gulp of wine.

"No, not exactly, but he has told me something."

"What? What has he told you?"

"That your real name is Gerald Perry and you have just been released from some mental institution… that you killed someone."

Greg was desolate, he could feel Gerald wanting to intervene, but he suppressed him.

He just stared at the floor.

"So, it's true," she said, clearly reading the signals.

Greg was trying to get his words right, Gerald would never

have been able to, not under these circumstances.

"What do you know about schizophrenia?"

"Nothing, it's a bit freaky," she said abruptly.

"No, it's not; it's an illness, it's just that you can't see it. I spent a long time getting well, they said it was caused by the trauma I had when I found my mother and father. It's not the Bruce Banner thing; I didn't rip my shirt and turn green or anything, it's not Jekyll and Hyde either. It's an illness"

He was desperately trying to keep the mood light, trying not to frighten Maureen; it had clearly come as a shock to her.

"Why didn't you tell me?"

"It's not the best chat up line is it; 'hi, I'm Greg and I'm a fruit cake'."

She almost smiled.

"I was going to and would have told you, at the right time. We've only been together a couple of weeks and everything's moved so quickly. I love you and I would never, never harm you in any way. I would do anything for you."

"Did you say that to Lindsey? I assume it was her you hurt."

A low blow which was unbecoming of the tenor of the conversation, but Greg understood her anger.

"No, I didn't. But that was a long time ago and I have spent hours of counselling and been fed drugs that make you shake and throw up and I am better now. That's all in the past; think about it, they wouldn't have let me out if they thought I was a threat."

Maureen could see the logic but wasn't letting go.

"But you killed someone?"

"Yes, I regret that deeply. I still don't know why or how. I have no recollection of the incident whatsoever."

"How do I know it won't happen again?"

"It can't. I'm better. Look, if you're at all concerned, I'm having to visit a psychiatrist every month as well as a social worker. They are monitoring me."

"So, these were the meetings you had in the office."

"Yes, you could come with me if you like, the next one, and ask questions. I really don't have anything to hide. Now it's out in the open, I'm glad. I had no intention of lying to you. You've done more for me than you'll ever know. You have given me back my self-respect, my life in fact. They could never do that in the hospital. I am no longer hiding from the world. It's like being reborn."

There was silence. He couldn't do any more. The ball was in her court.

Greg made the first move to break the tension.

"What are you going to do?" he asked.

"I don't know. I need some time to think. I'll phone my dad, see if I can stay with him for a while. I don't want to go back to the flat after the car thing."

"Then stay here, there's no need for you to go, please; I'm begging you. I can protect you and I will give you space, whatever. Nothing will harm you, I will see to that."

"No, I should go and it's best that we don't communicate until I can get my head around it all. It's been a lot to take in."

A feeling of acquiescence hung over Greg; he knew there was nothing more he could do.

"Look, I do understand. Just come back as soon as you are ready. I won't put any pressure on you. You must make up your own mind. I'll always be here for you."

Greg could feel tears beginning to well up, but he wanted to keep his emotions under control at least until she had gone.

She went upstairs and packed some things and he helped carry them to the car.

"This should keep me going until the weekend; I'll make arrangements to collect the rest, I just need time."

"I know, and I'm sorry, there's nothing more I can say but

I don't want you to leave. You'll never have any trouble from me. I promise," he said, trying one last time.

Greg stopped himself; he was starting to enter the world of emotional blackmail; he wasn't going to do that.

"If you need anything, any time just ring, promise?"

"Yes, I will," she said, and she got in the car and drove away.

Greg put his head in his hands and cried like a baby.

Chapter Eighteen

The emptiness Greg felt was unimaginable; he was inconsolable. He walked back into the house, his emotions in shreds. Gerald was definitely awake and ready to take over.

Just a push would all that it would take.

He sat in the lounge just staring at the wall; he was in a bad way. Greg was entering a well of depression and Gerald kept making random appearances which he was unable to suppress. He thought of Chapman and Dacombe. 'Gerald' thought Chapman was getting off far too lightly and his spilling the beans on his past to Maureen; well, he needed to pay. Anger, revenge boiling up inside like a pressure cooker with no outlet for the steam. Greg's head was ready to explode.

As for Dacombe, he was the main protagonist; 'Gerald' was in no doubt; too big for his boots; needs taking down a peg or two. Anger and revenge.

Greg tried everything to retain control. The breathing exercises were only having a limited effect but the fact that Greg was at least remembering to use them was a positive sign. One key factor was keeping him together; he must get Maureen back and win her trust. He could not function without her, he might just as well be back in Trenton or perhaps he should extinguish life altogether. Without her there would be no life.

But there was always a chance; she had not gone. She just needed time to think; that's what she had said.

The early evening dragged, he couldn't settle, wrestling with his demons. He went upstairs and opened Maureen's wardrobe. Most of her clothes were still there. He flicked through the dresses and jackets, visualising her wearing them.

He opened the drawer where she kept her underwear. The lingerie she had modelled for him on Saturday night was on top. He picked it up and put it to his face; he could still smell her perfume. She was all around him; she had not gone.

He rested his hands in his head to ease the pain; he had developed a headache and went back down to the kitchen to seek a cure. He opened a bottle of paracetamols and poured out a handful of the white pills. This would do it he thought for a moment, but then what's the point in that? Who would get the justice for his grandparents? Thoughts of them came back. In his self-pity he had forgotten his mission. That responsibility had been given to him, that's why he had come back, to the house, it was his destiny.

He thought for a moment. It was as though some unseen forces had directed him back to Taskers End to discover the truth. Everything had been leading him in that direction, perhaps his grandparents were controlling events from beyond the grave. He had never believed in spirits or ghosts and disregarded it as bunkum, but he shivered at the thought, his mind was in freefall.

He kept the prescribed two tablets and put the rest back and swallowed them with some water. Coffee, that always help helped him focus, gave him a lift, a buzz.

He poured water into the kettle and switched it on; a loud pop indicated the fuse had blown.

"Shit, that's all I need!" he said to himself. He opened his bits and pieces drawer and rummaged around. No fuses, no, they were in a box in the garage. He sighed in resignation. He went to the front door and out into the drive. It was a dark damp night; mist was rolling in over the heights of the Peak District and dropping a white swirl over the Rivelin Valley. His Audi now covered in a film of dewy moisture was still on the drive.

The security lights kicked in and created a theatrical back-drop to the old house. Taskers End was watching in the eerie white gloom like something from a Dracula movie. He activated his remote control and the roller door to the garage slowly raised allowing access. He went to the workbench on the right-hand side and fumbled in the dark for the light switch.

It happened quickly.

The polythene bag, a sudden plastic curtain, drawstrings being pulled tightly around his neck. He grabbed frantically at the ties, his head was jerked back by his assailant. Strangulation or suffocation. He gasped for breath; as he inhaled instinctively, the synthetic membrane clinging to his nose and mouth created an impenetrable barrier cutting off his air supply. He fought against the force trying to bend his head forward, but the pressure was relentless.

His hands flayed wildly as his survival instincts cut in; he was fighting for his life. His right hand swept the workbench and a familiar shape suddenly came into his grasp. He was grateful that for once he hadn't bothered to return it to its rightful place on the wall. He grabbed the handle; the sharp point was facing away from him. His strength was now almost super human, driven by his will to survive.

He blindly plunged the screwdriver back over his head and he felt resistance and a piercing scream. The drawstrings relaxed, and Greg pulled at them allowing air into the canopy. He ripped the bag off his head and gasped for air. He sunk to the floor on his knees trying to recover. The screaming continued and then stopped, a whimper, then silence.

Greg staggered to his feet, focussed his eyes and found the light switch above the workbench; he switched it on illuminating the garage in neon. Still holding his neck, he looked on the floor and there was a trail of blood. He followed it to the inspection pit and he looked down at the motionless body of David Chapman. The screwdriver was sticking out of his eye at an acute angle.

Greg went down the stone steps to where Chapman lay in a crumpled heap and checked for a pulse, there was none. He looked at his face. Using his medical knowledge, he could see that the screwdriver had entered his eye from the top, piercing his eye lid and rupturing the outer membrane; it had travelled downwards through the vitreous humor, puncturing the prefrontal cortex of the brain. Death was inevitable. A steeper angle may have saved him, but fates had decided otherwise.

Greg was still in shock but desperately trying to hold it together. Breathing exercises were useless, he was way beyond that. Coping strategies were just words, psychobabble. But it wasn't Gerald climbing over the wall trying to take control, not this time, something else was happening, something very strange.

Greg and Gerald had begun a metamorphosis; they were becoming as one. A fusion, a much more potent force, stronger, more determined, more cunning, fired with rage and fuelled by hatred for those that had caused their world to be so violently disrupted. Something had tripped and short circuited his brain. Suddenly a calm swept over this new entity, the mind now completely focussed, everything else had been shelved.

He examined the scenario. The body of David Chapman was lying at the bottom of the inspection pit. He replayed the action in his mind. Chapman had clearly staggered backwards and fell; the trail of blood was in spots. Chapman's clothes would have absorbed most of it.

The sensible course of action would be to phone the police, it was self-defence after all but who was going to believe him; stabbed with a screwdriver, the irony.

It would have to be concealment.

He went back to the house and down into the scullery. He knew what he was looking for; the box containing the remnants of his medical stuff. He found his sterile gown, gloves and shoes. Not that they would be sterile now, but blood stains and any other forensic material would be contained, and he could destroy the outfit later. He stripped off completely and put on the gown and shoes. He felt like a patient in a hospital waiting to be attended by a doctor. He put on the surgical gloves and then checked his own clothes. He could not see any blood, but to be on the safe side he would destroy them. He took out a large plastic carrier bag – the one from Maureen's boutique, from one of the kitchen drawers and put his jeans and shirt inside.

Back to the garage in his ghostly uniform, he set to work. Bleach would get rid of blood stains and, because they were still fresh they would not have had chance to be completely absorbed into the concrete. He believed he would be able to prevent any detection. In his mind, Greg was back in his lab in Leeds.

Forensic scientists use three types of chemical methods to detect haemoglobin, the constituent part of blood and with modern technology being so sophisticated Greg knew he would have to use all his skills to foil a fellow-professional.

He poured on the chlorine and scrubbed the spots thoroughly.

He reached the pit and looked inside and here the blood was much more prevalent, but he knew he could ignore this; he had other plans.

He collected his wheel barrow which was propped up against the wall on the other side of the garage. Here it was pitch black and out of range of the security lights.

He filled the wheel barrow with rocks from the pile at the edge of the drive. Greg checked Chapman's pockets. His wallet and car keys, the Mercedes from outside Maureen's flat; he kept those for the moment. He pulled the screwdriver from the head and wiped the blood on Chapman's shirt. It would have to be disposed. He then systematically placed the rocks over the body until it was completely covered and then put another row on top. It was back-breaking work, but he knew it had to be done.

The fog had thickened and continued to billow around the front of the house as Greg continued his endeavours. It was a surreal spectacle.

The pile of sand which had also been left over from the renovation work would also be put to good use and Greg poured several loads of it into the pit until the rocks had been completely covered. That would do for tonight. He lacked the necessary resources to complete the job.

Before closing the garage, he swept the floor with a broom. He picked up the plastic bag that Chapman had used and put it in the dustbin. He would complete his work tomorrow.

He went back into the house and checked the time it was nine forty-five. He may be too late for tonight but there was a loose end which would have to be dealt with. He was certain Chapman would have told Dacombe about his visit this evening and the disappearance would have been reported.

Greg needed time.

Then another thought occurred to him. "Shit...!" Chapman's car. He wouldn't have walked, where would it be? Then a brain wave. Of course, the Pines car park, but that would be alright; nothing to link him to it. Greg put Chapman's keys and wallet into the boutique bag with his discarded clothing and the screwdriver, for later disposal. He thought about what he might need for the next stage of his enterprise. He took a box of matches from the drawer in the kitchen. He was ready.

On the way to the Audi he had another thought and went to the dustbin and retrieved Chapman's plastic bag. That could come in handy. This was Greg and Gerald in concert.

He started the car and headed out towards the main road. As he got to the junction, he scoured the Pines car park which was bathed in an ethereal misty haze from the arc lights; super troupers with the building centre stage. Sure enough, parked at the front, a Mercedes S class numbered DC 15: it had to be it.

He turned left and within fifteen minutes was driving along Ridge Lane. The fog was intermittent but quite thick in places and would certainly help his cause. About two hundred yards beyond Dacombe's house there was a left turn into a small wood, a beauty spot regularly used by dog walkers, and he eased the TT into the area and killed the lights. He got out of the car and put on his surgical gloves, checked the matches and plastic bag and walked back along the Lane.

The weather had clearly deterred any late-night travellers but, despite the absence of traffic, he felt conspicuous in his forensic gown and kept in the shadows of the high hedgerow. He moved quickly and after about a hundred yards, climbed over the small wire fence that surrounded Dacombe's property. The fog, which was now swirling in thick pockets, made it a chill night, but it would lessen any chances of detection. Greg seemed totally oblivious to the climatic conditions. He made his way across the paddocks towards the house. It was only about two hundred yards to the back of the bungalow from the fence. Through the fog Greg could see the front of the property was lit up as it was on Saturday.

He could just make out Dacombe's Range Rover, but there was no sign of Barbara's Mercedes. Perhaps she was out for the night. There was, however, another car on the drive; it looked like a Fiesta.

Approaching from the rear of the house Greg quickly reached the back wall next to the kitchen door. There were no lights on inside. There were security lights and sensors at each corner but hadn't been activated; probably on a timer, thought Greg. He slowly made his way around the side of the house and to his right were the stables. He could hear the noise of horses, snorting and nickering in their guttural tones, but not in alarm.

He came to the first window and there was a light on. Although the curtains were drawn they were not fully closed, there was a gap of about three inches at the bottom, as though they had been pulled together in a hurry. Partly curiosity, partly necessity, he slowly lifted his head and peered into the room. It was a spare bedroom and the bedside table light was on. He couldn't believe his eyes. There was Pippa knelt on the bed on all fours, totally naked, being enthusiastically serviced by Dacombe from behind. Greg dropped down again retaining the memory of the vision.

That answered one question; Dacombe was definitely at home. There was a stifled scream and then giggling; Greg was keen for another peek but couldn't take the risk.

He made his way to the front of the house. Remembering Dacombe's habit from Saturday, Greg was sure he would be appearing shortly for a smoke after his exertions. Greg hid behind one of the mini-tractors by the side of the stable block and waited. The mist was descending again it was thick now and he could not see the main road.

Ten minutes later, Greg heard the front door unlock and a figure walked towards him. With the mist, and, silhouetted against the arc-lights, it looked like an alien creation, but it was soon clear it was Dacombe, dressed in a tracksuit. He sauntered forwards while fiddling in his pocket. Greg watched him take out a packet of cigars and approach the stables. He stopped just short and lit up. He put the packet back in his pocket.

He walked past Greg's hiding place to the stables as if to have a look at the horses and Greg followed him in a crouched position ready to pounce, like a tiger stalking its prey. The first stall was empty and, as Dacombe got level, Greg struck. He pulled the plastic bag over Dacombe's head and tugged the drawstrings tight, just as Chapman had done to him earlier. But Greg was much stronger and would not make any mistakes and gradually Dacombe legs gave way. The cigar dropped from his fingers and lay on the ground. Greg lifted him up and dropped him into the vacant stall which was full of straw. Greg quickly took off the plastic bag from Dacombe's head.

There were several cigar butts dotted around the area; this was obviously his preferred place for a smoke. Greg picked up the lighted butt and placed it beside the prostate Dacombe. Greg didn't check if he was dead, he may well have been unconscious; it wouldn't matter. Greg struck a match and lit a patch of straw next to Dacombe; he watched the flames take hold. He put the dead match back in the box. He didn't want to make this easy for the forensic team. The fire started consuming the dry straw and, within a few seconds, Dacombe's clothes were on fire.

Greg made his escape the way he came and when he reached the fence he looked back. Through the murk he could see flames coming from the back of the stables. There was the sound of agitated horses. He thought he could see a figure running about; it was difficult to tell in the gloom.

"That's for Nanna and Granddad," he said out loud.

He hurried back to the car and exited the beauty spot in darkness but turned left in the opposite direction so as not to pass the house. He waited until he was along the road before he put on his headlights. He was back at Taskers End in twenty minutes.

There were still things to do before he could think about sleeping. He went to the kitchen and took out another carrier-bag from the drawer. He placed his forensic gear, shoes and box of matches with the plastic bag into it. There could well be DNA from Dacombe's saliva.

He went upstairs and changed into his jeans and another sweatshirt and took the two carrier-bags and put them in the boot of the car. Focus was total. He picked up a couple of rocks from the few remaining next to the drive and put one in each of the carrier bags and tied the handles together. He started the car and headed through the gates once more. He turned right in the direction of the Peaks and the big dam that was traversed by the main road. The water would be at least a hundred feet deep.

He drove carefully, the fog was still quite thick, the road deserted. It took him another twenty minutes to reach the lake and the bridge that crossed it. There was a viewing bay in the middle, he stopped there, opened the boot and dropped the bags into the water and was away again before anyone had seen. He drove for about two miles before he found a suitable place and did a U-turn and went back to the house.

He returned on a high and opened a bottle of wine to see if he could reduce the adrenaline rush. It was gone midnight, but he felt wide awake. Only now did he start thinking about the consequences.

The next morning, he was up early. He'd slept badly, in fits and starts and when he had, the nightmares raged. One moment he was being pursued by unseen predators, chased until his legs could no longer work and then the spectres of his beloved grandparents appeared, troubled souls searching for their lost grandson. He could hear them speak. "Have you seen him…? Have you seen Gerald?"

At four o'clock he woke in a sweat, panting for breath. He dreamt he was he was deep under water; he could see the carrier bags which he had followed down into the turbid depths of the reservoir; he was trying to swim back to the surface, but something was holding him back.

He went downstairs to the kitchen to fetch a glass of water. He looked out of the kitchen window into the darkness and kept repeating, "why me... why now?"

He had also been thinking about Maureen, he missed her so much.

As he sat drinking his first coffee of the day, Greg started to analyse the events of the previous evening. How had the regression happened? He was doing so well. Although Greg felt he was now firmly back in control, the fragility concerned him. Physically his stomach was doing cartwheels; he had lost his appetite and was constantly running to the loo. He was trying his breathing exercises but with negligible effect. He was having difficulty putting the thought of his excessive behaviour behind him; back in its box where it belonged.

He was trying to re-engage his coping strategies, but they had not been designed to deal with the extremes he had experienced. It would not be repeated he told himself; it was a one-off, a blip. Gerald was back behind the wall; the metamorphism undone, but now the guilt was starting to overwhelm him.

He tried to rationalise the events of the previous evening; get it into some kind of perspective, something he could mentally handle.

Chapman's death was self-defence, not of his making; no doubt about that. He had been quite content with the humiliation Chapman would receive from his departure from Cathcart Rivers; an appropriate punishment which Greg could have savoured from a distance.

Why did Chapman have to interfere? Greg was entitled to defend himself; it was life or death; him or me, he thought, but who would ever believe him; he had been left with no alternative.

The question of concealment was a 'no brainer' - his recently discovered expression. From his forensic background he knew that blood from Chapman's wounds would have contaminated any container or vehicle that would have been needed to transport him to a new point of disposal. Ok, it was on the doorstep but with a bit of time and effort the chances of the body being discovered would be minimal. It was the right decision.

As for Dacombe, well he would have surely known that Chapman was going to come after him and would tell the police as soon as Chapman was reported missing. Dacombe had to be kept quiet. More importantly of course, he was responsible for his grandparents' death and Greg had worked it out when everyone else had given up.

But Greg knew that, despite the evidence he had amassed, nobody was going to give credence to the meanderings of a schizophrenic. 'Freaky' that's what Maureen had said. That had hurt him, but everybody would say the same. No, it made sense; Dacombe had to be bought to account; it was the only way his beloved grandparents would get justice.

Greg snapped out of his ruminations, he had important work to do if he was going to maintain his deception and by eight o'clock, he was on the phone to a DIY hire centre and ordered what he needed. It would be delivered by ten o'clock. He didn't know whether to ring Maureen or not; he desperately wanted to speak to her. Instead he just sent her a text. "Just to let you know I love you and am here for you when you are ready Greg xx". He hoped that it would make her aware that she was not forgotten without putting any pressure on her.

At nine forty-five, a builders-merchant's truck came into the drive and unloaded several bags of sand, cement and coarse aggregate. A few minutes later another delivery arrived from the same suppliers with the other item he needed, a mixer.

This was going to be demanding work, but he hoped he had calculated the requirements correctly and ordered enough materials. With the truck driver's help, he managed to get the cement mixer next to the garage. The driver gave Greg some details on its mechanics; it would mix around two-hundred and fifty kilos of cement at a time, he said. Just as well, Greg would need around three cubic meters which was quite an undertaking by himself. But after further instructions on its use, Greg was ready to go and, as soon as the truck had left, he opened the garage door. There was a strange smell, a mixture of chlorine and something else, like excrement.

Greg quickly got the mixer revolving and had opened the bags of cement and sand. He decided to mix one-part cement, one-part sand, and two-parts gravel, the builders' recommendation for foundations, a strong mix. He would use the hosepipe connected to the outside tap as he had for his car cleaning, as his water supply. He was not new to this; he had navvied for his grandfather during the school holidays when he was doing the odd bit of building work around the house.

There was a roll of chicken wire underneath the workbench which granddad Sinclair used to patch up the fence at the bottom of the garden to keep out badgers and foxes. This would come in handy and while the first load of concrete was mixing he cut off three lengths with a pair of pliers and placed the first over the sand. It would help strengthen the mix and lessen the shrinkage.

He started with a flourish and soon had the bottom of the inspection pit completely covered, but, as time wore on, so it became harder and harder. By lunchtime, his back felt like it was breaking, but he had over half the pit filled. He put a second layer of chicken wire over the concrete. He had to finish today, Queenie would be working tomorrow, and he didn't want any questions raised, too much opportunity for gossip.

With a quick break and feeling refreshed Greg got back to it. With a foot to go he laid the final piece of chicken wire. By five o'clock it was finished. The final layer he carefully levelled with a plank. It could never be exact; the colours and mix would be different and of course there would be some sinking. As concrete dries, so the mixture was likely to shrink and despite the chicken wire, he realised he may have to put another layer over in a couple of days. The best result would be to screed the whole garage floor using a latex based compound. This would naturally level the floor; he would consider this once the pit had dried.

There were three bags of cement left and a couple of sand and gravel, so his calculations were not far adrift. The DIY shop had said he could have a credit note for any returns. He would use this towards the screed.

The heavy work had proved therapeutic; it had given him much-needed focus, and though very tired, he was pleased with his day's work. He put his tools away and headed into the house. The concrete mixer would be collected at six o'clock. As he reached the front door a young lad on a push bike arrived with the evening paper. Greg thanked him and went inside, eager to read the news.

He didn't have to look too far.

In banner headlines; *Local businessman dies in fire – police investigate.*

Greg read the article with eagerness.

Police and forensic experts were today examining the scene of a fire at the home of wealthy businessman Peter Dacombe, where a man's body, believed to be that of Mr Dacombe, has been found. The fire which happened around 10.30pm Monday evening destroyed a stable block. The stable-maid, Pippa Freeman (24), managed to release the horses and none were injured. Two fire appliances attended the scene. Chief Fire Office, Dan Clark told the Evening News that it was too early to say whether foul-play was involved. It is known that his property empire was in difficulties following the recent banking crisis.

Dacombe Properties, company profile, see Page 10.

Greg flicked through the paper and on page four, there was another article which required his attention.

Police seek missing Solicitor.

Police were last night looking for local solicitor, David Chapman (49). His wife reported him missing after he failed to return from a game of squash on Monday night. His car was found at The Pines Care home in Rivelin where he was a director. Mr Chapman was also a director of Dacombe Properties. Police are not, at this stage, linking his disappearance with the death of Peter Dacombe whose body was found last night following a fire at his house. See page 10.

Greg sat at the kitchen table and suddenly the picture from Saturday night of the Dacombe family on their yacht sprung into his mind. He needed the toilet again.

The sound of hissing air brakes and crunching gravel announced the arrival of the Tool Hire lorry and Greg went outside and helped load the mixer. Greg paid in cash; save the VAT he was told. He opened the garage door and parked the Audi over the now filled-in inspection pit as usual.

Greg went back to the paper. He turned to page 10 and there was an article discussing the problems being faced by Dacombe Properties detailing some unfinished projects where, it was said, moneys had run out. There would be more to come out, Greg was sure.

While Greg had been covering his tracks, earlier that day at the offices of Cathcart Rivers, Arthur Cathcart had two visitors; it was around nine-thirty. Maureen, despite everything, had gone into work, knowing that it was going to be busy, and took the men into Cathcart's office and made them coffee.

She'd ignored Greg's text, for now.

"Thank you for seeing us Mr Cathcart, I'm DI Draper this is DC Harper, we're investigating the disappearance of your business partner, David Chapman."

"Former business partner..." he quickly asserted, not picking up the inference. "He left the practice yesterday by mutual consent."

The detectives looked at each other.

"Can you give us more detail?" asked Draper.

Cathcart hesitated. "It was a mutual parting of ways; he wanted to pursue other avenues."

"I see," said the officer. "Only, the reason we're here is that he's gone missing."

"Missing?" asked Cathcart.

"Yes, he didn't return last night from a game of squash."

Cathcart was in deep thought.

"Hmm, no, I don't see how I can help you," said Cathcart, showing appropriate concern. "I've not heard from him since he left yesterday."

"And, you say…" The DI checked his notes. "He left the practice yesterday… you mean the partnership?"

"Yes, by mutual consent, as I said."

"Ok… Are you able to tell us anything about his relationship with a Peter Dacombe, by any chance, from a personal, not a professional perspective?" asked the DI. "We understand they were business partners."

"I believe so," said Cathcart. He paused for a moment. "'Were'?" he clarified.

"Yes," said the officer. "Mr Dacombe was found dead at his home last night."

"Dacombe…? Dead you say, and Chapman missing?" said Cathcart with a quizzical look.

"Yes, as part of the investigation we're looking at Dacombe's business and various financial dealings, which is why we're anxious to speak to Mr Chapman."

"Yes, I see… No, I'm sorry, I can't help you, I'm afraid… Dacombe was one of David's clients and I have no knowledge of his affairs."

They continued the questioning for another half-an-hour, but they left with little more information.

Outside the office, the detectives compared notes. There was nothing really helpful, but the split from the partnership was interesting. Mrs Chapman had not mentioned it, and, in fact, she had said that the office would be worried about him not turning up for work.

"You don't think Chapman killed Dacombe and then disappeared?" said Harper.

"I don't know, but it's a line of enquiry," said the DI and the officers headed back to their vehicle.

After the officers left, Cathcart sat thinking.

"Chapman missing and Dacombe dead?" he said to himself and smiled.

He called Maureen in and told her of the events. She too was deep in thought.

Chapter Nineteen

At police headquarters, speculation continued that there was a connection between Dacombe's death and Chapman's disappearance, but there was nothing to corroborate that theory. Chapman's involvement in Dacombe's death had not been ruled out.

Another avenue of enquiry linked his death to a possible gang-land killing in Rotherham a few months earlier which remained unsolved. It was believed that Dacombe Properties owed a considerable sum of money on several building projects and the bank was about to pull the plug. Various unsavoury characters were being questioned. This seemed the most promising lead.

Despite a thorough examination at the stables, there was no forensic evidence at the scene of the fire to help police. It was difficult to prove that it had been started deliberately. One theory they were progressing was that Dacombe had had a heart attack whilst smoking and collapsed into the stall. They would need to await the post-mortem results.

Taskers End, Wednesday morning, and Greg was reading the Yorkshire Post and a lengthy article about Dacombe's demise. The disappearance of Chapman was also taking some column inches. A sum of ten-thousand pounds had been offered by the family as a reward to anyone able to throw some light on his whereabouts.

This morning Greg needed to check his handy-work in the garage to see if further attention was needed. He had thought more of the screed idea and, as soon as the concrete was properly hardened, he would contact the DIY shop again. This time he would need some help.

At eight o'clock he heard the front door open followed by a

cheerful "cooee."

It was Queenie. "Are you there? I've got somebody who wants to meet you."

Greg left the kitchen and walked towards the front door. Queenie had taken her coat off and was helping someone else with theirs. She turned around.

"Hello Gerald."

He stared for a moment trying to make the connection and then, recognition.

"Mrs Horley? Alice? Is it really you…? After all this time," and Greg went to greet his guest. She hugged him like a lost son.

"It's so lovely to see you again… and the house, it looks so different." She paused and looked around.

Queenie interjected. "Mum phoned out of the blue on Monday night and asked if she could visit for a few days. She'd managed to get a lift from one of her neighbours who was going up to Leeds and turned up yesterday afternoon. I've been telling her all about you and she's been dying to see you again. Haven't you Mum?"

She turned to the older woman who was still looking around the hallway.

"Would you like a drink and I'll show you around?" said Greg and he led the pair into the kitchen.

"This is lovely," said Alice as she entered the room. "So bright and airy, I always thought it was a bit gloomy in here. I said to your Nan that she needed to brighten it up a bit."

She went to the kitchen window and looked across the garden to the woods at the back.

"This hasn't change at all. It's just as I remembered it."

Greg looked at the woman; Queenie had already taken over coffee making duties.

Alice looked well, a tanned complexion, hair grey but thick

and healthy. The lines on her face gave her character rather than age. Greg tried to remember how old she would be; early 70's, he thought.

While they drank their coffee, Alice told Greg how she had moved down to the 'Island' all thanks to the money from his grandparents' will; she would always be very grateful. She said how good everyone had been to her and how much she had missed them after the 'accident'.

Her voice tailed off and then, for no apparent reason, she started to cry.

"Are you ok Mum? Whatever's the matter?" said Queenie, quickly coming to her aid.

Alice continued sobbing and it was a while before she had composed herself sufficiently to speak.

"It's, it's all my fault," she stammered between deep sobs.

"What's your fault?" asked Queenie.

"The fire, it was my fault," she whimpered.

"What do you mean?" asked Queenie.

Greg was listening but confused.

"That morning, the day of the fire," she continued, her voice quivering with emotion. "I was cleaning as usual and Mrs S said that she and your grandfather…" she looked at Greg; "had been worried about someone trying to take their house away from them and they'd not been sleeping very well. So, I said to her, 'have you tried aroma therapy'; I swear by it."

Alice looked at Greg again. The words poured out as if she was trying to expunge years of guilt.

"She said she hadn't, so I popped back home later and brought them a packet of my candles. I told her to light one and lie down for a few minutes and it would relax her. When I turned up the next day it was all roped off and the police were looking around, they said there had been a fire. I didn't twig at first. They asked me if I knew anything. Then they asked me if your grandfather smoked at all and I told them he smoked a pipe, but nothing else." Alice started crying again.

"It's alright, Mum. It's alright, nobody blames you. It was just an accident."

"But they said in the paper that Mr Sinclair caused the fire by smoking in bed and that's not right. I didn't tell them she wouldn't let him smoke in the house. I should have, but then I thought I would get the blame and go to prison," she said and started crying again.

Greg was trying to take this in. He went to cupboard under the kitchen sink and rummaged around at the back.

"Are these them?" he asked, showing her the old packet of candles.

"Yes!" she said in astonishment. "Where did you get them?"

"They were under the sink, been there all the time I expect. The builders must have put them back after the new kitchen was put in. I noticed them the other day, we had a power cut."

Greg was trying to keep his thoughts in check. Gerald was on the warpath again.

"Do you want to go home, Mum?" asked Queenie. "I think it's been a bit too much for her coming back," she said looking at Greg. "You don't mind if I drop her back, do you? I won't be long."

"No, of course not," said Greg.

Greg gave Alice another hug. "I'm so sorry," she said, "I am so sorry."

"That's alright," said Greg. "It was just an accident, that's all."

Queenie took her mother and left, leaving Greg in all sorts of trouble; his mind hardly able to process the course of events.

It made sense. There was no way that the candle could have survived the blaze, it would have been totally consumed in the conflagration and, of course, the naked flame was much more likely to have caused the type of fire that killed his grandparents than a smouldering cigarette or pipe. An accident, as the coroner had said, just a different cause.

Greg put his head in his hands wondering at the course of events his actions had triggered. He really needed Maureen now, but she seemed as far away from him as ever. She hadn't answered his text from yesterday or the one he sent this morning. He didn't know what to do, he was totally on his own. He sat in the kitchen looking out at the woods in the distance trying to make sense of everything.

Queenie telephoned about half-an-hour later to say that she was going to stay with her mum and would finish the cleaning in the morning; if that was ok, she said.

Greg could hardly focus on the call.

"Yes of course," he said without any enquiry as to Alice's well-being; his mind was completely elsewhere.

It was just after one o'clock and Greg was still in the kitchen when he heard the distinctive sound of a throaty exhaust and the crunching of gravel. Maureen?

Sure enough, the Mini was pulling up outside the front door just as he reached it. His face lit up expectantly but quickly he could see that this was no social call.

"I'm not staying, Greg, I just need to collect the rest of my stuff."

He was mortified. "Can I get you a coffee, something to eat maybe?" he said totally ignoring her remarks.

"I don't think so. Can you give me a hand please?" she said quite sharply.

"Yes, of course, of course. How are you? I've missed you so much," he said.

She ignored him again and went through the hall and up the stairs with Greg following like a puppy.

"Please stay and talk… there's so much I want to say," he pleaded but again she paid no heed and went to the closet and started to pile the rest of her clothes on the bed. Then the drawers; she checked them twice to make sure there was nothing left.

She had a couple of carrier bags in which she put her underwear, make-up and tops. The rest she just draped over her arms.

"Are you going to help me, or do I have to make another trip?"

Greg was full of resignation.

"Of course," and he picked up the two bags and led the way back down stairs. Wrestling with the load on her arms, Maureen managed to open the car door and placed the dresses carefully on the passenger seat and then went to the boot. She took the two carriers from Greg and placed them inside and locked it.

She took one last look at the house, then at Greg who was stood like a school boy on the front door step looking completely lost.

"Sorry Greg, but I'm going away for a while. Please don't try to contact me. I've changed my mobile number so please don't bother texting."

She got in the car and drove off through the gates.

Back at the South Yorkshire police head-quarters incident room, detectives were busy collating information relating to the death of Peter Dacombe and the disappearance of solicitor, David Chapman. They were now convinced the two incidents were related.

Detective Superintendent Mike Amos was heading the investigation. With the offer of a reward and the media interest, the phone lines were busier than usual. Yet another call came in. They were being filtered by a team of three detective constables.

"Gov, there's another call from someone with information on the missing solicitor," shouted one of the DC's across the room where DS Amos was discussing the case with another officer. "This one sounds promising."

The DS picked up the phone. "Amos," said the Superintendent sternly.

"Is the reward still open for info on that missing solicitor?" asked the voice.

"Yes," said Amos.

"Then I have something for you."

"Who am I speaking to? You won't be able to claim the reward anonymously; we'll need you to make a statement," he said.

There was a pause as the caller thought things through.

"Yeah... ok, ok... the name's Terry... Terry Baker."

Baker poured out his version of events to the policeman. He obviously couldn't say what he was really doing so he concocted a story that he'd been doing some surveillance work for Chapman as part of an insurance case that the solicitor was working on.

He continued. "I was in me van when this nutter climbs in and offers me some money to do Chapman over. Said he got a grudge against him or something." Baker laid it on thick.

"When was this?" asked the officer.

"Couple of weeks ago... Offered me fifty-grand, but I told him to get lost."

"But why you...? Why did he think you would do it?"

"No idea... he said he'd been watching me... Fucking freaked me out, I can tell you... a right nutter, he was."

"Go on," said Amos.

"Well, I seen the story in the newspapers, you know, about Chapman going missing... and I thought it might be him.

Maybe he's found somebody to do him in."

"Ok, thanks... Did he give you a name, by any chance?"

"Yeah, told me to call him Greg... I've got his mobile number... if that helps."

Amos wrote it down.

"We'll need you to make a statement. Can you come down to the station and ask for DS Draper?"

"Yeah, be down this afternoon," said Terry

The thought of ten thousand pounds was like a moth to a flame.

It was an easy job finding Greg's full name and address from the phone number and Amos decided to pay him a visit but first he wanted to call in on Mrs Dacombe; it was on his way. He was accompanied by a female colleague, DC Trueman.

They arrived at 'The Fairways' and took the opportunity to revisit the crime scene. The stables were just a shell and the smell of smoke still hung in the air. They had been cordoned off with yellow tape, although the forensic people had already concluded their investigations.

Amos had read the preliminary post-mortem report. The cause of death would never be established conclusively. The damage to the body was extensive and all internal organs had been destroyed. There were no broken bones, no skull fracture; so Dacombe had not been beaten, but that was about it for now. They were continuing their investigations.

Barbara answered the door, her face pallid and her eyes puffed.

"Sorry to disturb you Mrs Dacombe; Detective Superintendent Amos, and this is DC Trueman. Could you spare us a few minutes?"

"Of course, come in. Would you like a tea? Coffee?"

"No thanks, this won't take long."

They went into the lounge and Barbara invited them to be seated.

"Does the name Greg," he checked his notes, "Jensen, mean anything to you, Mrs Dacombe?"

Barbara paused for a moment.

"Yes, yes, he was a guest at a drinks party we had last Saturday. Peter said he was a potential investor and wanted to keep him sweet. He was also trying to get his grandmother a place at the Pines."

"Anything else? Anything at all?" asked Amos.

"Hmm... I think he said he lived in Loxley, with his grandmother, if I remember rightly, but he spent most of the time with Peter and David."

"David Chapman?" asked Amos.

Trueman was taking notes.

"Yes, they were in the den. I don't know what they were talking about."

"Anything else?"

"Not really, he said he'd been doing research in the States, he left quite early, around ten-thirty something like that."

Amos thanked Mrs Dacombe and the officers went back to the car.

"Why would he lie about his grandmother and where he lives?" asked DC Trueman.

"I don't know but something doesn't feel right."

As they were driving to see Greg, a call came through on the radio. Amos answered and listened. Right... thank you... thank you very much.

"That was Draper, guess what... Greg Jensen is really Gerald Perry, recently released from Trenton Court."

"Trenton Court?" said Trueman.

"It's a mental facility. He spent two years at Rampton.

Throttled his girlfriend and spiked one of his mates with a screwdriver in 2001. Released on license three weeks ago."

Twenty minutes later, they pulled into the drive of Taskers End.

After Maureen had left, Greg decided to take a bath to think things through. The front door was open, and the officers let themselves in.

"Mr Jensen," called the superintendent. "South Yorkshire police, we need to ask you a few questions."

They walked through the house, the kitchen, the lounge, no-one and then they could hear loud singing coming from upstairs.

"*Ying tong, ying tong, ying tong, ying tong, ying tong iddle I po,*"

Chapter Twenty

The police investigation at Taskers End was thorough. The forensic experts took away all the paperwork that Greg had put together about the death of his grandparents which included his doodling and meanderings he had committed to paper.

There were pencil diagrams, flow charts of possibilities, that Greg had sketched which clearly suggested that he suspected Peter Dacombe was responsible for his grandparent's death with Chapman also implicated. This gave the police a motive and they were beginning to think that Greg had killed both Chapman and Dacombe although it would be difficult to prove.

The body of David Chapman was eventually exhumed when the officers found the still-drying concrete in the garage under Greg's car. The post-mortem had confirmed that Chapman had died as a result of a stab wound to the head. A screwdriver was the potential murder weapon. An examination of the row of screwdrivers that were so neatly displayed in the garaged showed there was one missing.

The builders' yard that supplied the cement mixer and materials gave a statement that Greg was filling in the inspection pit and with Chapman's body in the bottom the police successfully argued that it was to conceal the killing and no-one else could possibly have done it. Greg was eventually charged with his murder.

The police had interviewed Queenie; she had turned up to finish the cleaning the following day, but she was unable to throw any light on the matter. Afterwards she did wonder to herself whether her mother's revelation about the Sinclairs' deaths had disturbed Greg in some way. She said nothing about it to the investigating officers nor mentioned Maureen's presence.

There were still many unanswered questions. What was

Chapman doing at Taskers End? They had found his car parked at The Pines and there was nothing to suggest he had been kidnapped so it appeared he had made the visit on his own accord... but why? There was a suggestion that Greg may have lured Chapman to the house for some reason and then killed him but that opened up the argument why hadn't he parked on the drive at Taskers End. Izzy Chapman in her evidence had stated she thought he had gone to the squash club, so why did he lie?

The police believed that Greg was also responsible for Dacombe's death. In one of his drawings he had put a red ring round Dacombe's name several times with such force he had almost gone through the paper. The words "it's him" was written in red with a large exclamation mark. However, the CPS confirmed that there was insufficient evidence to charge Greg with murder; there was no firm evidence to suggest foul play was even involved but it was left on file. The police would have loved to have asked Greg about it but that wasn't possible. He would be in no state to offer any defence.

Whilst locked away in a cell at the police station waiting to be questioned he suffered a complete mental breakdown. He was curled up in a ball on the floor rocking backwards and forwards reciting the *Ying Tong Song*. The officers could get no sense from him and a doctor was called.

Faced with being incarcerated again Greg had reverted to the Gerald Perry of six years earlier; worse if anything, according to the psychiatrists that later examined him. He had entered an impenetrable world; it was as if he had built a wall around him which he was sheltered and safe behind. The only person who could get any semblance of sense from him was Arthur Cathcart.

In his meetings with his client, Greg would mention a plastic bag, kept saying, "can't breathe, plastic bag" and would gag;

his face contorted in a frightening way.

With Greg's mental state having deteriorated to the extent he was unable to give any coherent statement there had been no formal trial, just an inquest presided over by a judge.

Cathcart initially argued that there was insufficient evidence to convict Greg with Chapman's murder, it was all circumstantial, but with the prosecution offering a strong case, the defence of 'insanity' was accepted; the charge reduced to 'manslaughter'.

The judge sentenced Greg to be detained indefinitely at Broadmoor.

In his review of the case, the judge was complimentary about Doctor Melrose's initial assessment report which was presented at the hearing, calling it insightful and should have sounded a warning bell. He was however critical of the social services' response who, he said, had ignored the psychiatrist's concerns. Dorinda Walcott was transferred from her position of social worker into an administration role.

Both the Melrose and Walcott reports recounted the fact that Greg/Gerald supposedly had a girlfriend, but no credence of this was made at the hearing. Although Doctor Melrose had met Maureen, she didn't believe his account of a relationship and thought it had been a figment of his imagination. Queenie was never asked about it and no further investigation in this aspect took place.

The case had roused a lot of interest in the media and of course they had a field day, criticising the Care in the Community programme. One newspaper ran a story headed '*Are we safe in our beds?*' using the Gerald Perry case as an example of where the experts got it wrong. '*How many more Gerald Perry's are there in your neighbourhood?*' it sensationally asked.

The Gerald Perry case became synonymous with poor decision making and gave grist to those who would lock up the mentally ill for ever.

Doctor Young as chair of the assessment panel who recommended his release was criticised by the subsequent Home Office report that followed the inquest and would never be in charge of such a body again.

One newspaper managed to track down the former Lindsey Jones, they didn't give her married name, seeking a reaction, but she refused to answer any of their questions and she spent a couple of uncomfortable days dodging the press and keeping her two young children away from the limelight.

Arthur Cathcart knew that the chance of any release, certainly in his own lifetime was remote and in the circumstances the decision was made reluctantly to sell the house.

The wrecking ball was soon smashing away at the fine old edifice that was Taskers End; the render quickly giving way to an overwhelming force. There was to be no last-minute reprieve. Cathcart was there that first day and so was another visitor, Queenie. The solicitor turned to her as they watched the workmen go about their work.

"How very sad... how very, very sad," he said.

The demolition was completed in three weeks; the old stone being recycled for some other development somewhere, taking their secrets with them. The adjacent wood was cleared, and four large properties were constructed on the site. The development was named 'Taskers Glen'. Starting prices for the houses were 'circa £1.2m'.

Cathcart sold most of Greg's effects and gave the rest to charity. A substantial sum was made available to ensure Greg/Gerald enjoyed the best possible conditions.

Following the deaths of Dacombe and Chapman, Dacombe

Properties went into administration and an investigation took place into the company's various dealings. Several banks lost money and Barbara Dacombe was forced to sell 'Fairways' which had been mortgaged to the hilt. It is not known what happened to her and the family.

At Broadmoor, Greg spent most of the time in self-imposed solitude. Doctor Melrose did visit him not long after he had been detained and Greg insisted on calling her Maureen. He wanted to know why she had changed her perfume and kept asking her what she would like for dinner. The doctor, although normally cold to any emotional attachment, was saddened by what she saw and requested to be withdrawn from the case.

The drug management programme was again prescribed; it would be sometime before he would be moved to a less secure unit. He was considered a high-risk category.

The day after Greg's arrest, Maureen was still at her father's but as the media interest grew she knew she had to get away. She was worried that her name might be linked to the incidents in some way and, after arranging cover at the office, she went to stay with one of her girlfriends in London for a couple of weeks.

When she finally returned to the solicitors, Cathcart called her into his office to explain the new working arrangements; a new partner would be joining the firm the following Monday.

As Cathcart spoke, Maureen could hold her emotions no longer and broke down in tears. She told him of the affair with Greg and her decision to leave him when she had found out about his mental health issues.

"If I'd have stayed, I know things would have been different," she said. "I did love him."

"Well, what's done is done," said Cathcart sagely. "Maybe

it was for the best."

"I do have a bigger problem," she said.

Cathcart looked at her over the top of his glasses as he was inclined to do.

"I'm pregnant."

Epilogue

The early newspaper reports had attracted the attention of the tenant of a run-down council-house in one of the many estates in Sheffield. He sat with a can of beer on the table next to him engrossed in the pages of the Evening Telegraph. He dragged deeply on a cigarette.

Having received confirmation that he would be entitled to the reward money, Terry Baker was upbeat. He had read the various articles with a great deal of interest. He couldn't believe that the man he had met in his van and whom he later shopped to the police for the ten-thousand pounds reward was linked to Taskers End. What a coincidence he thought.

His mind went back to an earlier job he had done for Chapman. He remembered the phone call.

"How would you like to make yourself a lot of money," Chapman had said.

Early summer 2005, it must have been, sometime around the beginning of June, when Chapman first called him. They were having difficulties convincing an elderly couple that they should sell them a large property in Rivelin Valley, he said, and they needed some encouragement. For five-thousand pounds he would do anything.

Another drag on his cigarette, he continued reading the article but only half concentrating, his mind was mulling over that job.

He recalled some of the ploys he had tried; the phone calls, the depositing of building materials, that was a laugh; he smiled at the recollection as he puffed away on his cigarette, the loud music, all designed to unsettle the elderly residents; nothing too heavy.

When these didn't work, Chapman had told him to, "up his

game". He remembered those precise words.

He decided to visit them, check the lie of the land, see what he was up against. He'd watched the couple from the woods for a while; how boring was that!? Then he decided to have a look around inside while they were asleep, never know, might pick up a souvenir or two, he thought.

Looking back, it was a bit optimistic; he would never get in through that small window. He soon realised that once he had managed to lever it open. He would need step ladders.

He would need to try another tack and decided to make a call; he made up an excuse that he was an insurance seller. He chuckled at the thought. Yeah, life insurance; now that's ironic.

He sipped from his can.

A few days later he followed them to the supermarket and put a knife through the tyres of their car. He remembered thinking it was a crap car anyway, at least ten years old, and with all their money they could have afforded better.

He recalled that Chapman was beginning to get impatient and threatening to pull the contract. "I need results," he said.

Terry realised he needed a different strategy and he came up with a plan which he thought would work. He remembered thinking at the time; if there was a fire, the house would have to be demolished and would probably be sold at a knock-down price, even better. He chuckled at the 'knock-down' reference. You never know Chapman may even give him a bonus, and if the owners accidently died as a result then there would be nothing to stop the sale. Now that would be a result, he thought.

It would be the middle of July about the 17th, if he remembered right; he left his van in the Pines Car Park and walked the short distance to the house. He rang the doorbell and it was the man again who answered. He recollected he had a cardigan on even though it was the middle of summer.

Terry could even remember the pattern, probably knitted by

his wife, he thought, poor old sod.

Terry recounted the confrontation.

"I've already told you I'm not interested in any life insurance," the man said.

He remembered barging in, knocking the man to the floor in the process. It was quite easy to over-power him and a blow to the head with a cosh was enough to render him unconscious. The lady proved a little more problematical. Terry initially couldn't find her; but, when her husband had not answered her calls, she came into the hall. She put up quite a fight, he remembered, but again a blow to the head did the necessary.

Terry took another slug of beer, put his cigarette out in the overflowing ashtray and opened another pack of twenty.

Taskers End was a large house and he did a quick look around and decided that he would use the bedroom. The couple would be asleep, no-one would know anything different. There would be no evidence. He carried the unconscious couple one by one up the two flights of stairs to the third floor and put them on the bed. The woman was as light as a feather, the man a little heavier. He recalled how peaceful they looked side-by-side.

He checked the room, tidy, everything in its place, and so clean, family photos of a young boy, black and white; another, in colour, a portrait of a young woman. There was a small unused candle on the bedside table and he wondered what that was for; power cuts most likely, he thought.

Click… he pressed the trigger on his cigarette lighter and lit another cigarette. He re-enacted the motion flicking his lighter on, then off; on, then off, and he watched the flame bouncing into life, then extinguished. It was like that, he remembered.

Their fates were sealed as he bent down and lit the corner of the bed sheet. He thought he could hear the old man groaning; he might have been wrong. The fire started gaining its own momentum; he watched at the door ensuring the bedding was well-alight and the curtains ablaze. Some of the furniture was starting to burn. He shut the door and went downstairs checking there were no tell-tale signs of any struggle; there would be no DNA. Then he let himself out and took the short walk back to the van... job done.

He remembered the newspaper reports and the inquest; the accidental verdict; it was what he'd expected, but there was to be disappointment. It had been all in vain; the property was saved before any extensive damage was done and, despite the death of the occupants, there was to be no sale.

He took another drag on his cigarette. What a coincidence though.

The End

Alan Reynolds

Also by Alan Reynolds

Breaking the Bank

Flying with Kites

Smoke Screen

The Coat

The Sixth Pillar

The Tinker

Valley of the Serpent